When the Rabbit Jumps

Allan David Mowat

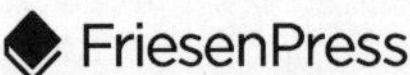

Suite 300 - 990 Fort St
Victoria, BC, V8V 3K2
Canada

www.friesenpress.com

First Edition — 2017

My thanks to all the boys I met over the years through my volunteer work. Their honest and quirky comments and personalities all became part of the character of Lucas.

ISBN
978-1-5255-0572-0 (Hardcover)
978-1-5255-0573-7 (Paperback)
978-1-5255-0574-4 (eBook)

1. FICTION1

Distributed to the trade by The Ingram Book Company

This novel is dedicated to the memory of Dorothy, Margaret, and Jock, the most wonderful parents.

Part 1
LAMB, WHAT LAMB?

Chapter 1

The weary man's great-grandma, in her refined English manner, would have maintained that some primordial instinct had triggered his actions. His paternal grandmother would have insisted that only a "celestial jolt" could spur an act so out of character. Without a doubt "Gramps," as his mom's father was called, during one of his inebriated reminiscences of his war experiences, would have explained his grandson's unusual behavior as an involuntary reaction to a desperate situation. The old man reasoned that actions taken under stress were usually spontaneous and might have been quite different had more thought gone into them. Finally, his father, who, not long afterwards, felt the need to desert the family, had made a comment that came across as quite disturbing at the time. He claimed that most of us, at least one time in our lives, take some action over which we seem to have no control, an action prompted by neither motive nor reason, and this action will undoubtedly have major consequences . . ..

Jarrod Wakefield slumped in one of the window seats of an idling Silverfox Line bus as it sat on the outskirts of a small Wisconsin town. His long fingers ran nervously through his mop of stringy hair, which should have been cut weeks earlier. Flecks of grey were noticeable amongst the dirty-blond strands. Although his facial features were soft, his unshaven jaw, tired eyes, and a ruddy complexion made him look every one of his forty-two years. His lithe yet muscular six-foot frame sat motionless, but Jarrod's eyes were alert to every movement outside the grimy window that supported his tired head.

The 1970s and early 1980s were a transitional period for those who risked large investments in the financial markets. Many young people were just getting their feet wet in penny stocks that were suddenly the rage. For every stock that tripled in merely a few days, dozens went directly into the toilet as investment brokers raked in their clients' money. A gambling addict who played in the fast lane, Jarrod had plunged into an abyss filled only with debt. Listening to one hot tip after another, he had risked investments in every gold and silver mine imaginable. Casinos became his weekend retreats. He even wagered on sporting events that he hardly followed.

It was the spring of 1984 when his world came crashing down. Barely six months earlier, having never stolen anything in his life and with no regard for the consequences, Jarrod felt a sudden need to purge his debts. With no time for remorse, he felt his life imploding. Driven by fear and desperation, he plunged into a life of crime. Over a sustained period, he embezzled money from his employer as he attempted to keep up with his mounting losses.

After several days on the run, Jarrod was still a free man, but he felt the noose tightening. His only interest was to avoid capture by keeping on the move. There was no time for any future plans. The transient embezzler could only sit and stare through the smeared glass as another long day faded into the inevitable cloak of darkness.

Jarrod hated buses. They were not only a wearisome but also a stressful mode of transportation. They made poor beds, smelled of stale smoke and urinals, and were often driven by men who resembled mechanical robots motivated solely by the haste with which the next rest stop could be reached. Either the largest or most foul-smelling person on the planet always made a point of sitting next to him. Trying as much as possible to pretend he was asleep by sprawling across two seats, any new passenger, after scrutinizing other options, was guaranteed to tap Jarrod's shoulder and ask if the seat next to him was vacant.

However, restricted by a lack of funds in his present fugitive state, Jarrod found himself seated on the idling Silverfox bus. The particular late-evening rest stop in an inconspicuous Midwestern town blended in with dozens of others along the bus route. The driver had announced the town's name over the intercom, but Jarrod hadn't been listening, his mind suspended between thoughts of a sordid past he would like to forget and a future that held only uncertainty. At that moment, he was merely a nervous transitory figure whose destination was as muddy and unclear as the view outside the window he peered through.

Although the thought had not yet entered his weary mind, perhaps there was some truth to the assertions of his relatives from a bygone era. Jarrod could never explain his own actions or the subsequent series of events that transpired on that cool, early November evening. Yet that night's exploits merely served as the precursor to an adventure that might best be described as cursed.

The westbound bus had been barely half full, but now only Jarrod and three soundly sleeping passengers were on board. The others were inside the bus depot restaurant, either freshening up (bus travel could be a clammy experience) or forcing down some tasteless food. With little enthusiasm, Jarrod munched on a stale bag of tortilla chips between sips from a lukewarm coffee he had purchased while stretching his legs. He was fidgety and wished the rest stops weren't so long. At least when the bus was moving, the distance between him and his former life was always increasing.

With smoking allowed in last few rows, the unmistakable smell of cheap pot lingered in the rear of the bus. Jarrod, who was seated halfway down the aisle, craved for a soothing drag on some good weed, or at least a few puffs from a cigarette. Both were habits he had given up years earlier. Try as best as he could to relax, events of the last few weeks kept spiraling through his mind.

At last, passengers began to drift back onto the bus. Outside, the driver was engaged in idle conversation with a police officer, perhaps the local sheriff. They appeared to be old pals, but at times their talk and gestures took on a serious tone that Jarrod found disconcerting. He tried to ignore them by reading a day-old newspaper, but his eyes continually drifted back to the uniformed men, who conversed under a dull fluorescent light. As the last of the passengers shuffled down the aisle to their seats, the driver boarded, and the officer wandered toward the bus depot. Considering his rotund physique, it was likely that he was off to purchase the first of many snacks to be enjoyed during his lengthy night shift.

The bus driver, identified as "Stan" by a name plate above the front window, was a grizzled, cantankerous man in his late fifties who, by all appearance, had lost interest in his job long ago.

"Have your tickets ready, please," he announced bluntly in the lifeless tone of a recording. He placed sardonic emphasis on the word "please."

Stan proceeded down the aisle, punching holes in some tickets and tearing others from their booklets. Those passengers unfortunate enough to be sleeping received an unceremonious shake and were jarred awake to the cheeseburger smell of Stan's breath as he admonished them for not hearing his announcement. It was obvious that diplomacy was not one of Stan's finer attributes. One elderly woman only produced her ticket after repeated fumbling through her handbag. Unfortunately for her, the first item that came out of her purse was her dentures. That aroused a series of stifled giggles from a mother and her young daughter seated across the aisle.

As Stan handed back his wrinkled ticket, he gave Jarrod's sullen face and his long, unwashed hair a squinty, suspicious look. Although the look made him feel uncomfortable, Jarrod let it pass as an overactive imagination. Finally reaching the back row, Stan took the ticket from a jittery young man who had quickly stuffed a small bag under his seat. Either unaware of, or preferring to ignore the aroma that lingered there, the exasperated driver finally made his way back up the aisle. He counted heads as he walked to the front. After making a brief notation in his logbook, Stan once again picked up the microphone.

"Federal regulations permit smoking only in the back four rows of the bus. Alcohol and illicit drugs are not to be consumed on the bus."

A few mocking coughs could be heard along the aisle. Perhaps the onions on Stan's burger had distorted his sense of smell, as the distinctive odor of smoldering pot continued to waft throughout the bus. Even as Stan recited the warning, the fidgety young smoker was rolling a fresh joint for the road. As long as no one had the nerve to complain, what did the surly driver care?

About to pull the door closed for departure, Stan realized he had forgotten to deliver a parcel to the depot manager. "Damn, will we ever get out of here?" he mumbled, stepping off the bus once again.

Just as Stan started across the parking lot, the little girl with the giggles informed her mother that she had to "go potty."

"Come with me, Missy," her mom said. She hustled her daughter toward the rear of the bus, where a tiny washroom was nestled in the corner next to the last two rows of seats. The nervous smoker fumbled to hid a baggie half-filled with marijuana. When the mother tried to push down the handle that opened the lavatory door, it wouldn't budge.

"What's wrong, Mommy?" Missy asked nervously.

"The door's stuck, honey. I'll get the driver." She gave it another jiggle and then headed to the front of the bus.

Stan was just stepping onto the bus when he saw the mother motioning him to the rear. He was already behind schedule and obviously annoyed with any further delay.

"What's the problem, ma'am?"

"The bathroom door seems to be stuck. My daughter has to go really bad."

After walking down the aisle shaking his head, Stan wiggled the handle a few times, cursing to himself. "Anyone in there? Are you all right in there?"

No response.

Stan turned and scanned the passengers. "Did any of you see someone go in there?"

A few shook their heads. Others appeared to show little interest. The pot smoker shuffled nervously in his seat, his head shaking emphatically. After stomping to the front of the bus, Stan yanked on the metal lever that threw open the passenger door. He stepped off the bus one more time, reassuring himself that no one could be sick in the washroom, as all the passengers were accounted for by his head count.

Little Missy rocked back and forth as she stood anxiously next to the washroom. Her jaw dropped when the door handle began to move ever so slowly. Her mother failed to notice the lever move, as she was looking out the window at Stan. The driver was trying to raise the door to a side compartment of the bus while motioning to the sheriff, who was seated inside the restaurant next to the window.

Leaving his half-finished meal behind, the overweight police officer strolled toward the bus. He had a brief chat with Stan before lifting himself gingerly onto the first step of the bus entrance.

"Mommy, it's opening!" Missy exclaimed, still standing next to the bathroom door. Her mother grabbed Missy's hand.

"I've got a gadget in the toolbox that'll open that damn door. Be right with you, Klem!" Stan hollered to the officer as he continued to struggle to open the latch that secured the luggage compartment on the side of the bus.

The officer, whose badge identified him as "Sheriff," waddled down the aisle, which seemed to get narrower as he squeezed past each headrest. He puffed and wheezed as if he were completing the final leg of a marathon. The lavatory handle stopped moving as the sheriff, with a firm wave of his hand, motioned Missy and her mother to return to their seats.

"I can't wait much longer," Missy whispered, tears welling in her eyes. Her mother sat beside her as if in a trance, never considering the depot restroom as an alternative.

The pot smoker was so agitated at the sheriff's presence that he bounced up and down in his seat. He need not have been concerned, as the large man with the badge had bigger problems on his mind. Most important was getting back to his burger and fries before they got cold.

"If someone's in there trying to bum a free ride, you might as well come out," Sheriff Klem announced, grinning slightly as he realized his unintended witticism. "We'll have this door open in a minute."

Just as the sheriff was about to issue another warning—he even considered drawing his revolver—the door to the tiny restroom burst open.

What emerged was a diminutive blur!

Jarrod, who was already concerned about the sheriff's presence, followed the entire affair with increasing interest. His attention focused on two wide, frightened eyes that searched desperately for an escape route. They were the eyes of a cornered animal, yet the body that held them moved upright on two legs. The pint-sized figure was wearing clothes that could best be described as discarded items pulled from a dumpster. He was the skinniest, most terrified-looking young boy Jarrod had ever encountered.

In his desperate panic to escape, the fleeing stowaway ran directly into the startled lawman's well-endowed midsection. After bouncing off the spongy impediment, the boy was about to bound toward the front exit when a steel-toed, size-twelve boot halted his progress. Although gasping for breath, the sheriff recovered quickly for a man so large. Unable to grab hold of the wiry boy with his puffy hands, he brought his closest foot down on the heel of the boy's left sneaker. The fleeing youngster's momentum sent him sprawling face-down onto the filthy aisle, the battered sneaker slipping easily from his foot. His flimsy knapsack was sent flying to the floor.

Several passengers gasped. Most of those close to the scene watched in a state of shock, frozen to their seats. Missy let out a piercing scream. Jarrod was by far the most alert to the desperate situation as the boy lay spread-eagled in the aisle just ahead of the seat he occupied. Unwilling to give up, the youngster bounded to his feet like a scared rabbit. Unfortunately for him, the sheriff was moving like a well-stoked locomotive. The boy had no chance of escape.

At that instant, Jarrod did something for which he later had no explanation. It was spontaneous and perhaps that one action his father had either predicted or foreseen. Although rather foolish in view of his own tenuous situation, it was a simple yet devastating act. He merely stood up in the aisle and allowed himself to be flattened by the charging locomotive. The wild confusion that followed only served to foreshadow an endless series of consequences that would stem from that single act, the most immediate of which was allowing the one-shoed boy to bolt for the exit.

Stan, meanwhile, had heard all the commotion and reached the outside door just as it flew open. It was no contest. He was hit with such an explosive force that, at fifty-eight years of age, Stan performed his first somersault. He tumbled backwards over an empty trashcan, landing firmly on his buttocks against the loading platform.

Sheriff Klem, not without a great struggle, regained his footing. After cursing a warning to Jarrod that he would deal with him later, he continued his pursuit, his lungs gasping desperately for air. Too late. A jackrabbit doesn't need much of an opening to escape. Not only had darkness set in, but the newly acrobatic driver was too stunned to offer any help. He wasn't even able to tell the sheriff who or what had hit him, and certainly not in what direction it had escaped.

While Stan and the sheriff consoled each other and tried to regain their breath, Jarrod was suffering great pain himself. He struggled to inhale, certain that the collision had bruised, if not cracked, some ribs. Pain stabbed his side at the slightest movement. Others about him were recovering from their shock, mumbling to themselves and each other, picking up purses they had dropped, and wiping spilled drinks from their clothing. Missy's mother had more than coffee to wipe up, as Missy really couldn't wait any longer. The pot smoker had slipped into the restroom, where he dragged heavily on his unbranded cigarette, not caring who might notice.

After sitting briefly on the armrest of his seat, Jarrod recovered enough to pick up the boy's backpack, which lay in a heap next to him, along with the torn sneaker which had landed under Missy's seat. Only the elderly lady with the dentures noticed Jarrod gathering the boy's belongings. Undoing the single strap that secured the backpack, he opened the flap. A feeling of guilt swept through him as if he were infringing on the privacy of a desperate boy. To be expected, the pack's contents were sparse and pitiful. Jarrod had never been one to worry much about the lives of others, especially children. He was perhaps familiar with self-pity, but when it came to others, compassion was not a familiar emotion. He hardly regretted stealing from the company that had been his employer. Yet for a brief moment, as he sorted through the woeful backpack's meagre contents, the ache from his injured ribs crept closer to his heart. Had this episode which defied explanation suddenly awakened a deep-rooted sense of caring?

Inside the flimsy backpack were two threadbare T-shirts, a pair of cut-off jeans, a faded sweater with holes in the elbows, a pair of mismatched socks, a dirty comb, and a yellowed toothbrush. What a fine wardrobe! Jarrod also found three crumpled dollar bills and some loose change, a travel guide describing the wonders of Canada, a folded newspaper clipping, and a wrinkled, water-stained letter that appeared to be written in a woman's handwriting. The letter interested him, but as he was about to examine it closer, the sheriff approached the bus.

Jarrod stuffed the backpack and shoe into his own nylon travel bag, which was not exactly overflowing with amenities. Forced to make a similar untimely escape from his previous life and employment, he had not taken long to pack. Staring toward the approaching sheriff's flushed face, Jarrod could only wince. Were his escape plans about to unravel?

Walking up to Jarrod, his breath still coming in pants, the sheriff pointed a threatening finger. "Pal, you're lucky I hate paperwork, or I'd run you in for obstructing justice. But I ain't worried; that kid'll freeze out there tonight. Snow's on its way." His wheezing forced him to pause.

"My ribs are sure telling me that I picked a bad time to stretch my legs," Jarrod said as a half-hearted apology. "Wish I knew what got into me. Do you know who that kid was? He looked as if he hadn't eaten in days."

For no apparent reason, the sheriff answered the question. "We know him, all right. His name's Lucas Kenny. He's a runaway from the youth home in Cherryhill. Not his first time either. That kid knows all the tricks, but he'll turn up hungry and shivering in the morning." Turning to leave, the sheriff glanced back and jabbed his finger in Jarrod's direction. "Don't let me see your face in this town again."

His breathing finally returned to normal, Klem turned to the elderly lady, who had remained the calmest during all the excitement. "Ma'am, did you see if that boy dropped anything when he got away from me?" In all the confusion, he seemed to recall seeing something other than a flying shoe.

Jarrod's eyes widened. With an imperceptible glance, the old lady's eyes met his as she replied with a toothless grin. "No, sir, I didn't see a thing, but my old ticker is still flappin' from all the excitement." She giggled softly at her little white lie.

Sheriff Klem was filling in for another officer that night and was annoyed at having a normally uneventful evening shift interrupted. He couldn't be bothered questioning anyone else. Instead, he lumbered back to the restaurant where he could unwind by ordering a fresh, full-course meal. His previous order went right to the garbage. Any paperwork could wait until morning.

Deep inside, Jarrod knew that getting further involved in the situation would only cause him grief. Already he held a great dislike for the town and its sheriff. But he also felt that one homeless kid was being tossed to the wolves with a shoe on one foot and no coat on his back. Besides, his left side was sending out pain warnings that fluctuated between dull throbbing and sharp stabs. Any further bus travel that night would only make the pain worse.

Stan had finally recovered from his tumble and was about to board the bus when Jarrod met him at the entrance, travel bag in hand. "I've decided to stay in town overnight. My side hurts like hell from running into your friendly sheriff."

"Well, I already punched your ticket. You'll have to explain your problem to the depot manager in the morning," Stan said, increasingly frustrated. "I'm half an hour behind schedule already. Too much damn confusion for one night. I hate when those stowaways sneak on when everyone's eating. That's the second time this year. Say, I hope you haven't got luggage underneath."

"Nope, this is it." Jarrod held up his travel bag as he stepped off the bus. Perhaps he had misjudged Stan's dedication to his job, not putting his bruised body and ego ahead of his time schedule. The last words Jarrod heard as the door swung shut was Stan complaining that it smelled like someone had pissed themselves.

As the bus backed out of its stall, Jarrod glanced up at the elderly woman, who strained to look out a window streaked with rivulets of muddy water. She mouthed the words "good luck" through her toothless gums. As a gesture of thanks, Jarrod winked back, smiled, and gave her a nod just as large flakes of snow began to flutter down from the starless sky.

Chapter 2

With his ribs aching, and still unable to rationalize his actions that evening, Jarrod gazed upward as if looking for guidance. Uncertain of which direction to walk, he made a complete circle before staring back at the departing bus. The smell of diesel exhaust puffing from it slowly dissipated as the noisy bus pulled onto the highway.

What the hell was he doing there? Jarrod thought. He fixed his eyes on the bus's taillights as it faded into the distance on Highway 27 West. He had to be going crazy.

Without warning, the answer to his query hit him like a thunderbolt as his mind flashed back to the small figure dashing up the aisle. It was the huge, darting eyes he remembered—the fear and the panic he saw and felt in the fleeing youngster. He could easily relate to those emotions. That was why he reacted without thought. It was instinctive.

Snapping out of his stupor, Jarrod circled to the left of the bus depot, not wanting the inhospitable sheriff to catch sight of him. A closed service station stood next to the depot. One long, flickering fluorescent tube cast dull white rays from within, exposing an open, empty cash register as a discouragement for petty thieves. Air hissed gently from a leaky hose hanging from an air pump that someone had neglected to shut off. Next to the service bay entrance, battered garbage cans overflowed with empty oil cans and rags, along with metal barrels and cardboard cartons piled with mufflers, cracked radiator hoses, and other discarded parts soaked with grime and grease. Altogether it was a large, smelly, eye-catching mess.

Still lost in a quandary of what his next move should be, Jarrod jumped at the roar of an engine firing to life, followed by the noise of squealing tires. He turned in time to see the sheriff's cruiser car tearing off in the opposite direction.

"Another disturbance in this guy's meal plans. He must be in a really ugly mood by now," Jarrod muttered to himself as he walked back toward the bus depot and entered the restaurant.

"That officer is sure in a rush," he commented to the young, tired-looking girl who stood behind the cash register. Wispy, dirty-blond hair drooped across her forehead.

"Yeah, Klem wasn't in a good mood. He just got a call. Some burglar alarm went off across town. That's the second meal he's left half-eaten."

After a quick scrutiny of her new customer, and while diligently cracking a wad of chewing gum, she nodded at Jarrod. "Say, are you all right? You seem to be hurting."

Jarrod touched his side. "Just some sore ribs. I could sure use some rest. Is there a motel somewhere near here?"

"There sure is. The Shady Lake Motel is about a block west of here, next to the Husky." She pointed toward it through the glass door. "It's the only all-night gas station in town. We're just closing up here—no business after that last bus."

"Great. Thanks. I'll take a couple of chocolate bars, please. Any kind." Jarrod winced as he forced a smile, pain stabbing at his ribs.

"Toothy's probably drunk by now," the cashier continued as she took Jarrod's money. "You'll know why he's called that when you meet him. He and his wife ran the motel for years 'til she left him some three years back. He's alone now with his cats, and he hits the bottle too much."

Jarrod was concerned that Sheriff Klem would return shortly for his meal and the talkative waitress would mention a certain sore-ribbed customer.

In fact, his fears were unwarranted, as Klem spent the remainder of his exhausting shift sleeping in the cruiser. Fortunately for him, it had been a false alarm. Before dozing off, he vowed to get even with the young deputy who had booked off sick from the graveyard shift, forcing Klem to cover for him.

Wanting to avoid further conversation, Jarrod thanked the cashier again. As she wished him a good night, she flashed him a doleful look that he interpreted to mean she wouldn't mind some company after her shift was over. Was that a silly male assumption? Likely he had simply misinterpreted the look. Besides, he already had more than enough problems.

Grimacing again as pain shot through his left side, he checked the time schedule posted at the depot and noticed that the first westbound bus left at 9:30 a.m.

With apprehension and much doubt, and still wondering if he had made a fatal decision by staying in that one-horse town, Jarrod started across the cluttered service station lot. The snow was falling heavier, and a chilly north wind cut through his jacket. While assessing his chances of finding a scared runaway boy in those dimly lit streets, his attention turned to a barely audible shuffling noise coming from the overflowing garbage cans. The feeling of being watched crept up his spine. The leaky air hose still hissed. A dim yellow streetlight cast eerie, grotesque shadows as its rays failed to penetrate the twisted rad hoses and rusted tail pipes. Then, without warning, one ghostlike shadow appeared to move ever so slightly.

What kind of alley cat would cast a shadow like that? he wondered, his heart pounding. Blinking snowflakes from his eyes, Jarrod peered toward the dimly lit barrels.

"Lucas? Is that you, kid?"

No response.

Jarrod pulled the weather-beaten backpack from his bag and held it up. "Is your foot getting cold? You may need this." He pulled out the sneaker and waved it back and forth. "Your pal, the sheriff, is long gone. That was quite a licking you laid on the bus driver, by the way," he added, hoping to draw a response. Almost certain that he could hear the shallow, rapid breathing of a child, Jarrod tried to lighten the mood. "You got that little girl so excited, she peed her pants."

His last comment must have worked. Hesitantly, a figure rose from between two barrels laden with trash. Jarrod could not help but stare. What he confronted might have been an apparition. The sad, dirty face contained eyes that were tired yet wide and apprehensive, a face that looked older and less innocent than the slender, sub-five-foot frame that supported it. The boy's brown hair was gnarled and matted, giving the appearance of a mop head. He was a sight straight out of a Dickens novel.

Stepping slowly toward Jarrod, the forlorn figure exposed further signs of wear and tear. A rough scratch across the boy's forehead and nose was vivid evidence of contact with the gritty bus aisle. Filthy toes protruded from the tattered remains of his sock. The Salvation Army would have rejected the remnants that clothed the rest of his body. An oversized jacket smelling of oil and gasoline was draped over his shoulders, likely a prize discovered at the service station.

"That's mine!" the small figure uttered in the confident tone of someone pretending to be much older and more mature than he was. He shivered uncontrollably as he pulled the shoe and backpack from Jarrod.

Jarrod stood motionless as he tried to accept the reality of the sorry-looking form that stood before him. "Look, I'm spending the night at a motel up the block. You're welcome to clean up and catch some sleep there if you want."

The boy shrank back. "Sure, mister. I know your type. Weirdoes who like to have fun with little kids. Forget it!"

"I take it you don't trust many people, kid," Jarrod said, annoyed by the accusation.

"Don't call me 'kid,' and why should I trust people?" the boy shot back.

"Oh, sorry, sir. I didn't realize you were an officer and a gentleman. Or is it admiral?" Jarrod's fuse was burning quickly.

The boy turned to leave.

Jarrod settled himself down. "All right kid—sorry, I mean Lucas. The fat cop told me your name and where you're from."

Lucas hesitated and then turned around slowly. Evidently, the oil-stained jacket offered little warmth, as he continued to shiver in the cold dampness of the falling snow.

"But call me Jarrod, not 'fag' or 'skinner.' Those names don't sit well with me. You're way off base there, pal, but I can understand your suspicion of some stranger interfering with the law and then returning your stuff. Pretty crazy. I have no idea why I did it." Jarrod winced again as pain jabbed his side. "Anyway, I've got to get to that motel before the owner passes out drunk. The offer's still open. I'm going to have a couple of beers and watch some TV, so drop by if you need a place to spend the night. My room won't have a car in front of it, but the lights will be on for a while."

Jarrod held up the two chocolate bars before tossing them to the boy. "Here, you look like you could use these more than me. It's supposed to snow all night. I hope you find a warm place to sleep."

Lucas caught the bars without saying a word. Although his mouth hung open, he was speechless—and confused. Could he not even trust the stranger who had made his escape possible? Was it the fact that men he thought he could trust in the past had let him down? Still shivering despite the additional sweater from his pack, Lucas watched wearily as the tall stranger hurried away, fading behind a curtain of gently falling snowflakes.

The waitress was right. Jarrod's first impression was that Toothy could have shared his incisors, canines, and bicuspids with a family of beavers. Working on his protruding, irregular teeth would have bankrupted any dental insurance plan. Years of pipe smoking had glazed not only his teeth but also his lips with a dull yellow film.

The waitress's second warning also proved to be accurate. Toothy was half-crocked when he finally answered the buzzer, which Jarrod had to press several times. Finally able to enter the warm office, Jarrod initially enjoyed the sweet smell of pipe smoke. However, the fragrant aroma was soon overpowered by the distinctive odor of cats and uncleaned litter boxes. His nose twitching, Jarrod let out two loud sneezes. Just when he was about to speak, he ducked instinctively as a black cat leapt over his left shoulder from its narrow perch on a shelf above the door. The cat landed with a thud on the desk, scattering a pile of registration cards.

"Get off the friggin' desk, Patches!" Toothy whisked the cat to the floor, where it scurried away to join its companions at the feeding dish.

"Have you got a single room for the night?" Jarrod inquired. He assumed by the lack of vehicles out front that all but two of the fifteen rooms at the Shady Lake Motel were vacant.

"Are you alone?" Toothy asked, scrutinizing his new customer. He was slurring a little, and his left hand cradled the bowl of an ancient pipe held together with electrical tape.

"That's what I said. Single room. No car. No pets."

Toothy pulled a registration card from the scattered pile. He pointed to a sign that leaned against a round fishbowl filled with matchboxes. Bold lettering showed the room rates: "$25 Single, $35 Double, $5 each pet."

"I can offer you fifteen dollars cash," Jarrod countered. He knew the place would not fill up that night. "I'm a little strapped for money. I missed my bus connection. The depot was closing when the waitress recommended your motel. She said you'd probably give me a deal." A slight fib, but why pay full price, especially when the owner was half drunk?

"Must be young Debby; she's always makin' deals. At least she sends you bus people my way. That friggin' old Stan, he'll never wait for the Eau Claire connection, even if it's ten minutes late. He's so damn worried about keeping to his schedule—scared that some younger driver will take his job." As he spoke, Toothy strummed his fingers along the counter like he was in deep thought over the business transaction.

After a brief pause, Toothy spoke again. His chatter seemed to be drawing him closer to sobriety. "Seems like someone's always gettin' stranded here, but at least I get a little business that way. I can give you the room for eighteen dollars, my best offer. No credit cards."

Jarrod agreed to the compromise, pulling the bills from a crumpled wad in his pocket. He surmised his donation would help push Toothy one step closer to oblivion. He signed the registration card as "James Smith, Buffalo, NY," the first name that popped into his mind.

"Here's your key, room number eight. There's a spare blanket in the closet. If you want to catch the westbound bus, it leaves at nine thirty, but I don't make no wakeup calls. Just leave the key in the room when you leave."

Jarrod visualized Toothy tossing back an early-morning beer in an attempt to relieve a throbbing headache. He wanted to grin, but his ribs hurt too much. With wavy pen strokes, Toothy filled out a receipt. "G'night," he mumbled as he staggered back to his bottle and the *Tonight Show*.

Snow continued to fall as Jarrod entered his room. It was simply furnished, drab, and lit with low-wattage bulbs, much like dozens of other motels he had slept in throughout his gambling sojourns. Countless trips to Atlantic City and Vegas flashed though his restless mind. Penniless return trips were far more common than the ecstasy of a winning weekend.

The motel room was the temperature of an icebox. He turned the electric heater to maximum before stepping into a hot shower. Although he tried not to dwell on the vulnerable situation in which the young runaway had placed himself, Jarrod couldn't get the poignant picture of the sad-looking figure out of his mind. But really, what business was it of his? Why did he suddenly care about someone else? He didn't have to remind himself that he was on the run as well, although for an entirely different reason.

Warmed by his shower, Jarrod sipped on the first of the two beers he had purchased at the twenty-four-hour Husky Station. He found that the less he moved, the less the pain stabbed at his left side. He sat up in bed watching a horror movie about some sorority girls and a corpse wrapped in plastic propped up in a rocking chair.

Even though he was half expecting it, the light rap at his door startled him. As he peered out the door with the safety chain still engaged, the dim light from the room exposed a pint-sized figure crusted with clumps of snow. It was Lucas.

With the door slightly ajar, the boy stood there speechless for a moment. "I guess that cop would have got me for sure if you didn't get in the way," he said finally. "Thanks for giving my stuff back." He shifted his feet uncomfortably.

"Hurry, get in here," Jarrod said, unlatching the chain, then opening and closing the door quickly behind Lucas. "You must have some angel upstairs who told me to get in the way of that jerk. I can't explain it any other way." He kept his father's words to himself. "I've got plenty of my own problems, but it seems that life isn't quite treating you to the best of times."

Lucas held out a ten-dollar bill. "Here, I pay my own way."

Jarrod waved it away and shook his head. "Forget it. The room's paid for."

"I don't take no charity," Lucas said in his most mature tone of voice.

Reluctantly, Jarrod relented. "Okay, but here's your change." He handed back five dollars. "The motel owner was pretty drunk. I talked him down to a reasonable price."

Taking the sawbuck, Jarrod detected the faint odor of stale whiskey. "Say, where did you get that money? There was only three dollars in your pack."

"I keep most of my cash in my sock. Luckily it wasn't the foot that slob stepped on. I've been robbed a few times. They only take what's in my pockets and backpack." Lucas gave his reply a little too quickly, the cunning smoothness of a con artist evident in his voice. The warmth from the baseboard heaters seemed to be feeding him energy. The boy's fast answer was part of living on the run, Jarrod knew. Yet he felt a pang of suspicion concerning this sudden cash flow.

"Anyway, first thing, please have a hot shower, and hang those wet clothes by the heater. I'm going to watch the end of this movie."

Sipping the remainder of his beer, Jarrod nodded knowingly when he heard Lucas carefully lock the bathroom door. He wondered if the kid could ever trust anyone, especially a stranger. Would he in the same situation? Certainly not.

About twenty minutes and several layers of grime later, Lucas emerged wearing his cut-off jeans. He hung his worn pants, damp shirt, sweater, and oil-stained jacket over a chair next to the heater. Besides being able to count the ribs on the boy's scrawny frame, Jarrod noticed an ugly purplish bruise running across his back between his shoulder blades. Numerous scratches and scabs dotted his torso, arms, and legs. The expression "been through the meat grinder" might adequately describe the pitiful human figure that stood before him.

"Is that nasty bruise on your back the reason you're on the lam, kiddo—I mean, Lucas?" Jarrod inquired, attempting to get the boy to open up a little.

"Lamb, what lamb?"

"Why you're on the run, I mean."

Lucas nodded. "Yeah, partly."

After a long hesitation, the apprehension and pent-up emotions within Lucas finally exploded. Without thinking, words began to flow from his mouth. "That place I stayed at was for kids with no parents. Maybe they were dead or just couldn't handle their kids. The older boys liked to take control. They used the younger ones like slaves, bossed them around. I hate those shitheads. Worse yet, they . . .." His voice trailed off, memories and hostility building within his confused mind.

"Go on," Jarrod encouraged gently. "I'm a good listener,"

Lucas paused for a moment to regain his composure before continuing. "The staff made us shower every couple of days. It was an open shower area. We got no privacy, and the younger boys showered in groups so they could protect each other. This one older asshole, I think he was sixteen, would sneak in and pick out some boy for his fun, usually on a Friday night when the counselors liked to party. They hardly ever checked the showers, and the younger kids were too scared to say anything. The group of older guys would back each other and make sure you got a good shit-kicking if you squealed. A couple of nights back, this jerk made a mistake and picked me. He managed to get me to his room, but I'll tell you, he's going to have trouble taking a piss for a while. My knee's still sore, but not near as bad as my back. The jerk-head threw me against a bookcase."

"Did he get caught?" Jarrod asked, shuddering as he tried to picture the scene.

"I doubt it. But I grabbed my shit and took off that same night. I'm sure he would have beaten the crap out of me when he recovered." Now that he had started talking, Lucas seemed unable to hold back his feelings.

"I take it this isn't the first time you've run off?"

"I've run a few times, but I always get caught. This time I can't go back." His brown eyes widened, displaying fierce determination.

"Have you ever had a . . ." Jarrod paused to search for the words. "A real home? Like with a mom and dad and all the trimmings?"

"Lots of foster parents, but most of those people just wanted the money they got for taking me in. They didn't give a damn about me." Lucas didn't know why he was telling so much to the stranger, but he couldn't seem to control himself. As he continued, deep-rooted feelings emerged, and his voice became more subdued. "I never knew my own mom or my dad. I heard stories that my mother was some high school girl who got knocked up. The state, or whoever, took me away from her and stuck me in these homes. They had a name for me."

Although the term "bastard" came to his mind, Jarrod suggested another. "Ward of the state?"

"Yeah, something like that."

"I saw a letter in your—" Jarrod began to explain, but quickly regretted his words when Lucas abruptly cut him off.

"You prick! Did you go through my stuff? That's none of your business!" His eyes widened with fury, his voice shaking with a sudden display of rage.

Jarrod held up his hands, trying to calm Lucas's temper. "Take it easy, pal. Don't worry, I never read it, just noticed that it looked like a woman's handwriting."

The boy's entire body trembled as he tried to control himself. Jarrod had thrown him the extra blanket, which was wrapped over his drooping shoulders. It was apparent that Lucas was rapidly losing interest in carrying the conversation any further. He looked pale and tired. Mention of the letter had obviously touched a tender spot and knocked the wind out of his sails.

"She was someone special." The words came out in a whisper. The mature demeanor Lucas had exuded was replaced by the tenuous voice of a lost and scared twelve-year-old. "She once said that she lov . . .." His voice trailed off, and he stared at the wall. Only his determined bravado prevented him from breaking down completely.

Feeling a lump rise in his own throat, Jarrod pulled an extra cover from his bed as he changed the subject. "Try to keep warm with this. You can have my extra pillow as well. I guess you'll have to sleep on the rug, but at least it's better than outside or in a cold garage. My side's still throbbing from my run-in with the sheriff, so I'll have to take the bed."

Without a doubt, Lucas was no longer in the mood to talk. He silently accepted the bedding and then settled quickly into his luxury accommodations on the carpeted floor beneath a small table close to the heater. He resembled a scruffy dog curled up before the hearth more than he did the vulnerable young human he was.

Jarrod shut off the television, switched off the lights, and sipped on the remains of his second beer. In the darkness, he made a silent vow to the small form he could barely make out beneath the table. *Kiddo, I sure as hell don't know what to do with you tomorrow, but one thing I promise: I won't desert you.* Was this merely the hollow promise of a desperate man on the run?

Chapter 3

Sleep that night was neither restful nor dreamless for Jarrod. Any movement he made brought a sharp complaint from his injured ribs. Concern of not waking in time to catch the bus also added to his restlessness. In the last of many dreams, and the only one he could remember, Jarrod was stranded on an ice floe drifting through the Arctic Ocean. As wind and snow swirled around him, he stood face to face with a hungry polar bear. The vivid image was quick to dissolve as he awoke abruptly to the reality that his room was as cold as the ice floe in his dream. His first thought was that a fuse had blown or that Toothy had shut off the power. But when Jarrod sat up, he noticed that the small window at the rear of the room was wide open. A cold breeze whistled through it. A quick glance under the table revealed only a crumpled blanket and a flattened pillow. Lucas had bolted, but why?

Before he had time to sort out the possibilities, and with his mind still not fully awake, Jarrod heard a rapid tapping at the door, an official-sounding knock. He pulled on his pants, and his heart skipped a beat as he peeked out a narrow opening between the curtains covering the window that faced the parking lot. Both Toothy and the repugnant, overweight sheriff (Klem! the name hit him like a sledgehammer) were standing outside his door. Another knock followed, and then the rattling of a key being inserted into the deadbolt.

"I'm coming, I'm coming!" Jarrod shouted as the door began to open. The safety chain caught.

"Police! Open your door, Mr. Smith. The motel owner would like to talk to you."

With no plausible alternatives (he could never fit through the rear window), Jarrod unhooked the chain and opened the door. Before him stood two of the oddest gentlemen that he could ever imagine: a rotund, bleary-eyed, unshaven sheriff and his mule-faced, dental wonder sidekick. As funny as the image might appear, Jarrod failed to find any humor in his predicament.

"Well, well," Klem began slowly and deliberately, "I thought I made myself clear that I never wanted to see your face in this town again."

"My side hurt too much for bus travel last night," Jarrod explained as calmly as possible.

"You got what you deserved, buddy." The sheriff let out a low growl to emphasize his point. "Toothy here had a bit of a problem last night. It appears that someone swiped all his cash receipts for the week while he was passed ou—sleeping. You were the last guest to register last night and—"

"Didn't hear a thing," Jarrod said. "I slept like a log," a remark that was far from the truth.

Noticing the rear window was wide open, Toothy threw his hands up. "What the hell's that window doing open? The heater's on full blast!"

Jarrod glanced back. "I . . . needed some fresh air to get to sleep." He tried to sound convincing as he shivered from the chilly draft. "I thought I'd turned the heat down. Sorry."

As Toothy went to close the window, Klem noticed the blanket and pillow underneath the table. "Say, you're kind of messy, throwing all this stuff under here." He lifted the blanket and, to Jarrod's dismay, out fell the tattered remains of a small sock.

"My, my, what have we got here? It appears Mr. Smith didn't spend the night alone." Klem held up the sock. He stated the obvious, "I somehow doubt this would fit you."

Jarrod said nothing as the sheriff walked to the open window, where Toothy stood, still grumbling. It didn't take Agatha Christie to detect that the screen had been pushed out, its twisted remains resting in a clump of fresh snow. With a look of satisfaction, Klem turned back to Jarrod. "I think Mr. Smith, or whoever you are, will be spending a few more days in our little town. Judge Bartlett will be making an appearance in a day or two. I'm sure he'd like to talk to you."

Sheriff Laurence "Klem" Klemchuk had suspicions that there was more to this out-of-towner than his rugged outward appearance suggested, and that nailing him would prove much more of a challenge than all the traffic violations, false alarms, barroom scuffles, and candy-stealing kids that occupied his normal workweek. Mr. Smith (probably an alias) reminded Klem of a modern-day spaghetti western cowboy. His piercing, deep-blue eyes and the determined manner in which he set his square jaw expressed a keen intelligence and perceptiveness not found in the common drifters that the sheriff normally hustled out of town. The lanky, confident intruder showed the composure of a foreign intelligence agent. The possibilities were endless. The sudden intrigue pumped energy through Klem's exhausted, underfed body.

Jarrod briefly considered making a fast escape, maybe even jumping in the driver's seat of the sheriff's idling cruiser. He quickly changed his mind when he noticed a large German shepherd sitting patiently in the passenger seat.

"What are you holding me for?" Jarrod inquired boldly, trying to cover up his concern. He held little hope of reasoning with the stubborn man, who had just reeled in his catch of the year.

"Well, why don't we start with harboring a runaway and obstructing justice, not to mention implication in the robbery of our friend, Toothy Reynolds?" Klem said with pleasure as he detached a set of handcuffs from his belt. He continued with a formal reading of the prisoner's rights.

Does this town allow any rights? Jarrod wondered.

"Don't forget, this guy owes me for an extra person," Toothy added, his teeth clacking together in agitation. "He only paid the single rate, an' that busted screen goes on his bill, too."

"None of those charges will stick, you know. How about I just settle up with Mr. Reynolds and get out of your hair?" Jarrod tried to sound confident in his last effort at freedom.

"Forget it, Mr. Smith. We'll let our competent judge decide. But first, I'm going to find out if that's really your name. Get your stuff, and let's go. You're going to like our new facilities." Hinting a surprise was in store for his prisoner, Klem's voice dripped with sarcasm.

Reluctantly, but with any form of escape looking hopeless in his present condition, Jarrod accepted the handcuffs and was escorted to a facility he could never have imagined. Three weeks earlier, with hard-wired smoke detectors failing in the middle of the night, the town's police station and holding cells had been ravaged by an electrical fire. Klem had no doubts that the curse of a new computer system had been the cause. The equipment had been installed only a few months earlier to update the station by linking it with the state law enforcement center and the FBI. Klem was just beginning to understand the new computer "gadgetry," as he called it, and could perform simple tasks on the console, when the fire destroyed it, along with the entire station. As a temporary replacement for the jail cells, Jarrod was taken to, of all places, the local dog pound. He could never have imagined such a facility. The two largest cages in the kennel had been modified with the addition of camp cots and portable toilets to imitate jail cells.

One cage was occupied by a soundly snoring man, who Klem mentioned was the town drunk. While wondering what rank Toothy would hold in the category of alcoholics, Jarrod was unceremoniously locked in the second holding "cell." The disturbance awoke two mongrel dogs that were caged in smaller kennels. They barked and yapped in unison, upsetting the sheriff.

"Shut up! You two are going down, and real soon."

Prior to his incarceration, Jarrod's belongings were listed and stored for safekeeping. It was during that procedure when Klem discovered Jarrod's identity from a card hidden in his wallet, ID that Jarrod thought he had disposed of. With increased suspicion, Klem faxed information on his prisoner to the state law enforcement agency in Madison, where any outstanding warrants or arrest records could be confirmed. Klem would have bet his life's savings that Jarrod was wanted for something, somewhere. Regrettably, his new computer gadget would have told him a lot faster.

After completing the paperwork he disliked so much, the sheriff received an answer to his fax. "Jarrod Wakefield, a name with a criminal ring to it, for sure," Klem surmised in the privacy of his cruiser. He had left a young officer named Hodgson with the task of monitoring the most prized prisoner to ever occupy the newly renovated "cells." That gave Klem time to consume a fast meal and catch a few more hours of sleep at home. Toothy had rudely awakened him from a brief sleep early that morning with news of the robbery. The sheriff felt certain he was close to solving that case as well. As he drifted into a deep sleep, his mind pictured the young runaway strutting around in a new pair of jeans and wearing a baseball cap that Toothy Reynolds had so generously funded.

Emotionally drained, Jarrod sat on the edge of his cot. Stone-faced, he munched slowly on a tasteless baloney sandwich and sipped a lukewarm coffee. The drunk was returning to life and complained loudly of his throbbing head and his need for a shot of whiskey. Hodgson released him to his wife just before noon. After hearing the man's wife tear into him with an earful of curses and admonishments, Jarrod understood why the fellow had turned to the bottle. The unfortunate man resembled a whipped puppy as his wife led him out of the kennel by his shirt collar.

As Hodgson watched them go, he shook his head. "That's Jake. He sleeps off his binges here at least once a week. It's a toss-up whether that witch of a wife he's got or the whiskey will drive him to an early grave. I'm betting on the wife." He smiled at his prisoner, who showed little interest as he sat dejectedly on his cot. Jarrod would refer to similar scenes over the years to explain his determined hold on bachelorhood.

"When's that judge going to be in town?" he inquired, already feeling confined in his cramped quarters.

"He's scheduled to be in tomorrow. But I'll warn you, Judge Bartlett is not fond of strangers disrupting life in our little town," Hodgson replied, his tone as discouraging as the words he spoke.

Chapter 4

During the next few hours of his confinement, Jarrod had plenty of time to think about his past, including his accomplishments and his indiscretions. He had invested nearly ten years of his life with a firm that manufactured sophisticated industrial parts, the terminology and jargon of which was beyond the concept of the average layman. Jarrod had watched the company grow from the embryonic stage to a firm that generated millions of dollars of business each year. It was fast paced, highly technical, and its market was ever expanding. By showing a keen intelligence and ingenuity, he zoomed up the ladder of responsibility, soon becoming a vital cog in the mechanism that drove the vibrant enterprise.

After an original underwriting was created to finance the company, penny stocks blossomed into shares that traded for over thirty dollars on Wall Street. That had particularly irked Jarrod, as a passion for gambling was the greatest driving force in his life, including his employment. Yet other than a few shares distributed as bonuses, he had never invested a nickel in the company. After failing miserably in his few forays into the get-rich-quick allure of penny stocks, it was one rainbow he had failed to chase. The potential gain of a company trying to get off the ground wasn't a fast-enough turnover for a guy who preferred the dizzying pace of the casino or the racetrack, places where money could be made or lost on a roll of the dice, the spin of a wheel, the turn of a card, or the photo finish of a stakes race.

Sure, Jarrod had enjoyed streaks of luck when nothing could go wrong, but like many gamblers, he didn't know when to quit. A steep fall inevitably followed those lucrative times. The most devastating of those collapses had occurred just over a year ago, when Jarrod got in far over his head with some unsavory and dangerous people. English was not their native tongue, and their high-interest loans were never forgiven. His debts soon exceeded $200,000, more than his salary or his extended line of credit could finance. The underworld heavyweights didn't accept written IOUs or American Express. They wanted a regular and substantial influx of cash, or else the leg-breakers threatened to make a midnight visit.

Jarrod was desperate. The position he held with his company allowed him the passwords required to access its computerized accounting system. Through his familiarity with the system and his experience as an analyst, he devised a plan that created fictional creditors. Over a period of eight months, he channelled over $80,000 from the company's operating budget into payments of imaginary accounts. He retrieved the checks from various post office boxes and then turned them into cash through an agency that retained a percentage. Suspicion is one safeguard not programmed into a computer. Jarrod's unsavory creditors were satisfied by the steady infusion of cash that they accumulated over the months.

Unfortunately, in gambling, as in life in general, good luck must come to an end. Less than a week earlier, Jarrod had found it necessary to close his affairs at home and take to the road. A downward swing in the economy had led to diminishing returns for the company. Every internal operation came under greater scrutiny. One of the newer, bright young employees caught some discrepancies while trying to correct a flaw in the accounts payable program. His brash enthusiasm propelled him over several heads to report his suspicions. Once alerted, management ordered an internal audit to begin immediately.

Aware of what the essential point of the audit would read, Jarrod booked off sick, closed out his meager savings account, borrowed as much cash as possible against his credit cards, and packed his bag while he still had the opportunity. At forty-two years of age, his apartment and furniture abandoned, he was officially on the run. Yet who would be his greatest concern, his creditors, or his former employer? Whatever the case, Jarrod knew he was in serious trouble. If only he had dumped that stupid ID before the meddling sheriff got hold of it. With no criminal record, Klem could never have traced Jarrod's fingerprints. Hopefully, the audit had not been completed and the police or the legendary federal bureau had not issued a warrant for his arrest.

No such luck. At about four o'clock, well-rested, well-fed, and beaming, Sheriff Klem returned to his temporary office. He sent Officer Hodgson out for some burgers and fries, enough to feed them all, including his special prisoner.

The news he had received across the fax machine at city hall had whetted his appetite and given him reason to celebrate.

"So, Mr. Wakefield, it appears we may not be the only ones trying to put you behind bars. It seems that some people back east want to question a man with your name and, by a strange coincidence, fitting your description. It concerns some misspent funds. I think they call it 'embezzlement.' My instinct told me you were different from the usual drifters that pass through town." Klem spoke slowly as he savored every word, confirming his prisoner's greatest fears.

Jarrod was speechless. Just a few hours of custody had already made him claustrophobic. Another ten years or so did not appeal to him at all. The reality of his situation struck him like a bolt of lightning. Suddenly riveted to his cot, he couldn't even find the strength to nod.

"Some gentlemen from the east should be down our way to interrogate you in a day or two," Klem continued. "In the meantime, we still have some matters of our own to take up with Judge Bartlett."

Hodgson returned with supper.

"Here, enjoy your meal. You can't say our fine town didn't feed you." Klem grinned like a winner as he passed a hamburger between the bars.

Sheriff Klemchuk proceeded to devour his own burger with two great bites. Grease dripping from his lips, he chewed and talked at the same time. "I'm instructing a defensive driving course tonight, but our young officer here will make sure that you're comfortable. You don't mind a little overtime, do you, Hodgson? Purcell can replace you at midnight."

Hodgson, his mouth stuffed with a handful of fries, nodded and mumbled a confirmation that he would stay.

Satisfied with the way the day was going, Klem let out a good belch and got up from his chair. With keys jingling loudly from the chain that dangled from his belt, he left the kennel to prepare for another of his important civic duties.

Desperation, panic, hopelessness . . . countless thoughts swirled through Jarrod's tormented head. He couldn't eat. Just the smell of the burger nauseated him. The bars of his cage seemed to press closer and closer, as if trying to squeeze the last breath from his body. His eyes, forced to squint as they teared up from the odor of greasy food, darted around the circumference of the room in an effort to find any hope of escape.

Please, give me anything, Jarrod prayed silently, squeezing his eyelids shut as he searched for inspiration. In the end, all he could focus on was a set of keys dangling from a tarnished metal hoop. The key ring hung teasingly from a wooden dowel that protruded from the desk fifteen feet away, where Hodgson was resting his size-eleven feet. In desperation, he examined the bars and lock on the cage which imprisoned him. Regrettably, the kennel was built to withstand the escape attempts of the strongest Doberman or Great Dane.

Then an idea struck him, a last resort. "Hey, officer, my toilet's plugged in here. Do you think I could use your restroom?" So strong was his urge to escape, his flimsy fabrication came out with a tone of complete desperation.

Hodgson was not one to be fooled easily. "Sorry, but the sheriff left orders not to let you out of there under any circumstances. You're a prize catch for him, especially with elections coming up next spring." Hodgson's duties were quite simple. His biggest concern was trying to adjust the fuzzy picture on a twelve-inch, worn out television.

Dusk and darkness came early on that late-autumn evening in northern Wisconsin. Jarrod stretched out on his lumpy cot, his ears filled with the hissing drone that came from the flickering TV. He forced his eyes to close as the smell of dog urine added to his nausea. Unable to lie still on his uncomfortable bed, his mind remained active. He conjured visions of a crowded courtroom, grim-faced judge, and confident prosecutor. When that scene faded into darkness, it was replaced with the view of a massive stone structure complete with turrets, razor wire, and thick steel bars. The grim building was perched so high on a barren hillside that low-hanging clouds floated across the tinted windows of towering guard posts that hid the dour faces of armed sentries.

It was at that moment, with Jarrod drifting toward unconsciousness, that the bars of all the kennels began to vibrate, slowly at first, and then rattling loudly as a muffled roar echoed throughout the building. The mongrels resumed their barking. Even with his eyes barely open, Jarrod noticed a flickering, yellowish light dance across the ceiling above his cell. As he stood up too quickly from his cot, dizziness swept over him, and a sharp pain jabbed into his left side. His legs wobbly, he stretched as high as the cage would allow him and peered through the bars at the window across the room.

Hodgson, as well, had felt the sudden tremor, heard the cannonading boom, and witnessed the strange, shimmering light that flashed across the dimly lit kennel. What he saw through the window made him leap to grab hold of his shortwave radio. About two blocks away, toward the highway and bus depot, flames leapt high into the black evening sky. From the suddenness and intensity of the blaze, he feared that maybe a tanker truck had exploded, and the inferno was engulfing his town. Unable to reach his superior on his radio (Klem had probably shut it off and was into his lesson on what a driver should do to get rid of a tailgater), Hodgson punched the school's number into the landline on his desk. Further panic struck him when he discovered the line was dead. Without concern for the consequences, Hodgson ran from the dog pound to his cruiser, oblivious to his guard duties and the mongrels' frantic barking.

Jarrod heard the familiar squealing of tires as Hodgson sped off in search of his superior. In an instant, he was on his feet and shaking the door to his cage with all his strength. His knuckles white, and with sweat dripping down his face, Jarrod was about to scream with rage and frustration when he froze, his wet hands still squeezing the smooth bars of his cage. He watched in dismay as the outside door to the kennel opened ever so slowly. When a small figure appeared, Jarrod blinked twice in disbelief. It was Lucas. The boy cautiously looked around the room before entering.

It didn't take Jarrod long to realize what must have happened outside and sense the opportunity it presented. His heart pounded with excitement and the return of not only hope, but also mobility in his limbs.

"Over there!" he blurted, pointing to the keys that dangled from the wooden dowel.

Lucas approached the cage and fumbled with three different keys before finding the one that matched the lock. Jarrod felt an enormous weight slip from his shoulders as his cell door swung open. The awareness of his imminent freedom sent a sudden rush through his body like no feeling he had experienced before. Overcome by the surge of energy, he came close to collapsing.

"I owed you one," Lucas said calmly. The maturity of his voice belied his youthful age once again.

"You don't know how glad I am to see you," Jarrod replied, his voice a sigh of relief. Instinctively, he gave Lucas a brief yet unreserved hug. Surprisingly, the boy accepted it.

It took one good stroke with a night stick to knock open the locked wooden desk drawer. Jarrod recovered his wallet and money from a sealed envelope. Then, after retrieving his travel bag and worldly belongings from an upright cabinet, the improbable duo made a hasty exit out the front door. Fortunately, other than the yapping mongrels, no one was in the vicinity to witness their escape. The only people in sight were running toward the inferno on the highway. Jarrod expected that scene would occupy the attention of every able-bodied person in town for the entire night and beyond.

Slipping down dark alleys and deserted roadways, making sure the smoke and flames were well to their backs, the escapees found themselves on the north edge of town in a short time. So far, the only sirens they heard came from the fire trucks approaching town from the east. Jarrod suspected the town would, at best, have a volunteer fire brigade, whose equipment was no match for the intense fire that engulfed the western horizon.

Familiar with that side of town from the previous day, Lucas pointed out three railway boxcars that rested on a siding along the side of a loading platform and warehouse. The building's corrugated metal walls, as well as the sides of the boxcars, were painted with countless shapes, letters, and scrawls that only a graffiti expert could decipher.

"I slept in that boxcar the other night, maybe we can hide there and—"

"The great marshalling yards of this upbeat community!" Jarrod interrupted, wondering how often a train actually stopped at the platform. It was likely that a whistle blast, an engineer's wave, and a rush of wind was all that most trains left behind on their journey to more important destinations. "We could hide in these boxcars, but they're not going to get us very far. It might be weeks before an engine hooks up to them. Sheriff Klem will have them searched long before then."

Lucas slumped his shoulders in disappointment.

"We're either going to have to hoof it, hitch a ride, or find some vehicle sitting around just waiting to take a little trip," Jarrod said. "The main thing is to split from this town as soon as possible." He had to ask one question. "Did you have something to do with that?" He nodded back to the bright glow that hovered over the trees and rooftops to the southwest.

"Maybe, just a little," Lucas replied. Jarrod could tell the boy was tired and had begun to withdraw into his own isolated world. Further questioning would be futile.

Jarrod paced across the dimly lit tracks, looking for anything that might be of use in their quest for escape. He considered hot-wiring one of the cars they had passed in their hasty movement through town but then rejected the idea, as the vehicles were all parked next to well-lit homes. Besides, he recalled his one effort to short-circuit a car's ignition when he was a teenager had been a complete failure, even though he was just trying to help a friend who had misplaced his keys.

Stepping across the slick, frost-coated tracks of the main line, Jarrod spotted something in the dim lighting that might be the answer to their transportation needs. Resting on a secondary set of tracks next to a wooden shed sat a strange contraption. Its exterior resembled a bombardier, a Canadian-made snow machine with tracks that navigated arctic regions. The blunt nose of the conveyance had the aerodynamics of a Volkswagen Beetle, whose tires had been replaced by steel wheels. A metal canopy covered the front half of the cab, but a canvas tarpaulin stretched over sturdy hoops was the only protection for the rear passenger area. The tarp was secured with metal clips and round snaps. A faded orange sign on the side of the cab read, "NW Angle Hydro." Jarrod visualized the odd machine, coated with ice and packed with a frost-covered crew, rumbling along the tracks on its way to repair downed power lines following an ice storm.

"Let's hope I can start this damn thing," he said, as much to himself as to his traveling companion. "I used to operate all types of equipment when I worked on road construction."

The vehicle had a gasoline-powered engine designed to turn over by depressing a button connected to the starter. However, an ignition switch had to be activated so the starter could draw power from the battery. As was often the case, especially with such older contraptions, the key slot was so worn that almost any key or facsimile would fit in and turn the switch. Finding that he still carried a set of old keys in his travel bag, for what reason he wasn't sure, Jarrod worked on the ignition switch until he was able to jam his old racket club locker key into the slot. Closing his eyes, he was beginning a brief prayer when the sound of a faint click made his heart jump. The key rotated clockwise a quarter of a turn, and a needle moved slightly on the voltage dial to indicate that the battery wasn't hopelessly dead. It took both hands to pull out the rusty lever that opened the choke. Then Jarrod depressed the red starter button and held his breath. The engine groaned its annoyance at being awakened on such a frigid evening. For an agonizing twenty seconds, the weary, old engine continued to sputter its opposition to firing up its dormant spark plugs.

Jarrod released his finger, which was turning numb from applying constant pressure. Even in the cold night air, he was dripping sweat. Realizing the battery was getting weaker, he gave it a short rest. As he pondered what other alternatives might be available, he glanced toward young Lucas, either for suggestion or inspiration, but the boy would be no help. He was curled up on the bench seat, shivering, exhausted, and lost in his own thoughts.

"What now?" Jarrod asked, his voice a whisper of gloom. He turned his head toward the small shed that sat next to the tracks. Could it hold anything that might help?

Grabbing a frigid wrench he found under the driver's seat, it took one swing for Jarrod to knock the padlock off the shed's flimsy door. A flick of the switch inside the door turned on a lone bulb that clung to the inside wall. Scanning the shelves that lined the interior, Jarrod spotted two items of interest. One was an aerosol can that was labeled Ether, a highly flammable liquid used as a starting aid for stubborn engines. The other was a plastic gasoline container, which turned out to be full.

Before topping up the gas, Jarrod had to make sure the engine started. After spraying an ample amount of ether into the open carburetor, he turned the ignition key, whispering, "Please," as he pushed the starter button one more time. The explosion and flame that shot out of the carburetor put an abrupt end to his companion's nervous fidgeting. They both jumped to their feet in shock, then sighed as the stubborn engine coughed to life.

The spluttering putt, putt, putt of the uncooperative engine echoed in Lucas's tired mind. "Sounds like the stupid lawn mower at my group home," he muttered. "Damn thing never wanted to start." Jarrod was too occupied to hear him speak.

The engine warmed slowly as the revs increased with the choke pulled open. After topping up the gas tank, Jarrod overcame one last obstacle by pulling down and rotating the handle that shunted the siding track so it aligned with the railroad's main line. With the gears engaged in a forward position, the vehicle sputtered and creaked onto the main tracks without the least concern for any danger that could be lurking. Before continuing, and not even questioning why the siding switch had not been locked to prevent vandalism, Jarrod returned the lever to its original position. He didn't want to be the cause of a derailment. Inside the cramped cab once again, Jarrod released the handbrake, eased the miniature locomotive into gear, and continued his westward journey. This time he was not alone.

How long would they have the tracks to themselves? Apprehension filled both passengers as they chugged away from town in their most unusual means of transportation. Jarrod pulled the throttle lever wide open. He hoped the attention of every person in town was diverted to the raging fire and no one's curiosity had been aroused by the noise of a strange contraption that belched smoke as it coughed and sputtered along the shiny tracks. Not until any sight of the crew cab was smothered by the vast darkness of a moonless night did Jarrod dare to activate the headlight. Frost on the tracks glistened in the beam of light cast by the powerful halogen bulb. Jackrabbits scattered in every direction as they tried to escape the intense, piercing glare that both frightened and blinded them.

Countless questions swirled in Jarrod's mind as he turned to look at his exhausted travel companion, who was curled up on the wooden bench behind the driving compartment. Any answers would have to wait. It appeared Jarrod would be the sole engineer and brakeman tonight. With the instrument panel partly illuminated, he found the toggle switch that started warm air circulating around the chilly cab. Even the squealing heater fan could not prevent Lucas, who had a dusty burlap blanket draped over him, from falling into the deepest of sleeps.

Dawn, and a new day, would come soon enough.

Chapter 5

Hodgson reached his superior in record time, racing through town as though the devil were chasing him. He broke every safety rule that Klem was teaching in his lecture, speeding up to the high school so quickly that his cruiser car peppered the windows of the principal's office with a shower of loose gravel as it slid to a stop against the entrance steps.

Out of breath, his heart pounding with excitement, Hodgson burst into the classroom. "Fire, Klem! There's one hell of a fire! I tried to call you . . .."

He caught Klem by surprise in the middle of a movie on the perils of losing one's night vision as a person aged. "Did you get hold of Fred Parker?" Klem asked. Fred was in charge of the volunteer fire brigade.

When Hodgson shook his head, Klem began to berate his deputy before realizing he had better take quick action. After getting as much information as he could from Hodgson, he ran (as well as a man his size could run) to the school phone and made the call himself. Although the phone line from the dog kennel was inoperable, the line between the school and Parker's home was still connected. Fred's wife told Klem that her husband was already in action, and reinforcements had been called in from the nearby town of Abbotsford. A combination of the closed classroom in a brick building and dialogue from the movie had blocked out the sound of the explosion.

"I should give Parker a badge and deputize him. He'd be better than what I have," Klem mumbled to himself as he squeezed into his cruiser. His safe driving class, not wanting to miss any of the action, was dispersing quickly.

Seeing smoke billowing into the sky toward the highway, Klem stuck his head out the window. "You get back to your damn prisoner!" he shouted to Hodgson. "I'll check this out and radio you if I need any help."

Klem sent stones and gravel flying as he raced off, lights flashing and siren blaring. Within two minutes, he was standing next to the bus depot among the crowd that had swollen to almost half the town's population. Two fire trucks from nearby Abbotsford were spreading a thick foamy substance on the remains of a gasoline fire. Apparently, the tanks had ruptured at the closed service station next to the bus depot. Smoke billowed from a pile of old tires, hoses, and refuse barrels on the side of the garage farthest from the bus depot. The crowd covered their faces from the stench of burning rubber. The volunteer fire unit hosed down everything in sight, rapidly depleting the water supply in its antiquated tanker. Quick action and a friendly westerly breeze had prevented the fire from spreading to the bus depot or to a laundromat north of the service station. Traffic on the highway was being detoured along the west service road. It was clear that Fred Parker should receive some sort of commendation for his quick actions and leadership role in fighting the inferno.

Klem found it hard to believe that an old brick high school could insulate his class from the sound of the explosion and subsequent sirens and commotion coming from the scene of the fire. Perhaps his interesting lecture had something to do with it. He was barely out of his cruiser when Debbie, the gregarious waitress from the bus depot restaurant, ran up to him.

"That sure scared the hell out of me, Klem," Debbie stammered, her body still trembling. She had been at home taking a bath when the explosion occurred. Wet strands of hair hung over her face, and her gum no longer crackled. She had swallowed it as she ran toward the fire in her pajamas. "If Mrs. Jones hadn't been walking her dog and seen it start up, that fire could have been a lot worse. It's lucky no one got killed when the tanks exploded. Fred should get a medal. He sure got them fire trucks here fast—"

"Did Mrs. Jones see where or how it started?" Klem interrupted the excited girl.

"She saw flames shootin' up from a trash barrel next to the garage. And get this: She saw some small kid running away from the station. She couldn't make out if it was a local kid. I'd guess he was movin' too fast." Her excitement kept Debbie talking. "If you want to speak to her, she's in the bus station. Her chest was aching, and she had to sit down."

Klem had blanked out the chatty waitress as a picture flashed into his mind. Just as he realized what likely had happened, a frantic call came over the radio in his cruiser.

"Klem, come in! Klem, are you there?" In his panic, Hodgson didn't bother with call numbers.

Klem grabbed the receiver and squeezed the talk button. "Go ahead . . . over."

"He's gone. The prisoner's gone! Someone let him out. The key's still in the lock." Hodgson's voice was quivering.

"You idiot! You were set up. I'll be right there," Klem yelled into the phone.

Forgetting his duty of crowd control, forgetting Fred Parker, forgetting Mrs. Jones, forgetting the smoke and the awful stench, Sheriff Klemchuk floored the accelerator of his patrol car. The vehicle fishtailed in its flight toward the dog pound, sending several onlookers scattering out of its path. Klem was livid, his blood pressure climbing well into the danger zone.

The ensuing conversation with Hodgson was one-sided and unprintable. Klem tore a strip off his deputy from head to foot. He only stopped ranting when he realized that his own health might be endangered. His condemnation and cries of stupidity came out between heavy puffs as his chest heaved up and down. Klem used words like "duped," "suckered," and "conned." He ended with the biting interrogative, "by a snotty-nosed brat?"

Klem was prepared to start the chase right away, with all barrels loaded and a pack of hunting dogs, if he could find any. Unfortunately, with all his manpower exhausted from the multiple tasks involved with fighting a fire, including redirecting highway traffic, he realized that an immediate hunt for the fugitives would be impossible. Some little brat had brought his town to its knees. All he could do for the moment was alert the state police and put out an APB. In the morning, he would search the town from top to bottom. Furious that any prisoner should escape his grasp, Klem vowed that if he ever caught them, those two would regret the day they set foot in his town. Somehow, someday, they would pay dearly for making fools of him and his police force.

Chapter 6

With the excitement, the crowds, and the lawmen far behind it, the miniature locomotive chugged along on its westward route. Unfortunately, even at full throttle, the speed of a camel lumbering across the Sahara would have rivaled its pace. While Lucas had fallen into a sound sleep, Jarrod was straining through bloodshot eyes to detect the impending approach of ominous lights. He kept a constant watch on the highway, which often came into view alongside the tracks, as well as the railway line, which stretched far into the darkness ahead of them. Frequent looks behind were also necessary. The threat of an oncoming train from either direction was enough to keep him alert. Physically, he was bone-tired, but he refused to let himself rest. Although enough heat circulated from the engine compartment to keep them both from freezing, Jarrod noticed Lucas continued to shiver under his burlap covers. The hard wooden bench made a poor bed. Placing his warm jacket over the boy, he impulsively rubbed his sore eyes, which were burning from the constant strain of the night vigil.

The night seemed endless as minutes stretched into hours. Clickety-clack, clickety-clack, the noise of steel wheels hitting the joints in the tracks echoed constantly in Jarrod's tired head.

The eye-straining vigil finally ended when dawn emerged, with the faintest of light shining through a vale of wispy clouds. It only took moments before the vivid colors of a crisp November sunrise celebrated the beginning of a new day. The backdrop that had shrouded the countryside in darkness was sliced open as if a sword had swung back and forth across the eastern sky, each stroke exposing a fresh streak of red, yellow, or orange as it shredded the night curtain. Rich rolling fields that would normally checkerboard the landscape with autumn hues were resting peacefully beneath winter's first blanket of white. The snow was thick and billowy in some places yet so thin in others that dark blotches of greens and browns were exposed like ugly scars. Jarrod, in his effort to stay awake, rocked his body to the rhythm of the rails. Clickety-click, clickety-clack, the rhythmic, mesmerizing sound continued along the frosty tracks. His eyelids gradually drooping, Jarrod was jarred to life by a loud sneeze from the rear of the cab, followed by a drowsy inquiry.

"Where are we?" Lucas asked in a husky voice as he muffled a yawn. He let out another huge sneeze and rubbed his hands in the warmth of the air blowing from the cab's heater.

"From the position of the sun, I would say we're headed northwest, hopefully many miles from that ugly town—and the even uglier sheriff who thought he owned it," Jarrod replied. "We can't travel much farther on this track. There's bound to be a train coming soon from either direction. I can't believe our luck so far."

"I'll get out of your hair soon, mister. I'm goin' north to Canada," Lucas announced with renewed confidence. He seemed rejuvenated by his night's sleep, although his dripping nose and persistent sneezing showed the first sign of a cold.

"Please, call me Jarrod, but I think we should stick together a little longer. We're not out of the woods yet. Say, why Canada anyway?"

"I'm looking for someone there." The brief answer was hesitant.

"By the way, do you want to tell me what happened back in town to get us both into such hot water? I was a little suspicious of that money you came up with suddenly at the motel." With his head full of questions, Jarrod pried carefully for some answers.

Lucas thought for a long moment before offering his explanation. Again, once he started talking, he couldn't stop. Apparently, his reluctance in accepting shelter from Jarrod the previous evening had been tempered by the snow and chilly conditions. Before trying to figure out which room Jarrod had rented, Lucas had peeked through the motel office window. The door between the owner's living quarters and the office was sitting open. Lucas had a clear view of Toothy, who was sleeping soundly with his mouth open and an empty whiskey bottle about to fall out of his hand. There, on the table next to him, sat a pile of crumpled bills, likely the cash receipts for several days' rentals. It was too great an opportunity for a hungry runaway to pass up. Since the office was locked and well lit, instinct led the young thief to the rear of the motel, where he found the entrance to Toothy's kitchen. With no deadbolt in place, Lucas easily jimmied the lock with a narrow metal shim that he carried with him for such occasions. The door opened slowly on hinges that screamed for oil, but Toothy, in his inebriated state, never even flinched. His profits quickly vanished.

Jarrod sat mesmerized as Lucas continued his storybook tale. At times, he felt as though he was interviewing a conman serving many years in prison rather than a twelve-year-old runaway. It was hard to envision Lucas was simply a child forced to grow up too quickly, fend for himself, and take on responsibilities normally left to an adult. There were no rules to follow when it came to scrounging for every meal and searching for a bed to sleep in. For Lucas, the transition from exuberant child to hardened adult could take place in the blink of an eye.

"A car door slammed and woke me up early at the motel," the road-weary boy continued. "When I looked out the window, I knew for sure there was trouble. I must have panicked. For some reason, I didn't wake you, but I felt bad about it later. Maybe it's just that I don't trust people, though I seem to be trusting you a little. Anyway, I knocked out the screen window at the back of the room—I'm surprised you never heard me. I had some trouble squeezing through that hole. Later, I got to thinking . . . you'd helped me out of a jam, so maybe there was a way I could pay you back."

Having seen Jarrod being driven away under escort, and overcome with an unfamiliar feeling of guilt, Lucas had stealthily searched the town until he discovered the police car parked outside the dog pound. He was unsure that the man who had aided his own escape was being held there until he overheard Jake, as he wobbled down the steps, telling his wife about the tall stranger locked in the cage next to his. The rescue plan had been simple yet effective. By starting a fire in a barrel of oily rags at the service station, where he had hidden the night before, Lucas hoped to create a diversion that would allow him access to Jarrod. Even in his wildest of dreams, he could not have imagined his plan working better. The flames spread to one of the pumps, where a small leak created a massive explosion. Lucas never planned on the enormous blaze that resulted from the gasoline fumes igniting.

So caught up in the man-child's story, Jarrod neglected his most important duty as a railway engineer. He failed to notice the series of lights that hung from poles on both sides of the tracks. Every light displayed a solid red signal. Because of his neglect, the miniature locomotive continued to rumble past the switch-lever box and siding track that could have diverted it to safety. Having served its purpose, Jarrod had meant to ditch their getaway vehicle on a siding as soon as daylight broke, but the long night vigil left him on the edge of exhaustion. The intrigue aroused by his companion's account of the last two days had also numbed his mind to the point that it broke his concentration on the more important task of survival. That distraction might well have proved fatal were it not for a casual observation from Lucas, whose survival instinct always kept him aware of potential danger.

"Jarrod, it looks like the tracks curve into those bushes up ahead." His comment was nonchalant as well as the first time he had called his older accomplice by name.

Realizing he had neglected his most important duty, Jarrod spun around and was immediately aware that the view of the tracks ahead was limited by rows of scrub brush and a long curve to the left. He chastised himself mentally for having missed the last siding track. "Get your backpack on. We may have to abandon ship. I meant to dump this contraption a lot earlier."

With tension knotting his muscles, Jarrod strained to see any small opening in the endless thicket of brush, which mingled with evergreens draped with fresh snow.

Sensing his older companion's concern, Lucas also concentrated his attention on the curving tracks ahead of them. His keener eyes were first to notice the trestle. "Look! There's a bridge ahead. Is that a river?"

Through bloodshot eyes, Jarrod focused his view on the stark black girders of an old railway bridge that spanned a river about the width of an eight-lane expressway. As the crew-buggy chugged its way closer, he noticed that the murky, slow-moving waters had not yet frozen in the cool late-fall temperatures. Trees that had collapsed during spring and summer flooding, dead branches, rotting logs, and other debris that had been swept downstream littered the sluggish waters. The bridge supports acted like a dam, clogging the river with a tangle of debris.

Instinctively, Jarrod slid his hand onto the mini-locomotive's throttle. He slowed the machine as it entered the eastern access to the bridge. Not a moment later, he noticed the thin, grey smoke of danger approaching. The shrill sound of a whistle reached out from the distance and stopped the breathing of both transients simultaneously. The sight of the approaching train made Jarrod gulp uncontrollably. He felt the tiny hairs on the back of his neck stand straight up. And what a train! Even at a distance of half a mile, he could see the shimmering tracks being devoured by three large locomotives. Trailing behind, like the body of a writhing serpentine, were a multitude of grain cars, box cars, and flat cars loaded with containers. The train seemed to have no end. Jarrod yanked the brake lever so hard he almost snapped it off. The crew-buggy slid to a grinding halt about one third of the way across the trestle.

There were few options for escape and even less time to think about them.

Chapter 7

Fueled by panic, the only choice was to jump from their conveyance. Lucas was wearing his backpack, and Jarrod instinctively grabbed his travel bag. Without looking back, their hearts pounded as they scurried toward the east end of the bridge along rough, wooden beams that ran along the north side of the tracks. Footing was treacherous on the slippery planks, which were saturated with creosote. It seemed like the more effort they put into escaping, the more they slipped and slithered. The recurring nightmare of many dreams had come to life.

Jarrod knew that the momentum of a freight train of that magnitude would carry it for several hundred yards after it struck the buggy, even after the brakes were dynamited. It was also possible that the train might derail on impact. Wearing runners that had little or no tread, Lucas continued to slip. Jarrod was forced to grab him by the hand, almost yanking the boy's thin arm out of its socket. Only thirty feet to go! In the blinding, early morning sun, could the train engineer even see the danger that blocked his path?

Although shots of pain gnawed at his left side, Jarrod moved with the dexterity of a high-wire artist, at least until his right foot tripped on a raised knot in the slippery beam. Unable to keep his balance, he pitched forward in an uncontrollable belly flop. His body splayed face-down on top of the cinders and greasy rail ties. Yet the effect of this unforeseen fall was even more devastating for young Lucas.

Before their tight grip could be released, the boy was sent spinning sideways into the wooden support girders that stretched skyward in a crisscross fashion. As Jarrod fell, his left leg struck a violent blow across the right hip of the much lighter boy. Now hopelessly off balance, Lucas tried desperately to clutch the angled girders, which were wet from a thin layer of melting ice. Totally helpless, he felt his body teeter on the edge of nothingness as his hands, slick with sweat and oil, failed to clutch hold of the bridge supports.

"No, no . . . I can't . . . Help!"

The boy's last words echoed between the sloping banks of the murky river. As if caught in a slow-motion replay, Lucas felt himself slide backwards off the bridge. Time slowed to a standstill as memories of twelve short years tumbled through his mind in flashes of light and crystal clear images. The scenes were kaleidoscopic, their vividness and clarity alarming him. Yet oddly, an inner peace and calmness flushed warmth throughout his slender body. The curious out-of-body experience ended abruptly as he landed backwards in the chilly water.

Jarrod's tumble landed him face-first onto a weathered railway tie, his nose striking the protruding head of a rusty spike. Scrambling frantically to his feet, he tasted blood running into his mouth from his smashed nose. After hearing the eerie splash that followed Lucas's agonizing last words, he reached the end of the trestle in three long strides. Leaping from the cinder railway bed to the muddy river embankment, Jarrod was airborne when his eardrums were pierced by the most deafening, high-pitched squealing imaginable.

The train had just entered the west end of the bridge when the engineer spotted the yellow obstruction in his path. In a desperate attempt to slow the momentum carried by tons of rolling steel laden with a bountiful prairie harvest, he activated the rampaging freight train's air brakes. The deafening sound of metal on metal tore apart the crisp morning silence. Like a Fourth of July celebration, sparks flared from a thousand screaming wheels, showering the black, criss-crossed wooden girders of the trestle before cascading toward the river below. Compared to the shrill cacophony, the muffled crunch of the first locomotive striking the tiny crew buggy resembled the popping noise of a prankster bursting a child's balloon. There was a dull hollowness to the impact, yet the small machine disintegrated like a grenade, sending metal shrapnel hurtling through the air. The cast-iron wheels spun wildly, as if attempting to climb the bridge supports in their effort to escape the onslaught. Bolts and rivets ricocheted off the girders like hollow-nosed bullets on a combat mission. The fuel tank burst into flames and spewed dancing, yellow ribbons in a graceful arc toward the river below, anointing the water with the sharp hiss of burning gasoline. Miraculously, the never-ending train continued to slide with relentless determination toward the eastern horizon with little regard for the tormented opposition of its locked wheels grating against the tracks.

Attempting to avoid the fallout from the impact, Jarrod had ducked beneath the eastern end of the bridge. The flaming gasoline had narrowly missed him, and a deflected rivet tore through his pant leg, but he was otherwise unscathed. Despite his smashed nose, all he could focus on was locating Lucas's small body in the muddy waters below. With frantic speed, he dropped down to the base of the riverbank, which had eroded into a gluey mass of clay and mud. Jarrod fell continually as he slithered downstream along the slippery shoreline. Clotting blood clogged his nostrils, restricting his gasps for breath.

"Lucas! Can you hear me? Lucas!" His shouts were drowned out by the screeching in the background. "Where the hell are you?"

Fallen branches and chunks of wood had piled up around the bridge supports, slowing the river's movement. Jarrod reasoned that the boy couldn't have been carried far in the sluggish current. He waded into the cold water almost to his waist, flailing at the floating branches and debris. Helplessness and dread filled his heart, causing his stomach muscles to cramp. He was oblivious to the pain from his injured ribs and smashed nose. In fact, at that moment, Jarrod felt a greater fear and a heavier guilt than when he had bet and lost his life savings on the gaming tables.

The dark, murky waters made any rescue attempt beneath the surface virtually impossible, and yet, Jarrod wouldn't give up. He couldn't. His muscles tightened, and his head felt like it was about to explode. Splashing downstream along the riverbank with panic speed, Jarrod came across a tree whose roots had recently pulled away from the embankment. The fallen tree's branches were still covered with leaves, which acted like a filter, gathering smaller debris from the current into a slime-covered pool next to the shore. It was in that stagnant backwater that he noticed something that made his heart jump. The faded, cloth material that floated on the surface looked all too familiar. It was a backpack! Grasping the material with numb fingers, Jarrod struggled to drag the pack onto the riverbank. It didn't take long to discover why the synthetic fabric resisted his pulls. The straps of the pack remained looped over the shoulders of its owner. Lucas was lying face-down in the mud and slime.

Jarrod responded swiftly and instinctively. Remembering what he could from a lifesaving course he had taken as a teenager, he concluded that mouth-to-mouth resuscitation was the only hope of reviving the unconscious boy. After dragging Lucas by his arms onto the muddy shore, he tore off the boy's pack and pressed firmly on his back, squarely between the shoulder blades. Slimy water drained from Lucas's mouth and nostrils. Then, after turning him onto his back, Jarrod tilted the boy's head back and tried to force open his jaw.

"Damn, open up!" he yelled as he struggled to separate Lucas's clenched teeth, almost dislocating his jaw when he finally pried it open. With fingers that had no feeling, Jarrod cleared mud and sodden leaves from the boy's mouth. Puffing badly from exertion, he took several deep breaths before clamping his mouth over Lucas's purple, lifeless lips. Pinching the boy's nostrils shut, Jarrod forced air down his trachea with short, rapid puffs, remembering that any youngster's lungs would be smaller than his own.

Steadily and continuously, he continued the procedure for over a minute, watching as Lucas's small chest continued to rise and fall. Blood dripped from Jarrod's smashed nose and trickled down the pale cheeks of the comatose boy. Lucas had so much mud clogging his nose that it was almost unnecessary to squeeze it closed during the resuscitation attempts.

Inhaling, exhaling, watching for some sign of life, Jarrod was prepared to give up on more than one occasion. His efforts seemed futile. One part of him kept asking what was the point of continuing, but a stronger inner force wouldn't allow him to give up. After what seemed like an eternity, but was only a matter of moments, Jarrod had to take a break. He was gasping for breath himself when, suddenly and unexpectedly, his aching eyes watched a miracle unfold. His young companion began to show signs of life!

The first sounds from Lucas were merely a gurgling whimper, but faint groans soon erupted into coughs of volcanic proportion as mud and sediment spewed from his tortured lungs and stomach. River water, mucus, bile, all kinds of disgusting liquids, flowed from his body in its attempt to cleanse itself. Continuing to retch, the boy gasped intermittently for air as his oxygen-starved lungs began to work on their own. With only the whites exposed, his eyes rolled aimlessly in their sockets, and he mumbled incoherently. Jarrod gripped the boy's shoulders as he continued to gag.

Practically shaking with relief and elation, Jarrod quickly stripped off Lucas's saturated shirt and jacket. He wrapped his own drier coat around the boy and held him tight, attempting to get warmth to his body. Getting Lucas to breathe solved his first problem. Fearing the effect that hypothermia would have on the youngster's thin, malnourished body, with pneumonia being a distinct possibility, Jarrod was at a crossroads as to what to do next. On one hand, approaching the train would mean surrendering to the authorities and suffering the consequences. Yet continuing to run might cost the boy his life. But at that moment, getting Lucas warmth was his first priority.

Delaying his decision momentarily, Jarrod carried Lucas and his sodden pack up the sloping riverbank to higher ground. Finding a place in the sunlight, he placed him on the comfortable and secluded bough of an evergreen tree. He did all he could to get circulation flowing by rubbing the boy's cold hands and feet. The soggy pack of matches in his pocket ending any hope of a fire, Jarrod climbed a nearby knoll and scoured the horizon in all directions that were visible through the foliage, searching for any sign of roads, service lines, or civilization. The deafening noise of the braking freight train had thankfully ceased, and the air was ominously still and silent. Looking to the north, where the murky river wound its meandering path, Jarrod's squinting eyes spotted dark grey curls of smoke rising into the sky, perhaps only half a mile away. The lodging, or wherever the smoke was coming from, was obscured by a mass of overgrown trees. It would be a rugged hike.

Still unable to communicate with Lucas—his eyes were closed and his breathing shallow—Jarrod did not know which way to turn. Leaving the boy as comfortable as possible, he walked back toward the trestle, not only to recover his travel bag, which contained dry clothes and just about everything he owned, but also to see the distance that the train's momentum had carried it down the tracks. Moving as low as possible along the shoreline to avoid detection, he quickly reached the railway. There, to his surprise, no one was in sight. Peering east down the tracks, he discovered the reason. Over one hundred yards away sat the tail end of the freight train, but no caboose was attached. Instead, hanging from the rear of the last box car was an oblong black box with a blinking amber light. As he recalled reading an article about cabooses being phased out as a cost-saving measure, Jarrod realized that the crew of train men would be almost a mile away, likely examining the damage to the lead locomotive. They would have already radioed for help and to warn others about the accident, and probably couldn't continue until both the locomotive and the rail lines had been inspected.

The more he thought about his brief time spent in "jail," the less interest Jarrod had in confronting the masses of people who would soon be swooping down to the accident scene. No doubt, law enforcement would be well represented. A pressing urge for freedom swayed him to a final decision—he and Lucas would make their way north toward the smoke and, hopefully, warmth and help. Looking among the scattered remains of the crew-buggy, Jarrod noticed the lifeless voltage-dial which, miraculously, was still intact, its needle sagged below zero. Grabbing his travel bag, he hurried back to see how his young friend was doing.

Lucas, who was barely aware that he had survived the river's icy grasp, managed a faint smile as Jarrod leaned over him and explained the plan of action. The boy's pupils were dilated, and his eyes could barely focus.

"We're going to head north along the river, buddy. I can see smoke rising not too far away. Maybe it's a farmhouse. Do you think you can hold on if I carry you on my back?"

Giving a nod that was more of a shiver, Lucas tried to speak, his voice barely audible. "I . . . I'll try. I'm ss . . . so co . . . cold," he stuttered through teeth that chattered uncontrollably. "Thought I was a gone . . . goner for sure. Lights . . . saw all thee . . . these lights."

"Try to hold on. We'll make it," Jarrod said. Taking off the damp jacket, he helped Lucas put on two of the flannel shirts from his travel bag and then looped the straps of the backpack over the boy's shoulders. He knelt so Lucas could clinch eight numb fingers and both thumbs around his neck. Two thin legs inside soggy jeans held a fragile grip around the waist of the man who had just brought him back to life.

So far, so good, Jarrod thought as he stood up, travel bag in hand and a larger, shivering burden on his back. Only then, as he began the difficult hike, was he aware of the constant pain that stabbed at his nose and the left side of his body.

Chapter 8

Few words were spoken as Jarrod clawed, stumbled, and groped his way through tangled underbrush, over spongy bogs, and around steep drop-offs, where, over time, the elements had eroded gaping furrows in the terrain. Combined with occasional contact with the mid-morning sun, the constant exertion warmed him considerably. Sweat trickled down the sides of his haggard face. Fortunately, some of Jarrod's body heat was absorbed by his rider, whose shivering diminished as he held on with every bit of strength he had left. With exhaustion soon taking over, breaks became more frequent, but at least each stop brought the curls of smoke a little closer. During those stops, Jarrod would pull clotted blood from his ragged moustache. His swollen nose was useless for breathing, but at least it had stopped bleeding. Its constant throbbing was a painful reminder of his nightmare encounter with a railway tie.

Jarrod was about to stop for a final rest when warm tears began to trickle down the nape of his neck, and sobs were muffled against his aching shoulders. At that point he realized that, rather than the hardened man-child he had met two days ago, he was carrying the body of a scared youngster on his back. The street-tough person he first met had been replaced by the form of a fragile boy. Yet his exhausted rider refused to complain, and neither would he loosen his grip.

For Lucas, the tears were unplanned, an instinctive reaction over which he had no control. Jarrod could not have known those emotions were fueled by the same thoughts generated when Lucas read a certain letter that lay soaked and smeared in his backpack. For the first time in many months Lucas was happy just to be alive. Although weak, tired, uncertain, and scared, he felt strangely at peace with his existence. Fading away were unpleasant memories of the group home as well as graphic visions he had faced recently as he tumbled from the railway bridge toward an icy encounter with the murky river.

It was close to noon when the exhausted travelers reached their destination. Struggling over one final embankment snarled with exposed roots, then circling a thicket of gooseberry bushes, Jarrod finally stood in the yard at the rear of a small farmhouse. Smoke rose gently from the stone chimney. A few pumpkins and bean stalks were all that remained from a vegetable garden. Several rusting farm implements sat among clumps of overgrown grass. Peacefully disintegrating, the remains of two vintage cars rested next to a barn that was in dire need of a coat of paint.

Releasing his grip one last time, Lucas slid gently to the ground, where he stood, with difficulty, on legs that were wobbly. Jarrod's two shirts hung well below his knees. The shirts' long sleeves hid his boney fingers, curled and stiff from the strain of locking around Jarrod's neck. Like two desperate tramps, a single glance at one another convinced both man and boy of their deplorable condition. Jarrod's clothes were mud-caked and streaked with sweat, his hair greasy and tangled, but what stood out even worse was his face. His nose was red and swollen. The blood vessels around both eyes had burst, leaving yellow and purplish bruises. He resembled a boxer on the losing end of a knock-out. Clotted threads of blood still hung from his moustache and unshaven face.

Lucas fared no better, his hair matted with a mass of mud and slime from the riverbank. The bruises and scratches on his face were barely visible beneath the hardened mud that his salty tears had streaked, resembling the pattern of rivulets trickling down the embankment of a streambed. His drying jeans and sneakers were caked to his body like the hardened plaster of a stucco repairman. His own mother (had she known him) would not have recognized him.

As he stared at the drooping barn, the small but well-kept white farmhouse, and the tilted outhouse, with a half-moon carved in its door, Jarrod realized it would take some fast thinking to explain their condition. Having entered the farmyard from the back, the sounds of mooing cows and clucking chickens reverberated among the rusted implements, but no humans appeared to be outside. Jarrod took a moment to explain to Lucas the story he was about to unfold.

After hearing a quiet, persistent rap, the woman who opened the back door to her home almost dropped the plate she was drying. From her shocked expression, Jarrod feared she might slam the door and run screaming to call the police. Instead, the plump farm woman with short, graying hair and wearing a pink apron over a lime-green smock simply stood on her doorstep with her mouth hanging open.

"Sorry to intrude on you, ma'am. I guess we gave you quite a shock," Jarrod began. His mind racing, words rolled out as he explained their predicament. He tryed to keep his voice steady and reassuring so as not to alarm the stunned woman. "We've had a bit of an accident. My son and I were hunting rabbits upstream there." Jarrod pointed in the opposite direction from which they had come, hoping it was as isolated as the area through which they had just tramped. "Jim here, it was his first time using a rifle, just a twenty-two mind you, but he got pretty excited when he spotted a rabbit. He chased it right to the riverbank and tripped over an old tree trunk just as he squeezed the trigger. Damn if he didn't pitch head-first into the water. I got into a real panic, because the boy isn't much of a swimmer."

As the bait seemed to be working, Jarrod gained confidence. "When I raced to pull him out of the water, I ran into a tree branch and smashed my face. Still don't know how I got him out—scared the hell out of me. I guess we got turned around, and the smoke from your house was the only sign of life I could see. We've been hiking most of the morning. Do you think we could warm up a little and change our clothes? Then we'll be right on our way." He hoped the story didn't sound too far-fetched.

"Oh, my goodness," the woman said without a moment's hesitation. "Get yourselves in here. I've got a fire in the stove, and soup and muffins are almost ready. Sonny, you get out of those wet clothes and have a hot shower. I'll throw those muddy things of yours in the washer. Your dad can take his turn next. There's plenty of hot water with our new propane heater."

Once this woman gets into action, she really moves, Jarrod thought. It always seemed that country folks were less inhibited than city people when it came to helping strangers.

Lucas thanked her as she showed him to the shower. The friendly lady couldn't help but notice the tight grip he held on his wet backpack. He wasn't about to release it to her.

"My son is about your size. He'll be eleven next month. You can borrow some of his dry clothes," she said, gathering clothing from her son's room without breaking stride. She slid the clothes into the bathroom before Lucas could shut the door. "Toss your wet stuff in the hallway. I'll throw it all in the wash."

A little out of breath when she returned to the kitchen, the woman seemed pleased to be of help. Jarrod was seated next to the stove, carefully peeling off his mud-caked boots and socks over an open newspaper when she introduced herself.

"My name's Julie Kane. My husband, Bert, is in town on some business. The kids are at school."

"Good of you to take us in, Mrs. Kane. My name's Bill Jackson. I was pretty scared back there," Jarrod said, coming closer to the truth than he cared to admit. "We left our car near that small town and started hiking—"

"You mean Spoonerville? That's where Bert's gone."

Julie was obviously anxious to talk about her own life. Jarrod had been about to explain how he got disoriented after bumping his head and was confused about his directions when she cut him off.

"We didn't have a good harvest this year," she said. "There wasn't much rain, and what did fall was always at the wrong time. Bert is trying to get financing to carry us over the winter. All we've got now are a few milk cows and some chickens. There's not much money in eggs, but we'll manage."

Jarrod eyed the stove, his mouth watering from the good smells. He glanced at Julie, who smiled.

"The soup should be ready now. I make it from scratch," she said as she ladled out a large bowl from a pot the size of a caldron. "Another five minutes before the muffins are ready." She paused to take a breath. "Sorry you can't phone your wife, but the line's been dead for a couple of hours. The power went out as well. Luckily, we've got an emergency generator."

Jarrod was curious if Julie had heard the noise of a collision just before the lights went out. He figured that pieces of flying metal might have struck the hydro and phone lines that paralleled the tracks. That meant crews would be investigating quickly. Looking back, he couldn't be sure if the engineer had seen him leaping from the east end of the bridge. Lucas would have already hit the water when the train's brakes were locked by a dynamite switch. Aware of the speed at which talk would spread in a small community, Jarrod was certain of one thing: they couldn't rest there for long. By nightfall, the train accident would be the talk of the town, and strangers, especially injured ones, would be viewed with great suspicion.

The soup was delicious, especially to a starving hiker. It was so thick with vegetables, beef, and potatoes that it was more like a stew. Jarrod had just finished a hearty bowl, along with a couple of fresh bran muffins, when Lucas emerged from the bathroom. He wore a red flannel shirt and faded, boot-cut jeans with patches on the knees. But without mud smearing his face, and with his borrowed clothes hanging loosely over his slender frame, he looked paler and thinner than ever. After a hot shower, old scratches on his face were exposed as bold, angry welts.

Jarrod noticed the astonished look on Julie's face when she saw how her son's clothes sagged on Lucas's frail body. He imagined what she must be thinking. *Does this man ever feed his son? Did he beat the boy and then make him hunt rabbits for supper?*

"Come in here, Jim. Have a bowl of soup and some muffins. You must be starved," Julie said, glaring at Jarrod, who was on his way to the shower. "Bill, leave your clothes on the floor, and I'll wash them, along with your son's." The deep sound of her voice came close to a growl.

Jarrod, who carried his travel bag with dry clothes in it, wanted to argue that they had to get going, but he wasn't sure how to word it without raising suspicion. Julie's look had been harsh.

As he passed Lucas, he leaned close. "We left our car at a place called Spoonerville," he whispered. "The phone is out. Let her do the talking." Then, raising his voice, he turned back toward their host. "Great meal, Julie, thanks."

With Jarrod in the shower, Julie had some work to do before she could question her young guest. After tossing their stiff, mud-caked clothing into her old Maytag, she spotted the sad-looking backpack resting against the hallway wall. As Lucas dug into his hearty meal, she began to unbuckle the flap that closed the pack.

"I might as well wash and dry whatever's in here," she said.

Lucas reacted so quickly, he almost knocked over the kitchen table as he jumped to his feet. "Don't bother! Mom can do that at home!"

Although startled by Jim's reaction, Julie continued to open the pack. "Don't worry, I've seen boys' underwear before. Got my own son, remember?"

As she pulled articles, one by one, from the backpack, she wondered if either of the boy's parents were fit to raise him. The clothing was in such humble condition that it all belonged in the rag pile. The letter and newspaper clipping were reduced to folded wads of soggy paper.

"Those are just my . . . old camping clothes," Lucas offered as an explanation when he saw the shocked look on Julie's face.

Realizing that washing the pieces of clothing might only hasten their disintegration, Julie stuffed them back into the pack, along with a toothbrush, a comb, and other personal items. After setting the backpack by the front door and starting the washer, she was ready to interrogate her young visitor. She pictured a strange story unfolding before her that could be more interesting than the afternoon TV dramas that she claimed to never watch.

However, to her disappointment, the boy evaded all her personal questions. Getting information out of him was more difficult than talking to her own son after a "gate night" Halloween episode. Most of the answers she received were so vague that she finally gave up, more confused than when the curious strangers first appeared at her door. Young Jim didn't seem to know what his father did for a living, except it involved a lot of traveling. He would say almost nothing about his mother. He blamed his stunted growth on a long illness that had kept him bedridden for several months. Either no one knew or they wouldn't explain what had been wrong with him. The only concrete fact (another fabrication) that she, in fact, believed was that today was the first time the boy had shot at an animal, and it wasn't the thrill he had expected it to be. He admitted sensing fear in the eyes of the rabbit and didn't even bother to get his rifle from the bottom of the river. Julie concluded that he was a very withdrawn boy from a very strange family, and further prying would serve no purpose.

Jarrod emerged after toweling his hair dry. His nose glowed so deep a red that he could have filled in as Santa's lead reindeer. Ugly, purple bruises circled his eyes. He had scraped off his three-day-old beard with a disposable razor and found fresh clothes in his travel bag. Wondering what kind of questions Julie had been throwing at Lucas, he was about to begin some small talk when the energetic woman brushed by him without a word. The washed clothing was ready for the dryer. Noticing her attitude was far from cordial, Jarrod kept quiet.

The dryer spinning in the background, Julie finally spoke. "That boy of yours can sure eat. He wolfed down two bowls of soup and three muffins. Sorry to hear that his health has been so poorly." She spoke in a cool tone without even glancing at Jarrod. He could see she had her suspicions.

Jarrod nodded slyly to Lucas. "Yeah, we hope to fatten him up soon. Cooking like yours would sure help. I should have listened to my wife and waited 'til he was healthier to take him hunting."

Jarrod was about to suggest that they should get on their way when an unexpected ring of the telephone startled everyone.

"I guess they got the phone line fixed," Julie said casually, picking up the receiver. She failed to notice the shocked look on her lunch guests' faces.

Both man and boy froze like statues as they watched the stout farm woman listening with interest to whoever had called. After what seemed like forever, she turned her head toward her immobile guests. The phone conversation continued.

"How long will you be, Bert? I've got a couple of visitors here—a man and his young son. They had a bit of a hunting accident and could use a ride to town." After pausing for a response, Julie continued. "An hour or two? Okay, I'll tell them. Drive carefully, honey. See you later."

She hung up the receiver. Fortunately for Jarrod and Lucas, neither Julie nor Bert appeared to be the suspicious type who might connect her visitors with the collision that Bert had just detailed over the phone.

"Bert told me that the eastbound freight train had some sort of an accident. It collided with one of those little crew buggies on the bridge just upstream from here—that same river you fell into, Jim. He and some of his buddies from town are headed up there to help clean up the mess. Bert said he'd give you a ride when he gets home."

"Anyone hurt?" Jarrod asked nervously, pretending to be interested. What he really wanted to know was if anyone had spotted them.

"I don't think so. Bert and the others couldn't figure out what the buggy was doing there, 'cause no crews were working on the lines. The engineer thought he saw someone jumping off the tracks, but no one was there when the crew got to the accident site. That should cause some excitement in our little town. I'm sure there'll be lots of people coming through to check it out."

Jarrod sensed Lucas was as anxious to get going as he was. "Thank Bert for the offer, but we should be on our way. My wife will be worried if we don't get back before dark. I would phone her, but it would only get her upset. She didn't want us to go hunting in the first place."

Convinced that this was one of the most peculiar families she had ever come across, Julie gave Jarrod directions to get back to the highway, where they could hitch a ride to town. Lucas offered to get back into his own clothes, which were still damp from the dryer. However, remembering the rags she had pulled out of his backpack, Julie insisted that her son was growing out of those clothes anyway and that Lucas should keep them. He didn't argue.

Jarrod thanked his hostess for her great cooking and offered her twenty dollars for the food and clothes. She adamantly refused the money.

"Just call it country hospitality," she stated proudly. Jarrod noticed she was still trying to figure him out. She likely wondered how a man, who seemed to be nice, could have a son who looked like an underfed orphan dressed in rags.

Jarrod was already out the door, travel bag in hand, when Lucas turned to Julie, another person who had been kind to him. There was a hint of sadness and regret on his face that he couldn't hide. He sincerely would have liked to spend more time visiting, maybe even meet her family. Undoubtedly, Julie felt the dejection in his parting words. "Thank you for everything, ma'am. You have a . . . a real nice home here."

"Take care of yourself, Jim," Julie said as she waved goodbye.

It was not until a few days later, after hearing newscasts and reading the local paper, which gave the train derailment a lot of coverage, that Julie discovered her visitors' true identity. Wanting no part of publicity or visits from the authorities, she and Bert kept the brief visit by two curious strangers to themselves. Julie had trouble accepting the fact that the polite pair who she had taken into her home on that bright fall day were, in reality, fugitives from the law. Yet somehow, from the final look the boy had given her as he left, she suspected he was hiding a life far more secretive than he let on. A mother's intuition had told her that the strangers were not a father and son hunting rabbits, but she had wanted to hug the child, not turn him in.

While cleaning up the house after her visitors left, Julie discovered a folded piece of soggy newspaper next to the laundry room door. It must have fallen from the boy's backpack when she emptied out its contents. Unfolding it carefully, she discovered a faded newspaper clipping that showed the photo of a Little League baseball team under the caption "Cubs, Local Champs." A short write-up explained how the team had won a trip to the zone final. The winning pitcher in the championship game knelt in the front row. "Jim," whom she had fed and clothed, was but a shadow of the beaming, healthy Lucas Kenny, who flashed a wide grin in the photo. Julie dried the clipping and hid it in her dresser. She kept it her own little secret, probably the only thing in her life that she would never speak about to her husband. On many occasions, while alone in the house, she found herself drawn to the faded, wrinkled piece of paper.

Yet she could only wonder.

Part 2
WHO DAT, MOMMY?

Chapter 9

The rutted, ungraded driveway that led from the farmyard wound its way to a section road, a straight, level gravel route that eventually intersected with the main highway. Along its way, the section road crossed a rickety, wooden bridge that spanned the river that had nearly been fatal to Lucas. The warped, rotting planks creaked their displeasure of a steady breeze more so than the relatively weightless footsteps of the foot-weary travelers who dared to step on them.

Jarrod would not have enjoyed driving across the shaky structure. Nevertheless, he had a new, developing concern much greater than a rickety bridge. Soon after leaving the farmhouse, Lucas had developed a perpetual hacking cough. Although recently fed and dressed in dry, warm clothing, his condition appeared to be deteriorating. Jarrod feared that a severe cold or even pneumonia might result if the boy did not receive treatment. Rest and warmth were major priorities. Unfortunately, Jarrod's toiletry kit contained nothing but a few Aspirin and antacid tablets.

They spent the first part of the thirty-minute walk to the highway mostly in silence, interrupted only by Lucas's consistent, raspy coughing. Both travelers were lost in their own thoughts. Jarrod's only comment was to emphasize the urgency of getting out of this state as soon as possible. He tried not to comment on his young accomplice's constant coughing.

"Our old buddy, Klem, isn't likely to sleep until he gets us behind bars again. The farther we are from that town he controls, the better. 'Out of state, out of danger,' might be one way to put it."

A further lengthy silence followed.

"Say, Lucas, I hope you didn't swipe anything from that nice farm lady. I suspect it would be hard to break that habit," Jarrod said, hoping to break the silence.

It worked. Lucas was incensed. "I would never steal from someone who treated me nicely."

Following another uncomfortable silence, the boy came up with a surprise question of his own. As if he were beginning to trust a stranger, the query came out of the blue. "Have you ever been married, Jarrod?"

Caught off-guard by the question, Jarrod suddenly felt old and vulnerable. His answer came slowly, a sadness crossing his face as his mind drifted back to better times. "I came close only once . . . lived with this woman—Beth was her name—for over a year. We got along great except for one thing. Actually, I should say two things, because she had two children from a previous marriage, a boy and a girl. The kids sure caused a lot of disagreements. I think they made a game of playing Beth and me against each other. Beth usually sided with her children, not unnatural I suppose. In any event, we finally split up, and I decided that marriage and children were not for me. Looking back on it, maybe I was just a jealous, love-struck, young fool. I blamed those kids for standing between me and their mother. I don't think I made much of an effort to get to know them." After a short pause, Jarrod continued. "Beth also didn't think much of my gambling habits, but that's another story and not the reason we split. We had a lot of good times together. I really loved that woman. Guess I still do."

Talking about his past, his good times and his failures, was not something that came easily to Jarrod. He seldom felt close enough to anyone to want to discuss his past or talk about feelings, both of which were, as a rule, very private to him. Yet something strange was happening to him. Had some mystical aura arisen from the boy's soul? An undeniable stillness filled the air, as if divine intervention was pulling the words out of Jarrod.

"After my experience with those kids, it was a mystery to me why I stepped out to help you. Anyway, I don't regret what I did. As far as I'm concerned, whatever happens now, we're in it together." The words, the feelings, continued to roll from the lonely man.

"By the way," he asked, eager to change the subject, "I noticed you had a tourist guide to Canada. Were you planning to visit up north? I can tell you from experience that it's not easy to sneak across an international border."

His coughing becoming increasingly frequent, Lucas felt himself relenting on his promise to never trust anyone again. Then again, he had already been spilling half his life story to this man, who had saved him not only from capture but also from certain death in the river. "Yeah, you probably figured out I wasn't just going there to sightsee. I'm trying to find someone. Tracy, that woman in the letter . . . the one you said you never read—"

"That's the truth. I didn't read it."

"Well, she was my foster mother, the last one I had. But she was different from all the others, an' let me tell you, I couldn't give you all their names, there were so many. I felt . . . I knew she really cared about me and didn't take me in just for the money. A counselor once told me that kids an' animals can sense when a person cares about them, is scared of them, or doesn't give a damn."

The fugitives came to a stop on the road as another coughing fit tore at Lucas's already tender throat. He wiped the mucus dripping from his nose on the sleeve of his oversized jacket. Then he continued, his voice low and hoarse, barely above a whisper. Jarrod had to lean over to make out what he was saying.

"Sh . . . she got me into cub scouts, baseball, all sorts of stuff. My baseball coach said I threw as hard as anyone he ever saw at my age." He forced a feeble grin. "I lived there for a year and a half, but Tracy had this boyfriend, Bob, who hadn't much use for kids. Maybe like you were." He noticed Jarrod shake his head. "At least, he sure didn't like me. Never came to any of my games. They were livin' common law. I don't even know how they were allowed a foster child in the first place. She must have had a hard time talking Bob into taking one in. I think she wanted kids of her own and hoped I might change his feelings toward them. Not a chance!"

After coughing again, Lucas continued. "Anyway, Bob got this job offer up in Canada. Chance of a lifetime, he said. I'm sure it was just a good excuse to dump me. He claimed that immigration wouldn't allow a foster child into Canada. He probably never asked, but Tracy believed every word he said, so, she had to make a choice. For a while, she couldn't seem to make a decision, but she was stuck on this guy, and he could offer her a good home, a future. Me, what could I give her but a headache? It wasn't like I was really her kid or anything."

Lucas was forced to stop once again, his breath coming in a raspy wheeze and his cough becoming more persistent. Never had he said so much at one time. His counselors had been lucky to get a nod and a grunt out of him. Still, he felt comfortable talking to the older man who had come to his rescue more than once in the last few days. A strange yet undisputable bond was growing between them. Continuing to cough, Lucas remained talkative as telephone poles came into view over a row of taller trees that lined the section road. The foliage was draped with fall colors. At last, the main highway came into view.

Lucas's voice began to crack as he completed his story. "Tracy had Bob return me to the 'boys' home,' as they called it. They didn't like to call it an orphanage. Although she had known me for not long over a year, Tracy said it hurt too much for her to come along. But she said to call or write her if I ever needed anything," Lucas continued, his eyes becoming moist. "She was supposed to send her new address, but all I got from her was this one letter. It had a Canada stamp on it but no address. Maybe she hadn't settled down or she just forgot . . .." Lucas was starting to pant, his words coming slower and slower. Yet the tone of his wheezing voice held on to the flimsy hope that Tracy had not closed him out of her life forever.

Jarrod pictured the scene—Bob hiding a wry grin as he dropped Lucas at the group home. He drew a cynical comparison to the father who had to go alone to the vet to have the family's old dog put down. He was sure that Tracy had been convinced to forget any notion she might have of seeing Lucas again. His impression of her was that she was weak-kneed and easily manipulated. Bob, who appeared to be the possessive, controlling type, would have insisted that, as a condition of her coming with him, she sever all connections with previous friends, including her foster child. He would have been furious had he known of her letter to Lucas, hence no return address. Yet it was obvious that Lucas still held an emotional link with his foster mother, an attachment so strong that he would set off to a foreign country in search of her.

"Do you realize how big Canada is?" Jarrod asked. "It's larger than the USA. Do you have any idea where Bob's job was taking him?"

"It was—or at least sounded like—Manoba . . . or Matoba. Sounded like an Indian name. I'm not sure if that was the city or the state."

"They're called provinces up there, not states," Jarrod said. "We'll pick up a map or a road atlas, and see if we can find it. Not counting the time I tried to sneak in as a teenager, I've only been to Canada once, at Niagara Falls. I don't know much about the country. When I was little, I thought

Canada was nothing but snow and ice all year around and that the people all lived in igloos. Later on, I realized that many of their cities are as big and modern as any of ours."

Finally arriving at the highway, Route 29, Julie had told them, Jarrod and Lucas looked not only lost but rather out of place as they surveyed their options. Although exhausted, both were wary that danger could come from any direction. Looking north, Lucas pointed out a road sign that read, "Spoonerville 12."

"You keep your eyes open for any cars with red lights on top," Jarrod said. "I'll try to get us a ride." He tried to sound optimistic as he explained his strategy. "Can you imagine trying to get picked up in the condition we were in before, covered in mud and all? I guess we still look like hell."

The boy's only response was an uncontrolled coughing spell.

Traffic was light on the two-lane highway. Two northbound cars sped past, the drivers both casting inquisitive glances at the hitchhikers but failing to slow down. The third vehicle, a slow-moving, dull-grey pickup, proved to be a better prospect. Jarrod gave the driver a big smile and a friendly wave. Much to his surprise, the truck pulled over several yards ahead.

The hitchhikers caught up to the good Samaritan as quickly as possible.

"Good afternoon. Thanks for stopping," Jarrod said pleasantly as he looked through the open passenger window. He quickly sized up the driver, who was clad in faded overalls, as a middle-aged, down-to-earth farmer. The smell of a barnyard permeated the cab's interior. No wonder the windows of the truck were fully open.

"I don't make a habit of pickin' up people hitchin' rides, but you two sure look pretty harmless to me," the driver drawled as drool ran over his lower lip. A large chaw of tobacco was pressed against the inside of his left cheek. Turning casually, he sent a long, yellow stream of spittle out the driver's side window and then motioned the hitchhikers to get in. "Your nose looks like an ol' punchin' bag. Did the kid sock your lights out?"

The tobacco chewer laughed at his silly joke, exposing stained and crooked teeth, which were complemented by stale breath that could only be described as vile. The cab was filled with the smell of uncooked sausages and hogs rolling in slop.

Jarrod put his head out the window and gulped a few breaths of fresh air before he could speak. Lucas, who sat in the middle, was coughing and sneezing. He couldn't smell a thing.

"I banged my nose on the trunk of our car trying to push it out of a swamp." After inhaling more fresh air, Jarrod explained their predicament further. "My son and I were out hunting rabbits when our car got stuck on a trail back near the river. I should've known better than to try to drive through that mud. I guess I'll have to hire a tow truck to get the car pulled out. Do they have one in town?"

Accelerating slowly as he eased the old pickup back onto the highway, the spirited farmer initially ignored Jarrod's question, beginning a one-sided conversation that lasted the entire twelve miles to town. He paused on numerous occasions to send a gush of brownish-yellow liquid out the window. Eventually, Jarrod got his answer. "I'm pickin' up the missus from her brother's place just east of town. I'll drop you at Bill's Truck Stop on the west end. He's got an ol' truck that'll pull you out. That snow we got sure as hell made muck out of those side roads."

After talking at length about the poor return in wages he got for all the hard work and long hours he put in tending to his hogs, the farmer expressed concern that the pale boy, whose cough continued unchecked, was coming down with a fever. Jarrod agreed, yet tried to downplay his obvious anxiety. He was relieved, at least, that no mention was made of the train accident.

As they entered Spoonerville, the sky darkened, a fresh band of clouds rolling overhead. The farmer pointed to a large sign outlined by chaser lights. Many of the bulbs had burnt out or simply given up chasing each other. The sign read, "BIL 'S TR CK ST P," the missing letters flickering sporadically. It stood in front of a row of fuel pumps, two service bays, a car/truck wash, a cashier's office, and a restaurant which adjoined it.

"You'll find someone to help you here. Bill or one of his boys will pull your car out," the hog farmer assured them as he brought the truck to a stop. "Nice meetin' you folks. Now you get yourself over that cough, son," he said to Lucas before shifting the truck into low gear and creeping back onto the road.

Just as Jarrod was giving a wave of thanks, one last yellow stain streaked the surface of the dusty parking lot.

Although he had no idea at the time, a couple of days later, the tobacco-chewer thanked his lucky stars he was alive when he realized he had given a ride to a couple of dangerous fugitives, as the local paper described Jarrod and Lucas.

Jarrod watched as the odorous truck pulled away. After taking several gulps of fresh air, he turned his attention to the service station lot, checking for potential trouble and the possibility of another ride. There were a few cars, which he suspected belonged mostly to locals who had stopped for their afternoon coffee and daily gossip. One semi-trailer unit was also parked facing north, but a cursory inspection found the trailer to be bolted shut. The Mack tractor's idling diesel engine emitted a noise like a death rattle as it belched acrid smoke skyward. The cab was small, with only two bucket seats. Only as a last resort would Jarrod approach the driver for a lift.

Another vehicle interested him more. It was a U-drive van with Michigan plates, a two-ton chassis with an enclosed cube-box separated from the cab (the type of vehicle people might rent when they wanted to save the cost of professional movers). It sat in the shadow of the semi-trailer unit, also facing north and out of view from the restaurant. After checking that no one was inside the cab, Jarrod tried moving the lever that secured the truck's rear doors. After three firm pushes, the steel shaft begrudgingly moved downward. The lever rotated in a clockwise arc, allowing the right door to swing open.

The contents of the cargo space clearly had not been packed by a professional. The interior was complete mayhem: couches, chairs, an assortment of tables, and a mass of boxes were piled to the roof. Mattresses, bedframes, lamps, rolled-up rugs, clothing, and stereo equipment were all crammed into the van in a disorganized arrangement that could be best described as an improvised packing job. With some fast rearranging, Jarrod made room for him and Lucas to sit on the one sofa that rested flat on the floor. From the precarious way that some of the boxes and lamps were piled, he was amazed that the entire load hadn't tumbled out the door when he opened it. Fortunately, for the sake of two cold travelers, plenty of blankets, pillows, and assorted bedding were visible in the dim lighting of the parking lot.

Lucas was dripping with sweat. Realizing that the farmer's diagnosis of a fever might well have been accurate, Jarrod wrapped the shivering boy in blankets and had him lie flat on the sofa, which he had cleared of boxes filled with housewares.

"You stay here, Lucas. I'll get us some food and try to get something for that cough of yours," Jarrod said, trying to hide the concern in his voice. The boy wasn't going anywhere, and his reply was unintelligible, spoken in a guttural whisper.

Carefully sliding the metal lever back into a closed position after he stepped out the rear of the cargo van, Jarrod left the boy and their few belongings safely hidden. Exhausted, his nose throbbing, his side aching, and filled with apprehension, he tried to focus on a crucial decision. Once again, what was the right direction to turn? Should he give up now and get help for the feverish boy or plod onward and hope for the best? Trusting that inspiration would strike eventually, he walked quickly, yet nervously, toward Bill's Truck Stop. An uncomfortable feeling was draped over his shoulders.

Chapter 10

Tom and Elizabeth Benning had been married for ten years. Their life together resembled a roller coaster, with its ups and downs and a multitude of sharp turns. Loving, peaceful times were invariably followed by heated arguments, with Tom's stubbornness usually coming out the winner. Their most serious disagreements arose over his management job with a department store chain. Every promotion he accepted invariably required the family to pull up roots and move on, often to a different state.

Elizabeth disliked their transient life. She would be getting adjusted to a community, meeting new friends, in general feeling like she belonged, when a new job opportunity would come up. Then Tom would convince her that it was time to move once again. What complicated the moves even more, but at least brought happiness to their marriage, were the births of two children, eight-year-old Cindy and four-year-old Timmy. The latest move didn't bother Timmy, but Cindy had reached the age when she hated to leave her latest group of friends. Tom's most recent promotion was taking the family from Sheboygan to Duluth, from Lake

Michigan to Lake Superior—a new state, new surroundings, and new beginnings.

The family sat inside Bill's Truck Stop, finishing an afternoon meal.

"Look, Liz, I keep trying to tell you, if things work out, this should be our last move for a long time. I promise." Tom looked up as the smiling waitress picked up two empty hamburger plates and the remains of two children's portions of chicken strips from their table. "Besides, we're going to a beautiful state. Minnesota is the land of ten thousand lakes."

"That's just the state's motto, Tom." Liz looked glum, her words skeptical as she took a short drink of water. "I hope you're right, but we've been through this time and time again." Liz let out a heavy sigh. "Stop teasing your brother, Cindy, and finish your milk!"

"We'd better get going, honey, so we can get to Duluth before it gets too dark," Tom said. He checked his watch, then glanced out the window. "Looks like storm clouds are rolling in."

"Take Timmy to the restroom first. We don't want any accidents," Liz said, nodding to Cindy as well.

Tom stood up and was leading Tim by the hand toward the men's room when he noticed a car pulling up at high speed. The mud-splattered police cruiser blocked a handicapped parking stall as it skidded to a stop in front of the restaurant door. What really caught Tom's attention was the immense size of the officer who, with great difficulty, squeezed himself out from behind the steering wheel and waddled through the restaurant door.

Wondering how any man so out of shape could possibly defend the peace, Tom pulled his son into the restroom. His attention diverted by the arrival of the officer, he didn't notice a tall, tired-looking man with bruised eye sockets and a red, swollen nose enter the men's room seconds ahead of him.

Once inside the restroom, Tom paid no attention to the fact that one of the two toilet stalls was occupied. His thoughts focused again on Liz and how she was taking their latest move. He was anxious to get going and hustled Timmy back to the booth without bothering to wash his hands. His visit to the men's room caused Tom to miss most of the conversation at the cash register.

"What brings you to these parts, Klem? I haven't seen hide nor hair of you in months," the balding man behind the register exclaimed, extending a friendly greeting to the obese officer.

"We had some trouble with a couple of jokers back in town, Bill, a wanted man and a runaway kid." After stopping to catch his breath, Klem continued to explain his unscheduled arrival. "The man's wanted back east. The boy set one hell of a fire before they escaped. I came up this way when I heard of the damn crash on the railway bridge over the river. I think those two may have been involved with that. Some crew buggy owned by the hydro company was stopped right on the main line. They figure it may have been stolen from our area, but there's not much left of it, just pieces scattered all over the place. Most of it ended up in the river."

"We sure as heck heard about the accident. Some of the boys drove up there this afternoon. It was lucky the freight train didn't derail," Bill said.

The Benning family approached the counter to pay their bill.

"Keep a lookout for these two," Klem said as he handed over a photocopy containing the descriptions of both fugitives. "Call that number if you or your staff see anything." He gave the impression that the desperados should be high on the FBI's ten-most-wanted list.

"I've been in the garage all day," Bill explained. "I just relieved Margo a few minutes ago, so she could have a break. I'll show the girls your poster. Are you staying for a bite to eat?"

Although tempted, Klem said he had to get on the road and distribute the rest of his posters before the criminals got out of reach. If only he knew he was standing only footsteps away from the jackpot. Klem did find time to grab one of Bill's famous giant cinnamon buns and a coffee for the road. Turning to leave, he almost collided with Tom and Timmy, who were waiting patiently to pay their bill.

"Why is dat policeman so fat?" Timmy asked his father in the innocent manner of a four-year-old.

"Excuse me, sir," Klem growled, ignoring the comment. His salivating mouth was already opening for the first bite into his cinnamon bun. With both hands full, he butted open the restaurant door with his tummy and, with greater difficulty, forced his rotund body behind the steering wheel of his cruiser. Puffing once again, Klem sat for another couple of minutes as he polished off the remainder of the giant bun and sipped the hot coffee.

As if the timing were preordained, Tom and Elizabeth chose that exact moment to usher their family into their U-drive vehicle, Tom checking the tires and making sure the rear cargo doors were secure. In a rush to get going, he didn't bother to check on the condition of the contents.

For one particular person, those brief moments felt like an eternity. Trapped in the washroom, one worried, blood-shot eye peered out a tiny opening created when the men's room door was pushed slightly ajar. No one noticed the eye, the haggard face behind it or the trembling hand that held a paper bag containing sandwiches, cough drops, a cold remedy, and chocolate bars. Margo, the cashier, would have known the man only as her last customer, but Margo was on her break, reading her romantic paperback in a corner of the kitchen. She had been a little curious of the tall stranger with the red nose and raccoon eyes. However, with her break approaching, she was more anxious to continue her literary romance than start a conversation.

The second turn of the ignition key was followed by a huge cloud of exhaust smoke as the U-drive sparked to life. Guiding the cube van carefully onto the highway, Tom only wanted to get to Duluth as quickly as possible. He felt himself getting tired and irritable. In his driver-side mirror, he saw the police car accelerating in the opposite direction. Briefly checking his other mirror, Tom caught a glimpse of a tall, solitary figure standing outside the restaurant door. Head bowed and shoulders hunched, the dark, dejected silhouette of a human held a firm grip onto a crumpled paper bag.

Chapter 11

In the past hour dark, billowy clouds had rolled across the autumn sky from the west, and light, fluffy, snowflakes began falling gently. The asphalt highway, which the sun had dried completely, was developing a thin sheen of water on its surface as the flakes melted on impact. Conditions became increasingly slick as the wet snow prevailed.

Except for Tom, the Benning family members were refreshed and in good humor after their meal. Yet even Tom joined in and felt his spirits lift when Cindy got them started on a verse of "Old McDonald Had a Farm." Liz laughed when her daughter asked quite seriously, "Does Wendy's have a farm, too, where they get their hamburgers from?"

Feeling more relaxed, now that the end of his driving was only a couple of hours away, Tom kept the van at a steady speed, but he failed to turn on the headlights as visibility continued to deteriorate. Perhaps he should have slowed a little to compensate for the slick road, but the heavy van seemed to have no trouble gripping the asphalt. The highway rolled gently through the pretty white-shrouded countryside. Curves were intermittent and gradual.

"What was that sheriff so excited about back at the restaurant?" Liz asked as the children entertained themselves.

"I didn't hear much, but it seemed he was looking for a man and a boy. I have no idea what they did to have that oversized cop chasing them." Tom grinned. "Even Timmy wanted to know why the guy was so fat."

"I hope you never pick up strangers," Liz cautioned in a serious tone.

Trying to hold his fading concentration on the road ahead, Tom replied with a nod.

The large snowflakes reminding her of Christmas, Cindy was leading the family in a chorus of "Jingle Bells" when Tom began to negotiate a downward slope and a rather sharp left curve in the road. He took his foot off the accelerator but tried not to use the brakes. It was Liz who first noticed the old, flatbed truck loaded with hay bales held in by wooden stakes protruding from the truck box. The vehicle was creeping onto the highway from a crossroad at the bottom of the slope.

"Watch out for that idiot!" she shouted, instinctively grabbing hold of Timmy, whose car seat had been left in the family station wagon. The others had their seatbelts fastened.

To Tom's disbelief, the old truck continued to turn north onto the highway, directly into their path. It was moving at a snail's pace.

"Damn!" Tom leaned on the horn. The solid center line, as well as a road sign, had warned of the blind intersection at the bottom of the hill. "Brace yourselves!" It was a warning he needn't have given, as his family was locked together in a death grip.

Pressing down on the brake pedal, Tom found the road surface to be slicker than he had anticipated. The loaded, cumbersome van began to slide awkwardly as the brakes locked. Tom quickly released the pedal, hoping to gain control of the steering, but he was rapidly overtaking the hay-truck. His jaw locked open, and his breathing stopped as he realized that, without changing lanes, a collision was unavoidable. There was only one hope. With a quiet prayer, Tom made a desperation turn of the steering wheel, crossing the solid centerline. Would another vehicle be coming toward them? In unison, his family let out a piercing shriek. By some miracle, the front wheels caught enough grip to swerve the van into the southbound lane, barely missing the rear of the lumbering truck. Fortune was on their side, as the oncoming lane was unoccupied. Fighting for control, Tom straightened the wheels, trying to avoid the west ditch. Unfortunately, the sideways motion of the weighed-down U-drive forced the left wheels into the soft, wet snow on the shoulder. The van slid to the left, the grassy ditch acting like an enormous magnet as it pulled the cumbersome vehicle into its grasp.

Only a combination of luck and instinctive driving prevented the van from rolling over in the wet grass. At times on two wheels, at times bucking like a wild stallion, the van bounced helplessly along the ditch. Plumes of snow exploded from the low brush and piles of dead grass. After what seemed like forever, but was actually a fifteen-second ride through hell, the U-drive came to rest against a culvert that protruded from a narrow crossroad joining the highway to a field of stubble. The Benning family breathed once again.

Never a religious man, Tom nevertheless looked up and gave thanks for their deliverance. He would never again criticize seatbelt legislation. Regrettably, he would spend many restless nights reliving the incident.

Liz loosened her vice-like grip on her children and let out a great sigh of relief. Trying to stop the pounding in her chest, she squeezed her stinging eyes shut. Both Cindy and Timmy released the tears that fear and tension had built up within them. The only injury appeared to be Cindy's sore elbow, which she had banged against the radio knob. There were no cuts, no fractures, and no broken teeth. The family's survival was truly a miracle.

After a moment's silence, Tom spoke, his voice quivering. "Wow. I can't believe we're all in one piece. I'd better check for damages. Our furniture must be a mess."

His shaken wife did her best to comfort the children. Tom's legs trembled as he stepped from the cab into the snowy ditch. In fact, they were so wobbly that he fell to his knees in the wet grass before regaining his balance. His anger toward the other driver diminished as the warm rush of relief spread through his body. He stumbled awkwardly toward the farmer, who had pulled over on the far shoulder and was walking cautiously across the highway.

As though he expected to be punched in the face for his careless driving, the aging driver spoke first. "God only knows how you kept that van of yours from flipping over, son. I know it's all my fault this happened. I'm sorry . . . so sorry . . . that damn hill." His voice trembled.

The man appeared to be in his late seventies. His face had turned pasty white from witnessing the near accident. Although his hair was steel grey, his skin weathered like parchment, and his walk displayed a slight limp, Tom judged that the man had been a hard worker all his life and was in good shape for his age.

Words came slowly to Tom, who was still shaken from his experience. “What’s done is done. At least we’re still alive.” He paused to catch his breath. “If the road had been dry, I could have slowed down easily.”

“I never saw you ‘til it was too late. Maybe your lights weren’t working,” the farmer said, his hands still trembling.

Tom glanced over at the U-drive and realized his lights had been off.

“I’ve got a chain in ol’ Betsy there,” the farmer said, nodding toward his truck, “We should be able to pull you out, if need be.”

“Let me check the damage first. We’ve got a load of furniture in the back. It should be in a real mess after that crazy ride through the ditch.” Tom’s voice was tired.

After checking the exterior of the U-drive for physical damage, and not being able to tell new scratches from old scratches, Tom walked to the rear of the van. The farmer waved a couple of passing vehicles to keep going, motioning that everything was all right. It was obvious the drivers had simply slowed down to gawk, and didn’t plan on stopping to help.

“Stand back when I open the door,” Tom warned. He pulled down the metal rod that secured the cargo doors and pried the right side open on hinges that had been jarred out of alignment. Sure enough, a couple of lamps and several boxes tumbled out the back. About to step into the cargo box, Tom hesitated. In the cold, still air of the box, he heard something that stopped him from moving. It sounded like a moan.

"What the hell is going on?" he asked, pulling more boxes and blankets out of his way. With the only light coming from the headlights of the distant hay-truck, the interior was almost in darkness. Tom stood inside for a moment as his eyes adjusted. He wasn't sure how safe it was in there. Then he heard the faint wheeze of labored breathing.

"Who . . . who's there? I can hear you." Tom tried to sound in command, but his shaky voice betrayed him.

Clothing and linen had spilled from overturned cartons onto a sofa that rested against the truck box's wooden liner. When the clothing moved slightly, Tom had to restrain himself from jumping out of there and locking the door. The small face that emerged from the linen shroud let out a resounding sneeze. The sight caught Tom so much by surprise that his jaw dropped open.

"Who . . . what?" he stammered, not knowing what to say. Dozens of questions spun around in his mind. The frail, sickly boy stared back at him through glazed eyes before a fit of coughing shook his shivering frame.

"You don't look well, boy." Tom's comment was an understatement as he erased the danger signs and got control of himself. "How long have you been back here?"

Silence.

Coughing.

More silence.

"You're lucky you weren't crushed when all that stuff fell to the back." Or would the desperate stowaway have been better off? "You stay put while I talk to Liz—my wife, I mean." Tom stammered, running out of questions.

The untalkative stowaway wasn't going anywhere. All the fight had drained from his emaciated body, his strength and courage depleted. Not only had the fever weakened him physically, there was no sign of his only friend. Reality struck home like a blow to the stomach, draining away whatever will to survive he had left. Lucas wouldn't have cared if the new stranger had simply rolled him into the snowy ditch and left him to die like a mangy old dog.

Tom rushed past the confused farmer, who had heard the commotion. He almost slipped in his anxiety to open the U-drive's passenger door. "Liz, you won't believe this," he said, stammering as he spoke, "but some kid has been riding in the back with our furniture. I haven't a clue how long he's been there."

"What?" Liz exclaimed. The children had settled down, their tears drying.

"He looks pretty feverish. I couldn't get him to talk. Do you think we should get him to a doctor and call the authorities from there?"

"Of course! You want to leave him here to die? Quick, bring him into the cab along with a blanket. He'll be warmer here. I should have some Aspirin in my purse," Liz answered without hesitation. "You kids will have to slide over to make room. Timmy, sit on your sister's lap."

As Tom walked around the back, the farmer was already getting a chain from his truck. If necessary, he would attempt to pull the U-drive back onto the highway. Three more vehicles had driven by, two of them almost veering into one another as the drivers stared at the near accident.

After wrapping the feverish stowaway in one of the many blankets strewn about the cargo space, Tom carefully lifted him from the sofa and stepped down to the ground.

"You gonna leave me here, mister?" The weak voice rose from the bundle that Tom held tightly in his arms.

"No, son, we're going to take you to a doctor. You're burning up with a fever."

Tom slid Lucas onto the seat beside Liz, who tried to cover up her shock with a few comforting words to the youngster. Leaving to repack the articles that had fallen from the van, Tom also wanted to exchange insurance information with the farmer. As he hurried to reorganize the whirlwind-like conditions in the cargo box, Tom failed to notice the weather-beaten backpack or the larger travel bag that hid beneath a coffee table and pile of bedding.

"Who's that, Mommy?" Cindy asked, having already forgotten her bruised elbow.

"Who dat, Mommy?" Timmy echoed.

"Did the stork bring me another brother?" Cindy asked in her comical way.

"Very funny, dear. He's just a sick boy we're going to take to the doctor," Liz replied as she tried to get the shivering youngster to ingest a couple of children's Aspirin. She had nothing in liquid form and had no success in getting the boy to swallow. He was in a cold sweat and drifted sporadically into unconsciousness.

"This boy's burning up with fever," she said as Tom got back into the driver's seat. "We have to get him some help as quick as possible."

Beyond tired, Tom mumbled an indiscernible reply as he shifted the roughly idling van into reverse. His first attempt to pull away from the culvert that had brought them to an abrupt halt sent the rear tires spinning wildly in the wet grass. Easing up on the accelerator, he rocked the van by shifting back and forth from forward to reverse. With the weight of their entire household making up for the lack of tread, the dual rear tires found just enough traction to ease the van backwards. Since the ditch was fairly shallow at that spot, Tom was able to angle the U-drive so it gradually climbed the slope. Moments later, he had maneuvered it back onto the shoulder. The chain wasn't necessary.

After exchanging insurance info as a formality, the farmer directed Tom to the nearest doctor, whose office was in a town some thirty miles farther north. He offered his apologies once again. Feeling much older than he had an hour earlier, the ashen farmer ambled toward his vehicle, a rusty chain scraping the pavement as it dragged behind him.

More cautiously than before, Tom continued his northerly route. For several hundred yards, the van's rear tires sent clumps of mud flying in every direction. The Benning family, still stunned by their near catastrophe, sat in silence for a long time. Liz hummed an old nursery rhyme as she rocked the shivering, nearly lifeless form that lay across her lap. The only other sounds were labored wheezing as their nameless passenger struggled to breathe.

"Liz, I was thinking. I wonder if this boy is one of the pair of guys that the sheriff back there was so anxious to find," Tom said.

Liz nodded. "That could be. Wherever he's from, he either wasn't fed, or he must have been running for a long time. He's so thin . . . so undernourished."

She held the boy tightly as he continued to shake in his delirious state. His eyes rolled upwards, the pupils disappearing as he mumbled incoherently. Liz caught only the odd word. "No . . . Jarr'd . . . I can't . . . watch out . . . the traaa . . . ain . . . won't go back . . . so . . . so hot." Then his eyes closed, and he fell silent. Whether a hallucination or a nightmare, Liz couldn't piece together the boy's delirious mumbling.

"How much farther to the doctor?" she asked with concern. "I don't know if he can hold on for much longer." Ignoring the fidgeting of her own children, Liz continued to grasp the sweating, blanket-wrapped boy, who began to thrash about in a tremulous state.

"Just a few minutes more, honey. I think that's the town water tower up ahead." Tom pointed at a tall, round structure between patches of trees that dotted the landscape.

"Is that boy going to stay with us, Mommy?" Cindy asked.

"Yeah, Mommy, can he?" Timmy pleaded.

"No, dear. We have to find out where his home is. His mommy and daddy must be very worried about him," Liz replied with some trepidation. A feeling of guilt crept over her, as she didn't really believe that the boy's past or future home life held much comfort or security.

"Here we are," Tom announced as he slowed the van on the outskirts of a small, nondescript town. Lexter? Was that the name? He had hardly noticed the sign. "According to the old fellow, the doctor should be down the first road to the left."

Turning onto the first gravel side street, which, to no surprise, was called Main Street, Tom spotted a large white house that stood tall and immaculate in the middle of a sprawling manicured lawn. The melting snow left a pattern of green and white swirls around the bases of neatly trimmed, ornamental shrubs. A wooden sign swung gently in front of the home: "Dr. W.S. Wilson, M.D. & Vet."

Chapter 12

"Vet?" Tom exclaimed as he turned into the massive driveway, which also served as a parking lot. He parked next to an old purple Dodge Dart. "This doc sounds pretty versatile. I hope he washes between patients." His weak attempt at a joke fell on deaf ears.

The youngster was not a heavy burden as Tom carried him through the front doors of the waiting room, which was obviously a later addition to the stately home. A slightly built woman seated behind the reception desk gave him a pleasant smile. She was dressed neatly in a crisp white uniform and chatted with an elderly lady seated next to her. Tom's mind, working in one of its peculiar ways, perceived the old woman to be the town hypochondriac, though her best medicine might simply be a good dose of conversation.

"Good afternoon," said the receptionist/nurse, Mrs. Wilson, the doctor's wife. She took one glance at Lucas and diagnosed him immediately. "Your boy looks very feverish. I'll get him in to see Bill—Dr. Wilson—right away." She turned to the older woman. "Mrs. Miller, you can let the boy in ahead of you, right?" Her words were firm, as if "no" would not be an acceptable answer.

"Sure. Go ahead. I'll survive," Mrs. Miller conceded, her voice a little bitter. It was apparent that Tom's inference came close to the truth.

Mrs. Wilson left briefly to speak to her husband.

A few moments later, the doctor emerged from one of his two examination rooms—the one set aside for four-legged patients. Beside him was a teenage girl carrying a small tabby cat. Tom could only imagine what Mrs. Miller thought of a cat getting in ahead of her.

"Muffin survived her shots," Dr. Wilson announced, smiling pleasantly to the group in the waiting room.

The doctor reminded Tom of old Doc Adams in the *Gunsmoke* TV series he had watched as a child, not only in appearance and his slow relaxed demeanor but also in his down-to-earth, considerate attitude toward his patients.

"Who have we here?" the doctor asked Tom and Liz, who were seated on a leather couch. Two of their children looked bored and wanted to play with the little kitten.

"The boy has come down with a fever. It's gotten worse. We heard you were the nearest doctor." Tom and Liz spoke almost in unison, as concerned parents are prone to speak. Initially, they failed to even mention that the child wasn't their own.

"You're right that I'm the only doc in these parts. It's mostly farm communities around here. Eau Claire has the nearest hospital. Please bring the boy into my examination room. I'll check him over." Then Dr. Wilson turned to his other patient. "Mrs. Miller, I'll be with you as soon as I can."

The elderly lady mumbled a reply that no one heard.

Tom carefully placed the patient on an examining table. Leaving explanations until later, he told the doctor that he would wait in the reception area with his wife. However, as he walked past the desk, he was intercepted by Mrs. Wilson, who explained that she needed the boy's medical history as well as all the necessary family data and health coverage. Was he allergic to any drugs? Penicillin? Antibiotics?

After explaining quietly that the boy was not his own and that he didn't know any of that information, Tom suggested he speak to the doctor in private. He was not anxious to talk in front of Mrs. Miller, whom he pictured to be the town gossip as well as its most frequently ill resident.

When he entered the examination room once again, Tom was greeted with an icy stare, a look that Doc Wilson reserved only for extreme situations. The shirtless boy lay on a cloth-covered examination table, exposing a bruised, emaciated torso. One slender arm was connected to an intravenous needle and bag containing a clear liquid.

"That boy is not ours," Tom said, noticing the icy glare. He then quickly explained the situation before the doctor could speak. "He's a stowaway. We just found him in the back of our moving van, about thirty miles south of here. We avoided an accident and ended up in the ditch. That's when I found him hidden in the back with the furniture and other stuff from our house."

Dr. Wilson hesitated. His anger was still apparent, but there was a tone of sincerity in the man's voice that the doctor's years of experience could acknowledge. His eyes soon returned to their kind, sympathetic look.

"You folks didn't seem like the type to abuse your children, but you never know these days. This boy looks as though he's been through one hell of a time. He has plenty of wounds from the past that won't heal and fresh contusions on top of them. I've given him some nourishment and medication for his fever. He's really burning up. But judging from his condition, I don't even know if he has the will to pull himself through. A lot of recovery is fight and determination. The animal instinct for survival is not always enough. A sick person must want to live for what tomorrow brings, even one so young." It was evident that Dr. Wilson had some background in psychology.

"We haven't contacted the police. We thought it more important to get the boy medical attention," Tom explained. "My wife and family, we're on our way to Duluth," he continued just as Liz poked her head through the door.

"How is he? Will he be all right?" she asked, her eyes showing concern.

"We hope so, dear. I'll be right out," Tom replied.

Dr. Wilson did everything he could for his patient, hoping the boy wouldn't react negatively to the liquid drugs that dripped slowly into his system. With Tom's help, he placed the boy in a bed under warm covering in an adjoining room.

"These two spare bedrooms serve as our hospital ward for patients that require overnight attention but whose conditions aren't life threatening or require a more sophisticated facility," Dr. Wilson explained. "We'll have to closely monitor the boy's condition for a while. Hopefully, we won't be forced to have him moved to a larger facility. I believe what he needs mostly is rest and nourishment. A good dose of love and caring wouldn't hurt either."

The doctor led Tom back to the waiting room. "I'd like to at least talk to the boy before we involve the authorities," he continued. "I think he deserves a chance to give his side. Are you and your family going to stay in town? We do have a small motel."

After a brief hesitation, Tom shook his head. "No, we really can't, but I'll talk it over with my wife. We don't even know this boy."

Dr. Wilson spoke quietly with his wife, who was no longer smiling. From her chair in the waiting room, Mrs. Miller let out an agonizing groan, making sure that another interruption wouldn't prevent her getting attention. Leaving their children occupied with coloring books (the girl with the kitten had left), Tom and Elizabeth walked outside for a talk.

"That boy looks like he's been abused," Tom began. "His body's covered with bruises. The doctor wants to keep him for a few days. He's afraid that calling the police right away might finish off any will to live that the boy has left. But we can't stay."

Liz's motherly instincts prevailed. "That boy needs someone. Can't we wait and take him to Duluth? Then at least we can make sure he's looked after and has a home… find out why he was running. Or we could . . .." Words, arguments, were coming so fast that she became incoherent.

"Look, honey," Tom said, trying to reason with her, "I've got work commitments. The company will only pay so much for our moving expenses. We would have extra motel bills we can't afford. Sorry, but we're leaving the youngster in good hands. Get the kids."

Frustrated with not getting her way once again, yet knowing further argument was futile, Liz stomped inside the waiting room to gather her children. She was angry and confused. Yet as always, she would abide by her husband's decision.

Tom wrote his new home phone number on his business card and left it with the doctor, who had already dispatched Mrs. Miller with her weekly supply of placebo pills. If the police wished to question him, they could contact Tom at home or at the department store in Duluth.

Dr. Wilson assured the Bennings that he would do all he could for the nameless boy, who was sedated and sleeping soundly in the adjacent room. Above all, he promised not to allow his patient to return to the environment that was responsible for his present condition. What the doctor didn't know was that the boy had heard these hollow promises before.

Loading up their bored and whining children, the Bennings prepared to continue their northern trek. Tom took a few minutes to sort and repack some of the boxes that were strewn all over the cargo area. While rearranging bedding that had spilled over when the rear door opened, he made an interesting discovery. Two items that didn't belong to his family—a travel bag and a beaten-up backpack—were jammed beneath the coffee table. A quick scrutiny of the contents revealed the clothing and toiletries of a man as well as the pathetic-looking remains of a boy's belongings.

Tom, even as tired as he was, saw pieces of the puzzle begin to fit together. For certain, the bag containing men's clothing showed that the boy had not been traveling alone. Tom was certain that the obese police officer at the last truck stop had interrupted a planned escape in the back of the U-drive. The lone figure standing next to the restaurant flashed across his mind.

Without telling his wife, who was trying to settle the kids down and buckle them in, Tom returned to the waiting room and left the travel bags with Mrs. Wilson. Her pleasant smile returned once again as she refused Tom's offer of payment toward medical costs. Without thinking that the bags might contain some clue to the boy's identity, she nonchalantly slid them beneath the reception desk.

The Benning family left town without another word. Cindy and Timmy quickly fell asleep, worn out from the day's exciting events. Their parents were lost in private thoughts. Liz was uneasy, feeling annoyed that she had given in to her husband once again but confident that Dr. Wilson and his wife would do the right thing.

The curves were gradual as the road wound north through gently rolling hills. The storm clouds were dispersing, exposing fields that were mostly bare, their harvest already collected. A harrow had cut a wide swath over many of the fields, leaving stubble protruding through the clumps of black soil. Round, elongated rolls of hay dotted the countryside, casting long shadows as the sun sank toward the horizon.

His wife sitting quietly next to him, Tom began to think more of the future, the new challenges in a new city. Yet in the back of his mind, he questioned, for the first time, his motives, his priorities. Silently, he promised himself that, from now on, he would pay more attention to Liz's opinions, suggestions, and desires. He thought that, in a strange, almost uncanny way, the wild events of the last few hours might prove to be a turning point in his life, certainly in his marriage.

Under skies that continued to clear, and aided by a gentle breeze, the U-drive plodded north, mud no longer flying from its tires. A new state—and a new life—was less than an hour away.

Chapter 13

Four hours earlier Jarrod took his first apprehensive step into Bill's Truck Stop. After making a cursory inspection of the customers, he identified the truckers as the group sitting at their own special table in the smoking section. Where were their big rigs? A greyish haze from the smokers drifted across the entire restaurant. The men, although diverse in ages, were decked out in peaked caps, cowboy boots, and denim jackets. Large wallets were chained to their belts and bulged from the rear pockets of oil-stained jeans. Keys jangling from tarnished rings were also cinched in some manner to the truckers' pants or belts, and hung below the folds of protruding bellies.

A couple of elderly women drank tea and shared a crumbly biscuit at a corner table, both reminiscing about the past and complaining about the present. They had no time to worry about the future. Two customers sat alone, munching on sandwiches and slurping large bowls of soup. One young family sat in a booth next to the window. Fortunately, no one paid attention to the new customer, who tried to keep in the shadows of the hallway adjacent to the restaurant.

Stepping up to a small lunch counter, its five stools vacant, Jarrod spoke to the only waitress he saw, a slim middle-aged woman with tight reddish-brown curls. Her white apron was soiled with tomato soup or spaghetti sauce splattered across the front in the form of a red dragon.

"Excuse me, do you have any sandwiches made up? I'm not fussy what they are. I'm in a bit of a rush," Jarrod said.

"Won't take a moment, honey. I'm sure Carl's got something made up," the waitress promised. (Were all men "honey" to her?) After speaking briefly to the cook through a small opening into the kitchen, she turned back to Jarrod. "Anything else? Sandwiches will be up in a sec."

Looking over a metal stand that contained everything from chocolate bars to lip balm, Jarrod picked out a packet of pills that claimed instant relief from colds, some cough drops, and a couple of Hershey bars. "I'll take these, and give me some change for the pop machine, please." His hand moved nervously into his pocket.

After totaling the bill, the waitress took a twenty-dollar bill from him and returned his change in coins. Carl handed her two cellophane-wrapped ham-and-cheese sandwiches that he had found in the cooler. She put everything into a paper bag.

"There you go, honey. Have a wonderful day."

About to comment on the condition of her customer's nose, the waitress noticed her boss, Bill, talking to the cook next to the grill. "'Bout time he gave me a break," she mumbled instead and turned away to join the meeting. The relaxed atmosphere would not last for long.

Jarrod was just about to drop some coins into the pop machine when, for no apparent reason, he glanced outside—and froze in his tracks. Through the front window, he saw a black-and-white car speed into the lot. On the roof of the muddy car sat two red beacons, neither of them flashing. As the patrol car slid to a stop at the front door, he recognized the familiar face of none other than Sheriff Laurence Klemchuk. Recovering from his initial shock, Jarrod turned and walked as casually as possible to the men's room at the rear of the restaurant. His grip tightened on the paper bag, which was clutched in the sweaty palm of his left hand. Several coins dropped from his other hand and rolled under the counter. His heart rate increased so rapidly that he felt it pounding against his rib cage.

Once inside the washroom, Jarrod locked himself in one of the cubicles and waited. Moments later, he heard a man talking to his young son, encouraging him to "go potty." When the man and the boy opened the door to leave, Jarrod heard the deep resonance of the sheriff's voice as he talked to someone, hopefully not the waitress who had just served him. He considered bolting from the restaurant through the emergency exit but then vetoed the plan. Klem would have those truckers chasing him like hounds after a fox. Considering his weakened condition, Jarrod wouldn't make it a hundred yards. And what about Lucas?

A few moments later, when the chatter died down, Jarrod chanced a nervous peek out the washroom door. Squinting, he made out the bulky form of the sheriff, who was now seated behind the wheel of his cruiser. As was his habit, Klem was stuffing some form of food into his mouth.

Seconds later, his tires spun as the police car backed up and left the lot in a cloud of dust. As if on cue, Jarrod walked from the washroom in a casual manner, hoping desperately that he wasn't too late. The waitress who served him was nowhere in sight. He assumed she was still on her break. Bill was clearing the dirty dishes from one of the tables, and Jarrod was careful not to look toward him as he walked past. The owner probably had a good description of the criminals Klem was chasing.

Stepping out the door into the brisk autumn air, Jarrod felt a lump rise in his throat. Breathing rapidly, he could only watch as the U-drive van pulled onto Route 29 north, its signal light flashing a sorrowful farewell. His tired brain straining for a solution to its latest dilemma, Jarrod stood like a statue, his pallid face etched with the look of a weary old man. One aching, bloodshot eye released a silent tear that trickled over the purplish marks above his cheek bone before dropping to the dusty ground.

Arousing himself with a rapid shake of his head, Jarrod was not about to give up. Suddenly alert, he remembered the semi-trailer unit he had mentally put in reserve as a last resort for a ride. Acrid, cloying smoke still belched from the diesel Mack as it idled under a dim light standard. The truck was a relatively small highway unit, having only one rear axle with dual tires on each side. An enclosed trailer about thirty feet long was attached to the Mack's fifth-wheel, a round, well-greased steel plate mounted on the truck frame behind the driver's cab. Walking slowly around the semi-trailer unit, Jarrod worked out his best method for getting a ride, quickly eliminating the trailer, which was sealed shut. The small cab was not equipped with a sleeper, likely a one-man unit used only on short runs. At least it had an extra seat for one passenger.

Having made up his mind how he would approach the driver, Jarrod watched as a tall, young man in his twenties strolled leisurely from the truck stop. He wore cowboy boots and a peaked cap displaying the Mack logo. A small cigarillo hung between his lips. As the driver strode toward his idling truck, Jarrod knew it was time to make his move.

"Excuse me, is this your rig?"

"Shoo . . . ore is, pal," the young man replied in a bogus southern drawl, casually removing his cigarillo and poking a toothpick between two of his bottom teeth. "Ain't she a beauty?"

"Yeah, you've got a great truck. Say, I've got to get back home real fast. My wife's gone into labor—our firstborn. The kid wasn't due for two weeks. I've been on the road—I'm a salesman, you see—then one of my regular customers got a call that my wife's on her way to the hospital. I guess I drove too fast in this damn slush . . . hit the ditch a few miles back. Busted the radiator."

Jarrod spoke with the staccato voice of a desperate man. He must have sounded convincing, or at least he touched a soft spot in the trucker.

"Hop in. I'm goin' as far as Duluth," he offered. "I know how you feel. Me and the wife have a couple of young 'uns. I was nervous as hell when she popped that first one. Guess I was scared somethin' would go wrong. Wait 'til your second. It ain't near as bad."

Jarrod climbed into the passenger seat, wondering if he could tackle another acting role. "Duluth . . . what luck, that's where the hospital is. I appreciate the lift," he said. "I was going to try thumbing when I saw your truck running. You've got a beautiful rig."

"I like her. The boys bug me that I talk more to her than I talk to the wife." The trucker treated his Mack diesel as if it were human, alive and breathing. "My dad and I are partners," he continued. "We get lots of short runs around these parts. I'm never away from the kids for more than one or two nights. I like it that way. Say, I don't mean to be nosey, heh, heh, but did someone poke you in the old honker?" The trucker laughed.

"Naw, nothing so dramatic. I just bumped my nose on the steering wheel when I went off the road," Jarrod replied.

"Sorry, but I've got one short stop to make a few miles up the road," the trucker explained. "Got to drop some stuff at my cousin's place. Shouldn't take long. You're probably a daddy by now anyway. Can't stop Mother Nature, can we?"

Jarrod nodded, his eyelids drooping.

So the fugitive's extended journey north continued, the Mack accelerating slowly on the wet pavement as her master shifted smoothly through countless gears. The trucker introduced himself as Randle, and Jarrod produced the name Bill, an alias that rolled out automatically. Randle drove confidently, handling the diesel tractor like it was an extension of his own body. His bushy, rusty-brown sideburns covered much of his pockmarked face. A thin, untrimmed mustache failed to fill in his upper lip. The frayed toothpick still hung from one corner of his mouth, and another cheap miniature cigarillo filled the cab with a thick, choking stench.

Despite the foul smoke, Jarrod was so exhausted that he found himself nodding off. Randle tried to carry on a conversation, reminiscing mostly about his trucking experiences. He mentioned a recent train accident but not a wanted man and boy. Margo had returned to the cash register when Randle paid for his dinner tab, yet no notice was taken of the sheriff's poster, which lay on top of a newspaper at the end of the counter. After clearing the tables, Bill had been busy outside gassing up a local car. He hadn't had a chance to mention the "wanted" poster to his staff.

Jarrod was sound asleep when the Mack came to a stop about twenty miles farther north. Randle dropped off a case of oil and some parts for his cousin's old tractor. The cousins chatted for several minutes. The delay was long enough so that, when Randle guided his rig down a certain steep grade with a dangerous left turn, the only evidence that remained of a near accident were deep tire tracks in the west ditch. Traces of mud still outlined the dual tire imprints which angled across the highway before fading away in the melting snow. Jarrod was still half asleep when Randle's rig overtook and passed a wobbly old stake-truck loaded with hay. No one noticed the white face of the nervous farmer who drove his time-worn vehicle at a speed not much faster than he would drive his combine. As he passed, Randle pulled on the chord to his air horn, displaying his aggravation as well as his concern for the hazard created by the slow-moving truck. The shrill noise caused the old driver to shudder even more.

Several miles later, Jarrod stirred when Randle began to down-shift at the outskirts of another town. The shifting caused a jerking motion inside the cab. After being jarred awaken from another deep sleep, Jarrod's mind was a tangle of cobwebs. His eyes had trouble focusing and, for a moment or two, he was totally disoriented. Had he been more alert, Jarrod might have noticed a familiar van parked on a street not far off the main highway. That sight alone would have made him jump from the Mack truck. As it was, he got to listen to endless country music and more idle chatter about Randle's travels.

"You awake there, buddy?" Randle asked. "I sure couldn't sleep when my firstborn was ready to pop."

"I drove all last night," Jarrod muttered, slowly untangling the web of confusion in his head. "How far are we from Duluth?"

"About an hour and a half. We're making better time now that the snow's melting. I hate it when the old girl gets messed up from all the slop on the highway."

Remembering the paper bag next to him, Jarrod pulled out a ham-and-cheese sandwich, offering the second one to Randle, which he declined. After swallowing a couple of painkillers to relieve his pounding headache, Jarrod quietly devoured the dry sandwich. His only memories of the remainder of his ride were a blur of grassy ditches and shadows, country music overpowering the steady hum of the Cummins diesel, the splish-splash of melting snow being dispersed by wide truck tires and, worst of all, the incessant drone of Randle's voice. A restful sleep was impossible as noises, inspirations, and graphic visions mixed together in his confused mind. He couldn't focus on any one thought, yet he couldn't block out the countless hazy images that floated about in his head as he drifted in semi-consciousness.

As dusk approached, Randle slowed his unit on the outskirts of Superior, Duluth's twin city. As the state border was oncoming, an orange, flashing light beckoned the Mack truck to pull over to a weigh scale. Aware that he was well within his weight limit and that his paperwork was in order, Randle confidently glided his semi-trailer unit up to the entrance for the in-ground scales. Only one tractor-trailer unit was stopped ahead of him. The interior of the Mack's cab exploded with a loud hissing sound as Randle popped out the lever that engaged his parking brakes. The noise was enough to snap Jarrod out of his restless slumber. He sat bolt upright in his seat.

"Why are we stopping?" he asked, a panicked tone in his voice.

"Gotta get my load weighed . . . won't be a minute. There's only one truck ahead of us," Randle explained, stepping down from the cab.

Wary that such places would be the first to get a description of escaped prisoners and runaways, Jarrod wondered if he should make an immediate exit. Sliding down from his perch in the cab, he kept an eye on Randle, who was inside the office talking to the scale operator. It was apparent they were acquainted, likely from previous trips, laughing together over some silly joke. Not looking any more suspicious than before, Randle returned. He noticed his passenger pacing nervously.

"Stretching your legs, I see," he commented. "We should be close to your hospital in twenty minutes. You look a little jumpy again. Worried about your kid?"

"That's for sure. I'm a bundle of nerves."

"A cop was around here a while back," Randle said, the comment catching Jarrod as much by surprise as it alarmed him. "He's looking for some guy traveling with a kid. He left some poster with a description of the two of them." Randle paused. "But nothing about some guy with a bashed-up nose about to become a father." He laughed. "So, I guess that lets you off the hook."

Jarrod smiled nervously, thanking his lucky stars that either Randle was awfully naïve or he had paid no attention to the poster Klem left behind. Or perhaps Jarrod's physical state bore little resemblance to the description on the sheriff's handout. Whatever the case, his ride would continue across the state line into Minnesota. The latest event had jolted Jarrod fully awake, his head much clearer and his heart pulsing rapidly.

Crossing the long bridge into Duluth, the "expectant father" stared emotionlessly at the cold water of Lake Superior. Several bridges spanned the St. Louis River, which emptied into the vast freshwater lake. A white lighthouse sat upon one of the spans, guarding the natural harbor and river estuary. The middle section of one of the nearby bridges rose laboriously, enabling a freighter, whose course was being monitored by several tugboats, to embark on its eastern voyage, its cargo hold swollen by a plentiful harvest of grain.

Within another ten minutes, after passing a new area of town, where modern homes and condos were sprouting, Randle pulled over to the curb. He was one block south of the Capital Health Center. Earlier, the young father-of-two had proclaimed the hospital to hold the finest maternity ward in the city and assumed "Bill's" wife would be there. Jarrod agreed quickly, inwardly thanking Randle for the name of a local hospital. His first child would come into the world only at the finest facility. Had he been prodded, Jarrod would have been unable to name even one hospital in Duluth.

"This is as close as I can get you, pal. There's no truck route nearer the hospital," Randle explained.

"This will do fine," Jarrod assured him. "I can't thank you enough for your help. Don't know how I would have made it here without you."

"Glad I could help. Hope everything goes well with your baby. The way you look, I hope you don't scare the wits right out of your young 'un. Maybe we'll meet again somewhere along the road. I'm surprised we haven't run into each other before." Randle was about to ask why his passenger had no luggage but then let it slide. The poor guy had enough on his mind.

After exchanging waves, Randle was on his way, his Mack truck puffing black clouds into the twilight sky as the noisy diesel pulled away from the curb. His mind working hard as it explored what possible action to consider next, Jarrod watched as the muddy rig faded away in a solid stream of traffic. Then, instead of rushing to the hospital, he walked directly to a nearby phone booth and paged through the local directory.

"Cross Country U-Drive." He could picture the faded lettering on the side of the truck box. Under the dim light cast by a tiny light bulb in the booth, Jarrod located an address. With a broken pencil that someone had left on top of the phone, he scrawled the street name and phone number on the remains of his paper bag, which still contained one sandwich and a chocolate bar. The pills were in his pocket.

He left the phone booth with a feeling of hopelessness weighing on his aching shoulders. The clothing he wore was not only his entire wardrobe but everything he owned in the world. A thin wallet in his jacket pocket contained his remaining funds. Yet as disheartened as Jarrod felt, the information scrawled on the torn and wrinkled paper bag served as the one ray of hope that might remove the dismal gloom that hung over him. The inexplicable connection between himself and the boy seemed to grow even stronger. He had to continue his search.

Chapter 14

Sounds of shallow, labored breathing flowed from Dr. W.S. Wilson's recovery room. Lucas either slept or was in a delusional state for almost twenty-four hours. His sleep was deep, but it was anything but peaceful. Instead, it was filled with dreams, images, and nightmares that invariably led to him rolling and thrashing about in the bed. Verbal gibberish flowed occasionally from his hoarse throat. The fever sent tremors through his emaciated body, forcing out sweat and dialogue that resembled a form of exorcism. Dr. and Mrs. Wilson made continual checks on him as he remained in a comatose state, but neither of them could piece together the mumble-jumble string of words he was uttering. They were unable to decipher even one coherent phrase, much less get any clues to the boy's past.

It wasn't until midafternoon the following day that Lucas's fever broke. Mrs. Wilson was mopping his head when his deep-brown, unfocused eyes were suddenly exposed as his eyelids lifted, drops of moisture clinging to his long eyelashes. It was as if an invisible curtain had risen to announce the start of a stage play—lights, drum roll, action. The sweating, the trembling, and the incoherent ramblings all ceased. Although barely audible, he uttered the first words which, in fact, formed a brief sentence.

"Where am I?"

Mrs. Wilson could barely hear the words. Caught by surprise, yet relieved that her patient had finally awakened, she took a moment before she replied. "You're in a small town called Lexter, at the home of Dr. Wilson. I'm Mrs. Wilson. You were lucky that a nice family brought you here yesterday." When he didn't respond, she added a note of reassurance. "You're safe here."

She wanted to ask many questions, but instead, Mrs. Wilson silently changed the sweat-soaked sheets and bedding and got her patient a dry flannel nightshirt. She moved him around like a limp ragdoll, finally hand-feeding him a bowl of warm chicken broth. His dehydrated and weakened condition left him unable to grip a spoon, but he was alive.

As Mrs. Wilson kept herself busy, trying to decide what questions she could ask, Lucas strained to recall the events of the last couple of days. He remembered Jarrod leaving him in the back of a van. Why? The memory came back. Food. That was it. His friend had gone to get food. Why didn't he return? It was so dark in there . . . then the truck started swaying and bouncing. Boxes . . . everything started falling around him. Was it real, or was it all a nightmare? Hot! He was so . . . so hot. And so very tired. Vaguely, he recalled someone lifting him . . . carrying him. He was lifted higher . . . and higher. Beams of light bounced off everything around him. People rushed toward him . . . hundreds of people. Their faces were white, like chalk . . . or were they human faces? Then he entered a tunnel . . . it seemed endless and dark. His body felt like it would explode. He tried to run, but his legs wouldn't move, like they were embedded in concrete. His eyes burned from the strain and the searing heat of the tunnel. Finally, one last memory of his dream? Delusion? . . . a shaft of light, so intense it blinded him.

But there he was, lying in a strange home, awake, alive, and squinting from the bright afternoon sunbeams streaming through the window next to his bed. It all seemed so real. Yet how could it have been?

It wasn't long before reality crept back to him as Lucas became more aware of his situation. It was far from good. He had reached the end of the line once again. Soon they would drag him back to the group home—or a worse place, if he got charged with theft and arson. There was no doubt he had lost the one person who seemed to care about him, whom he had grown to trust, the man who had put himself in danger trying to help him, whose friendship had given him hope that maybe his life could change for the better. Was Jarrod gone forever? Gloom and despair suddenly overwhelmed him. Lucas wished that he had never awakened.

"That's enough soup for now," Mrs. Wilson said, aware that her silent patient had lost interest in eating. He appeared to be in a trance, his mind off in another world. "The doctor will want to have a look at you." She felt it was not the time for further questions. After placing a thermometer under the boy's tongue, she left to get her husband.

Dr. Wilson was treating a scratched puppy when his wife entered the examination room reserved for four-legged patients.

"The boy's awake," Mrs. Wilson said. Her tone was not enthusiastic.

"Has he said anything?"

She shook her head. "Not much. Just asked where he was. He seems to be in shock or in a stupor of some sort. But I heard something interesting on the last newscast. Apparently, some out-of-town sheriff has been making inquiries in the area. He was looking for a man and a boy who escaped custody. The news report made them out to be a modern Jesse James gang, robbing and pillaging towns, leaving a path of destruction in their wake."

Dr. Wilson laughed heartily, scaring the puppy. "Do you think we're treating a pillager?"

"Of course not, dear, but I thought you'd be interested." She failed to connect the newscast with the travel bags that still lay in a heap under the reception desk.

"You know how the media likes to sensationalize," her husband said.

Having bandaged the puppy, he washed his hands before walking casually into the room where his young patient lay, staring at the ceiling. He pulled the thermometer from Lucas's mouth.

"Glad to see you're feeling better," he said as he noted the boy's temperature was less than one degree above normal. "What's your name, son?"

Dr. Wilson had caring eyes and spoke in a tone that was soft and yet confident. From the blank stare he received, he sensed the boy had scars much deeper than the superficial bruises that patterned his skin.

"Jim . . .." The monosyllable answer came out in a hesitant whisper. Lucas's mind pictured Jarrod's rugged face frowning at him, as if telling him to keep quiet.

"Where are you from, Jim?" the doctor asked gently.

Silence.

"Maybe we can help you. Don't worry, we're not running to the police. You're under my care, and you're safe here as my patient."

No response.

"Well, we can talk later. "Mom," my wife I mean, will fix you some great chow." Dr. Wilson's patience didn't waver, but he realized his patient wasn't in the mood for questions.

Leaving the bedroom, he passed Mrs. Wilson. "Try him on some solid food," he whispered, "and find something to entertain him, maybe some comics. You're always better than I am at getting reclusive kids to talk."

After her patient picked at a meal of scrambled eggs and hot cereal, Mrs. Wilson questioned him again. Perhaps a combination of her soothing manner and the hot food in his stomach enabled her to gain some headway. "Jim" offered bits and pieces of information, explaining how his parents were always fighting. His dad drank too much and then beat both him and his mother. He had been on his way to his aunt's place in Minneapolis when he lost his bus ticket and hadn't enough money to buy another. Instead, he hitched a ride in the back of a U-drive.

Although skeptical of his story (why was he headed north when Minneapolis was to the west?), Mrs. Wilson listened intently and with interest. At least he was talking. Her mind balanced somewhere between disbelief and faith that the boy was at least telling bits of the truth. She offered to call his aunt, but once again, he became distant, uninterested, and mumbled something about losing her address and phone number. At that point, their conversation over, Mrs. Wilson realized his entire story was a fabrication.

Morning arrived on the third day of Lucas's recovery at the Wilson home/hospital. He had remained reticent about discussing his past, where he came from, where he was headed, and even his last name. After seeing much improvement in his physical condition—Mrs. Wilson's fine cooking playing a big part—the doctor knew it was time to find out the truth. Since the boy provided no answers, he resorted to calling a friend at the local newspaper to see if he could dig up more information on the pair of escapees. Toward suppertime, his friend called back. The doctor listened intently as he learned that the man on the news was wanted for embezzlement, not murder. His young accomplice was Lucas Kenny, a runaway from a boys' group home. The two were accused of setting a big fire to help them escape as well as causing a train wreck. Hanging up the phone, the doctor felt numb as he tried to assimilate the new information. At least now he could approach his patient with something concrete. He still wasn't ready to involve the authorities.

While her husband was on the phone, Mrs. Wilson, who was helping a new patient fill out medical forms, came across the travel bags that lay under the reception desk. How could she have forgotten? She called her husband over.

After a quick scrutiny of the bags' contents, Dr. Wilson realized the torn and filthy backpack must belong to the boy. Gripping it tightly, he entered the bedroom, where

Lucas lay flat on his back, an open comic book resting on his stomach, his unblinking, glassy stare focused on the ceiling. His eyes showed no emotion, casting the blank look that a corpse lying in the morgue might display. His distant gaze was unwavering and blocked out the presence of the latest intruder to enter the room. Dr. Wilson felt the boy's profound depression reach out toward him like an icy hand. He realized this was not the time to confront the youngster, who might simply bolt out the door. Should he call the police? No. First, he would discuss the situation with his wife. He needed her calmness and strength, but, most of all, her approval.

Before leaving, the doctor laid Lucas's backpack at the foot of the bed. "I believe this belongs to you, son. The good folks in the van left it behind. It's yours, isn't it?" Rather than his normal display of assurance and comfort, Dr. Wilson felt a quiver in his voice.

His opaque, half-open eyes moving slowly to view the limp pack resting next to his feet, Lucas nodded imperceptibly. "Yeah . . . it's mine," he whispered, his tone displaying little interest.

With emotions taking over from reasoning, Dr. Wilson could say no more. He silently slipped out of the room.

Lucas had to force himself to eat his evening meal. His body ached for nourishment, but his mind balked at the thought of food. Eventually, hunger got the best of him, and he cleaned his plate, perhaps a premonition that coming events would require a need for nourishment. No one bothered him that evening. For hours, he stared, without interest, at a television that sat on the dresser, endless laugh tracks droning from its raspy speaker. At about ten o'clock, his swollen bladder forced him to visit the washroom down the hall.

After finishing up in the washroom, Lucas looked toward the den at the end of the hallway. The light was on, and its door was partially closed. Feeling not quite as down as before, he decided to at least say goodnight to the Wilsons. They had certainly been good to him, and so far, they had kept their word about not reporting him. As he approached the den, Lucas heard a subdued conversation behind the partially closed door. Always wary of people talking behind his back, he stood very still behind the oak door, making sure his shadow wasn't visible.

As the Wilsons talked, his sharp ears picked up the odd word or phrase. Words like "orphan" and "running" made him concentrate even more, but one word jolted him wide awake and sent him scurrying back to his room: "Kenny!" Doc Wilson said his surname. They knew!

Lucas lay on his bed in a cold sweat. He knew it was time to leave. Since his fever had broken, part of him had given up, lost hope, even wished his life would end. But suddenly it was as if a force he could not control had taken over his body. The passion that gave him strength was intuitive. It was the will to survive, an animal instinct that drives the young and the untamed, even those whose lives and whose futures hold little promise. Just as the street children of the world would steal, prostitute themselves, do anything to survive, Lucas was controlled by some inborn drive. The urge to continue his journey was with him once again.

As if some cosmic power was instrumental in urging him forward, an inexplicable spark regained his feeling that he could find happiness somewhere up north. Was Canada the light at the end of the tunnel? Was it a place where peace and freedom existed, where his running could end? Lurking somewhere in the boy's puzzled mind was a man with a smashed nose and a crooked grin urging him on, giving him the strength to follow his dream.

Chapter 15

Lucas left that night. First, he closed his eyes and pretended to sleep until Mrs. Wilson came in to check on him. Then, when he was certain the Wilsons had gone to bed, he dressed in the warm clothing Julie had given him. He put on practically all the clothes he owned that were above the level of rags. The remainder he left behind with the backpack, which no longer served a purpose and would only slow him down. He stuffed most of his money in his shoe, keeping a few dollars in his pocket. Water had ruined his pamphlet on Canada. The newspaper clipping was nowhere to be found. The ink had smeared on his letter, making it totally illegible when Mrs. Wilson had tried to decipher the writing. Lucas stuffed it in his pocket anyway. It was still the only link to the one time he had experienced true happiness, when the woman he lived with felt like a real mother to him.

Before leaving, he scrawled an unsigned note that Mrs. Wilson would find in the morning. She read over the heart-rending words several times before even showing the note to her husband.

Thank you for yur help
I must go now, sorry for being a bother good by.

Lucas left the note on top of the pillow in his bed. He thought briefly of leaving some money for the Wilsons but then realized he would need every penny he had for the long trip ahead. He did feel somewhat guilty after helping himself to a cozy knit hat that he found in the closet. Slinking silently down the dark hallway, he exited through the kitchen and screened porch at the rear of the house. Fortunately, the Wilsons' didn't have an alarm system. The doors weren't even locked.

How would he travel? Hitchhike? No, certainly not at that time of night. Besides, the locals would know everyone in the area. He was a stranger. Not only would his age arouse suspicion, but the police would have given his description to the local press and radio. He and Jarrod were probably the favorite gossip of the day.

Trying to get his bearings, Lucas walked toward the lights of the main street, which turned out to be the highway through town. Searching for any clues as to where he should be heading, he chose to turn left. Within half a block, he saw a sign that read "29 North." At least he was starting off in the right direction.

The town of Lexter was shut down at that time of night. If it had any sidewalks, they would have been rolled up. Even the service station was closed. As the cool night air energized him, Lucas began moving quickly. Was it fear, or was he just trying to keep warm? It only took him a few moments to leave behind another easily forgotten town as he continued his northern trek on foot. To avoid being seen by passing vehicles, he walked along the inside line of the barbed-wire fence that paralleled the highway's west ditch. Whenever he saw the lights of an approaching vehicle, he ducked for cover behind tall clumps of uncut grass or one of the long rows of straw that lay across the field awaiting the baler.

After barely an hour of hiking, fatigue set in. In addition to the physical drain from his fever, the biting chill in the air led to a rapid loss of stamina. His eyes scoured the hayfield in search of a place to rest. A gibbous moon was rising to his right. Silver moonbeams glinted across the water droplets that clung to the strands of barbed wire. Less than fifty yards inside the fence line, a dark silhouette rose from the field. Closer inspection revealed three rows of neatly stacked bundles of hay. After separating a couple of the outside bales, Lucas formed a small pocket, where his tired body could fit. The tiny cavity would serve as both bed and shelter for the remainder of the night. As his shivering subsided, he quickly dropped off to sleep.

At the first sign of dawn, Lucas awoke to the stale odor of an old bull nibbling at his shelter, only inches from his head. The surprised animal greeted him with a loud mooing sound. The smells of cow breath and damp hay mingled with the crisp morning air were enough to rouse the tired boy. Rubbing sleep from his eyes, he felt surprisingly warm in the insulated sleeping quarters provided by the hay bales. Stretching the stiffness from his joints as he brushed bits of straw from his clothing, Lucas said a brief farewell to the hungry bull before continuing his walk north under the pale sky of early-dawn. Breakfast consisted of three oatmeal cookies he had discovered in the Wilsons' kitchen during his hasty departure.

Still careful to keep out of the sight of highway traffic, Lucas continued to move along the inside of the fence line next to the west ditch. Bulrushes, tall thistles, and the occasional tree provided cover from the few vehicles that passed by. The ground, hard and frozen from the night's frost, was dotted with patches of snow. Doubt and concern crept into his mind. He wondered how many more nights he could survive without shelter, not to mention food. The days were getting shorter and colder. It was the wrong time of year to be traveling north on foot. Was the unrelenting, powerful force that urged him onward actually drawing him to his eventual cold demise? Shaking off such morbid thoughts, Lucas focused his attention on any and all opportunities that crossed his path.

Squinting as the early morning sun blinded his vision, prospects of a ride seemed bleak when Lucas saw a blue-and-white van zip past and then pull over onto the north-bound shoulder about one hundred feet ahead. Thinking that the driver had spotted him, he ducked behind a clump of brush. After the four-way flashers came on, he watched as the driver stepped from the right side of the van holding a large brown parcel. Lucas realized that opportunity had come knocking. Bold lettering identified the cube van as a postal truck. Since the package was too large to fit in the mailbox, the uniformed driver walked up the narrow drive-way toward the house. Any foot-weary boy would not miss such a chance. Keeping low as he checked for traffic, Lucas scurried across the highway.

The sliding door on the right side of the van was partially open. The postman would never expect an intruder on such an early morning. The boy slipped through the narrow opening and peered into the dark cargo area. Although the postman was out of sight, who could guess what furry companion might be lurking in the shadows of the cube van? When no fangs greeted him, Lucas crawled over the parcels and neatly bundled letters and slid behind a stack of empty mail bags at the rear of the van. He had barely got himself settled in, partially covering his body with the empty bags, when the postman slid the side door open and hopped into the van. Lucas's ears rang when the door slammed shut.

The next few hours were a swaying roller-coaster ride. The stowaway was serenaded by the sounds of tires spinning on loose gravel, which sent tiny rocks deflecting off the van's wheel wells. The crescendo of a noisy muffler exploding every time the mail truck accelerated provided the climax to the orchestral nightmare. The van went up and down an endless string of country roads, dispersing its load of bills, parcels, and junk mail. The driver also picked up mail along the way, tossing it into a bag mounted on a stand next to his seat. Fortunately, all his deliveries were organized within easy reach in the front portion of the van, and he had no need to open the rear doors.

The warmth and swaying motion of the mail van eventually relaxed Lucas, as his ears tried to block out the constant noise that resonated throughout the cargo box. He was lulled into an uneasy sleep, only to be awakened by the squeak of another flag being raised on a mailbox, followed by a lurch as the van accelerated toward its next destination. Lucas recalled a movie he had seen, where a group of teenagers drove down country roads in a convertible and knocked mailboxes off their posts with a baseball bat. Whack! Whack! With every rut in the road, the sound of a wooden bat striking its target echoed in his head.

Without warning, one vivid memory flashed through his wary mind. Although it felt like ages ago, only a year and a few months had passed since Lucas had pitched in his Little League championship game. It took place in Oshkosh, the city where he had lived with Tracy and Bob. It was the ninth inning, and his team was up by one run. He struck out the first two batters on eight pitches. Then the third batter hit a slow roller right at Lucas. He picked it up easily, but his arm almost locked when he tried to throw the ball to first. Luckily, the first baseman caught it on one bounce. The game was over. His team mobbed him. Only eleven years old, that was the last time he could remember being thrilled.

The musty bags that hid Lucas were spares to be used to collect unsorted mail on its way to a central post office. So far, as the load of new mail was light, there was no need for the extra bags. The stuffy smell, combined with the dusty roads, brought on more than one sneeze, which Lucas smothered in the sleeve of his jacket.

The postman entertained himself by listening to oldies music on a small transistor radio that hissed and faded in and out as the mail truck got beyond range of the signal. He hummed and strummed to country classics, completely unaware of any sounds coming from the rear of his van.

The day wore on as a series of stops and starts, the postal truck swaying back and forth as it continually pulled over to the side of the road. The mailman stopped briefly so he could devour a sandwich and an apple he had brought with him and then hurried to continue his route. His wage was not based on the hours he worked. The sooner he finished, the faster he got home. On one occasion, he tossed a full bag of mail toward the back of the van. It slammed on top of the sacks that hid Lucas, sending up a cloud of fine dust. The thumping noise of the sacks colliding, along with the distinctive voice of Johnny Cash singing "Walk the Line," disguised Lucas's loud sneeze. Fortunately, the postman kept an extra mail bag up front and never had any need to open the rear doors.

By midafternoon, the mail truck came to its final stop alongside a loading dock at a postal depot located in another Wisconsin town, its name unknown to Lucas. His pupils dilated from the darkness where he hid, Lucas became alert for danger when he heard the postman complaining to a fellow worker.

"What a long day, Sam," he said. "I swear I delivered as much junk mail and parcels today as I did last Christmas. I'm sure as hell not looking forward to the holiday season."

"You're just getting fat and lazy, Frank," Sam kidded.

Rest period was over for the young runaway. Expecting the rear doors to be pulled open at any moment, he slid between the mail bags and crouched behind the driver's seat to check out an escape route. He listened to the two men talking just outside the partially open driver's door.

"Did you bring those magazines for me?" Sam asked.

"Oh, right, I almost forgot. They're just here behind the seat," Frank replied as he slid open the driver's side door.

Glancing down, Lucas saw that he was kneeling on the well-endowed breasts of a woman on the cover of a magazine. It was now or never.

The postman had one foot on the front step of the van when he saw a small, shadowy figure move with the speed of a greyhound.

"Wha . . . at?" was all Frank could stammer as the stowaway bolted out the passenger's door, which slid open with a thundering crash.

Shock and surprise froze the two men in their tracks. They could only watch as the pint-sized figure streaked across the lot and down a back lane.

"Damn, how did that kid get in here?" Frank asked, knowing it was against federal regulations to carry any passengers in the postal truck.

After thinking for a moment, he handed Sam his magazines. "Here, take them. Let's not mention seein' that kid run off. That supervisor of ours is always after me for not keeping the truck locked. I'll only get into trouble if he finds out I was giving some kid a free ride from who knows where."

Sam nodded in agreement as he slipped the magazines into his mailbag.

So, the young stowaway's presence in town would be kept a secret, a comfort not known to Lucas, who continued to dart through yards and alleyways to assure his escape. After checking over his shoulder several times, he was convinced no one was following him and stopped running in a residential lane. His pulse racing, he leaned against a garbage bin and gulped air as he tried to catch his breath.

When he could finally breathe normally, Lucas turned his attention to the hunger pains that gnawed at his stomach. The nourishment of three oatmeal cookies had worn off long ago. Deciding to count the wrinkled wad of bills he had stored in his shoe, he tallied almost ninety dollars that remained from Toothy's night receipts. There was no need to starve for a few days yet. With a careful and practiced ritual, he tucked all but five dollars into his left sock, making sure his sneakers were tied tightly.

Following back alleys, an intuitive sense of direction led Lucas to the town's central business section. A spacious mall, where crowds flocked on that late Friday afternoon, dominated the shopping district. An out-of-town boy would easily go unnoticed in the bustle and confusion of the dozens of local children wandering the mall. Without having to look far, Lucas found a fast-food restaurant, the Whoppo Burger Palace. Its marquee claimed it had served thousands of burgers locally. Food at last! Getting over a dollar in change from his five dollars, he purchased a double burger, fries, and a drink. In a matter of moments, the starving boy wolfed down his meal.

His hunger taken care of, Lucas decided to wander through the mall. The warmth that came from being inside spread throughout his body. School was out for the day, and it wasn't long before Lucas turned his attention to a video arcade, where kids his own age crowded around an array of machines. Some of the latest games were computerized, digitally displaying scores, while others were older and shot silver balls against bumpers that pulsated and flashed. Dazzling colored lights and the sound of top-ten songs filled the arcade. Whirring, bleeping, shooting, screeching, even grunting noises rang out from speakers on the rows of games. Bells and sirens went off as pinball machines awarded replays for skillful play. The students of the games stood transfixed as they watched the masters battle their electronic foes, scoring points by the thousands or millions. The machines never quit, only rested momentarily, flashing a "GAME OVER" sign until a fresh transfusion of coins brought them back to life, renewing the battle. "INSERT COIN TO CONTINUE . . .." The blinking words issued the challenge while counting down the seconds, a warning that the game would end shortly.

Never able to afford to play—even stolen money could be put to better use—Lucas had often watched as kids fed quarter after quarter into the electronic monsters. Like junkies, the kids were hooked, entire allowances spirited from their pockets. A contagious spell had overtaken the particular group he watched. Several of them had discarded their warm coats on the arcade floor in the heat of battle. Remembering his chilly nights on the road, it was the jackets that caught Lucas's attention. His eyes roved from the flashing games to the floor, then back to the games. No, he couldn't take the chance. As entranced as they were by the video games, the kids would chase him down like hungry predators. He could never outrun them all.

While Lucas was eyeing a jacket with a large crest on the back, he caught the attention of a stocky boy, whose oily, pimply face displayed the telltale afflictions of puberty.

Perhaps thirteen, the boy was not accepting the transition of his body with ease, and he showed his bad disposition by taunting and bullying many of the other players. Lucas was a fresh target, a new person to dominate.

"Hey, kid, what are you looking at? You want to steal my jacket? You think I got money in there?" The bully was warming up for a confrontation.

Lucas shook his head and took an instinctive step back. "Naw, I'm just watching the games."

"That's not the way I see it, punk. You're probably the one who stole two bucks out of my coat last week," the bully continued, not wanting to miss the opportunity to harass his new victim.

"Leave the kid alone, Rocky," a blond boy about twelve years old cut in. "He never touched your jacket."

"Screw off, Chris. This jerk looks like a thief to me." Rocky stepped toward Lucas. "Let's see what you got in your pockets. Come on, hurry up."

"Forget it. I never stole a lousy dime off you," Lucas replied, his heartbeat quickening as anger surged through his body. He'd met lots of boys like Rocky in the group homes. He knew that even if he gave in, the bully would laugh and continue to humiliate him.

"If you don't show me, I'll have to see for myself," Rocky threatened as he grabbed Lucas by the arm.

Lucas shook himself loose and turned to leave the arcade when Rocky's right hand slapped him across the side of his turned face, causing a small nick in the corner of his lip. The blindside hit stopped Lucas in his tracks.

"Show me! Now!" Rocky bellowed.

Never having a long fuse, the salty taste of blood trickling into his mouth sent Lucas into a rage. He didn't care that Rocky outweighed him by at least forty pounds. He flailed away, raining a flurry of punches on Rocky's body. Unfortunately, his strength was still well below par, and his blows had little effect on the older boy, other than catching him off guard.

"Is that your best?" Rocky sneered. He grabbed Lucas and pushed him viciously to the ground. Planning to finish the fight quickly, he aimed a savage kick at Lucas's head as he lay on the arcade floor, but to the bully's dismay, the wild swing of his foot only glanced off the shoulder of his prone opponent.

Standing well off to the side, a woman who exchanged bills for coins in the arcade wanted nothing to do with the fight.

Breathing heavily, his face flushed with anger, Lucas was not one to give up easily. He saw his opportunity when Rocky was sent off balance by his errant kick. The bully's face glistened with red spots. Jumping to his feet with the nimble grace of a gymnast, Lucas used all the strength he had left to bury his head into his pimply-faced adversary's unprotected stomach. The force of the impact not only winded Rocky but also drove the shocked and staggering bully backwards against a pinball machine. The "TILT" sign flashed its authoritative "GAME OVER." Rocky's lower back was driven into the ball plunger, which protruded from the right front corner of the machine. The game *was* over, as the fight came to an abrupt end. Rocky knelt on the floor, his hands grasping his back as he doubled up in pain.

His breathing came in frantic gasps. The young audience let out an audible groan but was otherwise speechless. No one could believe what they had just witnessed.

Lucas wasn't about to hang around for congratulations. Staggering from exertion, he bumped into more than one of the young onlookers as he stumbled away. It only made sense to leave the arcade quickly before security guards showed up, or another boy decided to prove how tough he was and take over for Rocky.

Lucas needn't have worried, as the only person to follow him was the blond boy, who had no intention of fighting. The boy, Chris, caught up to Lucas in the parking lot.

"I haven't seen you around before. Are you just visiting, or did you move here?" Chris asked as he ran alongside the fleeing stranger.

Realizing that the boy meant him no harm and that no one else seemed to be following, Lucas stopped running. "Are you friends with that jerk?" he asked, his face still flushed and his breath coming in deep puffs.

"No. Never was. Rocky is always bugging the younger kids. No one likes him. You're the first to have the guts to stand up to him. I loved it." Chris smiled and introduced himself.

"I'm, uh, Jim," Lucas said. "Just passing through town on my way to . . .." He paused, remembering a road sign he had seen on the way to the mall. "Duluth . . . to visit my aunt. I've got to catch the next bus." His mind worked quickly, truth and fiction blending together as he spoke.

"Hey, that's cool. You won't believe it, but my folks and I are driving up to Grandma's place to spend the night.

She lives just outside Duluth. I could ask Dad if he'd mind giving you a ride. There's lots of room in our station wagon."

Without thinking for long, Lucas decided he had nothing to lose by accepting the ride. There was a cold night ahead, and the larger city might offer a better chance for shelter. Besides, it would be one more step in what continued to look more and more like a long journey to nowhere, to a place that existed only in a world of dreams.

"That sounds great, thanks," Lucas replied. "The bus doesn't leave for an hour or so. Are you sure your folks won't mind?"

Chris laughed. "Are you kidding? Not after I tell them what you did to Rocky."

With the ice broken, a natural connection developed between the two boys. Was Lucas getting softer in his willingness to trust others? The boys talked with the candid openness of youth as they walked the four blocks to Chris's home. The boredom of school, the sports they played, and cute girls were all part of their conversation. When asked if the light jacket he wore was all he had with him, Lucas explained that he had forgotten his winter coat on the bus that brought him to town from his farm, seventy miles to the south. "Don't worry, I wasn't going to steal one from the floor," he added.

"I've got an extra jacket you can borrow till you get back into town. I wear it for skiing—it's pretty warm," Chris offered. The young stranger who had just put Rocky to his knees had already made a firm impression on him.

The walk went quickly, the new friends entering a trailer park community where homes were either prefabricated or were trailers that rested permanently on concrete blocks. It was well maintained, and Chris showed off the seasonal swimming pool and rec hall. He and his parents lived in a double-width trailer with all the amenities of any modern home.

The first thing Lucas noticed when introduced to Chris's parents was the genuine sincerity they showed. The love amidst the entire family was very apparent. They quickly made Lucas feel at home, especially after hearing about his episode with Rocky. Everyone had a good laugh. Lucas realized what a real family life should be: happiness and caring for each other. A hint of sadness crept over him. He guessed Chris's parents were about Jarrod's age, although they did not have his road-worn appearance. They dressed in sweatshirts and faded jeans. Very cool. There was no hesitation in offering him a ride to Duluth, but they would have to be leaving very shortly.

"Call your aunt from here, Jim," Chris's dad insisted. "Tell her that you should be in Duluth by six thirty."

"Oh, thanks . . . I guess I should let her know," Lucas replied as Chris's dad showed him to the phone in the den. Not wanting the call to show up on the family's phone bill, he dialed the 555 information number and pretended to talk to his aunt.

"She'll pick me up at the bus depot around seven. She lives on the other side of town," Lucas told the family as they prepared to leave. He insisted they not drive him to her home.

For the first part of the ride to Duluth, Lucas remained subdued. He felt uneasy and had trouble accepting what life as a close-knit, caring family was all about. He couldn't find a way to fit in when Chris and his parents bantered back and forth, joking with each other. Yet Lucas sensed a bond that linked this family, a bond of love and respect. He recalled a similar feeling in his own life, yet on two occasions, he had been separated from the only people with whom he had felt a connection, security, maybe even love. Bitterness filled his mouth. Resigned that he would never become part of a family, his eyes were vacant as he stared silently at the passing traffic.

Chris was too outgoing to allow his new friend to remain out of the conversation for long. He got started with a wisecrack that Lucas should have been disqualified in his fight for head-butting. Before long, Lucas broke his glum silence and joined in the family chatter. It was unfortunate that he had to field a string of inquisitive questions with the deceitful skill of a professional conman. He had a quick and plausible answer to almost everything they asked.

The trip went quickly. Darkness closed in on the grey, late-autumn day as the station wagon crossed the state border and entered the bright lights of Duluth. Chris's dad, who had insisted on driving Lucas right to the bus depot, made one last, tempting offer.

"Jim, do you want to join us for dinner before we drop you at the bus station?" he suggested. "I'm sure your aunt wouldn't mind. We're early anyway."

Making a silly decision he would later regret, Lucas replied hastily and with little thought. "No, but thanks anyway. She said dinner would be ready for me. Besides, she's always early . . . likely left already."

Why was he not allowing himself to get close to this family? Was the whole encounter merely a sham, a distraction while some inner power continued its compelling mastery over him in the form of a crazy dream that pushed him relentlessly toward an impossible destination? More likely, it was the continual fear that his real identity would be exposed. When put to the test, even the kindest of people could not continue to ignore the obvious.

With some regret and a hint of sorrow, the new friends said their goodbyes. After thanking Chris's folks as they dropped him outside the bus station, Lucas promised to return the winter jacket when he got back to town. "But I'm not going back to that arcade," he assured them. Unfortunately, the first promise was one he was unlikely to ever fulfill.

Chris gave his new pal one last smile and a wave. Lucas sensed his blond friend realized the truth, that this was likely the last time they would ever see one another. He returned the wave but failed to smile.

Pushing open the door to the bus depot, Lucas brushed past two children who cut in front of him in their frenzied haste to get outside. The children's blank stares conveyed no message, no apology, and no words were spoken. It was almost as if two robots had stumbled past him on their route to oblivion.

"There's a couple of odd ones," Lucas mumbled under his breath. A rush of warm air drew the tired-out traveler into the bright lights of the bus terminal. Stepping into the well-lit waiting area, the young chaser of dreams had no idea he was walking into a nightmare worse than any group home he could ever imagine.

Part 3
ANTE UP, PLEASE

Chapter 16

Jarrod got directions from a service station attendant across the street from the phone booth and then began the six-block walk to the U-drive office. He recalled seeing the out-of-state license plate as he was checking vehicles at Bill's Truck Stop but decided not to risk asking over the phone for the name and address of a mysterious rental customer driving from Michigan. He was quite certain the man who had escorted his young son to the washroom at the restaurant was the driver of the moving van, but Jarrod's only real clue he was even on the right track was that, in his hurry to get on the road, the man had mentioned the city Duluth to his little boy.

The long walk gave Jarrod time to formulate a plan to get information on the rental van without arousing suspicion. He needed the name of the person who had rented the U-drive van in Michigan, intending to drop it off in Duluth. Regrettably, Jarrod discovered that entering the Cross-Country U-drive office just before closing time on a Friday was not such a good idea. The girl behind the counter, who was barely out of her teens, was obviously anxious to close up for the night. She was in such a hurry to get to an early dinner date that she barely looked up as the disheveled man entered the office. Faith, as her nametag read, appeared to have no concern that the man who approached her looked as if he had just escaped a back alley beating or might have robbery on his mind. Nonetheless, after she gave him a hurried glance, Jarrod felt certain he would not be considered a valued customer.

Sensing the girl's impatience, he skipped the preamble. "Sorry to bother you so close to closing, but my cousin, John Black, is moving here from Detroit. I expected him in town this afternoon. Would you know if he's arrived or been delayed by some problem?" He spoke quickly and businesslike, concerned his appearance might alarm the clerk.

After rapidly checking the day's log sheet, the anxious girl replied bluntly, her voice hissing with the sound of someone sucking on a breath mint. "No van due today from Michigan. No John Black on here. Sorry."

"I'm sure he said Cross Country U-drive," Jarrod pressed. "Could you check tomorrow's list? I might have the day wrong."

Exasperated, Faith grabbed the next day's log sheets from the manager's desk behind her, flopping them on the counter in a manner that was far from cordial. After checking her watch, she scanned the list with the speed of someone searching for a number in a telephone book. Leaning over the counter, Jarrod also skimmed through the list of vehicles due to return, but he wasn't looking for John Black.

"Nope, only one truck from Michigan expected in tomorrow, and it's not your cousin," she confirmed without a hint of remorse.

However, speed-reading the page from top to bottom, Jarrod had beaten the girl in spotting the Michigan plate and the name across from it: Tom Benning, Price Discount Store, 12A Central Mall. Years of experience at a variety of accounting jobs had conditioned him to scan columns of numbers quickly.

Memorizing the info, Jarrod backed away as Faith snatched the log sheets from under his nose. With a loud thump, they landed on top of the manager's cluttered desk. *An organized company, anxious for new customers,* he thought sarcastically. At least he had found the information he was after.

"Sorry I couldn't help you. Got to lock up," Faith said in a very unapologetic tone. She ushered Jarrod out the door and had already turned the deadbolt before he could thank her for her time, as short as it was.

Vowing never to rent a vehicle from that company, Jarrod didn't waste a backward glance. Leaving the office, he crossed the street to a fast-food outlet, but before ordering a basket of chicken nuggets, he called the Price Discount Store from a payphone just inside the front door. Several rings later, a clerk/receptionist, her high-pitched voice sounding like it belonged to a junior high girl, put him through to the manager trainee, who supervised the evening shift. A male voice, whose squeaky tone came across with the anguished pitch of a choirboy suffering through a change to his vocal chords, explained it was against company policy to give out any information concerning personnel. The youthful manager suggested that Jarrod drop by in the morning, when Mr. Benning would be in the store to get acquainted with his new staff. It was evident that Benning would be taking over senior management duties.

After thanking the manager trainee for his help, Jarrod hung up. He considered calling information to check for a new listing for the Bennings, but then rejected the idea of talking to them over the phone. Not only was it unlikely that a new service had been hooked up, but calling the family would give them the opportunity to alert the police before a meeting could be arranged. Most likely, the authorities were already involved. If Lucas had been apprehended, almost a guarantee in view of the boy's feverish condition, the extra travel bag that accompanied him would have led the police to the identity of his traveling companion. It was already evident that Sheriff Klem was determined to alert the entire free world to be on the lookout for the desperate escapees.

After he finished his meal, Jarrod was too exhausted to walk any farther and finally succumbed to using the local transit system. Riding a bright orange-and-green bus into the central area of town, his mind struggled with a recurring dilemma. Part of him fought to board the first westbound Silverfox bus, to put the last few days behind him, and to get as far away as possible from his former life, including Sheriff Klem. Yet the silent words he had uttered recently to a lost and desperate child kept stabbing at his conscience: *One thing I promise kiddo, I won't desert you.* The promise, the scared brown eyes, the look of desolation and fading hope, the memory of his own relief when air gasped into those water-congested lungs . . . Jarrod had to make one last effort, no matter the cost. The solemn promise, likely a futile one, had become part of his makeup, just as gambling had overtaken his life. He could not overcome an inexplicable bond with the youngster; instead, it seemed to be strengthening. His heart finally won the latest battle, but the war waged on. He would stay for a day or two, or at least until he knew his efforts were fruitless and there was nothing more he could do. He was not optimistic.

Worn out from the events of the last twenty-four hours, Jarrod stepped from the bus into an area that the transit driver told him was central Duluth. The downtown area would have once been the hub of activity, filled with theaters and restaurants, before large malls with acres of parking spread the action toward the outskirts of town. He stared at rows of older three- and four-story brick buildings, many deteriorating and in serious need of upgrades. Some were boarded up, deserted by previous owners. The streets were narrow, with few cars parked on them. In desperate need of some rest, he spotted a neon "Vacancy" sign that flashed on the front of an aging, three-floor brick hotel.

Jarrod dragged his feet as he pulled on the heavy wooden door that faced the sidewalk. It creaked open. The entrance led to a poorly lit hallway, which must have dated back to the early 1900s. Wooden moldings, baseboards, and a winding staircase were all worn, scuffed, and faded, badly needing a fresh coat of paint or stain. Brass railings, smudged with handprints, were so tarnished they had turned a deep amber. Perhaps sixty years earlier, the place had been majestic, but now it would have difficulty gaining a single-star rating.

The gentleman behind the front desk could well have been another Dicken's character. "Elderly" would have been a kind description, "fossilized" a more apt portrayal.

Hunched over the counter, his eyes squinting inches above the newspaper he was attempting to read, the desk clerk seemed shocked that anyone might be approaching him for a room.

"Evening, sir." The clerk spoke with a raspy croak that could only have resulted from years of inhaling unfiltered cigarette smoke.

"Good evening," Jarrod replied, his nose twitching from the moldy, dank smell that permeated the air. A purple haze hung over the lobby like an early-morning fog. "Do you have a vacant room for rent?"

"Do I have a vacant room? Hee, hee, hee." Through toothless gums and cracked lips, the desk clerk's laugh was piercing. The sound of piglets at feeding time might have been less abrasive. "Got your choice of the entire second floor," he replied, recovering from his fit of giggles.

His ears ringing, Jarrod winced, and he was momentarily speechless.

"I'd better show you the place first," the clerk said. Part of his job was showing new guests to their room before collecting the payment. Many chose to seek other accommodations.

After plucking a large ring of keys from a brass hanger behind the desk, the night clerk shuffled up a flight of warped stairs to the second floor. Each step the men took brought an agonized squeak from the wooden staircase.

"Now remember, if you decide to stay here, the front doors lock at midnight. You'll have to buzz to get in if you're out later than that. But I don't hear so good. I'll give you a room key, but the manager likes you to leave it at the front desk if you go out. And no visitors after midnight. This ain't no flophouse, you know . . . Hee, hee, hee." His shrill laugh echoed throughout the cavernous hallway on the second floor, its worn carpet patterned with the stains of countless spills.

As tired as he was, the list of rules still brought a grin to Jarrod. He remained quiet.

"Here's a nice room near the washroom." The night clerk said as he opened the door with one of the keys that dangled from the archaic steel hoop.

The rusty hinges squealed almost as loudly as the clerk's laughter. A switch on the wall let out an electric hiss as the clerk flicked it upward. A single unshielded bulb flickered briefly before casting its dull yellow light from a porcelain socket dangling from the end of a wire suspended from the ceiling. A narrow bed, its mattress sagging on overstretched springs, rested against one wall. A plain wooden desk and matching chair (matching only because both were slathered in layers of paint almost as thick as the wood itself) augmented the washed-out floral wallpaper. A heavy, dark curtain obscured the narrow window, which was not much of a loss, as the only view was that of a blank brick wall of the building next door. A tiny sink clung to the wall next to the desk. Years of water dripping from leaky dual faucets had stained the basin with brownish-yellow streaks. The effects of time and humidity had curled the pages of an old Bible, which rested on the desk next to a discolored beer glass, likely "borrowed" from the neighborhood bar.

"This will do fine," Jarrod said with a sigh. Too tired to search for a better place, he cringed when he thought of what he might find behind the "Men's Shower" door across the hallway.

"You'll have to pay me in advance for the night. Fourteen dollars includes the damn taxes. No checks or credit cards."

Following the old fellow as he shuffled back to the lobby, Jarrod glanced into the communal sitting room. The only television in the hotel droned dialogue and canned laughter in one corner of the room while two long-term residents argued over which was the worst sit-com. There could be no winner to the argument, as most of the other tenants had already dozed off to sleep in their favorite chairs.

"I'll let you know tomorrow if I'm staying another night," Jarrod said as he paid for his lodging. He knew there would be no bartering with the old codger.

"Check-out time is noon," the clerk warned.

"I'll remember," Jarrod promised, unable to guess what fate might be in store for him should he sleep past noon.

After the tour of his room and his cursory inspection of the TV lounge, Jarrod was convinced that the bar next door would offer a more suitable alternative for passing some time before trying to sleep. He was at the point of being overtired, and sleep would come much easier with a couple of cold beers in his stomach. Assuring the cackling clerk that he would return before curfew, and alone, Jarrod was on his way next door. As requested, he left his room key at the front desk.

"JACK'S BAR" flashed a pale blue sign as neon gas swirled and pulsed inside the twisted tubes that formed the letters. Both A's were so dull they were hardly visible. Perhaps vowels required more neon to illuminate them.

Pushing open another heavy door, Jarrod found himself in a surrounding that he could easily relate to, a place of comfort, so to speak. The bar's interior was similar to an old western saloon and was likely from the same era as his hotel. The high vaulted ceiling and the hardwood floors displayed the characteristics of a glamorous past. Years of contact with heavy boots and, perhaps long ago, even ballroom dancers, had worn rounded hollows in sections of the wooden floor. An elaborate, arched, rosewood crown rose above the central bar, which dominated the room. Several customers sat on round, wooden stools that surrounded the bar. The bartender, his sleeves rolled up and a soiled apron around his waist, pulled on a long tap handle as he poured a cold draft beer for Jarrod.

After ordering his drink, Jarrod said little, sitting on his uncomfortable barstool as he listened to the locals discuss sports heroes and bad politicians, both local and national. A television flickered and made noises on a shelf above the rows of liquor bottles. The bartender alternated his attention between the small screen and his regulars' puerile conversation, joining in the discussions only when they asked his opinion. More than one of the drinkers turned their heads away when they noticed the newcomer with the bashed nose and disheveled appearance sitting at the end of the bar.

Not much interested in the local gossip, Jarrod's attention wandered to the back corner of the bar, where he noticed a door open occasionally, exposing a smoke-filled room. Two circular canopy-style shades focused the room's lighting over a pair of octagonal tables. Before the door swung shut behind a waitress carrying a tray of empty glasses, Jarrod observed that one table was surrounded by several men holding playing cards and smoking cigarettes or cigars. The clinking of poker chips and curses from the participants were familiar sounds to him. Although poker was not his first choice for gambling, it was still an opportunity, or more of an urge, that he found difficult to resist. But tonight he would restrain himself from the temptation.

As fatigued as he was, Jarrod would be easy prey for the pack of local wolves, whose individual mannerisms would take a stranger to their game a fair time to assimilate. The "money" players, and there were always one or two, would read their regular, weaker opponents like an open book. The stronger players not only knew the odds but also recognized the subtleties of bluffing, especially with opponents they were familiar with. Even Lady Luck in her finest form might not be enough to allow a tired newcomer, no matter how much experience he had, to be a first-time winner in that game.

Bored with the local chatter and anxious to get some sleep, Jarrod poured back the last of his second mug of beer and said goodnight to the bartender, the only person with whom he had any conversation. He had blamed his facial injuries on a recent car accident. Directions to the mall where the Price Discount Store was located were given pleasantly and precisely. At first, the fellow behind the bar, who turned out to be the owner, was hesitant to confirm that any gambling activities might be going on behind closed doors in his establishment. But after Jarrod had settled his tab and was about to leave, the bartender admitted that at least one table was active almost every afternoon and evening.

New players were welcome as long as they went through the bartender and left a cash deposit. No credit was ever given for chips. As he was leaving the bar, Jarrod remarked that he might be willing to take a chance, perhaps soon, in one of the games. The seed had been planted.

Chapter 17

Regardless of two drunks who checked in late, then proceeded to argue for half the night in the room next to his, Jarrod fell into a deep sleep that even a fire alarm might not have disturbed. He awoke to a bright, cheerful day. The overall effect of a good rest and clear skies improved his mental outlook. His mind made up, he would postpone leaving town for at least a couple of days. Naturally, Jarrod's first priority was to attempt an important visit with a complete stranger. Using the bartender's directions, he set out on his route to the Central Mall, arriving at the Price Discount Store by mid-morning. Business was slow, and a girl working behind the only cash register in operation gave him a tired smile when he approached her.

"Excuse me, would the manager, Mr. Benning, be in the store yet?" Jarrod asked. "I'm an old friend." He sensed that the girl might have recognized him from last evening's phone call, but back-to-back shifts could be very tiring.

"Yes, sir, he is, but he's in a meeting with the other managers at the moment. I'm not sure how long they'll be, but if you know his wife, she's in the donut shop next door with their children."

It occurred to Jarrod that maybe Mrs. Benning and her children would be the ones to approach concerning a surprise passenger in their rental van. Lucas could never have opened the rear door on his own. They were likely to be more open and sympathetic than Mr. Benning in answering his questions. After thanking the cashier for her help, he walked the few steps across the parking lot, hoping the donut shop wouldn't be too crowded.

Fortunately, only one woman was sitting with her children inside Tom's Donut Palace. The kids were restless and arguing with each other, their mother scolding them as Jarrod entered. He quickly recognized the little boy he had seen standing next to the cash register as he peered out the narrow opening of the washroom door at Bill's Truck Stop.

Jarrod purchased a coffee and approached the family, trying to think of how to start the conversation. He hoped a morning shower had improved his appearance. "Cute kids you have there," was all he could think of to say as he seated himself at the table next to the Benning family. "They sure have lots of energy."

Liz looked up and flinched when she saw the stranger's rugged, unshaven, and bruised face. Although her first instinct was to grab her children and leave, Liz was overcome with an odd feeling that she should know this man, yet she certainly didn't recognize his face. She said nothing, not wanting to encourage any further conversation.

Words came out slowly. With a shaky voice barely above a whisper, Jarrod began. "I was traveling with someone a couple of days ago, a young boy—"

With her eyes widening to the size of the coffee mug that almost fell from her hand, Liz cut in, her heart pounding. "You! You left that sick boy there?" She was oblivious to her rambunctious children.

"Well, you all left before I could get back to the van. I tried to catch up, but—"

"How could you? That boy couldn't even stand. He was burning up with fever! For all I know, he might even have died." Her words were scathing, anger and frustration turning her eyes to burning coals.

The news of Lucas's condition would have come as no surprise, but Liz's blunt and angry response certainly triggered the shocked look on Jarrod's face. It took him a moment to reply.

"Where is he now? Is he all right?" he asked, his speech quivering and his throat dry as the words came out.

Sensing the obvious concern in the man's eyes, and certainly in his voice, Liz was slowly able to calm herself down. Reliving her hold on the sweating, shivering form that had rested comatose in her arms, her heart ached. Surely this man couldn't be the boy's father. If he were, she would have gladly continued to vent her frustration.

Her children had never seen their mother so upset. They sat unusually silent, their eyes fixed on her.

After taking a few deep breaths to calm herself, Liz was finally able to answer. "We left him with a doctor in some small town. He was very sick. The doctor promised to find out where the boy came from. He seemed to be a good man. I'm sure he did the right thing."

Liz was about to ask what relationship the rough-looking stranger had with the pitiful child when Jarrod began to explain the situation.

"Actually, the boy and I met by accident a few days ago in another small town. We were both alone and looking for any escape from the lives we were trapped in. Lucas was running from a situation he couldn't handle anymore." The rugged stranger failed in his attempt to sound calm. His voice was anything but steady.

"So, you're really not that boy's daddy?" Cindy asked. She had been listening, and her interest appeared to be growing.

"That's right, young lady, I'm just a friend," Jarrod replied, showing the hint of a smile.

"Mommy wanted to take that boy home with us. I could have had an older brother, but Daddy was in a hurry and—"

"That's enough, Cindy," Liz interrupted. "The man doesn't want to hear any more."

Jarrod could tell from Liz's face that Lucas had touched another person, although now he was certain that his relationship with his young companion had come to an end. Lucas would be in custody, probably on his way back to the Cherry Hill detention home to face the consequences of his latest string of crimes. Would he have the strength or the will to carry on with life under the conditions from which he was so desperately trying to escape? It was doubtful. As a feeling of hopelessness swept through his confused mind, Jarrod sensed the woman was churning with her own emotions. The look she gave him practically pierced his heart.

He was about to leave when Liz spoke again, this time her voice was barely above a whisper.

"He was delirious when I held him. His speech was a series of incoherent words that made no sense, but he said one name more than once. Jar . . . Jarrod, I think it was. Is that you?"

Answering with only a strained grin, Jarrod stood up slowly, silently brushing perspiration from his forehead as he walked from the donut shop. A nod was all he could muster to acknowledge the information Liz had given him as he bid her farewell. A hard lump blocked his throat, making verbal goodbyes impossible.

Her eyes glistening as she watched the door swing shut behind the downcast stranger, Liz sat silently with her children, who seemed lost in their own thoughts. Although she could still feel Lucas's shivering body in her arms, her empathy swung briefly toward the disconsolate man, who had struggled for words. She felt the caring, the connection he had with his young friend. Had they spoken longer, Liz would have only wished him luck in his desperate search for positive answers to a dilemma most likely destined to have an unhappy ending.

Trying to block out memories of the last few days and put thoughts of his future into perspective, Jarrod walked block after block, street after street, tracing a meandering route back to his hotel. His legs moved as if detached from his body. Time, distance, and physical exertion all lost their significance. Yet the more he walked, the more he could accept that, without any warning, chance had brought him into contact with Lucas, and the fickleness of fate would be equally swift in removing the boy from his life.

As the crisp morning air began to refresh him, Jarrod embarked on the difficult task of packing the memory of the last few days into a small but fundamental corner of his mind. The compact area was where memory cells containing past relationships and bygone friendships were stored like tiny crates made of sponge. The lower the crates were on the stack of memories, the flatter they became, the weight above finally reducing them to the tissue thinness of a forgotten moment in time.

At ten minutes past noon, Jarrod realized he had not yet turned in his room key. After taking a deep breath of fresh air, he stepped boldly into the stuffy lobby of his hotel.

Chapter 18

As he entered the Duluth bus depot, Lucas had to push open a second set of glass doors, which kept autumn's chilly winds from freezing the bus passengers. Groups of people stood about in the waiting room, shuffling their feet aimlessly with bored looks on their faces. A few were seated in molded fiberglass chairs joined together by chrome bars wrapped over the arms and bolted to the floor. Glancing to his left, he noticed a bulletin board plastered with posters and advertisements. A sliding metal bar locked the two glass panels that protected the bulletins and prevented unwanted postings. The most prominent poster displayed photos of missing or abducted children under the title, "Have You Seen Me?" Youngsters who had disappeared for long periods even had computer-generated images of what they may look like today, three or more years older than the day they went missing.

As if expecting his own photo to stare back at him, Lucas scanned the faces from top to bottom. No, he wasn't there, nor was he in any of the mugshots of fugitives wanted by the FBI. He had no idea that Sheriff Klem was distributing his own descriptions as he scoured the countryside in search of the two fugitives who were driving him to frustration.

Still flushed from the exertion of his day's activities, his strength drained from the lingering effects of the fever, Lucas went to the washroom to splash some water on his greasy face. Staring into the mirror, he realized how pale and tired he looked. The weak draft of air from a wall-mounted dryer was barely warm and only served to mat long strands of damp, stringy hair across his forehead. Leaving the washroom with his stomach growling for nourishment, Lucas regretted not taking up the dinner offer from Chris's dad. He flopped down onto one of the hard, molded chairs in the waiting room. Attached to each chair was a tiny black-and-white TV that offered half an hour of entertainment for fifty cents.

"Gee, only a buck an hour to watch that crap," Lucas mumbled to himself. Lost in their own thoughts, or going over life's problems with anyone who would listen, the people seated nearby paid no attention to the pale youngster.

After slowly scanning the waiting room, Lucas spotted a row of vending machines. They offered sandwiches, pop, coffee, candy bars, and cigarettes, but two signs suspended from the wall above the vendors bothered Lucas. In bold lettering, they read, "No Loitering" and "Depot Closed 11:00 p.m. to 5:00 a.m." He knew it was only a matter of time before a security person hustled him out the door. "Where's your bus ticket, kid?" they would ask, followed by "Why are you hanging around here?"

Before giving any thought as to where he could spend the night, Lucas walked over to the vending machines.

He felt hot again, as if the fever was returning. His spirit depleted, and feeling worn out mentally and physically, he stared at the rows of thin sandwiches. As he reached into his pocket for some change, he was startled by a female voice from behind his back.

"Cool night out there, young man, isn't it? Those tasteless sandwiches are stale and overpriced."

The calm tone of the words caught Lucas off guard. "Sure, but when you're hungry," he began, slowly turning to face the person who offered her advice.

One indelible feature of the woman he faced would haunt him forever, either lying in bed on nights that sleep was impossible, or awakening from horrific nightmares in a cold sweat. It was not her black, glossy hair that cascaded down her back, shimmering under the fluorescent lights. Neither was it her white, pasty skin or the hooded eyelids that mascara had streaked with hues of crimson and gold. It was not even the jagged wrinkles that ample amounts of makeup had tried to mask. Instead, the creamy-white powder merely spread the creases from the corners of her eyes to her cheekbones, sculpting her face into the look of a ceramic doll. Nor was it her long, slender legs encased in black, patterned stockings. So supple and fluid were her lower limbs, they had the appearance of tentacles. Were those actually feet inside her crafted, pointy shoes?

No, ultimately, the feature that struck Lucas most was her eyes, which smoldered like two phosphorescent coals. Through the transparency of her corneas shone a glow that was the color of aquamarine, as if the sea itself were splashing against the sides of her jet-black pupils. The grainy, white portion of her eyes held the power of a cresting wave, the tiny red blood vessels on the verge of bursting. Like living caves, her pupils pulsated as she talked to Lucas. First dilating and then shrinking, they drew him closer and closer with a mesmerizing grip. He could not pull away.

"Catherine and I were just going to join our friends for a hot bowl of soup and cookies. You're welcome to join us. In fact, please do join us." The hypnotic woman spoke in a comforting yet strangely menacing tone.

Lucas hesitated. He looked at Catherine, a freckle-faced girl about his own age. She gave him a smile so surreal that it could just as well have been painted on a mannequin. Although she appeared to be relaxed and pleasant, he felt that the way she moved and reacted was mechanical. Her dull eyes failed to convey any real feelings. Was she even controlling her own emotions?

"I have—we have—several children at our home. Catherine here is about your age. Twelve, correct?" Her dilated pupils continued to pulsate, as if emphasizing her insistence that he join them.

Was she sincere, or was he being conned? His intuition dulled by fatigue and hunger, Lucas could not reason clearly. But in the end, it was the woman's eyes that kept him from bolting out the door. The glow in those strange green eyes would not accept "No" for an answer.

"Well, I was planning to eat something," Lucas said, his words coming slowly.

"Then come with us, please. We always have extra soup and cookies for a hungry young friend."

Lucas glanced over at Catherine. She smiled mechanically, nodding like a puppet.

It was dark outside. As the three of them left the bus depot, the woman with the strange eyes introduced herself as Cassandra, or, as the children called her, Miss Cass. His guard down completely, or at that point not even caring what consequences might result, Lucas gave his real name when he was asked.

"Lucas, an interesting name," Cassandra commented. Certain he was on the run, she didn't bother to ask where his parents were or why he was hanging around the bus station.

After a short walk, the small group stopped outside a narrow storefront in the center of a block of older buildings. A young woman wearing a white baseball cap and carrying a bag of fresh-smelling rolls glanced instinctively at the odd group. Apparently in a rush, she hurried past.

Lucas looked up at a wooden sign that read in bold, capital letters, "MOUNT CLOQUET THRIFT SHOP." A "Closed" sign hung at an angle inside the front window, yet lights glowed in the shop as Cassandra snapped open the deadbolt using a key that hung from a worn leather strap connected to her handbag. The narrow thong, which had many clips attached to it, held an assortment of odd-shaped keys. Lucas was certain he saw the talon of a bird of prey as well as the skull of a tiny rodent also dangling from it.

Once inside the thrift shop, it was apparent that the floor space had been increased by knocking out the wall to an adjoining store. Lucas stared in awe. The floor, as well as countless shelves and counters, were laden with a multitude of items right out of a colossal garage sale: vintage chairs and desks, lamps with frayed chords and discolored shades, ironing boards, tarnished bread boxes, flowered canister sets, popcorn makers, piles of rusty tools, cracked oil paintings, faded prints . . . the list was endless. Scattered about the place was every conceivable household appliance that had ever overloaded a fuse: vacuums, toaster ovens, mixers, fans, humidifiers, even an old freezer. Counters were piled with yellowed books, comics, and magazines. Vinyl records protruded from age-worn sleeves, exposing their dusty grooves. Knick-knacks by the dozen, including porcelain frogs, dragons, and ballet dancers, adorned other tables. Half of the floor space was taken up with racks of used clothing, with sizes to fit all ages. Piles of folded sweaters were heaped in cardboard boxes next to rows of almost-new and not-so-new footwear. "Well-worn" or "moth-eaten" would best describe some of items that carried reduced price tags. Suspended from the high ceiling, a massive fan turned slowly, circulating the stale air that hung over the vast collection of second-hand goods.

"This is where our wonderful family sells all the nice things that good people have generously donated," Cassandra explained, attempting to sound humble.

"Doesn't look like you've sold much," Lucas remarked, his nose twitching from the musty air and thin layer of dust that coated many items.

"Don't worry, young Lucas, there's a long, cold winter ahead. People will be looking for warm clothing," Cassandra replied defensively.

A sliding door in the rear of the showroom led to a smaller room that was sparsely furnished, serving as a rest area and dining hall. A long wooden table, its legs held open by metal cross braces, sat in the middle of the room. Several children seated at the table were slurping down large bowls of soup or watery stew; Lucas couldn't really make out what the meal was. They barely took notice of the company entering the room.

"Is everything going smoothly, Florence?" Cassandra asked an older woman who stood next to a two-burner hot-plate, an item likely donated many years earlier.

"Very nicely, Miss Cass. The children have been well behaved." Florence ladled the remainder of the soup from a large iron pot into three bowls. The pot was so large it covered both elements of the hotplate. "They brought in some nice baubles today and had a fair amount of cash in their donation boxes. I haven't had a chance to count it yet."

Lucas wondered what in the world baubles were.

"Very good, children," Cassandra said to the blank faces that encircled the table. Intent on eating their meal, the youthful congregation barely acknowledged her approval. "We have a new friend I would like you all to meet," she continued, unperturbed. "Please say Hello to Lucas."

"Hello, Lucas," the children said in unison, glancing up briefly from their meal. The tone of their words was flat and lifeless.

Lucas nodded but didn't speak. His mind was filled with questions. Although the entire situation seemed bizarre, should he be concerned? Looking carefully at the bowed heads around the table, he recognized the two children who had almost walked into him at the entrance to the bus depot. These people didn't come across as a threat, yet there was something . . . the children's vacant expressions . . . Cassandra's hypnotic eyes . . . something was not right.

"Here you are, young man," Cassandra said as she placed a full bowl in front of Lucas, who had taken a seat at one end of the dining table. The soup consisted of bloated carrots, cabbage leaves, and bits of stringy chicken floating unappealingly in a bowl of tepid water.

"You'll enjoy this special broth that Florence has prepared for us all to enjoy."

"Thank you," Lucas replied, his stomach desperate for almost any food.

"Dip your roll," Cassandra suggested, handing Lucas a crusty, rock-hard lump, "while I prepare you a healthy cup of herbal tea. It will give you strength and warm up your body."

Without taking into consideration the boy's weakened condition, she began preparing him her special concoction of tea.

Trying to bite into the solid roll, Lucas was more concerned with breaking a tooth and paid no attention to the brewing of his tea. Had he noticed some of the additives, he might have accidently tipped his cup onto the linoleum floor. What did catch his attention was the aroma as Cassandra blended the tea. At first, he smelled the freshness of mountain evergreens, but then a strong, pungent odor bit into his nostrils. Why weren't the others offered this tea? Or had they already finished theirs?

After three small sips, Lucas decided he liked the unusual flavor. Almost immediately, it delivered a warmth that spread throughout his body. A tingling sensation spread to his toes and the tips of his fingers. As the warmth within him increased, so did his desire to finish the hot liquid. The barely perceptible smile on Miss Cass's face indicated she saw no need to offer a second cup to their new friend.

Only moments later, Lucas went from being engulfed with euphoria to a state of extreme dizziness. As a feeling of faintness crept over him, his head began to sway and droop. The people surrounding him drifted in and out of focus. Was it his imagination, or were the children's eyes glowing and staring at him? Cassandra's smile, so pleasant and welcoming at first, changed into the menacing grin of a crazed animal, her lips curling back to expose white fangs. Was this transformation real, or was he hallucinating? Even her face, so gentle and unblemished when he first drank the tea, took on the gnarled and weathered appearance of a witch. Her wrinkles, one moment subtly smoothed to a ceramic finish, widened into deep chasms that threatened to consume his trembling body.

Squeezing his eyes closed as he tried to refocus them, Lucas struggled to regain any semblance of control over his actions. He forced himself to his feet, but when he tried to walk, his legs had the rubbery texture of boiled noodles and refused to support his weight. Wanting desperately to leave, he was helpless. With nothing to support him, he collapsed onto the floor.

"You look so…sooo tired, young Lucas." Cassandra's words had a profound yet hollow echo to them, as if they were spoken from a vast cavern. "It's best that you come home with us now. We will look after you. Don't be afraid."

Gazing up from the floor through watery eyes, Lucas gave the woman (was she even human?) a vacant stare. He opened his mouth to protest, but no words came out. His head lolling from side to side, all he could see was the thunderous ocean in those green, translucent eyes. A frigid ocean that threatened to swallow him forever—consuming his body, his mind, and his very soul. He would never go with this creature!

In a desperate attempt to escape, Lucas struggled to his feet once again. He took two wobbly steps toward the door and then collapsed face-first onto the grimy linoleum floor. Having lost control of his muscles, Cassandra and Florence picked him up as though he were a limp doll. They propped him up in a chair next to Catherine.

"Please watch that your new brother doesn't fall over while we prepare for our trip home," Cassandra instructed sternly.

"You're my brother now. We're all brothers and sisters, you know," Catherine said, comforting Lucas as he slumped in the chair, not hearing a word. Her monotone voice lacked any hint of emotion. Did she really believe it, or was it merely part of the program that had been ingrained in her?

Lucas's head fell forward, almost touching his knees. Saliva and the pungent dregs of the horrible tea dripped from the corner of his mouth. His head was spinning, and his stomach roiled, a grim warning that it was about to heave. His tormented brain could only focus on the reality that these people had plans for him, and he could do nothing about it. Or were these even people? He had lost all control.

Still slumped over as his stomach began to cramp, Lucas slurred a few words of warning that he was about to be sick. Drool slid ominously from his open mouth, strings of saliva settling onto the knees of his jeans.

Sensing what was about to happen, Cassandra spoke quickly, her tone urgent. “Florence, get him into the lane as fast as you can.”

“Right away, Miss Cass,” the older woman said as she lifted Lucas onto his shaky legs. Struggling to support him, she ushered the boy out the rear door and into a poorly lit lane. He was so unsteady on his legs that she practically had to drag him out the door. Her actions were none too soon.

The rear bumper of an old Suburban truck offered a support for Lucas to lean on when the heaving began. For almost a full minute, he alternated between gagging and vomiting until his tortured stomach was finally empty. Trying to catch his breath, he gasped and sucked in several gulps of fresh air.

When vomit spewed on her shoes, Florence, feeling queasy herself, could watch no more. “I’ll be right back,” she stammered, pulling open the building’s rear door and disappearing inside.

Now on his knees in the slimy mess, mucous draining from his nose and mouth, Lucas slumped his head across the dirty bumper, still gasping for air.

“Please, just leave me alone. Let me go . . ..” The desperate captive mouthed his plea, but no words came out. The side of his head and cheek smeared with mud from the bumper, Lucas tried to raise himself to his feet, but his right hand merely slid across the Suburban’s tailgate. Through squinting, teary eyes, he noticed the smudge his hand had left on the rear of the truck. His tortured brain foresaw one last hope.

Unable to stand, let alone run, it took all his strength to drag his index finger across the muddy tailgate. He scrawled letters in the caked-on mud, rushing as fast as he could, afraid he didn't have much time.

Sure enough, the door to the building burst open before he could finish his desperate plea. Out marched Cassandra, hustling faster than normal, a wet cloth dripping from her clenched fist, obviously concerned that her new recruit might have escaped. In an impulsive attempt to divert her attention from the tailgate, Lucas tried to stand but then collapsed into her powerful arms.

"Didn't like our soup, young man? Or maybe my tea didn't agree with you?" Her voice was distant, the words merely gyrating in his head. "I may have made it a little strong for your taste. Your body was weaker than I expected, but you'll get to love it after a while. Everyone does."

Lucas wanted to curse her, tell her what he thought of her and all the others, but his voice was powerless, and the words remained lodged in his throat. Using the wet rag, Cassandra wiped the drool and vomit from his chin and flicked a stringy piece of chicken from the sleeve of his ski jacket. Shaking her head, she lifted Lucas to his feet and wiped the knees of his jeans, which smelled of bile and regurgitated soup.

Attempting to diffuse the boy's obvious hostility, Cassandra spoke gently to him. "Florence is picking out some clean clothes for you from the shop."

Taking Lucas firmly by the arm, she led him to the Suburban's right rear door, opened it, and seated him on the running board. Her attention diverted, she never got close enough to glimpse the vehicle's tailgate.

Just then, Florence emerged from the shop with a pair of corduroy pants and a woolen sweater. "I hope these fit," she said. "I'll get the others ready to leave."

As Florence went back to gather up the other children, Cassandra struggled to help Lucas get into his change of clothes. Despite their musty odor, the sweater and pants were a big improvement over the jeans and T-shirt she discarded against the building. Returning the warm jacket that Chris had loaned him, she helped her wobbly recruit into the Suburban.

His mind blurry as he focused on his latest blunder, Lucas cursed himself once again for not accepting the dinner invitation from Chris's father. What had he gotten himself into? If only he had never turned around and looked into the eyes of that beastly woman.

"Sit on the rear seat," Cassandra instructed, motioning him to the back row, where a bench seat was bolted to the floor of the luggage area. Returning to lock up the building, she was out of any view of the Suburban's tailgate.

Unable to protest, and with his stomach empty once again, Lucas crawled onto the rear seat. His eyes burned as he squeezed them shut. He rested his shoulder on the armrest and leaned his throbbing head against the smeared window. This was the last he would remember of his trip out of town. Even if he had the strength to argue, anything he had to say in the matter would have had no consequence.

Cassandra returned shortly with Florence and the other children, who knew exactly where they were to sit in the vehicle. There was no complaining, no arguing, and no one muttered a sound as Florence turned the ignition key. On the third try, the trusty Suburban's engine roared to life. With a sense of urgency, it began its well-traveled route back home, loaded with a cargo of women, children, and a coffee can filled with dollar bills and loose change. A basket that could have held the Easter bunny contained a few useful donations or, as Flo called them, baubles. Despite the cool evening, two windows of the Suburban remained partly open as the overworked heater blasted out a stream of warm air. The stinging aromas of regurgitated soup and a very special tea were drawn through the narrow openings to be absorbed by the frosty night air.

Chapter 19

Jarrod's decision to stay in town for a day or two longer left him in a quandary. The long walk back to his gloomy hotel failed to ignite his brain with any solutions. Instead, as an escape from the endless thoughts that troubled his mind, he lapsed into a world with which he was all too familiar, yet certainly one he could easily associate with: the perilous world of gambling and booze, complicated by the wanton desires that only a woman can satisfy.

While shuffling along a roundabout route back to his hotel, Jarrod stopped at a discount store and replaced some of the clothing and toiletry items he had left behind in the rental van. His new wardrobe, consisting of denim jeans and warm flannel shirts, fit easily into a mid-sized tote bag he acquired for a greatly discounted price.

Checking out of his room, Jarrod dropped off the key at the front desk. Any concerns about his tardiness evaporated when the day clerk, surprisingly, turned out to be more elderly than the cheery fellow with the piercing laugh. The clerk's eyes were so bloodshot and watery that reading the clock was an impossibility, hence there was no mention of any late charges. The ultimate lack of success from his morning inquiries had put Jarrod in an emotional state that might only be relieved by quaffing a few beers. Tension and anxiety still gripped him. Merely half an hour past noon at "Jack's Bar," the draft beer was sliding down too smoothly and too quickly. Around midafternoon, a warm sensation gradually replacing his mental stress, Jarrod noticed activity building in the back room. The same bartender who had been there on the previous evening stood by the television, trying to adjust the fuzzy picture. His old gambling itch increasing with each beer, Jarrod finally spoke. "Do you think I could get into that game back there?" He nodded to the smoky room at the rear of the bar. The door sat fully open.

The regulars all called the balding bartender/owner "Specs," a nickname derived from the small, half-lens style of reading glasses that rested on the end of his broad nose. After examining the stranger, whom he had met briefly the previous night, Specs nodded. "You look a little friskier today than you did last night. I'll check with the boys. They should have room for another player today."

Jarrod had noticed an improvement in the discoloring around his eyes and nose that hopefully might cast him in a better light. He also made a point of mentioning that he had no problem finding the Price Discount Store with the bartender's accurate directions.

Returning shortly with a tray of empty glasses, Specs nodded at Jarrod. "Okay, you can join the game, but since no one can vouch for you around this place, you'll have to leave me a hundred-dollar deposit. Tammy, the waitress back there, keeps her eye on the game. She kids around a lot, but she makes sure no one gets out of hand. She'll give you your chips and look after your drinks. Cash bar, no tabs, understand?" As he talked, Specs pushed the dirty glasses into a wet sponge inside the sink, then rinsed them quickly before stacking them on a grooved tray so they could drip dry. Calling them "spotless" would be stretching things.

"No problem," Jarrod replied, pulling out his wallet.

After satisfying Specs with two fifties, more than a third of his worldly wealth, the road-worn stranger carried his mug of beer into the back room. He noticed a couple of tables of backgammon and cribbage in addition to the felt-covered table strewn with plastic chips.

Jarrod walked directly to the poker table, only to be greeted with suspicious looks, one or two grunts of acknowledgement, but mostly indifference. Each player's concentration was held firmly by every turn of the top card flipped over dramatically by the dealer. It was almost as if every queen, king, or ace held the fate of the world. To a great extent, the plastic-coated clubs, diamonds, hearts, and spades truly were the world of the chronic gambler.

Only Tammy welcomed Jarrod with a pleasant smile as she counted out the chips that his deposit had covered. Clearly familiar with the procedure involving a new player, she wished him luck as she stacked three rows of colored chips in front of him. She had a slight twitch and jerkiness in her movements that gave Jarrod the impression she might have experimented with her share of drugs over the years. Unconsciously, he found himself attracted to her tall, slim figure, filled out with an ample yet firm bust and enhanced by a mischievous glint in her hazel eyes. A profusion of makeup added color to a face he suspected had been left pale by the conditions of her environment. Dimples and a few freckles gave her a girlish look, especially when she smiled. Her auburn hair had outgrown an old perm, the loose curls limp as they drooped across her shoulders. Jarrod imagined a hidden glow beneath her outward appearance that could only be exposed by her spending several days in the outdoors. (Or was the beer simply affecting him?) One thing for sure, she was smothering in that place. He guessed her age to be twenty-five, going on forty.

"Are you new in town? Haven't seen you here before," Tammy said, her soft, pleasant voice snapping Jarrod out of his mesmerized state.

"Ah . . . right, I'm just passing through," was all he could stammer as she helped him move his stacks of chips in front of the only empty chair at the table. He nearly dropped his almost-empty mug of beer when her warm, gentle hand brushed momentarily over his forearm.

"Want a refill?" she asked, flashing a friendly grin.

"Sure, why not?" Turning his attention toward the card table, Jarrod wondered how long it had been since his last fascination with the female gender. One thing for sure, it had been far too long.

The five players around the table left no doubt where they wanted the new player to sit when he joined their game. The vacant chair that awaited him sat next to a nervous, middle-aged man who chewed on a large cigar and mumbled something about rotten luck. There were no introductions as the regulars waited anxiously for the newcomer to sit down so the game could continue. Seven-card stud poker was not Jarrod's game of choice, but at that moment, he would have wagered on tiddlywinks. Without thinking, he glanced over his shoulder and received a wink of encouragement from Tammy, who had hesitated briefly before returning to the bar with a tray of empties. Finding the waitress more and more attractive, he tried to turn his attention to the poker game.

During the first several deals, the players engaged in a cat-and-mouse game, with the locals attempting to size up their new opponent and he, in turn, trying to determine who the skilled players among them were, the ones he considered dangerous. Experience had taught Jarrod to quickly classify those who were the sharks and which players were the fodder, donating much of the time. The players' subtler tendencies, mannerisms, and bluffs would take much longer to understand and catalogue with other factors to be used to the advantage of a professional. At that point, Jarrod was no professional. First, his interest in the game was more of an escape, and his concentration and mental toughness would surely be lacking. Second, the rate he was guzzling beer was a definite detriment to any gambler's judgment. Third, distractions outside the game that could throw off his focus and competitive edge had to be avoided at all cost. Tammy was one such distraction.

Trying to get a feel for the game, Jarrod began conservatively, dropping from many deals that he might normally call the bet or even raise for an extra round of wagering. He was more interested in observing his opponents, their shuffling of the cards, roving eyes, displays of nervousness, and any signs of cheating. After folding early in several deals, his attention diverted to Tammy, who seemed to follow all the action in the room as she wandered among the tables. She was constantly adding humorous comments as she served drinks and refilled bowls of munchies.

After about an hour, it became obvious that two of Jarrod's opponents, including the cigar chewer beside him, were easy prey and fed upon by the other sharks. They showed poor judgment, donating chips in too many deals as if folding their cards was a show of weakness, a lack of courage. Even more important, when they held good cards, their nervous habits made them as easy to read as an open book. Both were losers and would write checks almost every day.

Two of the others, the youngest players in the group—and cousins, as Jarrod discovered later—were much cagier opponents. They appeared to play together as partners, seldom staying in hands at the same time. They had the knack, whether through telepathy or prearranged signals, of knowing which of them held the superior cards. Trying not to appear too obvious, the one with the weaker hand consistently tossed in his cards at the first opportunity.

The last player in the game, a well-groomed man approaching fifty, Jarrod considered to be his peer in both skill and gamesmanship. The man clearly had the best card sense at the table. As a display of quiet confidence, an ornate pipe with a curved stem and meerschaum bowl hung from his pursed lips. A thin spiral of sweet smoke drifted upward through a bushy, yet neat moustache and across his wooden countenance and steel-grey eyes before settling in the thick haze beneath the colorful canopy shade that directed light over the table. The man's expression never changed. He chattered much less than the others, intent merely on increasing his pile of chips. It was no coincidence that he was the most consistent winner. Without being obvious, his attention was often focused on his new opponent. Did the shark consider the beer-guzzler to be a threat to his easy income, or was he concerned that some of his methods might be detected? The cat-and-mouse game continued.

Becoming increasingly comfortable as he drifted back to his old ways, Jarrod accomplished little in the first couple of hours except ordering beers from Tammy, tipping generously, and making eye contact whenever possible. He won a few small pots when everyone folded early, but mostly he just watched the others, surrendering plenty of his own antes. There were numerous breaks in the action, which gave the losers a chance to grumble about their opponents' luck.

Jarrod was down about twenty dollars when, in the third hour, Lady Luck graced him with her presence. His wins came often as he was consistently dealt down cards that matched well with his exposed hand. Even his seventh card bailed him out on more than one occasion. During a lucky streak, Jarrod's practice was to stay in many deals in which common sense and experience told him to toss in his cards. He was, as the saying goes, on a roll.

With even the better players donating a fair portion, Jarrod was up over $400 when the imperturbable pipe smoker called for another break. The cigar chewer took the sodden mass that hung between lips that were gouged by nervous bite marks and, with a show of disgust, mashed the smoldering remains into an ashtray already brimming with butts. A cloud of noxious smoke billowed upward.

"That's enough for me today. Our new player . . . I didn't catch your name, sir."

"William, sir, but call me Bill," Jarrod said, emphasizing "sir" with more than a hint of drunken sarcasm.

"Well, you're too damn lucky for me. I see even your pile isn't as high as usual, Cal," the sore loser commented as he glanced toward the acknowledged expert, who was carefully tapping the bowl of his ornate pipe over a clean ashtray.

"Harvey, even you get lucky on occasion," Cal remarked with a total lack of remorse, taking a final sip from his glass of soda and lime.

"Another refill please, Tammy." Jarrod's words were slurred. The copious beers were well on their way toward overtaking his body and dulling his perception. Tammy was taking on the look of a calendar girl.

Watching her count Harvey's few remaining chips before she relieved him of a sizable check covering his day's losses, Jarrod tried to act sober. "Have you worked here long?" he asked with genuine interest. "You handle those chips like an old pro." The effects of the alcohol were causing his head to rock from side to side.

"I've worked here pretty steady for the last few months, since I split up with my boyfriend. Got to keep busy, you know . . . pay the bills, feed the cat." Tammy paused for a moment, aware of the steady gaze that the half-drunk stranger directed toward her. "Are you in town for long?"

Jarrod tried to unscramble his thoughts and not make his desire for her too obvious. "A few days, maybe. I'm headed west . . . got a job offer in Montana that looks worthwhile." His words were hesitant, coming out a bit slurred. He was unconvincing.

"Where are you staying?"

"Oh . . . I guess a room next door will have to do," Jarrod answered, referring to the zero-star hotel he had just vacated. "That place doesn't seem to turn away drunks." No transit-bus driver would ever allow him to board in his present condition.

"Talk to me after the game finishes, I may be able to help you. That place is a real dump," Tammy said as she counted out additional chips for the remaining players, who were running low.

Trying to recoup his backgammon losses, a replacement for Harvey joined the game. Even the cousins, who normally dropped out after losing a certain limit, were adding to their depleted piles of chips. Apparently, no one still in the game thought the stranger's luck would hold up for much longer. Watching him get increasingly inebriated, the wolves were ready to pounce.

"Are we all ready to continue the game?" Cal inquired with a show of confidence. He had returned from the bar, where he allowed himself one double scotch on the rocks, an expensive single-malt import. He normally drank soda or tonic water or the occasional Perrier while the game was in progress. Once seated in his regular chair, Cal packed fresh tobacco into his fancy pipe's vacuous bowl.

"Let's deal!" he said, issuing the challenge.

Even the chips and pretzels that were brought regularly to the card table would remain a haze in Jarrod's memory.

Although Tammy tried to discourage him by serving his drinks slowly, he continued to order one beer after the other. His red, unfocused eyes burned from the cloud of smoke that hovered over the card table's green felt nap. The aroma of smoldering pipe tobacco, which smelled like butterscotch pudding one minute and like sweet marijuana the next, made Jarrod light-headed. His movements, his reactions, his judgment, not to mention his card skills, all slowed and dulled proportionately to the amount of alcohol he consumed.

"You forgot to ante, Bill," was a constant reminder from the others.

One thing was certain: Jarrod's streak of luck had ended. No longer could he stay in pots holding low-percentage hands. He spent his final hour in the game slumped over his dwindling pile of chips, donating regularly to his opponents. His watery eyes squinted in their effort to focus on the face-up cards around the table. Nearly three hundred dollars in chips had been spirited away before one lucky draw produced a straight flush, recouping a chunk of his losses.

Although aware that his condition was deteriorating, something continued to puzzle Jarrod. Occasionally during the afternoon, but more so in the early evening, he recognized a slight oddity in the game that was disturbing. At first, he blamed it on the smoky conditions that might have distorted his vision. Were his watery, aching eyes playing tricks on him? Squeezing them shut a few times as he attempted to clear his sight, he noticed the same peculiarity reoccur every ten or twelve deals. One or two of Cal's cards, and always his face-down or hole cards, appeared to have a slightly whiter or glossier tinge than the other cards spread out on the table, even when the decks were switched. Although the patterns on their backs were identical, the face-up side of the cards seemed shinier, as if they belonged to a newer or seldom-used deck.

When showing his winning hand, Cal would flip those cards quickly, a mannerism both annoying and distracting to the other players. They had only the briefest of moments to check that Cal really had his call before he slid all seven cards together into a neat stack, as if in a hurry to get on with the next deal, and then he would slap the cards between his palms and casually toss them toward the next dealer or on top of the pile of dead cards. Were his actions simply an irritating habit, or was some chicanery going on? Strangely, the cards involved in that day's game were always threes, sevens, or nines. None of the aces or face cards appeared to have that extra-glossy appearance.

To check if a different viewing angle would make a difference, Jarrod got up to use the restroom after folding on the first round of wagering during one of the deals. He braced himself, using the backs of more than one chair as he stumbled to the men's room. When he returned, Cal was raking in a healthy pot. Even through his watery eyes, Jarrod had a good view behind the winner. He saw that two of the questionable cards had nicely filled out a full house made up of nines over threes.

"I see where my 'old luck' has gone," Jarrod slurred, staggering back to his seat on wobbly legs. Unperturbed, Cal smoothly folded his cards together and slid them toward the next dealer, the backgammon player whose fortunes had not improved.

Despite his suspicions, Jarrod was having enough trouble just concentrating on his own game without worrying about what anyone else was doing. In fact, other than a throbbing head, he would have little recollection of ever leaving the poker game. The smoke and beer had finally taken their toll. Seeing his head begin to droop forward, Tammy moved quickly to Jarrod's side before he could collapse onto his own dwindling pile of chips. The predators were salivating.

"I think you've played enough for one day," she said, shaking him back to consciousness. "It's time you cashed in and took a break."

"He's all right, Tammy," one of the cousins said. "Just give him some coffee. Since Harv left, we need him to make up a decent game."

Like a shark attracted to blood, the cousin could sense the easy fleecing of a drunk. His money was there for the taking. The others, who resembled circling vultures, agreed that Tammy should let him continue. They argued that he still had plenty of their money.

"You guys are a bunch of . . . just a pack of . . ." she held back a string of swear words, "wolves. Can't you see the guy's drunk. He almost passed out right in front of you. Forget it! I'm cashing him out."

Tammy's voice was adamant. Familiar with her stubbornness, the players gave up arguing. They appreciated her control over their daily game. She was always kidding them that poker was just a game, not global warfare. Besides, she was a lot better looking than the previous waitress who had left four months earlier. With the number of players being depleted, the remaining group discussed what card game might amuse them for another hour. They never knew when to quit.

"I've got to get going shortly," Cal announced, checking his watch as if he had an important date. He disliked the other silly games, which involved a bunch of wild cards. "I'll cash out as well, Tammy." His own special skills in a few deals had put him well on the plus side.

As Jarrod stumbled over to the restroom once again to relieve himself and splash cold water on his face, Tammy counted his remaining chips, a couple of which had fallen onto the floor. She added his winnings to his original deposit, which she retrieved from the new bartender on duty.

"Not too bad for someone in your condition," she said with a smile as Jarrod returned from the restroom, water dripping from his stringy hair and unshaven face. She handed him $354 in cash.

"Am I up that much?" he slurred, his eyes barely open.

"Your deposit is in there, but you didn't do badly." She sounded impressed.

"Thanks for your help. I'd probably been broke in another half hour," Jarrod admitted, handing her a twenty-dollar bill, the last of many tips.

Tammy took the money without arguing. Tips like that were seldom seen in that place.

"You just about drank away your profits," she said with a grin, unable to add up the number of beers Jarrod had consumed.

"Wow . . . my aching head's starting to remind me. There's lots I'm trying to forget. How's the song go? 'Some drink to remember, but most drink to forget.'" Jarrod paused. The words he wanted to say wouldn't come out. Instead, he said, "I'd better find myself a room."

Tammy had already given some thought to her next suggestion, which came from someone who was lonely and bored with life. She fancied herself to be a good judge of character, and something about Jarrod intrigued her. On the surface, he was a drifter, a person with no roots and no direction. Perhaps she was simply romanticizing, but she felt that something special might be hidden behind his deep-blue eyes, his rugged countenance. Risking the consequences, she longed to discover it.

"I've got to work 'til one o'clock, but you can catch some sleep at my apartment. It's only a block away, and I'm sure it would be better than that crummy hotel." Her timid voice was out of character. Were misgivings sending that tightness into her chest?

Recalling the sly look of the girl at the bus depot, Jarrod found it difficult to understand what women could possibly find with him. He was a bloody, worthless drunk. Embarrassed about being picked up when he couldn't find the courage to express his own feelings toward Tammy, Jarrod took a moment before he replied. An offer to sleep off his drunk on her couch may have been what she had in mind, but his hungry body told him something else.

"I . . . I appreciate the offer," he said, sounding ashamed, his words rambling. "I just need a few hours' sleep to sober up. Did I make a real ass of myself tonight?"

"I've seen a lot worse. At least you're a quiet drunk who doesn't cause problems," she replied. "Most of the others start cursing and throwing cards when things don't go their way."

"Well, I won't impose on you for long. Thanks," he stammered.

With nothing of value at her place, Tammy wasn't worried about getting robbed. She gave him directions and a key to her apartment. "Don't worry about Fluffy, my cat," she added. "She's friendly, and will probably end up sleeping on your chest."

Jarrod stumbled out of the smoky room without a word to the other players. None of them even bothered to look up, engrossed in a childish game that included jokers and wild cards. Two of the crib players had been talked into joining the small-stakes game, which would continue until closing time.

Still unsteady on his feet, Jarrod wore a tortuous path as he navigated his way toward Tammy's apartment. He stumbled more than once.

Chapter 20

Tammy returned to her apartment shortly after one in the morning. Her place was chilly, and she had to turn up the heat. She found her snoring houseguest sprawled on the lumpy sofa, fully dressed, and covered with a moth-eaten quilt that he had dragged from a closet. Tammy poured herself a nightcap, Jack Daniels and water over ice, and then slumped into her favorite chair to unwind from a long shift at Jack's Bar, a place she was quickly getting tired of. Her long-haired Calico cat, Fluffy, jumped onto her lap and began to purr. Preferring to hide in the bedroom, Fluffy had rebuffed the drunken stranger, who had collapsed on the sofa, the cat's normal sleeping spot.

After her second JD, the stress and tension of the day began to fade from Tammy's body. With the subdued drone of an old blues melody playing from the speakers of her FM radio, she began washing a sink-full of dishes that had been stagnating for most of the week. Fluffy slithered her furry body between Tammy's legs, purring as she arched her back and rubbed against the exposed skin of her master's calves and ankles. Her cat's caresses momentarily aroused Tammy as her thoughts drifted to her snoring guest. Paying little attention to the monotonous task she was performing, a suds-covered plate slipped from her hand and smashed into pieces on the kitchen floor. Fluffy leapt in terror and scurried to her hiding spot under the bed.

The crash jolted Jarrod out of a deep yet uneasy sleep. He sat bolt upright, not realizing at first where he was. Squinting through dry, aching eyes, he tried to focus on the startled girl.

"I'm really sorry . . . got clumsy all of a sudden," Tammy stammered.

Jarrod squeezed his throbbing head between his sweaty palms. "No problem, no big deal," he mumbled, his addled brain finally grasping where he had passed out.

"Would you like a coffee or another drink?" Tammy offered, not knowing what else to say to her confused guest.

"No thanks." Jarrod's parched mouth felt like he had just devoured a ball of string. "Maybe a glass of water. Do you know the time?" he asked, wondering if he had slept all night.

"Just after two in the morning," she replied, running cold water from the kitchen sink.

The unlikely couple spent the next hour sitting at the kitchen table making small talk. Neither Jarrod nor Tammy wanted to talk about themselves, their scarred pasts and failed ambitions. As they shared a few laughs, the uneasiness of discussing personal feelings with a total stranger began to fade. A sensation of warmth and appreciation for each other's company crept through their bodies. Both were equally aware of what they desired physically, yet each was privately enjoying the verbal foreplay that came with joking about the evening's events.

"Did you see Cal's face when you drew that eight of diamonds to fill out your straight flush?" Tammy asked, laughing as she felt increasingly relaxed. "I thought he was going to bite off the end of his fancy pipe."

"Are you kidding? I could barely see my own cards at that point. It's a good thing you got me out of that game when you did. I'd have been spending the night in some gutter, or the local drunk tank." Jarrod's voice was soft, his appreciation genuine.

Even Fluffy joined in, leaping onto the table and knocking over half a bottle of stale beer that Jarrod had been nursing. The two newfound friends giggled uncontrollably, their hands finally coming together in a gentle yet firm grip. The warmth was hard to ignore as it spread up both their arms at a torrid pace. As time stood still, their eyes met in a speechless stare.

As inevitable as the affair may have been to each of them, both were still surprised when their lips met for the first time. For two shy and unpretentious people, what transpired during the remainder of the early-morning hours came as naturally as breathing. An innocent progression took place. Playful kissing led to gentle stroking. Embraces became less elegant, culminating with two bodies molded together as one, succumbing to passions beyond their control.

Jarrod relished the softness and the gentleness of his partner's caresses, the smoothness of her skin, the moisture and scents of her body. He experienced the passionate lust that has wreaked havoc on man since the first apple fell from its branch. He may have been a gambler, an embezzler, and a vagrant, but his desire to satisfy Tammy was pure and honest, as opposed to the ravenous appetite of a love-crazed animal. Jarrod was determined to please her, not only fulfill her desires but also make her feel at ease with his presence. He succeeded beyond expectations.

Tammy felt that the entire night was a fairy tale, a dream that would dissolve when she opened her eyes. She had also given in to her passionate needs, an enduring requisite of life. A rush she had not experienced for a long time, if ever to the extent she felt that night, coursed through her entire body. Nonetheless, never did the thought that she had demeaned herself enter her mind, nor did she feel that she had sacrificed her self-respect for a momentary thrill. In some way, Tammy had a deep feeling she had opened the curtain that concealed her love partner's private sanctuary, the place where secrets lay hidden. Behind that rugged, outer shell, she discovered a warmth she had always dreamed true love might be, a love that was unabashed and spontaneous, yet its power was more cosmic than any paperback romance could ever portray.

The young waitress was confident that never in her lifetime, or in several lifetimes, could that early morning experience be duplicated. As she lay back and reflected on—or, rather, basked in the pleasure of—her feverish love-making, she knew deep down that the affair was impulsive and would end as quickly as it began. She had been swept off her feet, but without a doubt, she was about to land back upright. Destiny had fashioned the chance encounter of two lost souls just as destiny would control the ending, as predictable as it might be.

Her houseguest breathing softly next to her, Tammy was still bathed in sweat as she lay awake in bed. What had possessed her to invite a drunken stranger into her home, let alone her bed? She had no answer for her actions. Only fate could have led him to the card table at Jack's Bar. Yet at that moment, she realized that life had a lot more to offer than what she had experienced until then. All she had to do was reach out and grasp it. From that one fateful encounter, she had discovered a quality within herself that she never knew existed. Suddenly, a sense of adventure was awakened, a powerful drive that threatened to spread her wings beyond the confines of her simplified world. Of more importance, she discovered an inner contentment and peace with life that she had never felt before. From that moment forward, disappointment would never get her spirits down. For some inexplicable reason, she felt prepared for all the challenges that life had to offer. With no restraints or limits as to how far she might reach, Tammy's attitude, her job, her entire life, would soon change for the better.

Chapter 21

Jarrod was perplexed. As he sat on the edge of Tammy's bed with both hands squeezed tightly around his bowed head, a song kept running through his confused mind. His persistent hangover dulled his memory. He couldn't put a name to the artist but remembered the lyrics from his wasted college years in Virginia, where he had failed to complete his accounting courses. He was sure he had watched the singer perform the song live. It was about a midnight watchman and a girl he picked up one night. The girl in the song walked out early in the morning, leaving a short note. Was he about to reverse the roles?

Sunbeams streamed through a narrow gap in the bedroom curtains. Jarrod dressed quietly while Tammy slept beneath a heap of sheets and a colorful duvet. One foot was exposed, hanging limp over the edge of the mattress. Strands of damp hair glistened against the background of a bright magenta pillowcase. The steady rhythm of her breathing was muffled beneath the duvet, which hid her flushed face.

Tiptoeing to the bathroom, Jarrod stared at a frightful image in the mirror. Although his head throbbed and his eyes were bloodshot, the purplish rings that circled his eye sockets and the ugly crimson welts that decorated his nose had been absorbed by his rugged complexion and were hardly noticeable. Nonetheless, it was evident that he was badly in need of a shower and a shave. With shaky fingers, he pushed his moist, stringy hair away from his forehead. A quick wash of his hands and face would have to do. Using a cheap, disposable razor that he found in the vanity cabinet, Jarrod tried to scrape off some of his beard, but the dull blade only tugged at the bristly stubble. After a few painful strokes, he tossed the useless razor into a wastebasket. He had to get some fresh air.

With the old song stuck in his head, and after leaving Tammy a brief note on the kitchen counter, Jarrod left the apartment as quietly as possible. Did he feel like a louse? Of course. Was he running like a yellow dog before his feelings could take over his actions? Somehow, he justified that wasn't the case. Tammy had told him that she had the next day off work, even suggested they might do something together. However, Jarrod had balked, explaining how important it was that he get on the road. Or was he simply afraid that an actual relationship might develop? He didn't mention another matter he was anxious to settle, one that would bring him back to Jack's Bar. He was glad that Tammy had the day off.

As he trudged away from the apartment building, the brisk morning air had an invigorating effect, clearing not only the fuzziness in his brain but also any regrets that lingered in his fragile conscience. Without thinking, he glanced back at the curtained, second-floor window, where the sun was struggling to gain entry. He was about to blow a silent kiss toward it when he realized how corny, as well as insincere, that would be. Sure, he was a jerk, but saying goodbyes would always remain a hopeless cause for him.

What Jarrod failed to notice were the orange feline eyes whose narrow black slits watched intently as he faded from view. Fluffy's long, puffed-up tail swung back and forth in a menacing arc as it stroked the lining of the partly-open window curtain.

Getting himself oriented, Jarrod set out in the general direction of the smoky bar that had so recently held him firmly in its grasp. He had unfinished business to take care of before he left town. A cramped, family-run restaurant provided him with a hearty breakfast. Bacon, eggs, toast, hash browns and copious coffee slid down his accommodating throat. Within an hour, his headache was subsiding, saliva was lubricating his dry mouth, and the fog that had muddled his thinking process was dissolving.

After taking time for deliberation, Jarrod was more determined than ever to get into the local card game one last time. He would remain in the game until everyone was aware of the deceitful edge that a certain player held that contributed to making him a consistent winner. Once he had exposed the cheat and performed his duty as the white knight, though secretly clothed in a black cape from his sordid past, Jarrod would slink out of town on the next available bus. His running would continue as he searched beyond the vague and distant horizon for whatever life still held for him. Although ghosts from his past would continue to haunt every step he took, Jarrod knew for certain that he had to keep moving. The ghosts would follow him to the edge of the earth, and the tiny sponge crates in his memory banks would have added pressure put on them from ensuing events, whether designed or unforeseen. But if Jarrod tried to analyze all his mistakes, misadventures, and poor judgments, what could any future possibly hold for him?

With breakfast finished and his thoughts consumed by the task ahead, Jarrod spent the remainder of the morning walking aimlessly as he digested his ample meal. He shared the sidewalks with shoppers, commuters, and delivery people. He passed by mothers with their youngsters as well as seniors struggling to get about with their canes and walkers. All the others on the streets seemed to have more purpose in their movement than he did. They were going somewhere, and he was going nowhere. His facial expression blank and disinterested, Jarrod stared at mannequins in store windows and watched squirrels scurrying around a treed park in preparation for winter's onslaught. But basically, he was just passing time, stalling until his winding route led him to Jack's Bar, where drinking, small talk, and gambling were cheap commodities.

Pushing open the heavy wooden door once again, Jarrod was surprised at how many regulars were seated on the row of uncomfortable wooden stools that circled the bar. Overhead, fresh smoke already lingered in the vaulted alcoves and crevices as the broad blades of a large ceiling fan slowly circulated the air. It was barely twelve-thirty.

It came as no surprise that the afternoon bartender was Specs. He and his regulars were combining their minds in a joint effort to complete the daily *New York Times* crossword puzzle. Trying to adjust the rolling picture on the TV, a constant adventure for whoever worked the bar, Specs looked up at his latest customer.

"Well, look who's back. Did you have a good night?" he asked, giving a sly wink. Obviously, Tammy's offer of accommodations had not gone unnoticed. Specs seemed unconcerned that his best waitress would do such a thing.

"Tammy's a bright girl," Jarrod retorted. "She could do a lot better than slinging beers in some smoky old bar like this place."

The group seated around the bar tried to stifle their laughter

"Hear that, Specs?" the cigar chewer with all the bad luck said. "You'd better give Tam a decent raise, or she'll run off to some executive job on Madison Avenue."

His casual jibe brought on a series of comments. Finally, the laughter at the bar was no longer muffled as everyone took turns tossing out their own wisecracks.

Specs, his crooked little magnifiers bobbing as his nose twitched with laughter, held onto his bloated belly but couldn't keep it from jiggling like a bowl of gelatin.

"The way you guys tip, I'm surprised Tammy didn't leave after her first day on the job," he said in a mock attempt to scold the others.

The laughter and mockery continued.

"I can see that all you clowns respect is the glass of whiskey in your hand or maybe the card that fills in your straight. Or probably not even that," Jarrod responded. Annoyed with their childish joking, he was close to getting up and allowing the group to continue to get fleeced. Why should he want to help people who would gladly take advantage of a drunken opponent? The answer to that question was ingrained in his fabric. He clearly disliked cheats. Or was he simply a modern-day Robin Hood?

"Oooo . . . what a shot," a couple of the regulars moaned.

"I guess Tammy felt pretty safe sending a guy in the condition you were in back to her apartment. She seems like a sucker for stray mutts and homeless kittens," Specs added, not wanting his regulars to be outdone by some aimless drifter. Was that the class in which Jarrod qualified? Surely not. He was hardly a vagrant. He paid cash for his drinks and wasn't an obnoxious drunk, so Specs was in no rush to lose his business.

Jarrod accepted the locker-room fun that the guys were having at his expense, refusing to get caught in a game of one-upmanship. With another matter on his mind, he merely ordered tonic water with a slice of lemon and ignored the conversation.

"Ready for another, Harv?" Specs asked the cigar smoker, whose noxious blue-grey plumbs had already filled several rows of wine glasses, which hung upside down, dangling precariously from a slotted wooden rack above the bar.

"Sure, why not?" Harvey replied. "Our game should start soon, so I'd better get in the right frame of mind for my usual string of bad luck." With an attitude like that, Harvey could never be successful at any form of gambling. Those with a negative approach always expected the worst, and that's invariably what they got.

Since the centrally located bar was a popular lunchtime hangout for locals who worked in the area, Jarrod had been forced to accept the only vacant barstool which, just as in the previous night's game, happened to be next to Harvey. With his trademark, soggy cigar smoldering unmercifully in an oversized ashtray, it was obvious why no one sat there. Wanting to learn a little background about the adversary, whose techniques he wanted to expose, Jarrod wasn't upset with the seating arrangements. He let Harvey begin a fresh conversation.

"You going to give your luck another shot, buddy?" Harv asked, still convinced that fate controlled the outcome of all card games. "Your name escapes me. I guess I was too upset yesterday to remember it."

"Bill," Jarrod replied casually, taking a sip of tonic water. Last names were best left unknown around such bars. "Maybe I'll see my cards a little better if I don't pour back a dozen beers," he said. Then he asked his most important question. "Will Cal be in the game today?"

"Don't worry, Cal will be here for sure. He seems to make a pretty good living off the rest of us. Sunday and Monday are the only days we don't see him," Harv replied. "But he'll be ticked off today. Marty, one of his regular contributors, won't be here. He's got a funeral to attend. So, there should be no problem fitting you into the game."

"That's good. I've got to get on the road tomorrow, anyway." Jarrod paused for a moment before continuing. "How long has Cal been playing with you guys?" Jarrod would have wagered that Cal wasn't a local.

"He came out of nowhere near the end of last year. Am I right, Specs?" Harvey asked the bartender, who was going over the football odds in the sports section.

"I remember it was just after Christmas. He walked in here wearing some fancy red sweater," Specs replied, his nose still buried in the paper. "Said he was from Baltimore originally . . . big Orioles fan. All he talks about is the odds on sports bets, seems to follow them all. I'm sure he has a bookie. But he sure knows how to pick his suckers around here. You guys never know when to quit."

"Oh . . . I haven't done badly in the last month," Harvey argued, finally displaying a positive tone. The reality of it was that Harvey's three pizza outlets had become quite profitable, the increased income making his card losses seem less significant.

"You did pretty well in the games you played last week, Zeke, didn't you?" Harvey asked, turning to a balding man who was talking quietly with a friend farther down the bar.

"Felt like it, Harv," Zeke said with a laugh. "I think I kept my losses in the lower triple digits."

"How do the cousins generally fair?" Jarrod asked, still trying to find another winner in the game that Cal appeared to dominate.

"You mean Jimmy and Lance?" Harv replied, nodding toward a table where the cousins sat, away from the gossip. "Over the long run, they don't do badly, maybe breaking even. One or the other has had good runs, but never both together. When one's hot, the other just lets him ride the wave, doesn't get in his way. They play it smart most of the time, and both of them avoid the liquor." Although he never mentioned any signals or eye contact between the cousins, Harvey had just summed up Jarrod's original assessment.

Shortly after one o'clock, Cal sauntered into the bar. Pulling off his overcoat to expose a checkered cardigan sweater, he perused the customers, feigning casual interest as he assessed the day's victims at the poker table. After greeting the regulars, he paused momentarily when his roving eye spotted Jarrod.

"And how are you feeling today, my friend?" Cal inquired with a hint of sarcasm. After the previous night's drunken display, surely he was less concerned that his latest opponent might be an equal at any skillful card game. Perhaps a challenge to billiards, another game at which Cal was proficient, might be in the offing. His confidence had returned, yet his cagy smirk was hardly detectable.

"Still feeling in a bit of a fog, I'm afraid," Jarrod replied, happy to play along with Cal's renewed coolness. "But I'm willing to give the game another try." His words were hesitant, hardly the tone to raise fear in an opponent.

"C'mon, Beth, get your buns movin' and count out those poker chips," Harv chirped as only a regular could get away with. Beth was Specs's wife and filled in for the regular waitresses two or three times a week.

"Harv, go and shove one of your damn cigars where the sun don't shine," Beth shot back in her husky voice. Clearly, she could hold her own with the verbal jousting.

The afternoon card players wandered casually into the back room, those without ongoing accounts buying their stacks of chips from Beth. She had some wisecrack for all of them except Jarrod, whom she welcomed with a cunning wink. Was that about the previous evening, or could Beth foresee what was about to unfold? Telepathy was not likely the case.

Jarrod allowed the others to take their usual chairs before he filled in the last space between Harvey and Zeke. No one seemed to like the cigar. He sat opposite Cal, a position that gave him a prime view of his adversary. The two cousins and Tony, the friend to whom Zeke had been talking, made up the remaining players. Tony was a member of the rubber bridge club, a game some consider to be more skillful than poker. Yet today, most of the members were attending the same funeral that kept Marty from the game.

"I hope today's game will be your usual seven-card stud. Are you still using Cal's variations?" Tony asked. He didn't like the hi-low and wild-card games. He considered them to be childish, especially for a skillful bridge player like himself.

"I'm sure we're all agreed on that. We'd like to see you in the game more often, Tony," Harvey said sincerely as he glanced around the table. Most of the others nodded their approval.

Since the bar was unable to provide a house dealer (who would serve the drinks?), the deal rotated in a clockwise manner. Cards were flipped, with Zeke's ace allowing him to deal out the first hand. On Cal's suggestion, soon after he joined the game the previous year, a second deck was shuffled by the person sitting opposite the dealer. He explained that not only would the pace of the game speed up, the cards would receive a more even shuffle. No one foresaw that handling an extra deck would be to the advantage of a card manipulator. Tony added that having a second deck was the normal procedure in a game of rubber bridge.

Cal's simple variation of the game dealt the first, fourth, and seventh card down. Wagers began after the second card, with the middle down card a free round where no one bet. The rule kept in the suckers who might normally have folded. They couldn't resist seeing that second hidden card.

"Same afternoon limits as before?" Tony asked.

"Three and five, no changes," Cal replied, packing fresh tobacco into his pipe. He meant a maximum of three $5 raises per round of betting. The local crowd didn't like to fold their cards, so pots could get reasonably large. Antes remained at two dollars.

"King bets," Zeke reminded the others as Lance toyed with his down card. The other cousin had only stared at the floor between his legs since Zeke completed dealing the first round of up cards.

The game continued, each player displaying his own mannerisms, old habits that were hard to break. "The odds were against another heart showing up," was an example of Tony's commentary as he tried to take advantage of his bridge analysis and card-counting ability.

"I'm in; my luck's gotta change," was Harvey's standard line as his chip stack continued to shrink.

"Can I see your cards again, Cal?" either Jimmy or Lance would ask, nervously questioning the master, who was quick to show his winning hand and equally fast at folding the cards together with the rest of the deck. He had again beaten one of the cousins by a mere pip.

For Jarrod, the afternoon wore on uneventfully until around three o'clock, when a break was called. Perhaps a truce would be a more accurate description, as it put a cap on the griping, the analyzing, the squirming, and the annoying tinkling of poker chips. Tony had been the most consistent winner. Cal had been dealt some decent hands, which he had judged well, taking advantage of his opponents' mannerisms. Jarrod had watched closely for the expert to flip over cards that were shinier and filled out runs or full houses, but nothing out of the ordinary seemed to happen. Was this the day that Cal played straight up?

Clearly ambidextrous, the resident expert was at ease dealing and handling the cards with either hand. His riffling of the deck was as smooth as satin. To have any chance of exposing his card manipulating, Jarrod had to be certain which hand Cal used to palm the substitute cards. Besides being patient for a large pot to present itself, a card cheat must time his moves with precision. But one thing was certain. A false claim of cheating was a scandalous crime anywhere in the world of cards. Following a severe reprimand, "Bill" would surely be vilified, then ushered out of the room in a hasty manner, his chips scattered all over the floor by the person he accused. If, and when, the time came to expose Cal's methods, Jarrod had to be sure.

Chapter 22

"Shall we get started again?" Tony suggested, draining the last sip of his double Manhattan, a potent drink containing neither ice nor mix. He was convinced that an experienced bridge player should have the advantage over those who played less-skilled games.

"Beth, you got any chips left in your tray?" Harvey joked, noticing his pile was practically depleted.

"I've always got plenty of chips for you, sweetie. I just wish you'd win once in a while so I could see how well you tip," she said, rubbing it in.

"Very funny. You're nothing but a damn jinx. I was way ahead on the weekend."

"Sure, Harv. What did you do, rob your own pizza shop?" Beth was a tough old gal who loved to jaw back and forth with her customers, especially Harvey.

"I believe it's my deal. Does anyone want to raise the stakes?" Cal asked as he shuffled a new deck. The consensus was to keep the stakes the same. Higher limits were reserved for late-night games or special occasions.

"Jim and I'll have to work double shifts if the stakes get any higher." A wisecrack from Lance was quite unusual. The cousins were both well paid for their shiftwork and overtime on the docks in Duluth.

"Give them a cut for luck." Cal's energy level seemed to rise as he slid the shuffled deck in front of Harvey, whose fresh cigar spread clouds of smoke throughout the room.

In a display of showmanship, Cal snapped out cards to the players around the table. He was often deliberate to expose his soft, pink hands in some manner, either adjusting his ornate pipe or flicking lint from the green baize that covered the card table. His mannerisms were irritating but nothing that might arouse suspicion among the others. That's exactly what Jarrod had first noticed. Cal was just too smooth.

However, now something else bothered Jarrod. Each time he sat opposite the dealer, it was his turn to shuffle the second deck of cards. Something didn't feel right. Although two fresh decks were substituted following the break, the cards felt a little sticky. Perhaps someone's hands were wet from his drink, but something else was unusual. Was one of the decks too thin? Could it be missing cards? Jarrod decided to follow the deck until it was his turn to deal.

The first three deals produced small pots, which went to Lance, Zeke, and Harvey.

"How come no one raises me when I get a good hand?" Harvey lamented, not realizing how his body language gave him away when he held above-average cards. "Your deal, Bill. I'm sure that was my one decent hand for the day." Harv, his frustration evident, slid his winning hand and the dead cards across the table for Cal to shuffle.

Jarrod squeezed the deck he had been waiting for. With no time to count how many cards it contained without arousing suspicion, he dealt everyone their cards slowly and deliberately. He would try to count the number of cards taken by the players as well as the remaining unused ones. Luckily, the pot was well contested. Even Jarrod stayed in longer than he would have normally. When the betting finally ended, with Tony congratulating himself on his fine card evaluation, Cal and the other losers were distracted enough not to notice Jarrod count the short stack of cards that remained in the deck.

Sure enough, if his count was correct, thirteen cards should have been remaining. Remembering to account for the players who had dropped out prior to the last round of betting, Jarrod counted only eleven. They were playing with a deck of fifty cards. Apparently, two of them had disappeared.

"Nice draw of that king on your last card," Harvey grumbled. "When I stay in with two pairs, I never get the card I'm looking for."

"Neither of the kings or eights were exposed, so the odds—"

"Come on, Tony, get on with the next deal," Cal interrupted. He wasn't the only one fed up with the constant analysis.

It didn't take long for Jarrod's suspicions to be confirmed. Two hands later, the thinner deck was once again in play. The deal began to build up a healthy pot, which was ardently contested as Cal and three others bumped up the bets. Never consistent with his mannerisms, Cal was unusually fidgety. He peeked several times at his middle and last down cards before finally calling Harvey in the final round of betting. His cupped left hand hovered above one of his face-down cards. Then, like the curled talon of an eagle, it swooped down for a fast peek as though his short-term memory had malfunctioned. In all his years of gambling, Jarrod had never seen a man so slick with his magic act. In the blink of an eye, Cal had replaced both down cards with the ones he had hidden in the palm of his left hand. The missing cards from the second deck had been waiting secretively just for this moment!

"I've finally got you, Cal." Harv couldn't hide his excitement as he nervously turned over his face-down cards, exposing two tens and an eight. With his remaining cards, he completed a full house of tens over eights. Zeke and Jimmy both folded their hands. They were beaten.

With only two fives showing, Cal appeared to be another loser. Another five had been tossed away with Tony's hand, so four of a kind was impossible. Then, to the shock of everyone around the table except Jarrod, Cal began to expose his three hidden cards. One jack followed another. As the third jack was dramatically turned face up, poor Harvey flung his freshly lit cigar so hard that it shattered on the floor like a ripe melon.

"I don't believe it . . . that's totally unbeliev . . ." Harvey began as Cal started raking in the large pile of poker chips.

Prepared for the moment, Jarrod was not about to waste a second. He moved so fast that even Cal, a seasoned expert at such tactics, was caught off guard. Jarrod slammed his right hand onto the card expert's left wrist. Cal's fingers gnarled up as he attempted to pull away, his eyes widening like a predator about to strike. His ornate pipe dropped from his mouth, hot clumps of tobacco singeing the green felt. His saliva might well have been venom as it spewed from his drawn-back lips. With a powerful twist, Jarrod extracted two wrinkled cards from Cal's curled fingers. A black three and the nine of diamonds, the legendary curse of Scotland, floated like autumn leaves onto the pile of chips in front of the cheater. The coincidence was uncanny, as the cheat's birthplace turned out to be Edinburgh.

The chaos of the next few moments never reached the papers. Cal leapt to his feet in such a panic that not only his chair but also the heavy octagonal card table was sent flying. Stumbling backward, he retained barely enough balance to reach for an object under his pant leg, hidden next to his left ankle. The stunned card players, including the crib and backgammon opponents, were only beginning to react when Jarrod spotted the small-caliber revolver that Cal pulled from an ankle holster.

"Get down!" was all Jarrod had time to shout.

Cal took careful aim at the adversary who had abruptly ended his easy living in that town. On his knees and unable to move, Jarrod simply closed his eyes and prepared for the worst.

Perhaps shooting another human was not part of his makeup, or maybe deep within his greedy mind, Cal held a candid respect for his vulnerable target. In an unsuspecting yet dramatic fashion, he had clearly met his match in the sordid world of the gambler. Much to the surprise of the roomful of immobile spectators, rather than pulling the trigger, Cal gave a simple warning: "Any of you follow me, and I won't miss."

The card cheat was out the front door before either Specs or Beth could react to the crash of the table overturning. Loading her tray with a fresh round of drinks, Beth was caught off guard when Cal rushed by like a frightened gazelle, his expensive overcoat draped over his arm and dragging on the floor. Both she and Specs hurried into the card room to discover what had happened.

"You mean that bastard has been cheating us all along?" Harvey asked.

"I'm afraid so, Harv," Jarrod explained. "He's been toying with you guys ever since he joined your game. I'm sure he played straight up a lot of the time, but when he needed an edge, you could see how easy it was for him to manipulate the cards. That trick you saw today was likely only one of many he had tucked up his sleeve. He's an old cheat, just running out of places to use his talent—probably been run out of a few towns before now."

Mumbling a few choice comments about the man who had fleeced her paying customers, Beth began to clean up the mess that was strewn all over the patterned carpet—poker chips, cards, glasses, cigarette butts and ashes.

Specs eyed each player in turn. "You guys realize we've got to keep this little incident between ourselves. Luckily no one got hurt except for a few bruised egos. We don't want anyone in uniform wandering through here asking a lot of questions." Gambling clubs were still illegal in that town.

"Well, that guy won't be cheating anyone around this area anymore," Harvey said. "I'll make sure of that."

Little did Harvey know, but Cal was already loading his car as he prepared to make a quick exit from town. He had taken advantage of living cheaply with a divorced relative with whom he shared an interest in gambling on sporting events.

"I think we owe something to our new friend," Zeke suggested. "Without him, who knows how long that cheat would have got away with his shady games. How about we give Bill whatever money Cal has left in his account?"

The others didn't take long to agree with the reward. Although the cousins would have preferred to split the money between everyone, they went with the consensus.

Beth was glad to see a little generosity from the group. "Cal always kept a two-hundred-dollar balance. That way he never had to pay for chips. And you know what? I don't ever remember him adding to his original pile of chips or having to top up his balance at the end of a session." She had never been around when Cal suffered the odd minor loss, an event that didn't happen often.

"We'll have to divide up this mess of chips on the floor as best we can," Tony added. "Sorry, Harv, but you can't win the last pot."

"But without that cheat—"

"That's only fair," Zeke cut in, the cousins nodding in agreement. "We'll split whatever Cal was ahead today. It won't be perfect, but at least none of us will be a big loser for a change."

Satisfied with the outcome, especially since no trigger had been pulled, Jarrod added one more comment. "I hope you guys will be more careful who you let into your game after this. Players who aren't nearly as smooth as Cal can still take advantage of you. But I do appreciate your generosity. Thanks."

He peeled two twenties from the pile of bills Beth handed him. "Beth, I think everyone could use a fresh drink." No one disagreed. Even the cousins ordered a couple of beers.

So, the conversation went on, no one able to believe that Cal had gotten away with his antics for so long without arousing suspicion among the regulars. They were all very grateful to Jarrod, and the drinks flowed for a while longer. No more cards were played that day. Even the players from the backgammon and crib games joined in the lively talk.

Eventually, darkness set in, and Jarrod finally said his goodbyes. He grabbed his new travel bag from behind the bar and, for the last time, stepped out of Jack's Bar into the brisk air of another fall evening. Once again unable to explain his motivation, Jarrod had slid into the lives of another group of people, his actions altering the inevitable path of control by the hands of a cunning card manipulator. That one unselfish deed, along with the words of wisdom from a total stranger, would, for years to come, become part of the folklore of the aging establishment.

Directions from Specs started Jarrod toward the Duluth bus station. He walked slowly and deliberately, his mind still unravelling from the eventful day. Although thoughts of Tammy lingered and were hard to dispel, a renewed determination pushed aside any doubt about continuing his journey. Deep down, he knew she would find success and accomplish her goals. Yet why was he so fearful that a relationship might develop that he could not even say goodbye?

And why could he not get Lucas's fearful eyes and forlorn face out of his mind? The answers to those puzzling questions could not be explained simply as nobility. They would be rooted much deeper in the complex fabric that encased Jarrod's essence. Yet in an odd way, the unsought help he gave the naïve gamblers, whom he hardly knew, kindled a faint hope that maybe he could accomplish something more in his pathetic life.

Although thinking more positively, Jarrod strolled slowly, lost between thoughts of the recent wild activity and whatever his future might hold. He paid little attention as he stepped off the curb of a major thoroughfare, almost walking into the path of an oncoming vehicle. With headlights that were dim from a lack of cleaning, the dark-blue, mud-splattered vehicle was practically invisible. He jumped backward as the bulky vehicle swerved to avoid him, its tired horn emitting a sickly groan. Startled, his eyes missed seeing the driver's face. Instead, he found himself staring directly through the dirty side window just above the rear wheel. In that split second, Jarrod saw something that brought his heart to his mouth. He couldn't believe what his eyes had suddenly focused on, if only for the briefest of moments.

With his body slumped and his eyes closed, his head propped against the smudged window, Lucas came into full view of his old friend. Stunned, Jarrod's jaw dropped. He froze in his tracks as the old Suburban accelerated away from him into the light traffic. Unable to speak or move, he could only stare as four shaky letters jumped into his view from the vehicle's mud-covered tailgate: "HEL/." Was the last scrawl part of an "L"?

"No!" he blurted. He felt certain that Lucas—or whoever had written it—was trying to scrawl a "P" in the mud but never completed it. In its own fickle way, would fate once again interrupt Jarrod's travel plans? Without doubt, his journey west was about to encounter yet another detour.

Part 4
CRUSTY AND MOLLY

Chapter 23

The old Suburban's heater fan groaned incessantly as it attempted to circulate warm air among the tired passengers. Almost all the children had dosed off in varying stages of sleep, which was generally sporadic and restless. The calming influence of the early afternoon tea was wearing off, its lingering effect enhancing visions and memories in the minds of the carload of resting youngsters. For most of them, their early childhood was barely a fleeting memory. Only two children were still awake. One of them was Catherine, the girl who had tried to comfort Lucas earlier. She hummed a melodic hymn that she couldn't get out of her mind: "We are born, we are happy, we *skip* with rabbits, *swim* with swans, *dance* through fields of tulips . . .We love one another, we laugh, we cry, we are caring . . .." The song went on and on. She had learned it in one of her study sessions. It reminded her of fields filled with colorful flowers and bounding rabbits, fluffy clouds, and gentle breezes. Those were happy thoughts, yet why did sadness hang over her? Although she tried to think *happy* as much as possible, she didn't always succeed.

Lucas, the other child who was awake, didn't hum. Pleasant thoughts never occurred to him. His body ached for sleep, yet his mind was treading water as it tried to figure out what was happening to him. One minute he had been warm and free, the next he was shivering and captive. He couldn't imagine where Cassandra and Florence were taking him. He longed for freedom, but his body wouldn't respond. Even his eyelids abandoned him when they drooped shut just as a familiar face peered momentarily through the mud-smeared window that supported his head.

Although flakes of wet snow made the roads slick, the trusty Suburban seemed to knowingly wend its way along a familiar path home. Paved roads turned to oiled roads, which led to gravel roads. Those deteriorated into a rutted washboard surface that eventually eroded to become a mass of slippery gumbo. The winding trail led past rows of defoliated trees and shrubs, their naked branches casting ghostly shadows as a waxing moon rose to the east. The dark outlines of the tree limbs flickered across the narrow beams of light cast by the dull headlights. The muddy gravel path rose and fell like a carnival ride as it meandered through the foothills of a low range of mountains. The term "mountain" might seem rather overstated for the gently rolling hills.

"I'm thirsty," one of the children complained as she awakened from the vibration caused by the Suburban's wheels bouncing over the rough washboard surface.

"We're almost home, Marsha," Cassandra said. "There will be plenty of fresh spring water for you there."

Florence gently maneuvered the mud-covered Suburban up its final approach, a narrow driveway that led to a secluded hideaway. As the rising moon peeked through intermittent clouds, the outlines of several buildings came into view. Some residents might have called the place a commune, where everyone was family. Others would have called it a religious retreat. Yet more than one unhappy guest, especially the younger ones, would not hesitate to call it the resort from hell. Perhaps the single-word message Lucas had tried to scratch on the muddy tailgate carried more than one meaning. Unfortunately, his last cry for help was totally obscured by a fresh coating of grime.

The two adults had hardly spoken during the tedious hour-and-a-half trip, both anxious to get home. The tired vehicle slid to a halt as the driveway ended, exposing a better view of several dimly lit one-story buildings. Eyes adjusted to the semi-darkness would be able to make out the roughly hewn outlines of log structures that an adventurous person might call lodging for campers accustomed to rustic amenities. Some comparison could be made to the stark barracks of a military camp. A single dim lightbulb hung over the entrance to each of the larger buildings. Only one smaller cabin, which faced the driveway like a sentry post, was illuminated on the inside.

"All right, children, we're home. Everybody up," Florence announced as she turned off the ignition and clapped her hands. The heater fan emitted a low growling sound of submission as it ground to a halt. "Here comes Matron Crystal. She will lead you all in prayer before you go to bed. I'm sure she has prepared a warm drink for you as well."

The youngsters yawned and stretched as they stepped out into the cool night air. From one of the dimly lit cabins, a loose, threadbare coat draped over her square shoulders, a woman shuffled toward the group. Her grim expression did little to inspire the tired youngsters. They knew the routine and were about to follow the matron.

"Lucas, you stay behind with me," Cassandra said. "There's someone I would like you to meet. Crystal, you and Florence put the others to bed. Get Dirk to help you. Our new young friend can skip prayers for tonight."

After a couple of hours, the effects of the special tea, or rather a potion disguised as tea, began to wear off. Lucas found that he could stand once again as he slid from the Suburban's bench seat onto the ground. His head still ached, his mind was groggy and confused, and hunger pangs gnawed at his empty stomach, but he could do nothing but follow Cassandra as she entered the smaller log cabin which, compared to the others, glowed like a special jewel amid its black surroundings.

Cassandra lit a kerosene lamp that dangled from the small kitchen's ceiling. "Since you seem to have lost most of your supper, I'll fix you a bowl of cereal with dried fruit and nuts. It's a treat the other children seldom enjoy. But Lucas, you may have the opportunity to become someone special around here." In truth, Cassandra sensed a unique quality in the boy.

"Gee, thanks, but what if I don't want to stay with you people?" he replied. Although Lucas tried to be firm, his voice trembled from exhaustion. "You didn't exactly give me a choice about coming here."

"You were chosen, my dear. From what I could determine, I wouldn't imagine your life was going anywhere. You are one of us now, and your life will be much better in your new family." Her tone left no room for negotiation.

Lucas's face reddened with anger. "Like hell you can kidnap me and keep me as a slave at your stupid farm, or whatever you call this place. I'll get out of here; I can promise you that."

"Our sacred home is called a commune, young man. We have our own ways, our own rules. The outside world has no control over us. We are a union of souls. Our destiny is controlled within the foundation of our principles . . .." With a blank stare on her face, was she reciting the ideals of a pagan priestess?

"What makes you think I want to be one of your *souls*?" Lucas asked defiantly. "Thank you, but I'll be on my way as soon as I get the chance."

Unperturbed by the boy's petulance, Cassandra continued. "Your bravado is one of the reasons I chose you to be among us. Don't you think others before you have resisted? Very few children have tried to leave our lovely farm, as you call it. But when they return, or are returned, they are more mature, usually wiser, and certainly far meeker. Never again do they complain about their life as part of our loving family."

"Maybe you'll find me a little different," Lucas said, still displaying his stubborn impudence. "Do you really think I'll drink any of your damn tea again? What else will you try to poison me with? Maybe your crappy cereal." The great meal he had enjoyed at Julie's home flashed into his mind. He longed for the independence and friendship he seemed to have found with Jarrod. Right now, food, shelter, and security were less important to him.

"Don't resist, dear Lucas. You can have a safe and wonderful life among us. Tomorrow there will be a small treat in store for you," she promised.

"What do you plan to do, brand me like some cow?" asked Lucas.

Her failure to reply was anything but encouraging. "Please stay here and eat while I talk to our gracious leader, my partner and the father of our lovely daughters. Don't worry; nothing in this food will cause you any harm. But one small warning: Don't even think of running. The night is cold, and many hungry wolves out there would love to hunt you down for an evening snack." Cassandra's advice was ominous but unnecessary, as Lucas would never consider an escape on that dark, chilly night. Not only was his strength completely drained, so was his determination.

Leaving him to eat his cereal moistened with a pale, milky liquid, Cassandra entered a smoky room that was utilized as a small den. A male voice spoke quietly, yet with the calm conviction of someone in complete control of all that went on in his covert community.

"I overheard some of your conversation. Who is the young man with you?" A small but intense fire crackled in the blackened stone fireplace. The room was warm and well-lit from the glow of several oil lamps. The couple clearly held a special rank in the community over which they exercised complete control.

"Lucas was alone and had nowhere to go when our paths crossed at the bus station in town," Cassandra explained as she planted a brief, almost ritual, kiss on the man's cheek. "How was your day, my dear Auscan?"

The devout leaders of the secretive society had been joined in wedlock twelve years earlier in a simple, non-traditional ceremony. The commune was in its early stages of development at the time. The two continued to be a perfect match, their personalities blending together remarkably well.

His mind far from lucid, drifting aimlessly among many thoughts, Auscan Zapata took a moment to reply. Perhaps the thin wisps of smoke that rose gently from the marble bowl of his strange pipe held the answer to his random thinking. The transient lifestyle of a gypsy for many of his forty-five years was etched in the furrows that lined his rugged face with the pattern of a road atlas. The dancing firelight only accentuated his weathered complexion, the result of overexposure to the elements as well as the rigors of his nomadic lifestyle. Over the years, Auscan had risen from a religious zealot and follower to a leader in his own right. An aura and magnitude surrounded him that made others his faithful devotees. Even Cassandra was held firmly in his grasp, bound to him with a deep devotion.

"My day was uneventful," Auscan finally replied. "But tell me, Cassandra, what plans do you have for this boy?"

"I was thinking, since I cannot bear you another child, and knowing you would dearly love to have a son, we might raise him as our own. He already possesses your stubbornness and independence. In time, he, too, could become a leader."

"You know I adore our four daughters. They will grow to be fine women. Yet you are also quite aware that I long for a son." The stone pipe was cupped firmly in his left hand, a unique tobacco mixture glowing in the bowl as Auscan inhaled. His eyelids were closed as curls of blueish smoke spiraled up from his flared nostrils. After thinking about his next words for some time, his speech was slow and deliberate. "In a manner of respect to my past beliefs, perhaps we could name the boy Lazarus. Certainly, he has risen from the ashes, and two of his would-be sisters are named Mary and Martha." His words floated in the air.

"A thoughtful idea, but you must not be too anxious, my dear. First, we must indoctrinate the boy, and that may be a difficult chore," warned Cassandra. "He harbors a stubborn independence that we must somehow suppress."

"Of course, we must go slowly. First, a minor operation, and then a series of your fine, irresistible broths should bring the young man over to our way of thinking. He will succumb like the others before him," Auscan prophesied. "Once he adjusts to our ways, he, too, may rise above his humble beginnings and develop leadership skills."

"I warn you, this boy is different," Cassandra cautioned. "I sensed something special about him right away. That's what attracted me to him at the bus station. But it would be better for you to meet him in the morning. At the moment, he is tired and weak, but he holds the heart and determination of a streetwise child. He will not give in easily."

"Put him to bed with the others. I doubt he will try to escape, but warn Crystal to take some precautions." Auscan spoke slowly and precisely, yet his words ran together.

"I'll do as you say, my dear, and then I will join you again shortly," Cassandra promised as she left the den, rejoining Lucas in the kitchen.

"I see your bowl is almost empty, young man," she said. "You must have been hungry. Did you sip on some of our pure spring water?"

"It was better than that horrible cereal, especially with that fake milk you put on it. I had milk like that before in a home . . . ." His voice trailed off, then took a more defiant tone. "What do you want me to do now?"

"Our leader would prefer to meet you in the morning. You need rest, Lucas, so you will join Crystal and the others in the boys' quarters. Just remember how I warned you about trying to escape. It's a dark, cold night out there." Her words were ominous.

"Tell me about it!" he replied bluntly.

Lucas entered the boys' residence without resistance while Cassandra returned to her partner. Long into the night, smoke rose from Auscan's strange pipe as the two self-proclaimed leaders of the concealed and, apparently, self-sufficient community continued their profound conversation. With much to discuss, sleep was set back to the early morning hours.

Chapter 24

Jarrod's mind couldn't sort out the countless possibilities. Who was Lucas with? How did he get to Duluth or even cross the state border? Had he recovered from his feverish state? One discouraging look at his slumped body and pale face augured little optimism. Only able to take a quick glance around the interior of the vehicle that almost ran him down, Jarrod caught a glimpse of a group of children who appeared to be sleeping. Were they all street urchins? Where were they being taken? He had many questions but few answers. His only real clue was likely hidden in the letters scrawled on the muddy tailgate. They not only reached out as a cry for help but also conveyed an ominous warning. Whatever the danger, there was no way Jarrod could leave town. The sight of his young friend alive, and possibly captive, flooded his body with a surge of energy.

Fueled by the pressing need to solve his latest challenge, Jarrod could only think of one place to start. Where else but the bus station? Lucas seemed to follow that route of escape. Maybe Sheriff Klem would figure that out instead of running around the countryside with his stack of posters. Walking quickly, and finally with some purpose, Jarrod reached the bus terminal in fifteen minutes. Pushing open the two sets of outer doors, a blast of warm air greeted him as he spotted the wickets where bus fares could be purchased.

Passengers milled about the waiting area with groups of friends or relatives looking for gate numbers, checking schedules, purchasing tickets, or saying their goodbyes. Some stood next to overstuffed luggage bags, cardboard cartons wrapped in masking tape, or green garbage bags that bulged with clothing. Bus travelers were not often fussy about their methods of lugging their private possessions. Jarrod noticed that one female ticket agent, her eyes half-closed as if she were praying her shift would end, had no customers at her booth. Recalling the clerk at the U-drive office, and with his mind searching for the right words, he approached her with some discretion, trying to be as casual as possible.

"Excuse me, but I'm looking for a young boy, my nephew. He was going to catch a bus shortly but forgot to bring something from home," Jarrod began, hoping his impromptu story might jar the disinterested ticket seller's memory.

"I don't remember issuing a ticket to any kid recently," she replied in a monotone voice that reminded Jarrod of Stan, the bus driver.

"He's twelve, thin, a little pale, with brown hair that's probably in need of a good brushing. Does that ring a bell?" Jarrod persisted, refusing to walk away.

"I told you already, haven't sold any young boy a ticket all day. There's two other agents; maybe ask them. Sorry." Her words were blunt, and final.

Turning away, Jarrod was deciding which ticket agent to approach next when he heard the wistful, barely audible voice of an elderly man. The old fellow's speech was so low that Jarrod almost missed it completely. "Excuse me, sir, but I couldn't help but overhear your conversation."

The man seemed to appear out of nowhere, or perhaps he blended so well with his surroundings that he was practically invisible. Spinning around quickly, Jarrod found himself staring into the strained, red eyes of a street person, or that's what he perceived the aged gentleman to be. The long, soiled, grey overcoat, the unkempt beard and haggard face, the dirty-orange toque and lengthy, unwashed scarf wouldn't belong to a businessman.

"I've been in here off and on most of the day, at least since it started getting dark," the old fellow continued, his speech slow and hesitant. "I did see a boy much like the one you're asking about. Did he wear a red winter jacket?"

Before answering, Jarrod led the gentleman to an empty bench, where they could both sit down. "Wait here. I'll grab us a coffee from that machine. Black okay?"

The elderly man nodded. Jarrod couldn't recall Lucas having a red jacket. The farm lady, Julie, had given him a plaid coat that was mostly blue. Still, he was anxious to learn more.

After handing over the larger of the coffees he had purchased, Jarrod began, his words faltering. "This boy, did he carry a dark-blue backpack?"

"He might have, but anyway, he looked kind of lost. He seemed unsure, was looking around a lot, checking the posters on the wall. It was like he had no place to go. I know the feeling," the old fellow explained, his expression sad and resigned. He sipped his coffee, wincing when it burned his lips.

"Did you see him get on a bus?" The answer didn't surprise Jarrod.

"No sir, he sure didn't. That's the strange part . . . say, you wouldn't have a couple of bucks so I could maybe get a meal? This place closes soon, and there's a burger place . . .." The old man's voice had a desperate tone.

Pulling out five dollars from his recent winnings, Jarrod was glad to help. "Here, get yourself something hot to eat. So, if the kid didn't get on a bus, did you see where he went?"

"Thanks, much appreciated," the man said, pocketing the bill. His sad eyes were moist, either a reaction to Jarrod's generosity or from a perpetual irritation. "A tall woman with long black hair started talking to the boy. She was a strange-looking one, but something about her seemed familiar." He didn't realize that Cassandra was adept at changing her appearance from time to time. "There were two children with her. The young girl I recognized from a second-hand store not far from here. She helped me find this warm overcoat . . . cost me eight bucks."

"What happened then?" Jarrod asked, realizing the old fellow's mind was wandering.

"I didn't hear the conversation, but the next thing I knew, all four of them were walking out the door. That's all I can help you with, sorry." His tone was apologetic, as if he would have liked to have been more helpful.

Hesitating for a long moment, Jarrod finally spoke. "That boy, and I'm sure it's him, isn't my nephew." His voice was barely above a whisper and began to shake as he continued. "We met only a few days ago. He was alone and on the run—can't say I'm much different. We got separated . . . well, it's a long story. Anyway, thanks for your help. My name's Bill."

The old vagrant flinched and drew back when Jarrod extended his hand.

"They call me Crusty around here. I guess too many years livin' outside turned me into a dried-up old prune." The harmless street person grinned through toothless gums and finally took Jarrod's hand. His rough and calloused fingers still had a firm grip. "I know a bit about drifting all over the place. Myself, I could never settle down. I've seen a lot of the country, but I think this town's my last home. I'm gettin' too old to roam around anymore."

"You want a refill?" Jarrod asked as he walked toward the vending machines.

"Sure, it's a cold night out there . . . thanks," Crusty replied, nodding slowly. "Security will be chasing me out of here soon."

Returning to the bench with two hot drinks, Jarrod had one more question. "That second-hand shop, could you tell me how to get there?"

"You want a coat like mine?" Crusty asked with his toothless grin.

"Not a bad idea, but—"

"Two blocks up that way, then one to your right," Crusty explained as he sipped his coffee and pointed one shaky finger toward the glass doors. "But don't be buyin' all the good boots. I might be wanting a new pair." He chuckled as he looked down at boots held together with tattered, grey duct tape. "The store is called Mount Cloq . . . I'm not sure how to say it. But it ends in 'thrift shop,' so you'll find it easy enough. But it won't be open at this hour."

"Where do you stay on these cold nights?" Jarrod asked, his concern genuine. "I hope not on some park bench."

Crusty hesitated. Like many loners and street people, he was very private and somewhat embarrassed about how he lived. "There's this shelter . . . If you're down and out, or they pick you up drunk."

"Sorry, that's really none of my business," Jarrod interrupted, sensing Crusty's uneasiness. His next offer was spontaneous. "Here, will this cover a pair of boots from that place? You've been a great help. It's the least I can do." He held out a crumpled ten-dollar bill.

An extra layer of moisture built up in Crusty's eyes. He seldom saw such generosity. A few coins jingled when he pulled out a knit money pouch and carefully opened the clasp. Jarrod noticed a bright-red lady bug was embroidered onto the tan-colored material.

"That store has plenty of good boots for that price. God bless you." Crusty sniffled as he spoke, his words tentative and his voice barely above a whisper. Then, before parting ways from the stranger who had been so good to him, he offered some useful advice. "I don't know if you're concerned, but the last bus tonight leaves in half an hour, and a regular police patrol clears this place out. I'll be off now to make sure I get a mattress for the night."

Jarrod nodded and gave a friendly grin. He suspected that a portion of his food and boot money would likely go toward a cheap bottle of wine.

Crusty's long, ragged orange scarf waved a silent farewell as he pushed through the double doors without looking back. Jarrod hoped he might run into the old fellow again, a highly unlikely circumstance considering the transient nature of his new life. Little did he realize it, but his small investment in helping a homeless street person would one day soon be paid forward in a far different way.

About to spend another night in Duluth, Jarrod heeded Crusty's advice and left the bus station as soon as he finished his coffee. Walking quickly in the chilly yet invigorating night air, he found the Mount Cloquet Thrift Store without any problem. The store was dark, and a large "Closed" sign hung at an angle inside the front window. Continuing up the street in search of a place to sleep, Jarrod felt shivers go up his back when he recalled his previous accommodations in that town. Only moments later, he was surprised to come across a red fluorescent sign that flashed the word "ROOMS." Beneath the illuminated sign, painted letters read "Daily, Weekly, Monthly Rates."

"Another night in another seedy inn." Jarrod said quietly to himself as he pressed firmly on a tiny black buzzer.

Chapter 25

Morning wakeup came early at the Mount Cloquet commune. Before dawn, the adults in two of the rustic cottages began to stir. Although no formal alarm or bell was used as a wakeup, everyone seemed to abide by a routine. Fires were stoked, water was boiled, and personal hygiene was taken care of. Those in charge of everyday tasks, including laundry, cooking, and rousing the children, performed their duties at a steady, methodical pace. Other than a few "good mornings," there was little conversation among the adults who milled about the grounds. One man, whose turn it was to lead the morning's prayer ritual, appeared to be lost in a trance or some personal meditation. Others were busy adding logs to the pot-bellied stoves that warmed their residences throughout the day. It was apparent that each adult served some purpose in the confines of their controlled community.

Two of the other cottages were the children's quarters. Oddly enough, Matron Crystal supervised the boys' lodging, while a young fellow, whom they called Master Dirk, kept charge of the girls' residence. Cassandra had reasoned that boys were less likely to provoke each other, act up, or even act out their improper thoughts with a strict female watching over them. Similarly, the girls were less inclined to giggle, gossip, or even discuss boys when a serious young man was supervising them. For whatever reason, the system worked. The dour matron put up with little nonsense from the boys, and Dirk was equally strict with the girls. He was quite aware that any flirting or improper behavior on his part would have dire consequences. The *medicinal* drinks he took to stifle any such thoughts could be purchased at many places in town. "Happy Hour" never came early enough for the young man.

When they needed his help the previous evening, Florence and Crystal had caught Dirk dozing, his face flushed and a lingering odor of alcohol hanging over him, a condition that was becoming far too common in their view. Now a supervisor of children, he had been indoctrinated into the strict system since joining the commune when he was merely a child alone on the streets. Any life was better than living with a drunken, abusive father and a mother who only cowered. After trying his first drink after watching his dad pass out for the umpteenth time, Dirk discovered an escape from his dismal life. He was barely eleven. Unfortunately, his dependency on alcohol found a recurrence during his years at the commune. Duties, responsibilities, and the expectations of others weighed heavily on him. His difficulty with self-esteem and motivation never ended. Insecurity continued to haunt him.

Now almost twenty-one years of age, Dirk had developed from a skinny child into a strapping young man with tremendous strength. As a rule, the most arduous of chores were placed on his broad shoulders. In addition, if any child got out of line, which rarely happened, Dirk administered his own form of punishment. Hands that could pulverize a mound of acorns with one blow proved to be a great discouragement to rebellious youngsters.

Crystal had suffered through two failed marriages, drifted from one menial job to the next, and was generally fed up with society when she was recruited from a late-night coffee shop. Going nowhere fast, she was easy prey for a culture that was radical in some of its ways yet simple in others. It at least offered her a more stable life. There, under strict supervision, the males she despised so strongly could do her no harm. The Mount Cloquet commune was devoid of class structure, with no significance placed on gender, race, or background. Emphasis was placed on new beginnings and respect for the common ideals of the community as a whole. That did not mean the two leaders did not expect the others to hold them in high esteem. Auscan and Cassandra strictly controlled the overall operation and agenda of the "progressive" social order, as they liked to refer to it, common ideals notwithstanding.

"Come on, boys, let's get up and moving," Crystal said as she banged a wooden spoon against a tin cup. Not even the soundest sleepers could ignore the aggravating clatter. "Get washed up. Morning prayers are in fifteen minutes."

After numerous yawns and groans, one by one, eleven boys (the new recruit still slept) made their way to the horse trough that served as a urinal. It was a similar design to those found in older stadiums and arenas. Javex and urinal blocks were in good supply. It was Norm's turn, a boy yet to reach his teen years, to heat up the wash water for a communal basin. Since birthdays were never acknowledged in the *one-for-all* society, the age of many commune members was often a guess. Apparently, talking was a discouraged pastime. Words were few as the boys slowly dressed and splashed water on their faces.

Only Lucas, who had finally fallen into a deep sleep, complained about the harsh awakening as the cup was banged next to his ear. "Come on, Crissy, let me sleep. I got in here the latest." The name had innocently jumped into his mind. Even so, his lack of respect was apparent to everyone in the room.

A couple of the boys grinned at the nickname given to the matron, but most of them stood in shock. Crystal was scathing in her response.

"Young man, you will call me Matron Crystal. While I am in charge, I expect your utmost respect and attention. Do I make myself clear?"

"You think I chose to be here?" Lucas asked defiantly.

"You are one of us now and must abide by our rules. The sooner you accept that fact, the better. You will no longer consider yourself an individual. Your thoughts, actions, your entire life has one sole purpose, and that is to serve your new family. Only our great leader can decide what fate is in store for us. Showing a lack of respect for any of your superiors will be dealt with harshly. Consider this a final warning." Crystal was breathing heavily by the end of her reprimand, reciting it like a quote from the testament. It was evident that the society's rites had been woven throughout her entire makeup.

Aware that any further argument was hopeless, Lucas did an about-face, speaking with his most apologetic tone. "Okay, okay, I'll try to fit in. But I've got to eat something before I can do my part *for the family.*" His appetite had returned.

"That's more like it, young Lucas. Wash up first. Normand has heated up the water. I'll use some to make us all a hot morning drink." Unaccustomed to insubordination, Crystal took a few moments to calm down. Beads of perspiration dotted her forehead.

"I'll pass on your tea. It only makes me throw up," Lucas explained politely.

"Don't worry; the lemon drink I make tastes much better. It has many vitamins and will give you strength," Crystal promised. "No one gets sick from my drinks. Right, boys?"

While some washed and others got dressed, the group nodded and spoke in unison. "Yes, Miss Crystal." Apparently, "Miss" was allowed to replace "Matron" on occasion.

"Morning prayers will begin shortly. Only after we give thanks to our spiritual leader, the man who bonds our great community together, can we consider breaking our fast with a morning meal. Little by little, Lucas, you will learn the ways of our wonderful family," Crystal explained, continuing the lecture so well entrenched in her mind. She spoke of Auscan as if he were God himself.

The obscure community, so estranged from mainstream society, was severe in following its principles. Caring and looking out for the group was pushed to the extreme, insomuch that individuals lost their personalities. Original ideas and input were frowned upon. That was the unfortunate aspect of its members' lives. Yet weren't many of those people, especially the ones who struggled to function on their own in the outside world, better off in a disciplined setting with specific obligations? At the very least, their basic needs were being met.

Nevertheless, the new boy in camp was not the type to be controlled. The regimentation Lucas faced there was no different from that in many of the group homes in which he had spent time. The adults ruled, not only rejecting input from any youngsters under their control but also putting the blame on certain individuals for anything that went wrong or items that went missing. Lucas hated it all. If not a total rebel, he was clearly a person who thought for himself. He would have preferred to live under a crumbling bridge to living with those people.

"What crap," Lucas mumbled. "These people are all brainwashed. Do they ever think for themselves?" Yet for the moment, he would keep his comments to himself. Taking a chance, he decided to drink the hot liquid that Crystal offered him. The tangy, citrus flavor gave a burning sensation on its way to his stomach. The taste wasn't bad, and his energy level seemed to get an immediate boost. He just hoped it wouldn't make him sick.

Looking out the tiny window in the cottage door, Crystal saw the other family members making their way to a secluded location beyond the barracks, a setting nestled in an outcropping of rocks at the base of a steep hill. Moments later, smoke began to rise from an opening in the granite ledge that rose vertically above the entranceway.

"Hurry up, boys, or we'll be late for prayers," Crystal said, concern showing in her voice. If her group disrupted the routine, she would surely hear about it later.

Donning the ski jacket that Chris had loaned him, Lucas trailed behind the group as they dispersed from their cottage. After a short walk, Crystal and the boys entered the mouth of a yawning cave. Although nature had formed it at the base of the steep precipice, the commune members had altered the entrance with mounds of rocks, wooden planks, and corrugated metal sheets. As well, a heavy canvas tarp that hung over the opening protected the sacred meeting room from the elements. The tarp was neatly folded back to allow entrance to the cavern. A roaring fire that burned in an open pit at the rear of the room was vented by a natural fissure in the cave wall. The location had been chosen carefully and obviously played an important role in the Mount Cloquet family's routine.

Neither Auscan nor Cassandra attended the morning's prayers. Both were sound asleep after a late night filled with discussion. As a rule, one of them would lead the service only on Sundays. On the religious side of the unconventional society, that was the day that still retained its biblical overtones. The revered leaders had chosen the most mature members of their community to conduct weekday prayers. Sermons or "sharing the word," as Auscan referred to the lectures, were seldom part of the weekday services, which tended to be much shorter than those on Sunday. Fundraising activities and schooling took precedence during the conventional workweek.

As the straggling boys were finally ushered through the entrance of the holy shrine, the adults and young girls had already taken up their prescribed positions. There were no pews, and except for one man in a wheelchair, everybody stood. The crackling fire produced a drying effect on the humid, fusty air, which clung to the congregants' skin. A natural flue drew the smoke outside, air circulating from the myriad of cracks in the natural stone façade.

The man whose turn it was to lead the morning's prayers stepped onto the top of a slim, flat slab of granite. A pulpit constructed from a rich, deep-red wood, perhaps mahogany, stood in front of the rock. The sides of the podium were draped with thick strands of braided hemp, the fibers frayed and dotted with flecks of soot from countless fires. Several candles were nestled in hollow niches along the uneven rock walls. Their flickering light bounced off the irregular walls, casting eerie shadows across the community members' faces. With hardened paraffin encasing their brass holders, two wax tapers stood on either side of the pulpit. Withered vines, choked lifeless ages ago by the cloying darkness, hung from the cave's roof, almost touching the surrogate preacher's shoulders. Only a foot above his head, the talons of an unknown bird of prey, perhaps a hawk or an eagle, dangled from a thin wire. Colin, the man who stood at the pulpit, continued to struggle with a childhood stutter. With everyone's eyes focused on him, he nervously cleared his throat in preparation for a well-rehearsed recital.

As Lucas entered the shrine, he noticed the adults were gathered in the center of the hard-packed clay floor facing the pulpit. The girls were lined up on the left side of the preacher, and the boys were assembling to the right. Having no intention of standing anywhere close to Crystal, his eyes roved across the row of heads before he spotted Catherine at the far end of the group of girls. Sliding behind the line of boys, he was oblivious to Crystal's stern glare. Despite the anger building within her, she remained motionless, fearing that any action she took would disrupt the ritual.

As Lucas wedged himself into a small space next to Catherine, a low, guttural sound rose from the preacher's throat. Sounding more like a man with a breathing problem, the choking noises were, in fact, the beginning of a rhythmic chant that spread throughout the congregation. Eventually, everyone except Lucas was humming a strange lyrical melody. With eyes closed and heads swaying from side to side, bodies tensed in unison as their voices reached a high-pitched crescendo and then abruptly fell silent.

As the odd, wordless chanting subsided, Catherine turned her head slightly and noticed the newest family member standing next to her. She returned his wishful grin with a careful sideways nod as a warning sign before turning to face the preacher. Fraternizing with the boys was frowned upon at any time but especially during prayers.

Lucas noticed right away how much clearer and more alert her eyes were compared to when he first saw them the previous night. Since their ride back from the city, he sensed that Catherine stood apart from the others. After seeing her that morning, he was sure she didn't belong with the rest of the odd group. Not only that, but Lucas couldn't help but feel a certain attraction toward her, a sensation he had never experienced before. He could best describe it as a tingling in his lower belly.

Just as Lucas was about to say something to the impassive, freckle-faced girl, the nervous preacher began to recite from a three-ring binder that rested on the pulpit, shrouded in braids of hemp that shimmered in the light from the intense fire. When she noticed that Lucas was about to talk to her, Catherine quickly put her index finger up to her pursed lips.

Most of the recital that followed was mere gibberish to Lucas. The preacher droned on about the virtues of *oneness* and how, "We need no God because we have ourselves for strength." Had Auscan put himself on a higher pedestal than God? "The answer to the mystery of life is within us all. Working together as one body, we can access the power of the universe . . .." On and on, the importance of union and harmony among their "family" was hammered into the heads of the mute congregation. After several minutes that seemed endless, the "sharing of the word" thankfully ceased.

After pausing to catch his breath, the preacher read from a separate piece of paper. Before going to bed, Cassandra had slipped the message into a special announcement box that sat next to the lectern.

"We are pleased to welcome a new member to our great and wholesome family," he began. "A young boy named Lucas has received the endorsement of our great leader. Could you come forward, Lucas, please?"

The congregants turned toward the group of boys. More than one member was shocked to see their latest recruit standing on the opposite side of the room.

The hell with you all was the first thought that came to Lucas as the others stared at him in anticipation. Standing his ground, he refused to budge until a soft, gentle hand touched his arm. The pleasant smile and affirmative nod from Catherine was the only thing that could have changed his mind. Begrudgingly, Lucas stepped forward amid subdued applause.

"Welcome to our family," the stand-in preacher, Colin, announced. His right hand trembled slightly as he held it out toward the disinterested boy. Showing no expression, Lucas refused to accept the handshake. Instead, he turned back toward his place in the congregation.

At that point, infuriated beyond the point of controlling herself, Crystal stepped forward and took Lucas firmly by the arm.

"I'm sure our new member is a little shy, but soon he will come to love us all," she stated with an unpromising tone, her voice shaking with anger as she ushered Lucas to the far end of the boys' line.

Grumbling as he winced from her vise-like grip, he called Crystal a name that would have curled the hair of her deceased mother. Fortunately, she didn't hear it.

As morning prayers ended, a prescribed order was observed for exiting the rustic chapel. The adults filed out first, following each other in a routine fashion. Some went off to do meal preparation. Others had clean-up duties. One woman remained behind to tend to the fire and extinguish the candles. As the boys were closest to the exit, they followed. Waiting patiently, the girls were the last to leave.

"Master Dirk, could you stay behind for a moment?" Crystal asked. "You stay as well, Lucas," she said through clenched teeth as her powerful hand continued to grip his right arm, giving the insolent boy little choice in the matter.

The children returned to their quarters as Dirk approached Lucas for the first time. Only Catherine had the courage to give Lucas a hopeful glance on her way past.

"What can I do for you, Crystal?" Dirk asked.

"This young man has barely joined us, but he already shows a great lack of respect for his superiors." Her face took on a scornful look.

"Yeah, sure, I should respect people who drug me and drag me here to this hellhole?" Lucas said, continuing his defiance.

"You have a poor attitude, young man, but it will change. That I can promise you," Dirk warned as he clamped his enormous hand over the boy's thin shoulder. Lucas could not respond as a searing pain shot across his neck and the back of his head. "I should imagine we will perform a small procedure very shortly. After that, respect will come much easier for you."

Lucas felt a fine spray of saliva as Dirk hissed those final words into his left ear.

His grip was so tight that a trickle of blood began to drip from Lucas's left nostril. As brazen as ever, tears of pain filled his eyes as rage flooded throughout his body. With a distorted face and his jaw clinched tightly shut, his words became slurred. "Not if I can help it, you bas . . .."

Chapter 26

Shivering from his chilly walk from the bus depot, Jarrod continued to stand outside the office door of the small motel he had just discovered. After several seconds, he released the doorbell button. There was no response. Finally, after a second prolonged push on the buzzer, he heard movement behind the locked door. An overhead light came on, a small hand turned up one corner of the curtain that covered the door's narrow window, and two cautious eyes surveyed his face. After a long pause, two deadbolts snapped open, and the door made a groaning noise as it swung inward.

"Sorry . . . you been standing there long? Guess I had the TV too loud . . . watching *Mash,* my favorite show." A sixty-plus woman wearing a fleece housecoat and slippers let Jarrod inside. "I didn't expect anyone to show up tonight," she said apologetically. "It's usually pretty quiet this time of the year."

"I read the bus schedule wrong and missed my connection," Jarrod explained quickly.

"Not the first time. Most of our one-nighters ride the bus. Lots of them have trouble sleeping in those cramped seats—too much bouncing and snoring, they claim," the woman said as she walked toward a desk strewn with advertising for Duluth attractions. A glass bowl was stuffed with a collection of matchbooks and business cards displaying ads from previous tenants. "I don't imagine you'll want a kitchenette?"

"Just a comfortable bed for a little shut-eye," Jarrod replied.

He filled out the registration card as the woman turned to watch the end of her TV show. She showed no concern that he might have wanted to rob her. The name scrawled on the card read "Bill Jackson," with an address in Detroit.

Taking the completed form, the friendly woman smiled, glancing knowingly at the generic name, not unlike previous guests, the Bob Smiths or the Tom Cooks. "Our midweek cash rate is twenty dollars for the night."

"That's fine," Jarrod agreed, returning her smile as he dug into his pocket for the money. "Do you own this place?"

"My husband and I own it. Fred's out of town visiting his ailing mother." She sighed. "Hope he's back soon. I could use a break."

"Do you have a coffee machine?" Jarrod asked. "That walk from the bus station gave me a chill."

"I put on a fresh pot before the show started." She turned toward the twelve-cup coffee maker, which sat on a counter behind the registration desk. The closing credits for *Mash* rolled down the screen in the background.

She handed her new guest a steaming Styrofoam cup of coffee. "They call me Molly. The name may have something to do with all the cleaning I do around here." She grinned. Taking the two ten-dollar bills that had a smell of beer on them, she handed a room key to Jarrod.

"Thanks, Molly." Hoping the woman didn't have another TV show to run off to, he asked, "There's a second-hand store down the street. Do you know when it opens? I could use a warmer jacket . . . maybe some boots."

"My husband donated an old coat just last week." Her regular television programs over, Molly seemed pleased to have someone to talk with. "The place is run by some religious group or colony. They're a strange bunch. Even the children seem to be a bit odd when they come in here every couple of months for donations. They take clothes, books, any old junk, but I won't give them cash. The young ones hang out at malls and street corners with their little wooden boxes, trying to look sad and poor. I think they dress in the clothes donated to them."

"Are they open tomorrow?" Jarrod asked hopefully.

"They're open on weekends for sure, but during the week, you never know when the place is open. You'll just have to check for yourself."

"I thought that I saw a tall woman leaving the store," Jarrod continued casually, attempting to get more information. He recalled Crusty's brief description. "She had long black hair."

"I know who you mean. That woman gives me the creeps. Her hairstyle, color, her whole appearance, it always seems to be changing. Just last month she was a curly blond. But her eyes, there's something about her eyes . . . it's like you can't pull away. You're mesmerized if you make eye contact. I stay away from her altogether."

Normally, Molly wouldn't get into a conversation with her guests until she got to know them, but she felt compelled to answer Jarrod's questions. And besides, she was lonely for some company.

"Thanks for your help," Jarrod said, taking the room key from Molly. "I'll let you know in the morning if I'm staying longer."

"You mean you might miss another bus, Bill Jackson?" Molly asked with a wry grin. She was enjoying the chat with her latest guest. There was something out of the ordinary about him, a sense of awareness and intelligence that she seldom saw in other guests. A certain aura hung over Mr. Jackson that she couldn't explain.

"You just never know," Jarrod replied, returning a smile that was more dejected than reassuring.

"Well, don't even think about getting fresh," she continued jokingly. "There's a big trucker who stays in the room right behind that wall—"

"I hope you're kidding."

"I'm known as a bit of a joker. Have a good evening," Molly said sheepishly, retreating to her living quarters as Jarrod walked down the hallway toward his room.

The following morning brought a break in the weather. The sky was clear, and an overnight south breeze made the air temperature bearable. Jarrod suspected he'd be spending another night and left his new travel bag in his room. Walking past the Mount Cloquet shop on his way to breakfast, he noticed the "Closed" sign still hung in the window. How long would he have to wait before the place showed any signs of activity?

After an invigorating walk and a leisurely breakfast of pancakes and bacon, Jarrod made his way back to Molly's motel just after noon. With unfinished business ahead of him, he planned to pay for another night's stay. Although catching the next bus out of town would have been the smart thing to do, he could not make himself leave. He was sure that the secret to finding Lucas hid behind the thrift shop's locked doors. He was more determined than ever to discover what those people were up to and what interest they had in his young friend.

Passing the front of the thrift shop once again, Jarrod decided to take a closer look through the window. He squinted through tinted glass that was smudged with fingerprints and road dust. His timing was perfect. A sudden flash of light coming from the right rear corner of the store caught his attention. At first, he thought that a light had been turned on and off, but then he realized that the rear door had opened and closed. Backing away from the window, he expected the lights to come on as someone approached the front door to unlock it. But nothing happened; the store remained in darkness. After more than a minute, Jarrod decided to peek once again into the shop, trying to keep himself hidden behind a cardboard box that blocked part of the window.

Although the interior was still dark, he detected the faint outline of a pair of shadowy figures standing next to the rear entrance. Two men were barely illuminated by the glowing embers of what Jarrod assumed to be a cigarette. His mind changed when the cigarette was passed from one person to the next. The glow was brighter and longer this time, exposing the rugged faces of two men that he would prefer not to meet face to face, especially in a dark alley. At that point, it was clear to Jarrod that more went on in the shop than selling second-hand clothes.

If what he was witnessing was some form of drug deal or negotiation, then Jarrod would have been wise to stay well away from the place, but if those people were involved in kidnapping Lucas, he had to find out as much as he could. Squeezing through a small passageway between two brick buildings, Jarrod made his way into a narrow alley behind the row of stores that included the thrift shop. Coming into view at the rear of the second-hand store were two parked vehicles—a short, mud-covered, army-style Jeep and a larger black luxury car that was in a much cleaner condition.

Hiding behind a bulky, graffiti-covered metal refuse bin that could only be raised by the forks of a specialized truck, Jarrod watched with interest as both men came out from the rear of the shop. Each of them glanced suspiciously around the alley before shaking hands and getting into separate vehicles. The man who got into the luxury car wore a dark trench coat and carried a large package wrapped in brown paper under his arm. The other man, who accelerated at high speed up the lane in his Jeep, had a more unkempt appearance and seemed anxious, his eyes darting in every direction. Jarrod would never have guessed that the man was the revered leader of a secret and thriving society.

Moments later, Jarrod's pace was rapid as he returned to his motel.

"Good afternoon, Bill Jackson," Molly said, displaying her usual smile as she almost collided with him as he opened the motel's front door. The deadbolts were not fastened during the daytime. Her arms were piled with bedding on its way to the wash. “Hope I didn’t spook you last night. Just having a little fun. I’m always claiming he’s a pain in the ass, but I miss Fred’s company.”

“No problem. I’m usually good at taking a joke, but I think life has been too serious for me the last while.” Jarrod was still uneasy from his encounter at the thrift shop. “I’ll pay for another night. I’m still not ready for a long bus ride.”

“Did you find that coat you wanted?”

“Not yet; that shop’s still closed.”

Jarrod sensed that Molly might know more about the people who ran the shop than she let on.

“You were saying the kids from that religious colony, or whatever you called it, were kind of odd. Did they seem unhappy to you?”

Shuffling her feet as she hauled her load of laundry, Molly appeared to wonder why her guest had such an interest in the thrift shop, but she seemed to be in a talkative mood. “The smiles of those kids don’t seem real. Even the adults around that place act pretty strange. They claim to be a religious order of some kind, even have a license. Those children don’t go to any regular school. They’re taught at home on some farm. It can’t be too far from town.” She paused for a moment, eyeing Bill Jackson curiously. “How come you’ve got such an interest in these people?”

“It’s a long story . . . don’t know if I can tell you right now,” Jarrod explained reluctantly. “I think there’s more to that store than selling used clothing and books. If I ever get to the bottom of it, you’ll be the first to know.”

“What are you, an undercover agent?” Molly asked, a touch of anxiety in her voice.

"You couldn't be further from the truth," Jarrod replied, unable to restrain a grin.

"There's something about you. You're not the usual drifter from one job to the next that we normally get here," she confessed.

"My past isn't all that pretty."

"Like I couldn't figure that out," Molly deadpanned.

"One other thing, have you run across a fellow named Crusty, a street person?" Jarrod asked.

"He's a well-known character," she replied, "a harmless old guy. I don't mind giving him a handout now and then."

"I talked to him last night. He seems to use that store quite a bit, gets his clothes there. I'm not sure what my point is, but he was helpful to me. I would appreciate it if you kept your eye out for him. He could freeze in the winter if . . .." Jarrod's voice trailed off as he wondered why he had even brought up the subject.

"Don't worry. Twice a week I serve soup and sandwiches at the drop-in center. I know about the problems homeless guys have, women, too. It's a sad life sometimes, but many of those people prefer life on the street. Lots are loners. They don't like rules, they don't like routine, and keeping a steady job is out of the question."

Molly found herself talking even more than usual. She could sense a caring in Jarrod that many humans, especially men, had difficulty exhibiting. She could only guess that the trait had been passed on by his parents or whoever brought him up. Would she ever get to know more about this tall stranger and his endearing qualities? Even in her own little fantasy world, she had her doubts. Yet her eyes could not help but follow him as he wandered slowly down the hallway toward his room.

Chapter 27

In the army or at summer camp, they would have called it the mess hall. At the Mount Cloquet commune, it was referred to as the dining lodge. It was a separate building, constructed with logs and mortar, its sloped roof covered with various shades of surplus asphalt shingles that a construction company had discarded. The eating area was sparsely furnished, containing five long tables with wooden benches that were not only uncomfortable but also quite unstable. The simple kitchen included two stoves and a large oven used mainly for baking bread and rolls, which frequently came out dark and crusty. The cast-iron stove was fueled with wood, the other stove with propane from a two-hundred-pound tank propped up against the outside of the building.

The cooks had prepared an enormous pot of hot oatmeal, which was served with bread, some loaves warm from the oven, and others left over from the previous day. Little food went to waste. A pale white liquid they called "milk," in addition to a granular, brown sugar, complemented the hot cereal. The adults mingled at two of the eating tables, but the children remained segregated, boys at one table and girls at another. As was the unwritten rule, conversation was kept to a minimum. Almost everyone present was eagerly devouring their hearty breakfast.

Catherine was a slow eater and looked up expectantly when Lucas was led into the dining lodge, a hand gripping his upper left arm. Most of the others had almost finished their meal. As the door opened, the noisy muffler of a Jeep could be heard as the vehicle retreated down the slippery driveway. Lucas was rudely placed at the far end of a bench, at the table reserved for the boys. Catherine noticed the dark smudge under his nose.

"Enjoy your first meal with your new family," Crystal snarled through curled lips. She released her vice-like grip. Feeling hot and agitated from the harsh treatment he had just received, Lucas pulled off his jacket. He was wearing a T-shirt, and one of his sleeveless arms displayed deep-purplish finger-sized bruises. Although a trace of dried blood was still visible on his upper lip, the other children pretended not to notice.

Still grimacing from Dirk's powerful grip, Lucas remained silent. He was served his morning meal just as most of the others were returning their dirty bowls to the kitchen. Crystal and Dirk ate at the adult table but kept a watchful eye on the disrespectful newcomer. Should he make the slightest wrong movement, they were ready to pounce.

Even though his shoulder and arm ached, Lucas was determined to get a message to Catherine. As the children filed past him, the matron's view was blocked, and Dirk was busy with his meal.

"Can I talk to you this afternoon?" Lucas whispered. "Try to get away from the other girls."

Catherine realized he was talking to her. Only she and one or two other girls could hear his low voice. She acknowledged his words without turning her body, making an "okay" signal with her thumb and index finger as she continued walking. Lucas understood.

The children, and everyone else not involved in clean-up duty, had left the dining lodge when Crystal spoke once again. "Well, young man, I hope that a nourishing meal has changed your attitude. I received word that Miss Cass would like to see you at her cottage. Here, wipe your face with this." She handed Lucas a damp cloth. "No need to concern her with a little dried blood."

Fearful of saying something that might cause him more pain, Lucas did as he was asked and remained silent. Words and actions would come later.

"Dirk, will you check that all the children are preparing for today's lessons?" Crystal asked. "I'll take care of Lucas."

"Certainly, Crystal," Dirk said. "Sometimes it takes a little pain to learn how we respect one another around here." As he made the absurd statement that contradicted itself, his eyes shot a warning as he stared directly at Lucas, who refused to make eye contact. If Dirk only knew his problems were just beginning.

After finishing a small portion of his stodgy oatmeal and leftover bread, Lucas walked ahead of the matron as they made their way to the cramped yet well-maintained cabin he had visited the previous night. He sensed a nervousness in Crystal.

"No need to take your coat off," she said. "We'll only be in there a few minutes."

"You wished to see young Lucas," Crystal said as Cassandra opened her cabin door. "He's been quite a handful already." She spoke with some trepidation in her voice.

Much to Crystal's chagrin, Lucas shed his jacket at the doorway and threw it on a nearby chair. Cassandra couldn't help but notice the recent bruises.

"This boy was so much trouble that you had to do this?" Cassandra asked, her voice scathing. "He didn't appear to be very dangerous when I left him with you last night."

"Well, Miss Cass—"

"Is Dirk involved in this? Sometimes the two of you get carried away," Cassandra continued. "Our leader is to meet the boy this afternoon. What will he say?"

"But . . . he wouldn't listen . . . showed no respect," Crystal stuttered. Uneasiness from the sudden admonishment showed in her eyes.

"Auscan and I were considering—" Cassandra stopped herself. For the moment, she would keep their plans to herself. "I'll talk to you and Dirk later. Right now, go back and help with the lessons. I'll return Lucas to the classroom as soon as we're through."

"Yes, Miss Cass," Crystal replied, her voice quivering. Opening the door to leave, she shot one last glare toward Lucas. Was it a warning, a threat, or both?

"My husband and I had a long talk last night," Cassandra began as the door slammed shut. "Please sit down." Touching Lucas's left shoulder, she pulled back when he flinched in pain. "What else have those two done to you?"

"Well . . ." Lucas began, sensing the opportunity for sympathy, "they didn't like where I stood during prayers, and I wouldn't shake hands. They kept talking about respect, but they sure as hell don't give much of it."

"We have rules, Lucas. Our children are taught to listen and to behave. Acting like a rebel is unacceptable, but sometimes those two can carry punishment to an extreme."

Pausing for consideration, she decided to postpone the mandatory operation that was planned for Lucas. It was apparent he had been put through enough discipline for one day. "My husband would like to meet you this afternoon. He had an errand to run, but we had a discussion about your future. I can see that the two of you are alike in many ways—"

"You think I like the smell of that stuff he was smoking?" Lucas interrupted. "I didn't ask to come to this damn place. What did you do, drug me? Then you all dragged me here. All you want to do is control these freakin' people, and nobody says nothin.' Except for maybe one, they're all a bunch of mindless goofs."

"That may be your opinion, Lucas," Cassandra said, trying to calm his rebellious attitude, "but you haven't gotten to know us. We are one big happy family. We really do care and look out for one another."

"Tell that to my shoulder." Lucas shuddered, wondering what he could expect when Dirk got hold of him the next time.

"Should my husband decide that you are a worthy brother for our four beautiful daughters, then things will be different. There will be a new place for you to sleep. You will take your lessons and prayers with the others, but your duties and responsibilities will be different. In town, the younger children need someone they can look up to, a person to lead them, to encourage them to work hard with their collections. That person could be you someday. My husband and I have much to offer." As encouraging as Cassandra tried to sound, she still sensed defiance and a stubborn resolve in Lucas that would be difficult to overcome.

Lucas didn't take long to reply. "Anywhere away from those two creeps would be better," he said, referring to Crystal and Dirk. "This guy, they called him Auscan, is he 'the man' around here? Everyone treats him like he's some sort of god. I guess I'll see for myself when he gets back."

Cassandra was relieved to see the boy showed at least some interest in going along with her latest proposal. Yet, deep down, she sensed he might be more of a danger than an asset.

"I can tell that you held little respect for adults in your past. Yet you show the character of one who can take charge and may grow up to be very much like my partner, a true leader." Hoping to promote a better attitude, Cassandra focused on the positives. Beneath the compelling garishness of her appearance, her mesmerizing eyes and slithering legs, she bore a natural insight and intelligence that only her husband could appreciate. It was unlikely that Auscan could even function without her close alliance. Truly, much of her outward bravado and swagger was merely an act.

"Is it alright if I stay here until he gets back? My shoulder's really sore. I don't think I can sit through lessons today,"

Lucas said with the art of every convincing youngster trying to skip out of school.

"I suppose for today we can make an exception, but our rules are strict. Children almost never miss their lessons. Education is important." As strange as it may seem, Cassandra found herself compelled to follow his wishes.

Education for what, being stupid? Lucas wondered.

Leading her prospective son into the den, where embers from a late-night fire still smoldered in the fireplace, Cassandra went to prepare a light lunch for her husband. Seldom did either of them eat the bland food in the dining lodge.

Entering the small den, Lucas was greeted by an odor that spread through the walls and rustic furniture. Although burnt incense sticks protruded from cracks in the stone fireplace, their fragrance failed to mask an aroma that was neither sweet nor pungent, more so hinting at the odor of special pipe tobaccos. Older boys in one of his group homes had experimented with drugs, even passing their smoldering joint around to the younger kids, mainly to keep them from talking. His one attempt at inhaling the smoke had left Lucas with a coughing fit, his lungs burning. He never tried it again, but he would always remember the aroma.

Two elaborate pipes chiseled from a patterned stone, likely marble or onyx, rested on a short oblong table. Their bowls, turned black from daily use, had round, thin wire screens pressed into them. The pipes leaned upright against an old coffee can that was partially filled with sand. The can overflowed with the burnt remains of twigs, buds, and seeds.

Scattered about the room were notepads and sketchbooks, a few sitting open to expose grotesque, wild-looking beasts with prehistoric heads, scale-covered bodies, and long curled tails. Some doodles and sketches were cartoon-like, others gruesome and threatening.

"Was I supposed to see these drawings?" Lucas asked himself. Could they be some sort of warning to him? Having scrawled similar cartoon figures as he sat through boring math classes, he found them amusing. Just as he was about to browse through one of the older, more-yellowed drawing books, Cassandra stuck her head into the den.

"My husband likes to put his thoughts down on paper. He is very creative and believes that our innermost feelings can be expressed through drawings," she explained, appearing not unhappy that Lucas had discovered the sketchbooks.

"He did all these?" Lucas asked, wondering what really went on in the community leader's mind. Did he fantasize the grotesque creatures had human qualities?

"Yes, those are all his. I have many expressions of my own thoughts, some in poetry and others in the form of art. But mine are not so elaborate, and I keep them out of sight. Auscan doesn't mind sharing his artwork with others. He is very clever in using his drawing skills." Cassandra spoke with obvious admiration, but her look was quizzical, as if she questioned why she was revealing her thoughts to a youngster she barely knew.

Lucas shuddered. He could not imagine life with those two as his parents.

Cassandra went off to continue her chores. Left alone once again in the den, it wasn't long before Lucas focused his mind on how he could meet with Catherine away from the others. He had so many questions he wanted to ask. Should he take the chance and slip out now or wait for his meeting with Auscan, the great leader, the man who may want to adopt him? There wasn't a chance in hell of that happening. The offer of him being given an important role in the community was no temptation. All he longed for was a way to escape that place.

It was evident that Auscan didn't welcome many people into his personal sanctum, rejecting help from others for even menial chores, including cleaning. Cassandra doted on her husband as if under a spell. In addition to raising money in town, running the thrift store, and recruiting new members, she was expected to perform all the housekeeping duties in their cottage, not to mention meal preparation. She had little time to spend with her daughters, who boarded with the other girls and shared in all the children's tasks. Yet she was offering special treatment to Lucas. Like the bond with her husband, the boy had a trait that she found intriguing. Yet she either chose to ignore, or even believe he was an imminent danger to her community.

Bored from the long wait, and starting to become dizzy from the nauseating odor that wafted throughout the den, Lucas glanced out the only window in the log wall just in time to notice movement outside the teaching lodge. The children appeared to be on a break, wandering aimlessly in an area that would have been a playground had there been any balls, nets, or structures on which to play. None of them were smiling. They reminded Lucas of the child zombies he had seen wandering through a cornfield in an old horror movie. Even though the way his own life was going had little chance of success, at least he had some control over it. What choices did those kids have? What chance did they have when their every move was programmed or controlled?

Just then, his roving eyes spotted Catherine. He did not hesitate to seize the opportunity. While Cassandra was busy cleaning up in the bedroom she shared with her husband, Lucas snuck out the front door, careful to close it behind him. Slipping into the shadows of some burly oak trees, it took him barely a moment to intercept Catherine, who was walking toward the girls' residence.

"Hey!" Lucas called. "Come over here. Quick, quick!" He motioned to her as he knelt in a shaded area between a gnarled oak and an enclosure containing lengths of firewood waiting to be chopped.

Stepping toward the shadows, Catherine was clearly on edge. "They're going to notice if I fall behind," she whispered. "The girls won't say anything, but Dirk, he'll be waiting. I know he must have hurt you this morning."

"I've had worse done to me," Lucas replied bravely. "When can we talk? I've got lots of questions about what's going on at this place."

"About an hour after classes," Catherine answered timidly, "Dirk gets together with a couple of the adults. I think they drink some liquor, because his face is red when he comes to eat. Some days he's meaner than others. Sometimes he's happy and jokes with the girls." She glanced toward her cottage. "I've got to go. I'll try to meet you about half an hour before dinner. This is a good spot but behind the woodshed."

"Okay, but don't get into trouble because of me," Lucas replied, showing his concern. He felt that strange feeling again in the pit of his stomach. His heart fluttered as Catherine turned to leave.

"I've got to get back to that old witch," he said. "See you later."

The youngsters parted quickly before anyone except a couple of the girls noticed anything unusual. Fortunately, neither was a daughter of the esteemed leaders.

Lucas got lucky. He returned to the den just as Cassandra came out of the bedroom carrying a bundle of bedding and clothes that she had gathered for wash day. He had only been gone for a few minutes.

"Did you have a look at Auscan's library?" she asked, poking her head into the den once again. "He has an interesting assortment of books."

"I saw some books on gardening, plants, and hydropontifix or something," he replied, huffing slightly. "The smell in this room, that's the same stuff I smelled last night, isn't it? It sure didn't come from the fireplace. That smell kind of burns my nose. It even makes my chest feel funny."

Although Lucas had mentioned the odd smell before, Cassandra was slow with her response. "Oh . . . Auscan likes to mix his own tobacco. He has some special blend. I'm used to it and don't even notice the smell anymore."

Nice recovery, Lucas thought sarcastically. *I'm sure you don't know the mixture he smokes.* Without flinching, he stared fearlessly into Cassandra's strange green eyes.

In a weird way, the tables seemed to turn when Lucas's steady glare made Cassandra uncomfortable. Even her eyes lost their hypnotic glow. She turned away quickly as she continued gathering towels and articles for the wash. "I've got to get these things over to the wash building. I'll be back in a few minutes. Auscan should be returning shortly."

Cassandra's nervous reaction was the first sign that Lucas had seen of any vulnerability in her. His confidence seemed to upset her. As his curiosity increased, he used the opportunity of her leaving the cottage to conduct a further search of the den. Of particular interest was a square wooden cupboard built into the wall to the right of the fireplace. The cupboard doors were stained with water marks and the soot from countless fires. Smudged across their surface was a random array of fingerprints, most likely from the same person. A tiny unlocked padlock dangled from the latch. Auscan was either careless or unconcerned that someone might look behind those well-worn doors.

The cupboard doors swung open easily on their tiny brass hinges. On three wide shelves set into the wall, Lucas discovered a stockpile of paraphernalia that could only relate to the drug trade. On full display was a set of miniature scales, plastic bags, one tin containing seeds and another filled with plant buds that gave off a pungent odor. There was even a strange pipe with a center compartment filled with water or some other liquid. Surely the padlock was meant to be latched. It was quite obvious that Auscan did more around the commune than grow vegetables and lead his followers in prayers.

Carefully closing the smudged doors, Lucas left the tiny lock hanging just as he had found it. Then, to his surprise, as he was turning around, his foot caught against the edge of a rough log that protruded slightly just above the floor and directly beneath the cupboard. Curiosity made him bend down. Grabbing hold of the loose board, he tugged with all his strength. To his amazement, a square section of the log slid out from its camouflage at the base of the false wall, giving access to a narrow alcove. Inside the opening sat an oblong metal chest. It appeared to be solid and heavy, which Lucas confirmed when he tried to slide it out from the niche in the wall. He remembered a similar chest where one of his foster parents had stored old coins and documents. A combination lock protruding from the hinged top protected the contents from intruders.

Was that where Auscan hid the proceeds from his drug dealings? Was Lucas being set up? Did they expect him to snoop around in that room and have another excuse to discipline him? Or did Cassandra even know the chest existed? Many thoughts raced through his puzzled mind as Lucas hurried to position the sliding door back into the opening. Just as his knees had almost pushed the panel into place, and as only keen, young eyes might even notice, the room seemed to darken ever so slightly. Turning his head quickly, Lucas was sure that he saw a shadow—or was it a head?—move away from the only window that allowed light into the somber den. Was his imagination running wild? Whatever the case, Lucas had seen more than enough and would spend the remainder of his wait in a padded chair next to the smoldering remains of the previous evening's fire.

It turned out that he hadn't long to wait. The cabin door creaked open only minutes later. The noise jarred Lucas to attention. Was it the shadowy figure that had passed by the window? The answer to that mystery would have to wait. Right now, both illustrious leaders of the commune entered the cottage together.

"Are you there, Lucas?" Cassandra asked gently. "There's someone here who would like to meet you."

"Yeah, I'm still here," he replied. "Where would I go?"

Auscan frowned when he discovered the boy sitting in the room he considered to be his private sanctuary. He glanced involuntarily to the right side of the fireplace. Nothing appeared to be out of place. He turned back to Lucas.

"Well, young man—Lucas, I believe your name is—welcome to our family."

Lucas wasn't about to stand up and take the hand offered to him by the wiry man with the hooked nose and furrowed face who stood before him. "You know, it wasn't my idea to come to your little farm," Lucas stately firmly, still seated in his chair. "I was drugged and kidnapped. Is that how you got all these kids here?"

Now that it was her husband's turn to deal with explanations, Cassandra gladly left the room on the pretence of completing her laundry chores. Auscan could find out for himself the defiance and stubbornness that embodied their latest recruit.

"Of course we don't drug the children who choose to become part of our wholesome life, a life far better than their previous existence. We are simply one complete and happy family who prays to our own God together, looks out for each other, and does everything for the good of all our members." His words mimicked those of all the others around the commune. Although his voice was steady, he began to pace.

"Same old crap everyone in charge around here tells me," Lucas replied, his voice rising. "Nobody around here says squat. It's like they have no minds. What do you do, hypnotize them all?"

"You will learn someday that we are at peace with our lives here. There is nothing to fear from our past, and our future is protected. No one can harm us," Auscan continued, frowning. As a salesman, he had found a tough sell.

"How do you explain these nice little marks from your caring family?" Lucas asked, pointing to the bruises on his arm and neck.

"You are fighting the system, young man. We must work together as a united body. One person cannot cause disharmony. Disobedience will not be tolerated." Auscan reverted to his previous role of a persuasive preacher. "We can offer you a great life here. In time, you can become a part of our inner family."

"You're not convincing me with all this garbage. This life isn't for me, thanks," Lucas said, as defiant as ever.

"I'm afraid that once you have entered our commune as a child, you have joined our family. Without earning our trust, you can never leave, even to go to town. The few who have tried found they would sadly regret their decision," Auscan warned, his voice becoming acidic. His face strained to the verge of contortion as he struggled to control his growing anger. Was he morphing into one of the creatures portrayed in his sketches?

Realizing he might have to put his escape plans on hold, Lucas had thought over his response while waiting alone in the den. Concerned about the anger he had aroused, he realized it was time to change his tone. There was a long pause while both he and Auscan calmed themselves, allowing their heart rates to settle down. As a start to his newest scheme, Lucas embraced a condescending approach, not the first time he had a change of heart.

"Well, sir, maybe I could try to change, try to see how your family works. Your wife said she might have some responsibilities for me, maybe watching out for the younger children."

Lucas noticed the rather skeptical look he received from the sudden change in his attitude. The vaunted leader appeared to develop a sudden urge for his special mixture of tobacco. "Trust and responsibility must be earned. In time, there will be many opportunities awaiting you. But first you must learn the ways of our community and how to fit in among us. Do you understand?"

"I'd like to try, but I'm sure I'll need help to change," Lucas said, attempting to sound convincing. "Miss Cass said I might be able to stay somewhere different, someplace away from the other boys."

"That won't happen right away. Remember what I said: First, you must earn our trust. Only then can we make changes. It's apparent that Matron Crystal has not become your best friend. Both she and Dirk demand respect from all the children. There can be no exceptions." Auscan checked to see if his wife was returning. Was he getting hunger pangs, or did he simply crave some privacy so he could take a relaxing drag from his special pipe?

"A little late to tell me that," Lucas whispered. He recognized the power Auscan held over the others. As a leader, he was convincing and surely believed everything he said. Lucas could see why his followers were so loyal to him, but he still didn't plan to stick around long enough to earn his respect.

Auscan, on the other hand, realized that perhaps his wife was right. Lucas did possess some of his own characteristics, yet could they ever form a father/son relationship? Just then, Cassandra returned to the cottage with the dried washing.

"Since you missed lunch with the others, Lucas, you can enjoy a sandwich in our kitchen," Auscan said. "Then you must join the other children for afternoon classes."

"But Miss Cass said—"

"Remember, young man, around here you do as you are told. Understand?" His voice left no room for negotiation. "Now please go to the kitchen. Tell my wife I will be there shortly."

Lucas left the den without further comment as the door closed firmly behind him.

Twenty minutes later, his eyes glazed from a lengthy session with his ornate pipe, Auscan emerged from his sanctuary. His body moved slowly as he tried to organize the disjointed thoughts that swam in his head. When he gradually settled into the lunch his wife had prepared, Lucas had already left reluctantly for afternoon classes.

Cassandra knew better than to ask questions. Her husband would talk when he was ready.

Chapter 28

Jarrod was unable to sit in his motel room for long. By midafternoon he was walking past the thrift shop once again. The place remained dark inside, convincing Jarrod it wouldn't be opening that day. Reflecting on his conversation with Molly, he wasted some time wandering along the busy streets, even stopping to explore a downtown park. The sun's warmth rekindled his spirit, igniting a spark that only hope could keep alive.

While trying to focus his energy in one direction, he became increasingly determined to locate the community where the religious group resided. Since the thrift shop could provide no answers just now, he reasoned that neighboring businesses might offer some help. After a cursory look around the area, Jarrod decided that a small bakery on the street corner less than half a block from the thrift shop might be a good place to start.

Entering Murray's Bakery, he set off a buzzing noise that attracted the attention of a young woman adjusting the oven temperature in a room at the back. She walked quickly to the front of the shop, her hair tucked under a white baseball cap and a tray of warm, unsliced bread in her hands. The aroma of the fresh loaves brought saliva to Jarrod's mouth.

"Hi, haven't seen you in here before," the young woman said pleasantly. "We mostly just get regulars." Her bright even teeth gave her an attractive smile.

"I'm just passing through town. Been staying at Molly and Fred's motel up the road," Jarrod began, hoping to gain the confidence of Bonnie, the name on the tag pinned to her apron. Her "whites," as bakers tended to call their uniforms, showed numerous stains, some from the edges of hot trays and others from the toppings added to sweet desserts.

"I was hoping to buy a winter coat from that second-hand store across the street, but it never seems to be open."

"No surprise. They do most of their business on weekends. During the week, it's pretty hit and miss," Bonnie explained as she slid the fresh loaves onto a display shelf behind the counter. "How's Molly doing? She's been running that place on her own. Fred's been gone for a couple of weeks now."

Pleased that he had started off on the right foot, Jarrod grinned. "Well, she's quite a feisty gal, likes to joke around when she's not complaining about the extra work."

"That's Molly, all right, always the funny one. She'll be in here tomorrow," Bonnie said, turning to face the tall stranger. "She picks up a bunch of our day-old stuff to serve at the shelter. There's nothing wrong with it, but our regulars want everything super-fresh."

"Do they have any good buys at that thrift shop?" Jarrod asked, taking a sample slice of a fresh croissant that Bonnie offered him.

"You have to barter a bit with them, but I get good deals for me and my two kids. We're on our own, and this job doesn't pay much, so I can't afford all those brand names the kids want." Bonnie seemed like she enjoyed chatting, but she had trouble making eye contact with her new customer. Or was he one?

Jarrod sensed her uneasiness. "I'll get one of those fresh loaves. I can't resist the smell." After a brief pause, he continued. "Talking about kids, I saw some strange ones at the bus depot when I came into town. They acted like robots, just stood around with glassy-eyed stares and asked for money. Do they belong to some kind of fundraising group?"

Bonnie nodded as she bagged his bread and rang up the sale. "I know who you mean. Those children belong to the group that runs the shop you're interested in. They act like they've been schooled in begging. The kids usually look tired. They always act pleasant, but they don't really show much interest in what they're doing."

"Have you been in the shop recently?" Jarrod asked as he paid for his bread.

"I tried to go in after work a couple of nights ago, but they'd just flipped their 'Closed' sign and wouldn't let me in. The woman who seems to run the operation, I've heard them call her Miss Cass, was returning with some of the children who hang around malls and street corners with their collection boxes."

With most of her work done and no new customers, Bonnie seemed relaxed and open to conversation. "There was a lot of talk about that group a few years back. People were worried those kids might have been abused and weren't getting an education. Apparently, some state agency checked out everything. Nothing bad ever came out, and there's not much talk about them anymore."

Hoping for a few more minutes alone in the store, Jarrod still had questions. "Did you happen to see anyone new in that group the other night, someone you didn't recognize?"

After thinking briefly, Bonnie nodded. "Come to think of it, there was a thin boy I hadn't seen before. He looked hungry and a little confused."

Jarrod hesitated for a moment, his pulse racing and his mind not knowing how to continue. Seeing someone approaching the bakery, his words flowed quickly. "I've got to locate that boy. He's sick, and I've got medication for him. We were traveling together but got separated. Those people, whoever they are, must have either grabbed him from the bus station or convinced him to go with them. He's too bright a kid to just walk away with a group of strangers."

As a regular customer entered the store, Bonnie spoke quickly, her voice low. "My son's teacher knows a little about the group. They claim to be a religious order and live somewhere in the hills north of town. I'm going to a parent/teacher meeting at the school tonight. I'll see what info I can get from the teacher and talk to you tomorrow—if you come back here, that is."

Jarrod gave Bonnie a quick nod, thanking her for the bread as he brushed past a portly man whose eyes were focused on the creamy desserts.

Remembering a local deli that he had passed during his afternoon walk, Jarrod retraced his route and purchased some meat slices and cheese so he could make himself a sandwich or two. He had a renewed determination in his step as he approached his motel. It was time to quiz Molly once again.

Slipping quietly into the lobby, Jarrod spotted her watching a game show in the back room. Her television showed a wheel spinning to the loud applause of a live audience. She sipped from a stemmed glass, which Jarrod suspected to contain red wine.

"Hey, Molly, have you got a knife that I can borrow?" he said loud enough to be heard over the game show host.

"How do you always manage to interrupt my favorite shows, Mr. Jackson?" Molly said with her usual chuckle as she came to the front desk. She left her glass in the TV room.

"I couldn't resist this fresh bread, but I've got nothing to cut it with."

"It so happens that I keep this trusty weapon under the counter. I figure that maybe I could scare off some thief with it. Luckily, the situation has never come up," Molly said with a dry laugh. She handed him a serrated bread knife. "You might want to clean it off."

"Thanks, that'll do fine," Jarrod replied. "Bonnie, the girl at the bakery, told me to say hello. She expects to see you in the shop tomorrow."

"She's a sweet girl, does a great job with those kids of hers. I'm sure she has trouble making ends meet." If Molly hadn't forgotten her television program yet, she was about to when Bill Jackson began to reveal some of his past.

Jarrod began slowly, "Bonnie buys clothes for her family from that second-hand store across from the bakery. You talked about that place the other night—"

Molly interrupted quickly, as if she had to speak her mind. "Why don't you tell me your real interest in that store? I know it's not just for a pair of boots."

After hesitating for a moment, Jarrod confessed. "I'm convinced that those people kidnapped a friend of mine, a young boy. He was sick when we were separated a few days ago. He's a street-smart kid, so I figure that woman, Bonnie called her Miss Cass, must have taken advantage of his weak condition." Although out of character, it was the second time in an hour that Jarrod had opened up to someone.

"I figured there was more than just missing a bus that kept you around here," Molly admitted, her face showing interest. "How long have you known the boy?"

"Actually, we met by chance less than a week ago. Both of us were running from pasts that weren't very pretty, and we helped each other out of a couple of bad situations. He took sick, and we got separated. It's a long story, but I'm worried about his health," Jarrod explained, his voice low and his uneasiness noticeable.

Any concern that she was dealing with a criminal did not enter Molly's mind. She had always gone by her gut feeling, which told her Jarrod was in no way threatening. She wouldn't have cared if he was a jailhouse escapee. There was no hint of him being a danger to her or the boy he was searching for.

"Sounds like you've both lost an important friend," Molly said in a sympathetic tone, turning away briefly to hide her emotional reaction. She sniffled briefly. "I told you before those people running that store are some religious fanatics. They're forever collecting donations and cash wherever the law allows them. Rumor has it they recruit adults and runaway kids, basically people who are down and out. Some likely suffered from abusive relationships. Others probably just had no one in their lives. I've heard that these people get indoctrinated into their system. The group seems to be legitimate. When it's open, the store is a popular place."

"I understand that the children don't seem to act like normal kids. Did you notice anything unusual?" Jarrod asked.

"I know what you mean. They never show much enthusiasm and don't seem to have any personality. It's like they're being controlled in some way or brainwashed not to think for themselves." After collecting her thoughts, Molly continued. "But I recall one girl who has come in here a few times for donations of clothes. I've seen a sparkle in her eyes, and she's tried to start a conversation a couple of times. But the girls with her always interrupt and won't let her continue, like they're worried about something. I think they called her Cath. I get the feeling there's a bright personality buried by the environment she lives in."

"Looks like I'll have to wait until Saturday to find out for myself. The store should be open by then." Jarrod decided not to mention the other activities he suspected were happening at the thrift shop. "Maybe I should pay you for another night."

"Don't worry, a couple of nights more, and you qualify for the weekly rate." Molly couldn't help but laugh. "By the way, my friend from the police department will be dropping by soon."

The grin that crossed Jarrod's face disappeared.

"When Fred's away, he likes to check up on me once in a while. I give him a beer on his way home from work, so there's no rush in returning the knife." She must have noticed her guest flinch slightly.

"Thanks, Molly. Don't worry, you won't get any problems from me," Jarrod promised as he turned toward his room.

Molly noticed a slight tremble in Jarrod's hands as well as a wobble to his knees when he walked away. She chose to ignore the unmistakable evidence that her unnerved guest was a fugitive from the law. Her curiosity piqued, Molly began to think that maybe she was wrong. Instead of not getting to know more about her latest guest, she was about to become immersed in the complex life of this intriguing stranger with the obvious alias. Here was a person, likely a fugitive, who really seemed to care about the lives of others, homeless people and children alike. She imagined a real-life soap opera was about to unfold.

Chapter 29

Although not happy about it, Lucas entered the building that served as a classroom for the children as well as a study or reading area for the adults. Over twenty boys and girls were seated on an assortment of chairs, some wooden and some with metal frames. No two were alike. The chairs were likely received as donations or salvaged from the garbage dump. Writing desks had been assembled from rough, oddly matched pieces of plywood, their surfaces sanded and coated with layers of clear varnish. The presence of many more windows than were in the other buildings meant that lighting was much brighter in the classroom. Several bare, low-wattage lightbulbs dangled from wires that sagged between a series of wooden support beams. Put into operation only on the darkest of days, the bulbs were powered by an inverter connected to a twelve-volt battery system. A gas-powered generator sitting outside the building was used to recharge the system whenever necessary.

Florence, who was arranging a picture display of various mushrooms at the front of the class, greeted the new student. "Good afternoon, Lucas, welcome to our classroom. We have prepared a desk for you next to Peter. Please be seated."

Grunting a reply, Lucas noticed that the boys and girls were separated once again. Catherine was seated three rows to his left. Passing a note would be nearly impossible. The teacher was a woman named Val, who was making a series of hand gestures or signals toward a girl in the first row. Lucas realized that the youngster was deaf, and the teacher was using sign language.

Moments later, Val walked to the blackboard and erased the rows of numbers that had been part of the morning math problems. Her chalk squealing across the shiny surface, she drew the outline of a mushroom that appeared to be growing tentacles.

"Do any of you know the name of this toadstool?" she asked.

When no one responded, Lucas offered his opinion. "Looks more a squid to me." His remark elicited unexpected laughter among the students.

Glad that someone had at least commented, Val continued. "No, young man, that is a death angel, one of the deadliest of the mushroom family. Fortunately, none grow in our area. But Florence will show you the types of toadstools you might find in the hills around here. Very few are dangerous, the kind that must not be eaten with our meals."

The afternoon continued with discussions on the region's vegetation, followed by the promise that the following day they would learn about the fauna, or wildlife that thrived in the hills surrounding their home. Although the schooling was untraditional, it was practical. Lucas spent most of his time trying to get Catherine's attention, but she ignored him, careful to keep her eyes to the front.

"Young men, you're to meet with Dirk over by the woodshed after class," Val announced as the lessons wound down.

"He has some chores for you. And girls, I've been asked to send you to the laundry area. Matron Crystal has washed some recent donations that require ironing and folding. I'll see most of you in class tomorrow."

It turned out that Val had been a teacher in town. New to the education system, she had tended to be strict in her grading. When the mother of one of her male students disagreed with the marks Val gave to her child, she began a vicious rumor that alleged misconduct involving her son. Since the boy was afraid to contradict his mother, the baseless accusations continued to spread. Eventually, feeling severely ostracized when confronted by the school board, Val had difficulty defending innocent events that became highly exaggerated. Even a pat on the shoulder or a comforting hug could be misconstrued. Before long, she became an easy recruit for the Mount Cloquet community.

Still unable to get Catherine's attention when class ended, Lucas had no choice but to join the other boys at the woodshed. Waiting there patiently with an unpromising grin on his face, Dirk handed Lucas a heavy ax, known as a splitter. "Here, Mr. Tough Boy, show everyone how you can swing this little baby," Dirk barked, his words mocking.

The logs had been cut into one-and-a-half-foot lengths and stood on their ends. Straining just to raise the bulky tool over his head, Lucas swung the heavy ax in a downward arc as he attempted to split the rough logs in half. The smaller ones burst apart easily, but some were almost one foot in diameter, and the splitter jammed part way into them. Just the effort of prying the ax out of the hefty logs proved to be difficult. After less than ten minutes, Lucas's arms ached as much as his sore shoulder. Sweat dripped from his forehead.

"Do we switch off on this job?" he asked hopefully, his breath coming in deep puffs.

"You're supposed to be the tough guy," Dirk said sternly. "Show us what you're made of! Keep swinging until I tell you to stop."

He was obviously enjoying the entertainment. The other boys shuffled uneasily, knowing that their turn was coming.

Gritting his teeth, Lucas took a couple more swings before his sweaty palms finally lost their grip. The heavy splitter flew out of his hands, the thick, iron blade landing between Dirk's legs. As the ax handle bounced, it struck him solidly in the groin. Jerking backwards as he winced in pain, Dirk filled the air with a volley of curses.

"You idiot!" he screamed, his eyes burning with anger.

Lucas was off balance and had turned instinctively to run when primal instinct took over, and the heel of Dirk's right boot shot out. Striking the boy across his lower back, the impact sent Lucas sprawling onto his face into a pile of wood chips. Inner rage exploded as the image of Rocky at the pinball machine flashed through his mind. Seething with fury, Lucas scrambled to his feet just as a powerful hand clamped around his neck.

"I'm sure you'd like another chance with that ax, you little prick!" Dirk yelled as he squeezed his massive fingers.

Lucas came close to blacking out. Without warning, time came to an halt. Everyone at the woodpile froze in their tracks. An eerie stillness filled the air.

"Let go! You're going to kill him!" The voice was calm, firm, the words spoken with conviction, yet those few syllables came as unexpectedly as a snowstorm in summer. It was Peter who spoke, the quietest, most unassuming of all the boys. He was the boy who never talked back, who never complained, who did all his chores.

The speech was short, the words simple yet incredibly effective. Peter's piercing glare startled the rage from Dirk. He loosened his grip as if the Lord himself had spoken to him, and perhaps he had. Shaking his head as he regained his composure, Dirk's face remained flushed as he stared down at Lucas, who lay on the ground, gasping for air.

"You others take turns splitting the wood," he said, turning toward the nervous group of boys. "I want it all done before supper. And be sure to get cleaned up." Dirk tried to control his voice as he spoke, but his agitation was obvious. Then, still unnerved and embarrassed by the situation, he walked briskly toward the cottage he shared with the male adults, his hands gripped to a very tender area.

On his knees, Lucas spoke with a raspy voice as a deep redness drained from his face. "Thanks, Peter. He just about had me out cold."

"I don't know what made me do it. I've never talked back to Dirk before," Peter whispered, his body shaking like a leaf. "I . . . I shouldn't have done it. He's gonna find some excuse to give me a whipping for sure."

Before Lucas could respond, an older boy named Tom cut in. "Pete, you had the courage to speak up. I'm sure you said what we all wanted to say but couldn't. But what can we do? Maybe it's time we all stood up for one another. That guy has bullied us for long enough."

As the group looked around at each other, the murmur of agreement among the boys was unanimous.

Tom smiled. "You heard it, Peter, we'll all watch out for you." He then turned toward Lucas. "I hardly know you, but in the short time you've been here, we may finally be getting the nerve to look out for ourselves. It was hard to watch you stand up to that jerk, but something about it rubbed off on me, maybe some of the others as well."

There were several nods among the group at the woodpile, whose ages ranged from about eleven into the early teens. The youngest of the boys were back at their cottage.

"They've done something to all of you," Lucas began, his voice still hoarse. "Whatever they teach you or feed you has made you like . . . like spaced-out robots or zombies even, walking around half-dead. No one here has shit to say about what goes on. You might as well be slaves."

"You're right," Peter responded. "It's like we're addicted to those drinks they give us. I feel relaxed, but my energy goes way down, and I don't seem to care what happens, especially after that tea." He wasn't about to mention another control device that involved a simple operation. Every boy there carried a small scar as a reminder. Shaking his head, Peter continued. "But Lucas, you don't belong here. You'd be smart to get out as soon as you can."

"You know damn well I'm going to try," Lucas confided, to no one's surprise. The girls began to file out of the laundry cottage as Lucas continued. "If Dirk and Crystal have their way, I'll be in the hospital, or worse. But you're right. I've got to get out of here somehow. The sooner the better."

Remembering the promise he made earlier in the day, Lucas turned toward the girls. "I've got to talk to someone for a minute. You'd better finish the chopping. Watch out for Dirk, will you?"

Noticing the eyes of his new friend turn brighter, Tom nodded. "You bet we will, but don't be too long."

Making sure that the matron was nowhere in sight, Catherine separated herself from the other girls and ducked behind the clump of oaks that surrounded the woodshed. After spotting the group of boys, she knelt on a pile of bark and kindling, hidden only momentarily before she heard the rustling of dry branches.

"I was afraid you weren't going to come," Lucas said, pushing through the dried and crumpled leaves that hung from a clump of dead brush.

Her freckled face hidden in the shadows, Catherine glanced around. "It's so hard to talk around here. They always keep a close eye on us." Her smile disappeared when she saw the purple lines across Lucas's neck. "Was it him again?"

Nodding, Lucas tried to be positive. "Peter stood up to him. I think Tom and the others will follow. You're going to have to talk to the girls. These people want to control you all. I'm sure with something like the tea that made me sick, or even the soups. Can you tell me if—"

"We haven't much time," Catherine said. "Here, look at this." She leaned her head forward, exposing a tiny scar above the base of her neck. Obviously not a birthmark, it was likely the same concern that Peter was reluctant to bring up.

"What's that?" Lucas asked.

"Soon after you come here, they put this electronic gizmo under your skin. They call it part of your initiation. It's like a tiny round battery, and the machine that controls it is kept locked up. Only a few adults know where it is. Some kids like to rebel when they first come here. Most came from bad homes or just off the street, like you did. A few have tried to run away. I've never felt it, but others have told me they can send an electric shock to your head. They zapped one girl who never liked to listen. Later, she told me the shock went all the way to her toes. Her whole body tingled." Catherine glanced between the laundry room and her cottage.

"So, that's the surprise that Miss Cass had for me." Lucas shook his head. "I don't plan to hang around for it." He did his best to sound confident.

"About a year ago, a boy, Jerry, tried to run away. He was new here, but he started acting up and arguing all the time. Dirk gave him a few shocks, but it only made things worse. The poor kid was going crazy. He'd be screaming and yelling, and they would lock him in one of the sheds. They call it a time out. Finally, he tried to get away. I think they really hoped he would run off. That was the last we ever saw of Jerry. Crystal told us that he fell into the river, and no one could get to him in time, but I never believed the story. Whatever happened, it sure scared all the kids."

Suddenly anxious to leave, Catherine jumped to her feet.

"Wait, tell me how you ended up in this place," Lucas pleaded. "You're different. You don't belong with these people."

Her nervousness about being missing from her cottage evident, Catherine spoke quickly, sadness coming to her eyes. "I've lived here since I was seven. My folks were killed in a car crash, and my auntie took me in for a while. Then she heard about this commune and decided I'd be better off living here. I don't think my aunt wanted the responsibility. She never had children."

Turning away from Catherine as his mind drifted back to his own past, Lucas nodded. "I know just . . . just what you mean." The fading light reflected off the thin layer of moisture that suddenly glazed his eyes.

Looking up toward her cottage, Catherine gasped. "I've got to run. I see Crystal looking around. She knows I'm missing!"

"I'm getting out of here soon. Please, try to come with me . . .." The words flowed impulsively from Lucas as his freckle-faced friend ran off, making her way along the tree line and back to the other girls. His pleading words had fallen on deaf ears. Catherine neither responded or even looked back.

Staring off in the distance, his eyes unfocused and his mind filled with so many thoughts, Lucas didn't notice Peter approach him.

"Come on, we'd better get cleaned up. I hope Dirk didn't get into his liquor. He can get pretty mean when he drinks," Peter warned.

"Really? Dirk's got a temper?" Rubbing his neck, Lucas spoke cynically in his poor attempt at humor. He quickly rejoined the group of hungry boys returning to their cottage.

While continuing to chop wood, the group discussed how they might avoid drinking some of the teas and stick up for each other when the need arose. Unfortunately, their plans hit a roadblock as dinner approached. Peter's concern proved to be warranted, as Dirk had gotten into his whiskey. His temperament had certainly turned for the worst, and his attitude toward all the boys was anything but pleasant.

Chapter 30

Sharing the same desk with the television in his motel room, Jarrod sliced into the fresh bread, the knife slipping in his sweaty palms. He slowly consumed two pastrami-and-cheese sandwiches while waiting nervously in his room, expecting a loud rap on his door at any moment. An anxious hour and a half passed before the bang of the outside door announced the departure of Molly's friend. As he was trying to decide if he should return the knife and talk to Molly again, Jarrod was startled by a gentle knock on his door.

"Are you still awake?" Molly whispered.

"Need your knife back already?" Jarrod asked as he approached the door.

"No, it's not that. But my friend, the cop, told me something you might be interested in," she replied as the door to Jarrod's room swung open. "He's worried about me being alone and even had a second beer today. Usually, he doesn't talk about his work, but maybe because Fred is away he gave me the description of a man and boy who are wanted by a sheriff in Wisconsin. I think the man may be a guest of our little motel."

"Since the handcuffs never came out, I assume that's as far as the conversation went," Jarrod responded in a relieved tone.

"What, and lose a paying customer?" Molly said with a wry grin.

"Did he mention what terrible things these two were accused of doing?" Jarrod asked.

"Just something about embezzlement, a raging fire and a train derailment, nothing serious."

Molly laughed. Her sense of humor was infectious. How could she be so frivolous? Jarrod had stolen from his employer. He had caused a lot of damage. But harming others didn't seem to be part of his makeup. With his ruggedly handsome looks, Molly pictured him as a dashing character in one of her soap operas. On top of it all, a curious aura of compassion hung over her motel guest. She was enthralled. Her fictional world had turned into reality, and she wasn't about to give it up.

"Do you want me to leave?" Jarrod asked, "before your hotel bursts into flames?"

"To tell you the truth, I don't feel threatened at all. Over the years, I've become a pretty good judge of the people who pass through this place. You're different from other customers; you have this strange, caring trait about you. But if you're the guy the police are looking for, why did you steal? There are other ways to pay your bills." Molly's tone had become more serious.

"I guess I panicked. My debts were to the wrong people. Threats started to come. Honestly, I never stole before my stupid gambling losses went overboard. Anyway, I appreciate any confidence you have in me. You seem to understand why I've got to locate this boy. His name is Lucas, by the way." Jarrod struggled to understand why Molly had not turned him in.

"I can imagine you're two lost souls searching for a place to belong. I can feel your concern for the boy. I'll do what I can to help," Molly promised as she turned to leave, determined to continue living her own soap opera. "That store should be open tomorrow; it's almost the weekend."

"Thanks for covering for me—and for trusting me, Molly. See you in the morning."

Jarrod closed and locked the door to his room.

Feeling renewed excitement in her life, Molly wandered back to her evening television programs.

Friday morning began to drag as Jarrod awoke early, then waited anxiously for any signs of activity at the second-hand store. Finally, on his third walk-by, he noticed the "Open" sign swaying gently in the window. It must have just been turned.

As he entered the musty building's cluttered confines, Jarrod heard the roar of an engine as a vehicle pulled away from the rear entrance. He had no way of knowing the close connection the driver had with Lucas. Dirk was behind the wheel on his way to drop off a few of the older children with collection boxes.

Jarrod approached a pre-teen girl who was busy emptying the contents of a box of folded clothing. "With all this cold weather lately, I could use a pair of warm winter boots. Do you have any in stock, young lady?"

Showing little emotion, the sleepy girl pointed across the room to a rack containing shoes and boots.

"You kids must be in a special class to get a day off school and help out in here," Jarrod continued, hoping to get some reaction.

"School is very important, but we all get to come to town once a week. Helping in the store is one of our duties." Forcing a polite smile, the young girl's reply hardly seemed natural. It was more like a conditioned response.

"Do you all live around here, or do you come from out of town?" Jarrod asked casually as he looked over the few boots on display.

"We live up in the hills—" the girl began but then stopped as Florence approached from the back room with an armful of sweaters.

"Lil, go and help the others sort the items in the back, please." Florence quickly interrupted the conversation when she heard the questioning

The girl left the room quickly, her eyes downcast.

"I haven't seen you in here before," Florence said to Jarrod, her tone abrupt. "Are you from this area?"

"Just passing through," Jarrod answered. He felt an uneasiness in the woman's inquiry. "I met a fellow called Crusty who told me about your place. He's a street person. Said he came here often."

"Can't say I recall him. We get so many of those people through our store, usually looking for handouts," Florence replied, showing nothing in the way of sympathy. "Those boots you're holding are about the best we have right now. If you want them, they cost fifteen dollars, cash only."

As he dug into his pocket for money, Jarrod tried fishing for more information. "I recall seeing a couple of your girls at the bus station. Do you folks live out of town?"

Florence hesitated, clearly unwilling to divulge any information. "Our family has its own community. We don't live in town, but our children receive an excellent education. Sorry, but I can't talk any longer . . . we're going to be busy soon, and there's lots of work to do." She took the money for the boots and retreated to the back room.

Frustrated with the lack of answers, Jarrod left the store, hoping for better luck as he crossed the street to Murray's Bakery. Bonnie had just finished serving a customer, who was on her way out the door when Jarrod entered the shop.

With only the two of them in the store, Bonnie could speak freely. "I'm glad you made it back. I spoke to my kid's teacher last night," she began. "She's been at that school for a long time and remembers a former student who disappeared about ten years ago. His name was Dirk, but the kids at school called him Dirt. They teased him, because he wore the same clothes all week, and usually his hands and face were either filthy or bruised. Dirk was a loner, and the word was . . . he had an alcoholic father who beat him. He finally ran away from home."

"Did the teacher know what happened to him?" Jarrod asked, his interest growing.

"The talk around school was that the commune recruited him, and he seems to have been there ever since." With no new customers, Bonnie kept talking. "Not long ago, someone saw him driving the children who go all over town looking for donations. And this Dirk guy, he refused to talk to one of his old classmates who recognized him at a pool hall."

"Now I'm starting to understand how a child could disappear," Jarrod said. "Did the teacher tell you anything else?"

Bonnie shook her head. "Not much more. The group is very secretive. They homeschool the children and use them to raise money and collect donations for their store. You're the first person who seems concerned about where they live. Because they're polite and not overly pushy for donations, people around town don't seem to be concerned with their lifestyle."

"From what I saw at that store, I'm sure there's more going on with that group than the people in town are aware of. If they're holding the boy I was traveling with, it must be at some hideaway in the country. I may just pay them a surprise visit." Jarrod was open about his latest idea.

"Well, all I can do is wish you luck," Bonnie said as a well-dressed, businesswoman entered the bakeshop. "I hope you have the chance to come back and tell me how things turned out."

"I'll try to, Bonnie. Thanks for all your help," Jarrod replied, almost bumping into the new customer's unwieldly handbag as he turned toward the door.

Still uncertain what his next move should be, Jarrod began to walk slowly through an unfamiliar district of the downtown. The area was on the seedy side, consisting mainly of older businesses, bars, a vintage theater, and numerous boarded-up buildings, whose profits had dried up years earlier. After wandering for several blocks, his roving eyes spotted something that made his heart skip a beat. There, in plain view in front of him, an older, dark-blue Suburban was parked with one wheel on the curb. The dirty vehicle sat only steps from a run-down pool hall. Although no letters were visible on the muddy tailgate, the truck looked very familiar.

The paint was flaking on the sign that rested above the scarred, metal door that led customers into Eddy's Pool Hall. The door fit poorly in its frame, and it took a hard tug to pull it open.

Once inside, Jarrod discovered a place much smaller and far dirtier than the bar he had entered only a couple of nights earlier. Smoke stung his eyes as he tried to focus through the lingering haze. Although there were two rows of pool tables, eight altogether, only three were occupied. The young people playing, probably in their late teens or early twenties, seemed to all be friends and were joking around. One young fellow was leaning over the back of a girl on the pretense of showing her how to properly grip the pool cue. Jarrod remembered pulling the same stunt in his youth and knew just what was going through the young instructor's mind.

Jarrod walked up to the counter, where a lone man attended a small snack and liquor bar. His other important duty was distributing pool cues and change required for the coin-operated tables. Several quarters had to be inserted into yawning slots on the sides of the pool tables before a plunger mechanism released the numbered balls required for eight ball, or stripes-and-solids, as some people called it.

"Could I have a bottle of Miller, please?" Jarrod asked the scruffy attendant. Obviously, showers and haircuts were not a requisite for his job.

With a twitch of his right eye, the shaggy-haired man, looking much older than his thirty-some years, popped the top off the bottle. The cap flew onto the floor, spinning briefly before coming to rest among dozens of others.

"Don't think I'll need ID from you, bud," he said with a crooked grin. He sniffed constantly.

Jarrod recalled his one and only experience with hard drugs. He would never repeat it.

After paying for his beer, Jarrod's eyes adjusted to the lighting as he scanned the dimly lit area at the rear of the room. He saw one person sipping a beer at a small table at the back. The strapping young man would certainly require proof of age before ordering a drink. Could he be the driver of the Suburban?

Jarrod walked over casually to where the young fellow was slouched over his table.

"Hey, bud, feel like shooting some stick?" Jarrod asked, using the lingo from his pool hall days.

"Not really . . . just not in the mood today," the powerful-looking man replied. His words were hesitant, and he appeared surprised that someone would ask him for a game.

Seating himself at the table next to the sullen man, Jarrod continued to prod for answers. "I'm headed west, just killing some time on my way through town. Do you live around here?"

"I'm just in town for the day. I've got to leave soon," Dirk replied tersely, apparently uncomfortable talking to strangers.

Jarrod nodded as he sipped his beer. "It's sure getting cold around here. Do you know where a fellow can buy a good used coat?"

Dirk hesitated for a moment before replying. If he was suspicious, he didn't show it. "There's a second-hand store just a few blocks from here. I could give you directions how to get there."

"Thanks," Jarrod said. "I don't have a lot of cash these days. Been out of work since summer."

Appearing to relax more as they spoke, Dirk scribbled directions on the back of a coaster and then handed it to Jarrod. "Here's how you get to the store. I've got to leave in a few minutes." Could Dirk be eyeing the stranger as a candidate for the "new society?"

"Thanks again. Can I buy you a beer?" Jarrod asked, hoping Dirk, who couldn't have been much older than twenty, might be persuaded to talk more about his home.

Initially appearing wary of accepting the offer, Dirk nodded. "Sure, I've got time for one more."

Jarrod checked that the sniffling attendant was looking their way before putting up two fingers to order a round. "My name's Bill," he said, turning back to the table and extending his hand. "I'm from Detroit."

Still showing signs of uneasiness, Dirk nodded. Did his indoctrination teach him to be wary of all strangers? "I'm Dirk. I live on a farm not far from town." It was likely no one had ever offered him a free beer, and he wasn't about to turn down the gesture.

Reluctantly, he grasped Jarrod's hand like he was squeezing an ax handle. Jarrod winced in pain from Dirk's powerful grip.

Pulling his hand away, Jarrod realized that he had struck gold. He couldn't believe he was actually sitting next to the runaway whom his classmates had labeled "Dirt."

The fresh beers arrived as a myriad of questions spun through Jarrod's mind. He started probing slowly. "Do you raise cattle, or is your farm agricultural?"

"Well, we don't really—" Dirk began just as the bar phone rang, its noisy reverberation disrupting the conversation. The pool players looked nervously toward the interruption, probably hoping no one knew where they were. As improbable as a divine intervention would have been, the attendant called Dirk to the phone.

After a brief conversation, he returned to the table. "I've got to go. There're some people I have to pick up." Spooked by the sudden call, Dirk poured the remaining beer down his throat as fast as possible. It was evident that whoever was tending the thrift shop knew exactly where he spent his afternoons in town.

Aware that this might be the opportunity to discover the commune's hidden location, Jarrod left half his beer on the table and walked out of the pool hall just as Dirk was pulling away. He would have asked for a ride, but he was concerned that the woman in charge of the thrift store had already seen his face. His pace was quick as he walked back to his motel.

Jarrod could think of only one way that he might follow the group as they returned to their country home.

As he entered the front office, he was relieved to see Molly filling the coffee maker with fresh water. Out of breath after his brisk walk, Jarrod was about to speak, but Molly was quicker.

"What's wrong? You look like you just saw a ghost."

"I've already talked to two adults from the commune. No one wants to say much, but I'm certain the group lives in a secretive location not far from town. I saw that blue Suburban of theirs again. My only chance is to follow it somehow." Jarrod sounded desperate.

Molly's response was frank and without hesitation. "Fred and I have an old Pontiac. It's our second car. We call it the 'old beater' and keep it licensed so I have something to drive when Fred's away." Reaching into the drawer beneath the gurgling coffee machine, Molly pulled out a set of keys. "Here . . . the car's in the lane behind the motel. Get going!"

With time for only a grateful nod and a quick word of thanks, Jarrod ran into the lane. The Pontiac's starter balked at first, but after three attempts, the eighteen-year-old engine rumbled to life. The cold transmission thumped into gear, and the pursuit began.

Moments later, the car was parked on the same block as the thrift store but not close enough to arouse suspicion. Jarrod arrived in plenty of time, as several minutes passed before children began to file out of the shop. Like regimented cadets, they took their places on the Suburban's bench seats. Finally, Dirk, and the woman who had sold Jarrod his boots emerged, carefully locking the store's front door. Neither of them noticed the idling Pontiac as their well-loaded vehicle pulled away from the curb, Dirk behind the wheel.

After making a U-turn in the middle of the block, Jarrod kept a safe distance as he followed the slow-moving vehicle. He need not have been concerned, as Dirk was still a little inebriated from his visits to the pool hall, and Florence, exhausted from her duties at the store, began to doze in the passenger seat.

Nonetheless, when traffic became sparse outside of town, Jarrod eased off the gas and pulled back even farther as the Suburban began taking secondary roads. Both the Pontiac and Jarrod vibrated nonstop on the washboard surface of the uneven gravel paths.

As the narrow roads wound into a series of rolling hills, Jarrod noticed the surrounding land opening into broad fields and pastures. He was convinced the secret community occupied many acres tucked away in the sparsely populated, undulating hills. Eventually, when the gravel deteriorated into a texture of oozy clay, he noticed the brake lights ahead of him come on a few times more than necessary. Fearing that he may have been detected, Jarrod turned off onto a muddy path leading into a farmer's field. It was getting dark, and he couldn't follow any longer without putting on his headlights. After waiting a few minutes, he chanced following the rutted trail a little farther. It wasn't long before the Suburban's fresh tracks made a sharp right-angled turn onto a single-lane driveway. Here, the muddy tracks appeared to stretch sideways, as if the vehicle had come close to sliding off the road. There was no sign or even a mailbox at the junction, but Jarrod was certain he had found the entrance to the Mount Cloquet society's secret haven.

The final sloping path was far too dark and hidden to venture up that night, especially as it appeared to wind its way to the top of a steep hill. After an inquisitive look up the driveway, Jarrod retraced his route back to town, hoping that daylight would uncover the final clue to Lucas's location. His mind was already plotting the following day's return visit to the secret retreat, a place where the welcome mat would never greet outside visitors. With the following day being Saturday, there was a good chance the thrift store would be busy and require more adult supervision. That would make the commune less secure and, with some luck, more vulnerable to uninvited guests.

Jarrod could only hope.

Part Five
CALL OUT THE DOGS

Chapter 31

Friday, and duties in town would come soon enough for the powerful young man. Dirk was relaxing now, enjoying several drinks of his favorite beverage at the cottage reserved for the adult males. The pain in his groin was slowly subsiding. It took several reminders from his "happy hour" companions to persuade Dirk it was time to check up on his boys. Stumbling more than once, he fell behind his two drinking buddies as they hustled toward the dining hall.

The boys washed up quickly for dinner. They were a few minutes late and just about to file into the dining hall when Dirk approached the group. There was fire in his eyes as he staggered toward the anxious boys. It was obvious he had been drinking something other than spring water. Although strict about most rules and routines, the community leaders tended to overlook alcohol consumption. A few family members, both male and female, drank quite regularly. Since most of the drinking was moderate, little was said about it. In recent months, Auscan was beginning to have enough problems with his own addiction. As long as day-to-day routines ran smoothly, he was content to allow the adults a few pleasures of their own. Unfortunately, Dirk went overboard more frequently than anyone else. Not wanting to lose one of their few privileges, the others were forced to keep him under control.

"About time you got here," Dirk slurred. His face was flushed and his words hard to understand as he spoke to boys. "Did you lazy ashes finally get all the wood chopped?"

Realizing he meant to say "asses," a couple of the boys snickered.

"All but a couple of big logs," Tom replied. "They need to be cut into shorter lengths."

"If our big-shot new kid had finished his job, you'd have had time to cut them yourselves," Dirk roared. "Get into dinner before I lose my temper!"

Passing by Lucas, he turned to give the insolent boy a swat to the head. However, after tripping over his own feet, Dirk lost his balance and almost fell to his knees. His entrance into the dining area was anything but graceful.

The adults and girls waited patiently for the boys to enter the dining lodge. Once everyone was seated, one of the adults recited a short grace. Diluted bowls of soup were distributed to everyone. Catherine gave Lucas a discreet glance as he tried to get a seat as near to her as possible. However, a stern glare from Crystal convinced him that conversation would be impossible. His every move would be under scrutiny.

It didn't go unnoticed by their supervisors when several of the boys hardly touched their bowls of soup yet devoured the rest of the meal. Many of them heeded the caution from

Lucas about tea and soups having an adverse effect on them. With dinner almost over, Florence stood up and announced the names of those who would go to town the following day. Friday was the start of a normally prosperous weekend for the commune. The thrift shop would be open, and the most mature children would solicit donations from various locations around town. Generally, busy malls and the bus depot were the best locations for their colorful wooden boxes, which they hung around their necks. Although they might as well have been painted on, pleasant smiles always adorned the young solicitors' faces.

The remainder of the evening was relatively uneventful. Dirk, who was obviously ready for an early bedtime, carefully avoided getting involved in evening prayers. Used to his frequent alcoholic indulgences, the girls were accustomed to getting ready for bed without supervision. Catherine often took charge and made sure that all the younger girls settled down for the night.

Barely thirteen, Martha was Auscan and Cassandra's oldest daughter. Her sister, Mary, was two years younger. The youngest sisters were only five and seven years old. There was no need for control implants or special teas and soups for any of them. Indoctrinated into the system since birth, the sisters were completely docile, content to do their chores and sleep in the lodge with the other girls. They displayed little ambition and even less interest in becoming leaders. They simply followed directions. With Dirk snoring in the background (a curtain separated his bed from the others), the older girls could talk quietly among themselves. However, with the community leaders' offspring present,

Catherine had to keep most of her thoughts to herself. She didn't dare talk about the suspicions that Lucas had mentioned earlier.

With the intent of opening the thrift shop as close to eleven as possible the following morning, Dirk was assigned the duty of driving to town with Florence and six of the children, who were excused from class. Two of the younger girls and a boy would remain at the shop with Florence, helping her sort and arrange the latest donations. Dirk, meanwhile, had the additional task of chauffeuring Catherine, Tom, and Martha to one of the malls. Those three children were the most mature when it came to soliciting donations and normally had the best returns in their boxes. Their smiling faces were familiar to regular donors.

Friday morning came too early for the young man with a chronic hangover. Dirk quietly stumbled through his customary routine, leaving the girls to look after themselves. Although the city trips were always an uncomfortable experience for him, he never complained when his turn came to drive the others to town. Except for any chores that required heavy lifting, he was excused from most duties at the thrift shop. His shyness around people made him a poor salesman, and his organizational skills were almost nonexistent. Whoever was running the shop didn't mind him disappearing when his driving duties were not required.

Consequently, Dirk spent most of his time in town at a rundown bar and pool hall, where he drank beer alone, trying to hide from the other customers. He could never guess that today would be the day that a complete stranger actually offered to buy him a drink.

The beginning of the ride to town was a little exciting as Dirk struggled to stay alert. His driving was dreadful as the lumbering Suburban slewed from side to side along the slick trail that led to the gravel road. The children had to stifle their laughter when Florence laid into Dirk for not paying attention to the road. With clenched fingers and white knuckles, she gripped the door handle and bottom edge of the dashboard. Her crude, back-seat-driving language could never be repeated in front of Cassandra, yet her words had no effect on Dirk, who ignored everything she said. When they finally pulled up in front of the thrift store, Florence was so frazzled she had to get Tom to unlock the front door.

After the three older children were dropped off at a mall, where collections averaged higher than at other locations, Tom did his best to work as close to Catherine as possible. As a daughter of the commune leaders, Martha was not as close to the other children, who considered her to be more elite or special. Although she seldom was shown privilege in their supposedly classless society, Tom never felt that he could trust her. Regardless of her reserved attitude among the children, Martha showed great determination when it came to soliciting donations. Her smiles and thank yous abounded.

"Catherine . . . can I talk to you?" Tom whispered as they took up their locations outside a grocery store inside the mall. Martha stood next to the entrance of a multi-screen theater several yards away.

"You know what Miss Cass will say if our donation boxes aren't full, don't you?" Catherine replied. Her faith and commitment to the commune was deep-rooted.

Ignoring her question, Tom continued. "I know you talked to Lucas . . . I think you care about him. He said something to the guys when we were chopping wood. It made sense."

"He's going to try to run. I'm sure of that," Catherine said as she smiled at the passing shoppers.

"He believes that maybe they control us, keep us from acting up or having our own ideas, by giving us those drinks and teas . . . and horrible soups. I've been thinking . . . I sure lose my energy a lot of times. I don't seem to care at all." Tom also tried to remain pleasant as shoppers noticed his wooden box and printed sign requesting donations to help needy children.

"I know what you mean, but what can we do about it? Crystal and Dirk are so strict. They watch us all the time," Catherine said, her voice low, before thanking an elderly woman, who was a regular supporter.

"You think maybe you can talk to the girls, try to get them to stop drinking those crappy teas, maybe those tasteless soups, too? Something's sucking away our energy. Us boys have all decided to stick together and back each other up," Tom explained. "You won't believe it, but it was Peter who spoke up when Dirk started to strangle Lucas by the woodshed. You know, I'm tired of being pushed around. Don't you think we should have some say in at least a few things we do? It's almost like Lucas has given us some weird power. By the way, he sure thinks a lot of you."

Ignoring the last comment, Catherine spoke so quietly that Tom had to lean forward so he could hear. "It would be nice to have a little say in something. I'd like to be able to pick out my own book from a library or just talk to someone in town. I'm tired of always begging for money or donations. But the other kids seem afraid to speak to anyone on the outside."

"Let's be careful what we drink at the shop today, see if it makes any difference," Tom suggested. "But I'm sure that Florence and Dirk are going to notice."

"You're right that we all have to stick together for your plan to work. Martha and her sisters, they seem okay, but I don't think we can include them," Catherine said. Was it possible that she was beginning to question her faith in her "special family?"

It was a payday Friday for many people, and collections went well that afternoon. The children's pleasant attitudes brought back many regulars to see them every two weeks, even if they weren't sure about where their donations were going. As three o'clock approached, the young solicitors showed signs of hunger. Talking less to each other, they looked around for their ride. An afternoon break was just around the corner.

Glad that Dirk had gone to town, Lucas had no option but to spend the entire day in class. With a short attention span, he daydreamed, thinking of ways he could escape and convince Catherine to come with him. In charge of both the boys and the girls while Dirk was absent, Crystal was constantly making her presence felt. While helping to supervise the classroom, she sent the occasional nasty look toward Lucas when he wasn't paying attention. But mostly she just left him alone with his wishful thoughts.

"You haven't much to say today, Lucas?" Val asked finally. "Not even one of your humorous wisecracks?"

Lucas only shook his head and stared out the window. His mind was focused on how to avoid the operation that Dirk had promised for him, likely on the weekend. Somehow, some way, he had to make his escape soon. The shop would be busy tomorrow, and many members of the commune would be in town, hopefully both Crystal and Miss Cass among them. But what could he do about Dirk? The man would love to find any excuse to strangle the last breath from Lucas's body.

When classes were finished, Crystal directed Lucas and Peter to complete their chores at the woodpile. Dirk had left instructions that every log should be cut, chopped, and neatly piled. Without a doubt, he would be inspecting their work when he got home.

Once they were alone at the woodshed, Lucas turned to Peter. "You and Tom have to make sure everyone stands up to these bullies like we talked about."

"I felt a shock to my head once from that little battery gadget they're planning to put into you. It was a long time ago, but the pain was terrible. They warned us that it would hurt even more if we tried to remove it. No one has dared try it," Peter explained. He was afraid, yet somehow Lucas had uncovered an inner strength, an awareness of his own self that Peter had never found before or even knew could exist. No longer would he sit back, be pushed around, and have all his actions controlled. Watching what he ate and drank would just be the start of his move toward self-control and independence. But really, was Peter's dream remotely achievable in his current environment?

"Don't worry, I'll do what I can to help the others," Peter said. "We're all in this together. By the way, what are you planning to do, Lucas? I'll help you any way I can."

"I'm not having that damn operation! I've got to get the hell of here tomorrow, but I don't think you'll be able to slow down Dirk. That man would love to finish me off. Probably because I won't roll over and play dead." Still unable to figure out a realistic escape plan, his speech was agitated.

"Let's just see what happens in the morning." A mischievous twinkle flashed across Peter's eyes as he spoke. What was he thinking?

As time for an afternoon snack approached, Tom and Catherine continued with their collections at the mall. They gave each other a knowing look when Dirk came to pick them up just before three o'clock. His face was flushed, and he appeared to be more nervous than usual. With a familiar smell on his breath, Dirk hardly spoke on the ride to the thrift shop. Although the memory of it wouldn't escape his mind, he never talked about his unusual encounter with a total stranger, neither with the children nor with Florence. Seated next to him during the ride to the shop, Martha remained as passive as ever and took no notice of Dirk's anxiety.

Much to her surprise, Tom and Catherine turned down Florence's special blueberry herbal tea. Both asked for cold water instead. Even bowls of her nutritious soup were left half-filled when the children prepared to continue their duties. Were the two children not feeling well, or was there another reason for their behavior? Tom and Catherine each gave a lame excuse for not wanting the tea, their actions only increasing Dirk's uneasiness. It was apparent that he had felt uncomfortable since Peter's bold words embarrassed him the previous day. Was he loosing control of his own behavior, or was he merely following the route of his abusive, alcoholic father?

As Florence finished emptying the collection boxes, Dirk glared at Tom and Catherine. "It's time that you all get back to the mall. If you work a little harder this afternoon, maybe you'll be hungrier at supper time."

"Miss Cass won't be very happy unless you can more than double what you've collected so far," Florence added with a frown.

"We'll try our best," Catherine responded flatly.

After warning Tom and Catherine to concentrate on their duties (Martha's status excluded her, plus her work ethic never changed), Dirk left the three of them outside the same mall for the remainder of the afternoon. Still uncomfortable with his recent experience of talking to a stranger, he hoped to be left alone when he made a second visit to his favorite watering hole. He would return to pick up the children before six o'clock, chewing several breath mints before returning to the store.

As the day's activities wound down in a normal fashion, Dirk and the solicitors returned to the shop and prepared to close up. Florence seemed pleased with the day's events. The collections had gone well, the new clothing rack was filled, and there had been a fair amount of traffic in the store. Tired and hungry, she was glad to finally turn the "Closed" sign as everyone prepared to load into the Suburban for the homeward journey.

"Let's get back home for supper. Some of you didn't have much for lunch. I can't understand why," Florence said in a manner that was firm yet confused as she locked up the shop.

As they ushered the silent children into their mud-covered vehicle, neither she nor Dirk noticed an older car idling farther up the block. Only on the final rutted section of road that approached the commune did Dirk notice a vehicle in the rear-view mirror. He braked once or twice out of curiosity, but by then the other car was out of sight. Before turning up the final approach to their hidden community, he remembered the most important rule of checking that no one was approaching from either direction. As was normally the case, the Suburban was all alone. Dirk turned the final corner a little too fast, the heavy vehicle sliding sideways against the driveway's raised edge. Florence let out one last groan.

Although suppertime was pushed back over an hour on Fridays and Saturdays, the group returning from town was still late in joining the others in the dining lodge. Grace was not repeated for the latecomers. Lucas was seated next to Peter at the end of the table closest to the girls' section. Looking up as Dirk and the others entered, he was disappointed when Martha sat in the vacant spot almost beside him but at the girl's table. Catherine gave him a brief optimistic glance as she walked past. Tom, as well, gave an encouraging nod before sitting across from Lucas. It was evident that the two of them had communicated.

Cassandra decided to join her faithful community members that night for supper. She had prepared a light meal for Auscan at their cottage. His particularly mellow condition did not encourage the consumption of a large dinner. The role of organizing, as well as supervising activities at the commune, had fallen almost entirely on her shoulders. Her eyes roaming across the throng of eaters in the dining area, only at one certain table did Cassandra notice something out of the ordinary. The boys seated there were not only talking more than usual among themselves, but many of their soup bowls were left untouched. Their appetites normally voracious, the boys seldom wasted even a swollen carrot. With one look at Lucas, whose eyes were glued on the girls, Cassandra recognized the root of her suspicions. What had he said to the others? Was he more dangerous than she had imagined? Several doubts crept into her mind. There was much to discuss that night in the warmth and flickering firelight of the leader's den.

The latecomers were still finishing their meals when Cassandra stood up next to her table. Her tone left no doubt who was in charge. "Before you return to your cottages, be sure to check who will be going to town tomorrow," she began. "The shop will be busy. Collection boxes must be filled and supplies for our community replenished. Florence has the list of those who will participate. I will join you in the morning."

Ending her remarks with a no-nonsense expression, everyone nodded in agreement. Cassandra strode quickly toward the exit, carefully avoiding eye contact with Lucas. Her intuition sensed a unique quality surrounding him that she could not put her finger on. Overcome by an uncharacteristic uneasiness, she felt a sudden shiver as the tiniest bead of nervous sweat trickled across her textured brow.

Chapter 32

Jarrod couldn't hide his excitement when he returned to his humble quarters around nine o'clock on Friday evening. "I think I've found where those people have their hideout," he said loudly through the half-opened door of Molly's TV room. "Here are your keys."

Carrying a half-empty glass of wine, Molly strolled toward the front counter. "You seem pretty wound up. Do you think they suspected you were following them?"

"I don't think so. I hung well back but didn't have trouble following their tracks right up to where the truck turned onto a steep driveway. The entrance was narrow and muddy, but I'm certain that's where they're holding Lucas." With a poor attempt to keep his voice steady and controlled, Jarrod continued. "I know one thing about this kid. He won't accept being held captive. Escape will be the first thing on his mind. But if his condition is still as bad as when I saw him leaning against the window of that truck, he needs help, and quickly."

"I've been doing some thinking since you've been gone, and I actually came up with an idea." Her face a little flushed from the wine, Molly spoke deliberately as she flashed her impish grin. "I'm sure you plan to do all you can to get your friend out of that place."

She paused for a moment and took a sip of California merlot. "Fred will be back in a couple of days, and I shouldn't be needing the old beater. My sister, Doris, lives in a town called Baudette. It's up north next to the Canadian border." Molly was obviously relishing her role in a real-life soap opera.

"What are you suggesting?" Jarrod asked, his heart beating rapidly.

"Borrow the damn car! But you'd better gas it up first, before you get on your way to free your pal. That town's over two hundred miles away, so you'll be well out of this area. There's an empty gravel lot in town close to the business area. People like to park there for free. That would be an easy place to dump the car. I'll make up some fib for my sister and get her to take it to her place. I'll think of something. Just leave the keys under the front floor mat." Molly tilted her wine glass back and emptied it.

His mind racing, Jarrod took a moment to reply. "I appreciate your help, but I don't want to get you into trouble, Molly. Won't your police buddy be suspicious?" He spoke with concern.

"If it comes to it, I'll just tell him that the keys disappeared from behind the counter. I'm a very sound sleeper. Don't worry about me; I've told a few good stories in my life."

With no better plan in mind, Jarrod jumped at the surprising offer. "I'm thinking that tomorrow is the day to make my move. That store of theirs will be busy, and the kids will be collecting donations. And maybe other adults will be coming to town for groceries or whatever." Ideas swirled through his mind. "I'm sure they'll keep Lucas at the commune, but with any luck, it could be half deserted. Could you draw me a map, so I can find this border town and the place you want me to leave the car?"

"No problem, there's an old roadmap in the glovebox as well. What time will you be leaving?"

"Around eight o'clock. You said that the shop opens early on Saturday, right?"

Molly nodded. "It should open around nine or earlier. Don't worry; I'll be up, probably starting on vacuuming or some job that a maid should be doing."

"Thanks again for your help. I won't let you down." Jarrod winked anxiously as he walked back to his room, the car keys stuffed into his pocket.

Saturdays had the earliest start of the week at the Mount Cloquet commune. As the busiest day of the week there were no prayers, only a quick breakfast as those going to town got organized. Ten children were scheduled to work that morning. Collections for clothing and other articles would take place door to door. Those with collection boxes would hang around busy shopping areas and the bus depot, where out-of-town travelers could often be talked out of a dollar or two. Six of the children would travel with Crystal and Cassandra, while four others would go with George, one of Auscan's close allies, in the Jeep. An older pickup driven by one of the stand-in preachers was used to get weekly supplies for the commune. Jarrod's prediction was right. The clandestine community's country hideaway would definitely be understaffed. Unfortunately, Dirk appeared to be the sole person in charge at the home base. Auscan, the great leader, remained in his private sanctum.

As expected, Lucas also stayed behind with many of the younger children. Was that the group Cassandra had suggested he might one day mentor? As their supervisor, Dirk would make sure they all had plenty of chores around the farm. He didn't forget to remind Lucas about an important meeting shortly after breakfast.

"Don't make me have to look for you," Dirk growled, clenching his massive fists. "Things could get a lot worse."

At that point, everyone was finishing their pre-dawn breakfast in the dining lodge. The eastern sky showed the first signs of daylight. Dirk turned toward a slim African American man seated across from him. The man's black, tightly curled hair showed flecks of grey. "Don't forget, Paul, I'll need your help shortly."

Paul nodded in reply. His previous employment had been as an intern at a private hospital in Jamaica.

Lucas sat still and remained silent, but his mind was racing. His heart beat rapidly as he watched the others loading into the vehicles headed to town.

Suddenly remembering a priority, Dirk stood up and walked outside toward George, who was seated behind the pickup's steering wheel. Lucas saw a ray of hope. It was evident that Dirk's mind was focused on reminding the driver that it was his turn to pick up supplies for their afternoon refreshments. Could any trapped youngster resist the opportunity? Just moments earlier, Peter had given a little nod and glanced outside as he passed Lucas at the breakfast table. Lucas now realized what Peter had meant. The previous twinkle in his eye at the woodshed really had carried a message.

Mumbling something about getting to the washroom quickly, Lucas stood up and almost knocked over his bowl of runny oatmeal. Occupied in a conversation with the pickup driver, Dirk had no idea of the activity going on behind his back. Lucas displayed a surprising calmness as he slid out of the dining lodge and mingled briefly with the group of children who had purposely delayed getting into their vehicles. Acting as a screen to block the view from the pickup, Tom, Peter, and a few of the other boys were alert and prepared, quite aware of what was going on. His eyes darting from side to side, looking for danger, Peter motioned the fast-moving Lucas to slip behind the wall of bodies the children provided.

Keeping as low as possible, Lucas reached the men's outhouse after several long strides. Rather than opening the door, he ducked and shifted his route behind the smelly latrine without even looking back. Seconds later, he was out of the view of everyone preparing for their trip to town. His movement went unnoticed by almost all the girls, including the leaders' daughters. Lucas had noticed the pathetic looks those girls showed were no different from any of the others. Their higher rank in the community didn't seem to carry any extra benefits. Fortunately, both Crystal and Miss Cass remained preoccupied with organizing their trip, and none of the other adults realized what was going on. One exception was Catherine. She became part of the screen formed by the boys when she saw what was happening. So far, so good.

It wasn't until Peter watched Lucas's small form fade away, blending in with the surrounding brush, that he realized there was no escape route in the direction his friend was heading. Why hadn't he warned him about the fence? With no opportunity to catch up to him, Peter could only try to increase the time that Lucas had to recognize his mistake and alter his course.

Peter intercepted Dirk as he returned to the dining lodge. "I forgot to tell you . . . the last time I was in town, someone was asking about you."

The unexpected news stopped Dirk in his tracks. It was that boy again, the one who had dared to talk back to him.

"Whoever that was, they must be mistaken. I don't know anyone in that damn town." Apprehensively, Dirk spat out the words.

"The man said something about going to school with you . . . said he saw you driving us kids around town," Peter continued, trying to buy precious seconds. His story was, in fact, true.

"He must have me mixed up with someone else," Dirk growled, unable to look Peter in the eye. The boy had not only got him thinking, but also momentarily thrown him off an important task.

When Crystal yelled that he was holding everyone up, Peter ran back to the others, who were already seated in the vehicles going to town. He might have only gained Lucas a few valuable minutes in his quest to escape, but he certainly put Dirk into a state of confusion.

Lucas moved quickly toward the tree line that bordered the commune's west perimeter. After passing a couple of smaller barns that housed clucking hens, plump chickens, and screaming piglets, he came upon a much larger structure situated near the commune's western edge. The sloped roof on the south side of the building was comprised of several rows of thick, transparent panes. Most likely, rather than glass, the windows were made of Plexiglas, a material that was almost unbreakable yet still allowed sunlight to enter the building during every month of the year. As well, the taller trees on that side of the property had either been trimmed or chopped down, exposing the windows to as much light as possible.

Beginning to sweat from exertion as he circled the massive greenhouse, Lucas halted abruptly. His mouth fell open as he stared at a six-foot fence that stood in his path along the inside edge of the treeline. It stretched in both directions as far as he could see, probably surrounding the entire property. Unfortunately, rather than wooden or metal bars he might climb, crisscrossed wires and tightly wound strands of barbed-wire posed an impenetrable barrier. Thick wooden posts supported at least twice the number of strands necessary to enclose a cattle ranch. Each strand was separated by less than six inches. The edges of a single coil of wire at the top of the fence glistened like razor blades. Lucas might as well have been trapped in a maximum-security prison!

Why hadn't the other kids warned him about the fence? Surely, they must have known about it. Or did they not expect him to attempt an escape so soon? Lucas began to panic as he realized that Dirk was probably on his trail already. Adrenaline pumping, he saw one glimmer of hope. Using a good-sized rock that he pulled from the pathway, he smashed open the rusty lock that secured the only entry to the imposing building on the edge of the property. He hoped desperately that he might find some form of cutting device inside. He would gladly destroy a set of tree-pruners or garden shears trying to slice through the strands of wire.

As Lucas slid open the heavy door, it was not a big surprise when the powerful odor of mature marijuana plants stung his nostrils. The building was truly a greenhouse, and certainly a very profitable one. Overpowering humidity hung in the thick air that washed across his pallid face. Long tubes suspended from wooden beams emitted bright iridescent light that made him squint. A blast of warmth streamed from a noisy oil heater and circulated among the dense foliage. The rumbling of a powerful generator filled the expansive confines of the isolated building.

Lucas's frantic search for a cutting tool came to an abrupt halt when his alert ears picked up a faint muffled sound that froze him in his tracks. Far in the distance, the anxious howling of one or more dogs became louder and louder. Could Dirk be far behind? Without taking time to check if he had repositioned the entry door—the broken lock would be an obvious giveaway—Lucas, in his panic, clambered over several baskets of harvested plants, attempting to hide in the darkest corner of the building. His chances of running next to none, he could only hope that the dank, pungent smell of the lucrative harvest would camouflage his own scent from the approaching dogs, whose excitement was increasing by the second.

Crouching in the smallest possible space, Lucas's worst fears were soon realized. Time stood still as his canine pursuers strained their leather leashes to the limit, howling and yelping as they closed in on their prey. As the scent grew stronger, they were relentless in pulling their master toward the building. Kneeling with his head bowed, the terrified boy shook uncontrollably, and his breathing stopped momentarily when the frantic dogs lunged against the outside wall, which was his last protection.

Moving toward the entrance, it took only seconds for Dirk to notice the useless lock and mangled latch on the greenhouse door. He gripped the leashes of two nasty-looking curs, whose yelping only got worse when the powerful man forced the door fully open. Both dogs were in a frenzy as they pulled Dirk into the stifling warmth of the humid building. Just breathing the fetid air was a strain on the lungs.

"You're late for your operation, my young friend." Although winded from the exertion of holding back the canines, Dirk's words still dripped with mockery. Concerned they might ruin the special crop, he held fast to both dogs, although he neither heard nor saw any movement in the greenhouse. "I caught you snooping in our leader's den the other day," he continued. "You pulled something out of the wall. Auscan and I are the only ones who know about that secret place. You have already betrayed your new family. Your punishment will not be pleasant, but it might just be your last!"

So, the shadow I saw the other day wasn't my imagination, Lucas thought, his stressed body continuing to shake uncontrollably in its cramped hiding spot.

With no response coming, Dirk's deep voice was devoid of either emotion or remorse, yet his threat was real. "I'll give you thirty seconds to think about showing your face before I allow my four-legged friends to tear you to pieces."

To a cowering child, those words were as chilling as if they echoed from the depths of a medieval grave. His energy suddenly drained and his head spinning, Lucas felt he was about to faint.

Chapter 33

Three hours earlier in his cramped motel room, Jarrod rubbed sleep from his eyes. It was time to get up.

Seven hours in bed should have provided plenty of rest. However, an anxious man on the run awakens many times during the longest of rests, sleep coming in sporadic intervals. With a body that remained tired, only caffeine and adrenalin could get Jarrod through the hours to come. He dressed quickly, packed, and ate the leftovers in his room—bread, cheese, and a handful of grapes. The fresh bread was now day-old bread.

Hearing the gurgling of the coffee machine as he approached the front counter, Jarrod peeked into Molly's back room. She already had the vacuum going. "It's time for me to get on the road!" he yelled over the roar of the noisy appliance.

Shutting off the vacuum, Molly walked slowly toward the mysterious man for whom she had developed a peculiar degree of empathy. Jarrod sensed an emptiness in her body as she realized her intriguing guest was about to slide out her life, most likely forever.

Blaming her watery eyes on the dust, Molly stumbled to find the right words. "Good luck to you and the boy. I'm sure you'll need it."

She handed Jarrod a sheet of paper with directions to her sister's town and the drop-off location for the car. "Don't worry too much about the old beater. It's time we got a newer one anyway. I just hope it gets you there without breaking down."

"I'm sure the car will be fine. I'll leave it where we agreed," Jarrod promised, giving Molly an impromptu yet emotional hug. "I don't know how to thank you."

"You just did. Please . . . keep safe," Molly said, her voice shaking. She turned away so Jarrod couldn't see her tears.

"Oh, Molly, I almost forgot." Jarrod handed her an envelope. "Give this to your policeman friend in a couple of days. Just say you found it in my room. I think he'll be interested in some of the activities that go on at that so-called thrift shop." He even included the plate number of the black limo he had watched pull out of the lane.

Although it may seem strange that a criminal fugitive should be so interested in exposing another lawbreaker, Jarrod was strongly against forcing innocent people into a situation against their will. He felt there were some sinister control methods going on within the Mount Cloquet community. Even from his first encounter with those people, he saw in the children's dull eyes that something was not right. What he had no way of knowing was that many members of the secretive group he was so interested in exposing had joined to simply escape from a life they couldn't endure.

Miraculously, the old Pontiac started without complaint. Maybe the previous day's trip into the country had loosened some engine sludge. Easing the car out of the narrow lane behind the motel, Jarrod planned to begin his route by passing the thrift store. He was not surprised that the "Closed" sign still dangled in the front window. However, within twenty minutes of following a familiar route into the countryside, he approached a convoy of three vehicles amid a sparse stream of highway traffic. Two of them he recognized—the Suburban and the dirty Jeep. The third vehicle was an older pickup truck.

Slowing as much as possible without causing suspicion, Jarrod tried to scan the occupants of the three vehicles. Observing the drivers' grim faces, he recognized only the woman who had sold him a pair of used boots. She was driving the Suburban. Neither the young man he had bought a drink for nor the nervous drug dealer was anywhere to be seen in the convoy. Although he had little opportunity to glance at the faces of the many children in the vehicles, Jarrod was certain Lucas would not be among them.

Facing a clear sky and a gentle breeze, Jarrod retraced his path toward the low-lying range of hills that surrounded the Mount Cloquet enclave. Beginning to sweat, his palms struggled to grip the steering wheel. The old car slipped and slid along roads that deteriorated into narrow gumbo paths. Although his memory of the route was accurate, Jarrod could just as easily have followed the fresh tread marks of the three vehicles that wound toward a variety of Saturday obligations. Slowing as he passed the driveway that he assumed led to the compound, his plan was to hide the car beyond the entrance, out of view of any other vehicles that might enter or exit the property.

In case a fast getaway was necessary, Jarrod faced the Pontiac toward his return direction, finding a spot that the tires had reasonable traction on the sloppy road. Judging from the weeds along the path that continued beyond the driveway, it was unlikely that many vehicles had ever ventured that far. However, as an extra precaution, Jarrod uprooted a nearby sapling and did his best to rub out his vehicle's tracks. After discarding the now-leafless young tree, he crept along the inside edge of brush that camouflaged the winding driveway.

What did he have for a weapon? The thought hit Jarrod just as the small cabin that acted as a sentry came into view. Looking up, he watched as thin threads of smoke from a dying fire rose from the log building's soot-encrusted chimney. Without even a pocketknife—Jarrod had returned the bread knife to Molly—Jarrod scoured the ground in the dense brush for anything he might use for defense. The best he could come up with was a stubby, round wooden shaft that might have once been a table leg. His hands fit comfortably around the hardwood bludgeon. Its lacquered finish had long since disappeared, but as a defensive weapon it would have to do.

While his head was bent to examine his find, a ruckus startled Jarrod. The noise seemed to originate from a larger building set farther back on the secretive community's sprawling grounds.

"The damn kid's gone! I've checked every cabin and outhouse. He's trying to escape! Come on! You've all got to help me. I'll get the dogs!"

The staccato voice that resonated across the courtyard was familiar to Jarrod. Only the day before he had bought a beer for Dirk, the runaway who had progressed through the ranks of the Mount Cloquet society.

Had Lucas made his move to escape? Certain that he had, Jarrod was concerned that he had showed up too late to be of any help. Dirk sounded determined, and his dogs would be well trained in tracking their prey, either animal or human. What chance did one defenseless boy have?

To remain hidden, Jarrod was forced to move deeper into the brush that thinned out as he circled behind a log building that gave off the burnt smell of a failed batch of muffins. As the near-leafless trees provided a poor screen to hide behind, he kept as low to the ground as possible. When a second building came into view, Jarrod caught a glimpse of three men moving quickly away from him down a narrow path.

Clutching their leashes, Dirk was yanked forward by two large members of the canine family that lunged aggressively ahead of him. He was followed by two other men dressed in khaki hats and jackets. As they faded out of sight in pursuit of their prey, it was evident that the hunters were not pursuing rabbits. Jarrod cautiously entered the same path and easily followed the loud barking of the frenzied dogs, which he guessed to be shepherd cross-breeds trained as hunters or tracking animals.

It wasn't long before Jarrod, who was still gripping his wooden club, came to a sudden halt as an opening in the trees came into view only a few yards ahead of him. Before him stood a barn-like structure, half of its sloping roof constructed with transparent panes. He stood there for a moment, trying to catch his breath. Jarrod had a clear view of two men rocking nervously back and forth as they watched Dirk and the ravenous hounds barge into the daunting structure. It was evident that the snarling curs had picked up the scent of the game they were pursuing with voracious delight.

Before he could decide on a plan to get past the two sentries without a confrontation, Jarrod's predicament ended when both men turned toward him. He was barely able to duck behind a clump of brush as it became apparent that the cowardly instincts of Dirk's "posse" recruits had gotten the better of them. Wanting no part of the violence they anticipated would come quickly, the squeamish men retreated up the path at a rapid pace. Dirk had chosen the wrong family members for his hunting party. The two recruits were more suited for overseeing a prayer meeting or selling used clothes than participating in the bloodshed that was about to ensue.

Approaching the isolated building unhindered, Jarrod stopped abruptly when he heard Dirk's threatening voice ring out over the yelping of the dogs. The only words he overheard struck him like a bolt of lightning: ". . . my four-legged friends tear you to pieces!"

It was now or never! As an intense surge of energy pumped through his system, Jarrod burst through the door. He ran between the rows of leafy plants, drawing their powerful aroma up his flared nostrils with every breath. The noisy generator covered up any sounds from his running. After several long strides, he glimpsed Dirk on the far side of the building. It was evident immediately that the snarling dogs had cornered their prey. Distracted by the howling dogs trying to pull away from his grasp, the powerful young man had little chance to react when Jarrod overtook him like a hurdler approaching his take-off. The wooden club snapped in half as it struck the back of Dirk's skull.

By the time Dirk sensed the danger behind him, the shock of the impact was threatening to numb his mind. His motor senses ceased, his thought process going totally blank. The hollow thud of the table leg reverberated throughout the building. The sound resembled that of a ripe watermelon exploding as it dropped on a slab of concrete. Sprawling face-first onto the wood chips spread over the greenhouse floor, Dirk lost consciousness immediately. Blood trickled down his thick neck, and a chunk of torn skin hung from the severed end of the club that had felled him.

Sensing the danger his master was in, one of the snarling dogs turned instinctively and leapt toward the intruder, saliva dripping from its exposed fangs. Jarrod barely had time to react. Still holding a vice-like grip on the remains of the jagged club, he automatically thrust his arm toward his airborne attacker. Either by design or sheer luck, his aim was perfect. The sharp end of the stick smashed through the unsuspecting dog's front fangs and lodged firmly in its jawbone. The beaten crossbreed let out a deafening howl as it crashed to the floor and lay in a pathetic heap, its broken teeth scattered on the floor and its chest heaving.

Hearing the hollow echo of the thud as his pursuer was clubbed over the head, Lucas rose hesitantly from his hiding place. Even more surprising was the agonizing yowl of one of the nasty canines going down. With little time to think, it took him only an instant to realize that the second hunting dog had more interest in seizing its prey than defending its master. Lucas reacted intuitively as the snarling mongrel lunged at him. Grabbing a half-full basket of drying plants that lay beside him, he held his arms out firmly as the dog's head smashed into the woven mesh. The bottom of the basket absorbed the full force of snapping fangs as they sunk into the coarse hemp, but his attacker wasn't about to give up. Spewing slobber as he tore his mouth away from the mesh, the angry canine was about to renew his attack when, without warning, his tender underbelly caved in.

Jarrod was three-for-three, his aim again perfect as his boot thrust solidly into the lunging animal's solar plexus. Wood chips scattered as the second dog tumbled onto the ground, its lolling tongue and heavy breathing the only evidence of life. The animal lay prone on the remains of the splintered basket. Mature marijuana buds dotted the folds of skin on its pink belly. The fight was over almost as quickly as it had begun.

"I can't believe you're here," Lucas stammered. His voice and his body shook uncontrollably. Although brief, the hug that he gave to his old friend was firm and sincere. "I never thought I'd see you again."

"The last few days have been a blur to me—ever since that U-drive drove off with you in the back," Jarrod replied. "After I saw you in the back of that damn truck the other night, I haven't been able to get you out of my mind. It wasn't easy to find this place. Are these people on drugs or just crazy?"

"I think you got both right. The night I met these creeps, they gave me some weird tea. It made me puke, and next thing I knew, I was at this place. Then they tried to make me part of their family, or whatever they call themselves."

Realizing that the time for renewing acquaintances was over, Lucas changed the subject. His reaction to immediate danger was faster than Jarrod's survival instinct. "What do we do now? Those dogs and that jerk won't lie on the floor forever." He glanced toward the daylight streaming through the open door.

Jarrod nodded, still breathing hard. "You're right. That guy's far from dead. He's breathing just fine. I've got a car sitting out on the road, but getting to it won't be easy."

"Besides the guy you clobbered, the worst of these stupid people have gone to town. None of the ones still here care much about fighting. They're scared of their own shadows." Lucas suddenly remembered Auscan, the man who might have been his future father. "Except maybe for one."

"I'll take your word for it, but we'd still better be careful," Jarrod replied.

"Our only way out is through the front. There's wire as sharp as razor blades all around this place," Lucas explained, his legs still wobbly. "But we have to get past the crazy leader."

Just as the reunited friends were leaving the greenhouse, the first of the hunting dogs gave them a vacant look as its eyes rolled open. However, with no fight left in him, the injured animal crawled slowly on his belly toward Dirk. Despite its shattered teeth, the dog began to lick the nasty wound on the back of his master's head. Would Dirk ever forgive his two so-called 'brothers' for abandoning him?

Looking out constantly for signs of danger, Jarrod retraced his precarious route along the path, careful to keep his distance as he circled around the rear of the log structures that dotted the commune grounds. Lucas followed closely behind him. Although their rapid movement through the dry underbrush triggered cracking and snapping noises as twigs and branches broke under their feet, there was no sign of any community members. Showing little or no concern for the activity and turmoil going on outside, and with no one to give them specific directions, everyone chose to hide safely in their cottages. Lucas was right that they were a group of controlled followers, the adult males unable to push themselves into action without direction from a leader. Even the former intern, Paul, seemed disinterested in his next patient's escape. Was it fear, lack of confidence, or was the trauma of the unprecedented situation never programmed into their teachings?

Just as escape appeared imminent, one last obstacle had to be overcome. Lucas also turned out to be right about an unexpected danger lurking on the grounds. Auscan, the society's self-proclaimed leader, had stirred from his cozy den. Having barely awakened, his mood was edgy and his mind unfocused when he became aware of the commotion outside his private haven. Aroused by Dirk's yelling in the courtyard, and before even lighting his customary pipe, Auscan searched the cottage for his favorite weapon, a twelve-gauge shotgun that was normally used for hunting game birds. After locating the gun in the pantry, he slid two cartridges into the breech and leaned it next to the front door. However, before even considering his next move, Auscan entered his favorite room to take part in his morning ritual of calming his jittery nerves.

Resting comfortably with his marble pipe, and with no concept of the passage of time, Auscan maintained a vigil at his den's tiny window. Why did he not greet his followers? Why was he not taking charge of the situation? Was he on the verge of losing control?

After a lull in activity that lasted many agonizing minutes, Auscan was jarred out of his relaxed stupor. He became alert when his anxious eyes caught a glimpse of Lucas and a stranger moving toward the driveway. His response was automatic. Stumbling as he leaped into action, Auscan grabbed his shotgun by both barrels. Flinging open the cottage door, he ran as fast and as straight as possible for a person in his somewhat mellow condition.

"Halt! Stop! That boy is one of our family. He must be protected!" Auscan yelled as he raced toward the startled escapees.

The leader came to a stop, raised his shotgun, and aimed it at the tall stranger, who had slowed his pace as he turned toward the frantic yelling. Even without a decent aim, the mushrooming effect of the buckshot would have a devastating, if not deadly, outcome. With no time to react, Jarrod could only grimace as he anticipated the worst.

Lucas stood in disbelief when, without warning, and almost instantaneously, Auscan went crashing to the ground. His finger squeezed the trigger just as he went down, sending shotgun pellets exploding toward the sky. A flock of starlings scattered from a nearby stand of birch, two of them crashing to the ground with broken wings.

Auscan had not tripped. To the shock of everyone, a snarling four-legged beast stood over the downed leader. For some inexplicable reason, the second cross-bred shepherd, the one that had tried to attack Lucas, had renewed its mission. After recovering sufficiently from its injury, the dog had caught a renewed scent of its prey and bounded down the trail in hot pursuit. Perhaps confusion resulting from its injury had short-circuited the canine's thinking. As a result, the enraged dog attacked the first person it came across, the one whose piercing voice resonated throughout the still morning air.

Whatever the reason for the attack, Jarrod and Lucas weren't going to hang around to investigate. Scrambling down the winding driveway, neither of them looked back as several members of the commune finally jumped into action. They ran to help their fallen leader, who was engaged in the fight of his life.

It took four men with ropes and a hunting net to subdue the attack dog. There was little fight left in Auscan after the out-of-control animal was finally pulled off him. Fortunately, his right shoulder and forearm had taken the brunt of the attack, and the puncture wounds he suffered weren't particularly deep, which could likely be attributed to the dog's recent injuries. But one thing was certain: Auscan's interest in pursuing Lucas and the man with him had greatly diminished.

Where was Dirk, the one person he could rely on when situations involving conflict arose? Not only would Auscan soon find out the answer to that question, but he would come to realize the great mistake of bringing the enigmatic boy called Lucas into his community in the first place. His scathing tirade aimed at all those who sat around and watched as the day's events unfolded would have to wait until the following day's prayer meeting. Injured or not, he was certain to preside over that event.

After slipping several times in the slimy muck that covered the driveway and the road, Jarrod and Lucas were both panting when they finally reached their getaway car. Still worried that others with rifles would be right on their heels, Jarrod started the Pontiac with one firm turn of the ignition key. With tires spinning, the trusty old vehicle lurched away, bringing an end to its final visit to the remote enclave of the Mount Cloquet society. Jarrod and Lucas kept a close lookout behind them, unaware that any fears they might have were unwarranted. In addition to the turmoil going on inside the commune, the only roadworthy vehicles that could have been used in pursuit were in town performing Saturday duties.

Chapter 34

Getting over his concern that someone might appear in the car's rear-view mirror, Jarrod finally spoke. "Can you believe what that dog did? Its brain must have short-circuited. It went berserk."

"Maybe it just got you and that wrinkled old creep confused," Lucas replied. "You guys kind of look like brothers." He smiled for the first time in what felt like ages. "Would you believe that weirdo and his scary wife wanted me to be a brother for their stupid daughters? That'll be the day!"

"Well, I'm sure between your curved nose and lousy aim with a shotgun you could easily pass as the son of that withered monkey," Jarrod replied with a straight face. "Oh, sorry, I forgot the shotgun part was just a story we made up." He broke into a grin.

"Okay, you got me there," Lucas said, "but to tell you the truth, I'd rather have you for a father if I had a choice." There, he had finally got that admission off his chest. He had never in his short life respected even one adult male. His confession was unplanned and impulsive.

Caught off guard, Jarrod could not think of a reply. He looked straight ahead, the washboard road curving to the right as it approached the intersection of a paved highway. Pulling the car over to the edge of the drying mud, he stopped well short of the asphalt roadway. Aware that a left turn would be to the north, toward the Canadian border, he still wanted to familiarize himself with Molly's map.

After memorizing the route, and still without knowing how to respond to his young friend's words, Jarrod pushed down on the Pontiac's signal lever. When he realized the car was about to make a left turn, Lucas's face turned serious. "Wait! That's not the way to town!" His tone was anxious.

"No, it's the opposite way. But we're headed north—as far away from that place as possible. Is something wrong?" Jarrod asked, confused by the boy's anxiety.

"There's someone I've got to talk to before we go." Lucas paused, his mind confused. "A girl who lived in that dumb society, or whatever you call it. She doesn't belong there any more than I do. Maybe she can come with us. Pleeease . . . can we go to town just one more time?"

Hearing the desperation in Lucas's voice, Jarrod thought for a moment. Then shook his head. "That's too much of a chance. Someone is bound to recognize us—or at least me. We've probably been on the news, and Sheriff Klem will have his posters all over the place. And what if she did come with us? Don't you think we have enough problems with just the two of us?"

"Then just let me out here!" Lucas shouted. His words were impulsive, his inborn stubbornness taking over. Tears brimmed in his eyes as he tugged on the passenger door's handle.

"Okay, okay, settle down." Jarrod realized there was little chance of reasoning with Lucas at that point. "What did you do, fall in love with this girl?" When Lucas didn't respond, Jarrod continued. "But really, there's no way we can take the chance of going back there, sorry."

The words were barely out of Jarrod's mouth when the passenger door flew open. Lucas jumped from the car just as it was starting its left turn. With only the clothes on his back and a few dollars stuffed in his sock, the frustrated boy started to march toward town.

Exasperated, Jarrod drove a couple of hundred yards before he pulled over to the side of the road. What now? After all his efforts to locate the exasperating child, was he about to be separated again, barely an hour later? Without giving much thought to his next decision, his heart, not his common sense, won the battle.

"Damn, you're an idiot," he cursed, admonishing himself as he gripped the steering wheel and spun a U-turn in the middle of the highway.

"You'd better hope we can get lucky one more time!" Jarrod shouted through the open window as he skidded to a stop next to the impulsive boy. "Get in!"

Fortunately, there was no traffic on the highway. How could an urge be so powerful that it would send Lucas flying out of the car without a moment of thought? In any event, Jarrod wasn't about to let the kid fend for himself so soon after finally catching up to him. Would another stupid maneuver prove to be a big mistake? Jarrod was about to find out.

"Thanks," Lucas whispered as he got back into the car. "I kind of thought you'd come back—at least I hoped you would." His voice was hoarse with emotion. "I felt something strange when that girl was around me . . . I can't describe it."

Your first puppy love, Jarrod wanted to say, but he kept his thoughts to himself. Instead, with a wry grin, he offered nature's explanation. "You remind me of a love-starved male duck. With all his colorful feathers, he could float anywhere in the big pond, and yet he swims two feet behind the plain-looking female no matter which way she turns."

"I wouldn't call Catherine plain," Lucas mumbled, rolling his eyes as he stared out the window.

Although it was only midafternoon when the old Pontiac entered the western outskirts of Duluth, the late-autumn sun was sliding quickly toward the horizon. Making sure to obey every traffic law and speed limit, Jarrod kept to the side streets, taking an inconspicuous route toward the downtown bus terminal.

His sharp ears able to pickup the early-morning conversation, Lucas remembered that Catherine was one of the children assigned to collect donations from the travelers, or whoever hung out at the bus station. He was not able to catch the name of the person who would accompany her, but he hoped it was either Tom or Peter. Both boys had gone to town that morning.

Wary that danger might be lurking as they approached the bus station, Jarrod parked two blocks from the depot, easing the Pontiac into a vacant spot between two smaller import cars.

"Let's park on this side street. It's not too close to the bus depot. Maybe we can get lost in all the people wandering on the streets. Saturday seems to be a busy day around here." Jarrod sounded jittery and uncomfortable as he spoke. He was still skeptical, certain that Lucas's dumb idea was only going to stir up more trouble. As he led the way up the street, Jarrod was wary of all activity, anticipating the worst.

Negative thoughts have a way of leading to negative results. Jarrod shouldn't have been surprised that Curtis, Molly's friend in the police force, had drawn the Saturday afternoon beat in the downtown area. "Make the shoppers feel safe." Curtis had heard the words from his captain on many occasions. Little did he know that his normally mundane and uneventful shift was about to be filled with action.

Although he disliked it immensely, one duty that Curtis was expected to perform was ticketing illegally parked vehicles. The sky began to darken as he walked his beat toward the end of an incident-free shift. Glancing casually up a side street, to his surprise, he caught a glimpse of a familiar car: Molly and Fred's old Pontiac. It was parked in a red zone, almost on top of a hydrant that Jarrod had failed to notice. Why would Molly park her car there? She could have walked there just about as fast. Curtis debated whether he should ticket the car, finally deciding that a good scolding would be in order next time he saw her. Never did he suspect that Molly was not the one who had parked the Pontiac today.

Curtis's last stop before calling it a day was the bus station. Would he have to hustle Crusty or one of his buddies out of there again? That was another job he deplored, but loitering in public places was a breach of a longstanding town ordinance, and someone had to enforce it.

Pushing open the double doors at the entrance to the bus station, Jarrod was hit with the usual blast of warm air. The lobby and chairs were crowded with weekend travelers, including many who either looked confused or just shuffled about with bored expressions. There were few signs of enthusiasm.

Lucas's eagle eyes quickly scanned the waiting room, taking only a moment to spot a familiar freckled face. Catherine's smile, if not genuine, was at least consistent as she approached the travelers. Some looked tired and unpleasant, while others were good-humored and approachable as she held out her box and asked for contributions.

Forgetting for a moment where he was, and with his mouth dry as he approached his freckle-faced friend, Lucas had trouble thinking of what to say. "I got away . . .." were the only words he managed to stammer as he came within two paces of her, his hands trembling.

The shock of seeing Lucas almost made Catherine drop her wooden box. Only the strap around her neck kept it from falling to the floor. She was dumbfounded. "How did you get here?"

From a few feet away, a second familiar face appeared. It was Peter. With a stunned expression, he stood in disbelief that Lucas had escaped not only Dirk but the hunting dogs as well. Peter was convinced that only magic could have spirited him out of that place.

Seeing their shocked looks, Lucas was quick to explain. "I got help from a friend—an older guy I met on the road. We got into some trouble together a while ago . . . it's a long story." Suddenly, the tone of his voice changed. "Catherine, you've got to come with us! We've got a car, and we're headed north. You can't stay with these people." Lucas's words came close to pleading. "Peter, you should get away, too. There's no life for you at that place."

"I couldn't sleep last night . . . thinking about what you said," Catherine began. "You've got a few of us thinking for ourselves now, but the other kids still need us to help them, especially the younger ones. We know that Miss Cass and the others are trying to control us, that we're being used. But things are going to change. We'll stand up for ourselves. I really . . . appreciate your offer . . . but sorry, I can't leave the others. We've been together too long—"

"I feel the same way," Peter said, anxious to give his opinion. "Thanks to you, we're finally looking out for each other. But Cath is right. The younger kids need our help. No matter what happens, I've got to stay and see it through. Even if it means getting a beating from Dirk."

Lucas glanced over to where Jarrod was standing, staring anxiously at the bulletin board, where all the posters and notices were pinned. With disappointment and sadness etched in his face, Lucas realized that no convincing in the world would sway the minds, and especially the loyalties, of his newfound friends. He should have been pleased to see them display his own traits of boldness and unwillingness to give in. How stupid he had been to even think of asking

Catherine to leave with him. He was annoyed with himself, realizing he should have listened to Jarrod in the first place.

Unable to face either of his friends, Lucas stared at the ground. "Goodbye, guys, and good luck. I've got to get out of this place. Maybe we'll meet again . . . sometime." The chance of that happening was beyond remote, the sad thought rushing through the minds of all three friends.

As Lucas turned to walk away, Catherine was unable to control herself. She grabbed him by the shoulders and planted a firm kiss on his cheek. Embarrassed that he couldn't make himself face her due to the tears brimming in his eyes, Lucas pulled away and forged a path through the crowded lobby.

Not wanting to get in the way of Lucas and the freckle-faced girl of his youthful dreams, Jarrod had been careful to keep his distance. Moving slowly as he dodged the crowds, it wasn't long before he found himself staring at his worst nightmare. Displayed prominently behind the bulletin board's protective glass was an artist's drawing showing the likenesses of two wanted criminals. It was likely Klem who had provided descriptions of the escaped prisoner and his runaway companion. Surely the sheriff's determination was beyond the call of duty. The uncanny detail of their portraits could only have been sketched by a professional. Beneath their faces were not only physical descriptions but also a list of the dreadful crimes they were accused of committing (dreadful in the eyes of Sheriff Klem at least).

More desperate than ever to get out of that place, and as quickly as possible, Jarrod's attention suddenly focused on a reflection that, with cinematic clarity, stared directly at him from the glass panel that protected the posters. On one side, he saw the slim figure of Lucas, who was winding through the throng of travelers, but on the other side he had a clear view of the entrance to the bus depot. The hat, the jacket, and the badge were all too familiar. Unaware of the approaching danger, Lucas was directly behind Jarrod when the police officer began to stroll across the lobby, scrutinizing the crowd.

"Don't turn your head . . . we've got company," Jarrod said. The two fugitives froze in their tracks, their minds desperately plotting an escape route.

Either the mental stress of his thoughts or the spooked expression Jarrod displayed must have acted like a powerful magnet, because Curtis, for no apparent reason, glanced in his direction. No doubt, suspicion ingrained from years of experience led the policeman on a direct route toward the bulletin board, his left hand clutching a two-way radio that swung from his thick belt. Only the day before he had distributed several updated posters that a Wisconsin police department was sending across the country. His pace quickened as his mind began to focus on the descriptions of the wanted fugitives.

As soon as he saw the wiry youngster standing next to the man whose face he recognized from the stack of posters, Curtis realized he had uncovered a perfect match. However, just as he was unfastening the clip that supported his bulky radio, a familiar face staggered into his path: Crusty, the homeless man, stared directly into his face.

"Officer . . . you've got to help me. I've got this awful pain. Please . . . I think it's my heart." He grabbed Curtis's shirtsleeve and slumped to his knees. His attention briefly diverted, Curtis called immediately for an ambulance. Two bus passengers with paramedic experience witnessed the old fellow's distress and rushed to his aid. Despite the sudden commotion, Curtis's police training had taught him to concentrate on more than one task. His eyes continued to follow Jarrod and Lucas as they pushed their way toward the front entrance. Satisfied that Crusty was getting proper attention, Curtis rose to his feet and started toward the exit, calling for backup as his radio crackled with static.

The unusual activity in the bus station didn't escape Peter's attention. Aware that Lucas was in trouble, he dropped his collection box next to Catherine. "Here, make sure you hide this!" he shouted as he ran toward the front of the lobby. Catching up to Curtis just as he was adjusting the squelch knob on his squeaky radio, Peter was almost bowled over when he charged directly into the officer's path.

"Officer . . . please help me. I've been robbed!" Peter screamed.

The distress in the youngster's voice caught Curtis by surprise, stopping him dead in his tracks, the boy hanging onto his right arm. The radio dropped from his hand. "You're one of those kids who does church collections, aren't you?" he asked, trying to calm Peter, who was now on his knees.

"That's right, I've seen you before. You seem like a nice guy. Someone just grabbed my collection box," Peter explained, attempting to divert the officer's focus. There was just enough panic in his voice to sound convincing.

Looking out the plate-glass doors, Curtis watched as the two fugitives escaped up the street. He was caught in a quandary. Which way should he turn? After finally getting through to the dispatcher at his precinct with a request for backup, Curtis followed his heart and decided his community came first, allowing Peter to lead him to the scene of the crime. Yet in the end, all Curtis got was a vague description of a scary-looking thief. Catherine had hidden the collection box. Witnesses were fewer than scarce. The only certainty was that time was now in the favor of two fugitives who were about to skip town in a rundown old Pontiac that had been illegally parked next to a hydrant.

Chapter 35

It wasn't until the next day that Molly reported her keys missing. She also turned over an informative letter found in the room of her motel guest, Bill Jackson. Curtis's conversation with Molly was both eye-opening and confusing. It provided little help in locating the fugitives, and he left even more puzzled than before. His backup had arrived too late to get any leads on the fugitives' whereabouts. The duty sergeant was not inclined to start an all-out search for them, which would involve calling in off-duty officers. Curtis did receive a minor reprimand for not pursuing them himself. Finally, after reading an unsigned letter concerning the drug trade, Curtis realized that the faces he only knew from an artist's sketch were about to affect more lives than they might ever imagine.

When the truth eventually surfaced, Officer Curtis and his superiors were indeed pleased with the information they received from Jarrod. Molly's account about the stolen car keys was realistic. As her soap opera continued, she envisioned the back-lane drug dealers as the real villains of an ongoing mystery, and she had been part of her heroes' escape. It turned out that the driver of the limo was an unscrupulous character that the state police drug division had been building a case against for several months. But one major source of his drug supply had, until then, remained a mystery. Ultimately, not only the leaders but also the entire Mount Cloquet society was on the verge of collapse.

Ironically, one revealing note penned by a desperate fugitive altered the fate of a unique though eccentric lifestyle. Over the winter months, discreet surveillance of the thrift shop led detectives to an important source of drugs for the mysterious man who parked his shiny black limo in the same lane in which Lucas had scrawled his frantic plea on a muddy tailgate. A warrant led to a search of the clandestine society's property and the arrest of its leader, Auscan Zapata. Considered to be obtained through the profits of crime, the entire property was seized. The decision ultimately broke up the Mount Cloquet community.

The children who lived there without any parents or relatives to take them in became wards of the state and were placed in foster care. Catherine, Tom, and Peter were lucky enough to find permanent placement with fine families. All three of them thrived with their new-found freedom, yet a bond always kept them in touch with one another. Where was the one boy who had changed their lives forever? On more than one sleepless night, each took their turn wondering what fate had in store for the friend they hardly got to know.

Cassandra was the first to realize that her community was unravelling. From the fateful day she flinched when Lucas dared to stare her down, she knew something was changing. Control was slipping away from both self-proclaimed leaders. The children began to talk more among themselves, appearing to gain a sense of strength and independence that was never apparent before. Auscan seemed to be losing interest, spending more and more time in his private den. Did the dog attack send him over the edge?

Yet in the end, Cassandra proved to be the most resilient of all. She held together the remnants of the community, those who wished to continue life as a family, including the children who lived with their parents. Even her own daughters gained maturity and responsibility in a more relaxed atmosphere. The soups and teas became much healthier. Through an estate sale, the remaining group members were able to secure a bargain-priced property not far from their original commune. There was no massive greenhouse, and farming became more traditional. Still able to maintain a reasonable profit, the thrift shop continued to operate at its same location.

Other than Auscan, who was the only one to serve a prison term for drug dealing, the only real casualty was Dirk, the powerful young man who had been bullied as a child. Addiction to the bottle led him on a downward spiral. His life became a series of menial jobs and welfare checks. The last anyone saw of him, Dirk was travelling out west with a carnival that had passed through the area.

The demise of the Mount Cloquet society barely got a mention in the local paper, yet for the people who had spent much of their lives there, it had been a family, the only true family they had ever known. The commune offered them shelter and stability, two things that were lacking in their previous lives. In certain ways, perhaps Auscan and Cassandra were actually on the right track. They had provided a home for many lost souls. Unfortunately, their methods of control were not only unorthodox but also more than a little over the edge.

Convinced that the officer was right on their tails, Jarrod and Lucas dodged pedestrians and traffic as they ran like frightened deer toward their getaway vehicle. How were they to know that two people they had only met days earlier had made their escape possible? Not until they jumped into their getaway car did they realize no one was in pursuit. Nevertheless, the Pontiac's tires spun wildly as it merged into a maze of congested traffic on the main street, accelerating onto the shortest route out of town. An uncharacteristic impulse made Jarrod throw caution to the wind.

"What happened to that cop?" Lucas asked with amazement. "I thought he'd be right behind us." He was still trying to catch his breath from another hurried escape.

"I saw an old homeless person walk up to him, a fellow I talked to when I was trying to track you down. Maybe he stalled the cop on purpose. It's hard to say," Jarrod replied, trying to make sense of their fortunate escape.

"Catherine wouldn't come with us. I guess you figured that out," Lucas said in a tone that lacked expression. He had a blank look in his eyes. "She wanted to stay and help the other kids. I guess they're the only family she knows. But the leaders of that crazy place are control freaks. I think I got a few of the kids to stand up for themselves, but I hope it doesn't make things worse for them."

"I get the impression your feelings for that girl went deeper than just trying to get her out of that place," Jarrod conceded, carefully navigating the car through heavy traffic near the edge of town.

Lucas dug deep for an explanation. "That feeling I had was weird. Whenever I looked at her, there was this tightness way down in my guts. Even my heart started to beat real fast."

"Don't worry; it's just part of growing up," Jarrod said, a grin crossing his face. "There'll be plenty more of those feelings."

"Sorry I got so pissed off back there. Deep down, I really thought you'd turn around. But I was desperate. I guess pretty stupid—and I took a chance."

"I'll tell you one thing. I called myself a few names when I made that U-turn. But when it came down to driving off alone, I couldn't have lived with myself." Jarrod took a deep breath as he kept a close eye on the rear-view mirror. "It looks as though we got lucky again."

Remembering something, he reached into his jacket pocket for an important slip of paper. When his hand came up empty, a feeling of desperation crawled into the pit of his stomach. Molly's map was missing! After searching his other pockets, he asked Lucas to check the front seat and floor. The map was nowhere to be found.

"Damn, I must have lost Molly's directions. They showed us how to get to the Canadian border," Jarrod said, his voice shaking with frustration. With all the recent activity, he had forgotten the highway numbers.

"Do you remember any of the route?" Lucas asked.

"The town, Baud . . . Baudette, I could find on any map. But that's not what's important. What if I dropped that map near the bus station and the cops find it? They'll alert every town on the border. Do you think we'd have a chance?" Jarrod was almost shouting.

His mind still churning, Jarrod remembered to fuel up the Pontiac, pulling over at one of the last service stations on their way out of town. Rummaging through the glovebox, Lucas came across a tattered old state map. Unfamiliar with roadmaps, all the colored lines and numbers confused him, but he recognized the red dashes that showed the Canadian border and a place called Baudette right next to it. He figured the black line running north from Duluth was the highway on which they were traveling.

"Highway fifty-three looks like the road we take to Canada," he announced when Jarrod got back into the vehicle.

"That sounds familiar," Jarrod replied, glad they at least had a roadmap. "Maybe I overreacted when I couldn't find that paper with the directions. Anyway, what are the chances it would fall into the hands of the police?"

Lacking a better idea, Jarrod decided to stick with his original plan. Surely the priority of apprehending them didn't warrant roadblocks on every highway exiting town. Unless, of course, Klem had been the local sheriff.

Loaded with junk food and soft drinks purchased at the gas station, they set out on their ominous journey north as the great orange ball sank behind the western horizon.

Winding past the low range of hills that hid the entrance to the hideout of a secluded community, Jarrod couldn't help but glance towards the washboard road he had driven down more than once. As the highway straightened out ahead of him, the land became flatter. When darkness set in, the clumps of trees that dotted the countryside showed a vivid display of fall colors.

Within an hour, Lucas was slumped on the front seat with his eyes closed. The Pontiac's squeaky wiper blades were busy cleaning off light flakes of powdery snow, the noise keeping Jarrod awake and alert but having no effect on the exhausted boy. As traffic thinned out when the divided highway narrowed to a two-lane road, the lights of approaching vehicles became increasingly intermittent. The towns along the highway were so tiny, and their speed zones fluctuated so quickly, that Jarrod was continually on and off the gas pedal, carefully observing all the speed limits. He noted two road signs in particular. One was for the US Hockey Hall of Fame, and the other was for the Nett Lake Indian Reservation, a faded, wooden sign pointing west toward Pelican Lake. He figured that water birds of any kind would be scarce at that time of year, smart enough to fly south for the winter.

Late evening was approaching when a more crucial sign caught Jarrod's attention and jolted him to pay closer attention: "Canadian Border 10 Miles." They were nearing the border town of International Falls.

"Lucas, wake up," he called out. "Check that map again. This is where we turn west, isn't it?"

Blinking sleep from his eyes, Lucas yawned as he tried to focus on the wrinkled map. The folded edges were torn, making it tricky to read. Squinting in the faint glow from the Pontiac's interior light, he nodded. "Yeah, there's a crossroad up ahead. Turn left, and we won't have to go through town. It'll take us to Highway Eleven, the road that goes to that town you talked about. Bawdet, is that how you say it?"

"It's pronounced like an 'o'. . . Baudette. Molly said it was a French name."

"Do they speak French in Canada?" Lucas asked casually, sounding concerned that no one would understand him.

"If they do, we'll both be in trouble." Jarrod smiled. "Don't worry; it's only out east in Quebec where they speak mostly French." He hoped he was right.

Moments later, they found the shortcut that bypassed International Falls. After five or six miles along a road that suffered from an endless series of potholes that warning signs politely called "surface breaks," they intersected the only east/west roadway that paralleled the border. Its course meandered as it followed a swift-flowing river. A sign reflecting in the car's headlights displayed "Rainy River" as the name. That evening, it might have been more aptly named the Snowy River, as white powder showered its surface, melting on impact with the black, uninviting water. Although not heavy, the snowflakes were persistent as they continued to blow from the north, impairing visibility.

Jarrod was forced to dim the Pontiac's headlights when the elevated rays of light from the high-beams were reflected into his eyes by billows of swirling snow stirred up by oncoming vehicles. Some areas were protected from the continual north wind by stands of pine, spruce, and other evergreens that occasionally blocked their view as the road wound close to the open water on the right. At other times, when the highway curved toward the river, the powdery veil of snow shimmered in the headlights before the fragile flakes were devoured by the dark, silent waters.

"It feels like we're in the middle of nowhere," Lucas commented as he strained his eyes, anticipating any signs of life along the highway. Occasionally, the eyes of some tall animal glowed like hot coals on the side of the road and then disappeared as the animal darted toward the safety of the bush. Satellite dishes perched on the roofs of well-lit bungalows appeared to provide the only entertainment for residents of the few tiny villages that emerged along the highway.

"If the weather doesn't get worse, we should reach that town in about an hour," Jarrod remarked, trying to keep positive. Molly's estimate of time and distance had been too conservative. Should he have dumped the car or taken another route? His answer would come shortly.

"Do you think we'll ever find a place where we don't have to always be looking over our shoulder? Maybe I should have just stayed at that farm," Lucas said, his unemotional voice taking an odd philosophical approach. "But I couldn't take that gizmo being stuck in my head. To be honest, I'm tired of being on the run."

"It would sure be nice to quit running. Let's not give up hope just yet." Jarrod's response was terse, his stamina draining. "We've both come a long way so far."

Little was said for several minutes as Jarrod tried to figure out if, and where, they had any chance of getting across the Canadian border undetected. Making any move that night in the snow and the darkness seemed out of the question, or could the weather work in their favor? When they stopped in town, Jarrod would examine the map from the glovebox for any clues that an illegal entry into Canada might be lurking around the corner.

The rest of the ride went smoothly, and it wasn't long before a yellow, hazy glow on the horizon gave the first sign that civilization was imminent. Moments later, Baudette's streetlights reflected on the gently falling snowflakes, producing a series of flickering halos as the Pontiac crept into the outskirts of town.

Chapter 36

"Keep your eyes open," Jarrod warned. "It's unlikely anyone is looking for us, but we can't take anything for granted."

As the speed limit slowed, the local traffic increased. It was obvious that people didn't let the weather keep them home on a Saturday night in that northern town. Certain that Molly's directions to the parking lot led along the main artery through town, Jarrod kept pace with the traffic as his eyes checked both sides of the road. Not surprisingly, Lucas was the first to spot the open field not far from the lights of the local movie theater and a popular bar and restaurant. The cleared lot on the right side of the main road had no lighting of its own, and served as an overflow parking area for the adjacent shopping mall and theater. Cars were scattered in small clusters across the unpaved surface, and several recreational trailers rested in winter storage along the lot's outer edge. Jarrod recalled seeing the movie theater on Molly's map.

"There . . . that must be the place," Lucas began. However, after a tense moment of silence, the tone of his voice changed dramatically, its volume rising. "Don't slow down, Jarrod . . . I see something!"

Forced to keep his eyes on the road as he overtook slower traffic, Jarrod couldn't hold back his concern. "What is it, the police?"

"I think so. About four white cars with beacons are sitting in the far corner of that big field," Lucas replied, his voice cracking as he struggled to keep it steady. "A group of guys in uniforms are standing around talking. Maybe they're just on a coffee break," he added hopefully.

"Wishful thinking. You think a town this size normally has four patrol cars out at once? More likely some cop got hold of that stupid map. Or Molly's friend found out that we borrowed her old beater." Jarrod trusted she would stick to her original story. "We'll have to dump the car somewhere else. The border is still a few miles away, so we may still need it."

Just then, as a new wave of wet flurries once again taxed the wiper blades, the Pontiac's engine began to cough and sputter. The old beater could not have chosen a worse time. An uncontrollable shiver went through Lucas as his tired mind envisioned the worst of possibilities. As usual, the thought of losing his freedom was the most distressing.

Suddenly realizing that the fuel gauge read "Empty," Jarrod quickly pulled over at the first gas pumps he spotted, which happened to be in the lot of a convenience store. He was none too soon, as the gas-starved engine abruptly stalled.

"I guess I was a little cheap when I put gas in back there . . . ten bucks barely got us here," he said as he glided the car to a stop next to the nearest pump.

Lucas breathed a sigh of relief, mumbling something that sounded like, "El cheapo."

Although the sign read "self-serve," payment was required before the clerk behind the cash register would activate any of the pumps. Jarrod went inside with two five-dollar bills in his hand, while Lucas looked around anxiously from inside the car. Emerging moments later holding two overcooked hot dogs that had been turning perpetually on heated steel rollers, Jarrod inserted the hose and squeezed the filler handle until his cash deposit was fully depleted.

Young couples paraded in and out of the convenience store, smiling and giggling as they carried either six-packs of 3 percent beer or sweet and colorful slushy drinks. The liquids were accompanied by generous bags of munchies, mostly potato chips and pretzels. Cold and blustery Saturday nights didn't keep the kids at home. Jarrod even noticed a couple of cars with Ontario license plates, the Canadian province he was planning to enter soon.

Hoping he hadn't run the carburetor dry enough that it would require priming, Jarrod closed his eyes as he turned the key. After three groaning attempts, the gas-starved engine coughed, then roared to life when Jarrod pinned the gas pedal to the floor.

The car had barely started when Lucas barked a warning. "There's a black-and-white car coming! The beacons aren't flashing, but it's got a turn signal on. I think it may be coming in here!"

"Let's hope they're just looking for more coffee," Jarrod replied as he accelerated away from the pumps, cutting in front of a van that was filled with beers, snacks, and hormone-driven teens.

The occupants of the vehicle sent a volley of curses toward the old Pontiac and encouraged the driver to go after the car that had the nerve to cut across their path. Fortunately, one of the teens spotted the approaching police car. With a van filled with underage drinkers and open liquor, the chase was quickly called off.

Still shaken, Jarrod merged gently into the slow-moving traffic without anyone in hot pursuit. It was almost as if the old Pontiac had taken on a life of its own, including the responsibility of safely delivering its cargo of two desperate humans. Neither nasty weather nor dangerous pursuers were going to deter the faithful car from reaching its final destination, as only fate would ultimately determine.

Traffic thinned out quickly as they approached the west edge of town. Finally convinced that no one was following them, Jarrod decided it was time to check for directions. He pulled into a picnic area that became a turnaround for snowplows during the winter season. Once stopped, he took a closer look at the torn map that Lucas had been fidgeting with. The first thing he noticed was that the Rainy River, which paralleled the highway at this point, made a sharp turn to the north only a few miles ahead. The river flowed on a northerly route for ten miles or so before emptying into a vast body of water called Lake of the Woods. It had been evident from the movement of the snow-covered branches and other debris in the water that they were following the river downstream.

"It looks as though Canada is just on the other side of that river," Jarrod said. "Swimming isn't an option, but there must be another way to get across it." Jarrod tried to sound optimistic, but he was spellbound as he stared at the chilly black waters.

"Aren't there any bridges around here?" Lucas asked hopefully.

"Only at official border crossings, where they have plenty of guards that ask a load of questions. And those places are the first to get descriptions of people on the run from the law."

With a sullen look on his face, Lucas slumped down in his seat. Those cold, swirling waters did not look inviting. He had run out of suggestions.

"But look here at the map," Jarrod said. "A side road leads north to this little town, or maybe it's just a summer camp. It's called Wheeler's Point." Jarrod got little reaction as he pointed out the potential escape route to Lucas, who looked disinterested, curling up on the passenger seat without connecting his seatbelt.

The map showed an immense lake dotted with islands, the entire region isolated from any populated areas. There was no sign of a town or even a village on the Canadian side anywhere close to the US border. For all Jarrod knew, the area could be the private summer playground of the rich and famous. Actually, he had come closer to the truth than he realized, with wealthy individuals laying claim to their own private islands. The tear in the map ran along a series of dots and dashes that designated the international border as it bisected the lower portion of Lake of the Woods before turning sharply to the west, where it joined the southern border of the central Canadian province of Manitoba.

When he heard Jarrod casually mention the name of that province, Lucas surprisingly showed a renewed interest. "That's the name!" he blurted, suddenly wide awake.

"What are you talking about?" Jarrod said, startled by the sudden outburst.

"The place my foster mom and Bob were talking about. Where he said he was going to get a job," Lucas explained excitedly, his words coming at rapid speed.

The kid sure has determination. He won't quit. That woman must have really meant something to him, Jarrod thought. It wasn't the time or the place to show discouragement. "You're still a long way from getting there, but at least you can see the place is somewhere on a map; it really does exist," Jarrod said, his voice displaying a positive tone. "But first, let's figure out how to get into Canada."

Aware that the Canadian border stretched for thousands of miles, it seemed inconceivable to Jarrod that the entire length could be patrolled. Besides, wasn't Canada a close ally and trading partner of America? Rather than humans, wolves, deer, and moose were likely to wander the paths that wound throughout the vast wilderness that spread across the isolated stretch of land. Crossing back and forth between countries would be of no concern to those animals.

Their tired minds mesmerized by the Pontiac's high beams reflecting off the snow-shrouded pines that lined the highway, Jarrod and Lucas almost missed the sign that pointed north to Wheeler's Point, the tiny hamlet shown on the map. The old car slid sideways as Jarrod attempted to make a right turn at too high a speed. Not used to winter driving conditions, he discovered that applying the brakes only made turning more difficult. After almost sliding off the road, Jarrod released the brake pedal, the car getting just enough traction to complete the right turn. He was fortunate not to spin in a complete circle.

"Whew, that was close," he mumbled, regaining control just in time.

"Nice driving," Lucas said rather sarcastically. "Did the map show how far to the camp?"

"Not really, but if I read the mileage scale right, it should be only ten or twelve miles. But it'll be slow going in this weather. We should have enough gas."

"I hope so, cheapo." Lucas was glum, but he couldn't help his innocent wisecrack.

As the Pontiac slipped and sloshed along the secondary road that received minimal plowing, even in the midst of winter, the wet snowflakes appeared to gain size and density. Lucas was wide awake and kept a close eye on their route, commenting on every set of eyes that glowed in the headlights. His voice grew louder when he saw a large black bear turn and amble into the thick brush. Fortunately, none of the creatures darted into the path of the trusty old beater as it wandered from one side of the road to the other, the tires trying to get traction in the slushy conditions. The temperature was just around the freezing point.

Slightly over half an hour later, Lucas spotted the first sign of civilization. Almost obliterated with wet, sticky snow, a metal sign reflected a welcoming message. Yet the village of Wheeler's Point appeared to be deserted. In place of a welcome committee, its scattered buildings were engulfed in darkness and a fresh layer of snow. The few dull lights that were activated by timers failed to illuminate the hamlet's narrow streets. The tiny community consisted of boarded-up summer homes and rental cottages as well as groups of small businesses related to boating, fishing, and camping supplies. Other that the faint smell of a wood-burning fire, any evidence of human activity was nonexistent.

When Jarrod noticed a sign that pointed toward a launching area for boats, it took only two short turns for the Pontiac to reach the bank of the river they had been following. Close to the shore sat a row of rectangular, brightly painted wooden huts resting on thick beams. They were likely ice-fishing shacks that had no use until the water froze over, probably in January. What really caught the attention of both driver and passenger was the vast undulating body of water into which the Rainy River emptied.

Lucas fidgeted nervously as he gazed over the enormous lake that intimidated his young imagination (he had yet to experience the ocean). While his eyes fixated on the endless expanse of water, the billowy clouds overhead began to dissipate, and a magical autumn moon sprinkled its silver beams across the gently rolling waves that spread out to the north as far as the distant horizon and likely many miles beyond. Hopefully, the waxing moon that was approaching its full phase bode well for the end of the stormy weather pattern. Without doubt, the sprawling waters were instrumental in bringing on increased humidity. Combined with a gentle breeze from the north-west, the dampness ate through to the bones of the two tired fugitives as they stepped from their vehicle and stared at the vast lake, the endless water daunting to their weary eyes.

Chapter 37

Moments later, after getting over the shock of seeing such a huge stretch of water, Lucas spoke, his teeth chattering from the dampness in the air. "What do we do now? Start swimming?" His trivial question was spoken with a tone of resignation

"You're getting tired and grumpy, you sarcastic little bugger," Jarrod shot back. "It's pretty obvious this place is some kind of fishing camp. There must be plenty of boats around here."

"You saw how well I can swim," Lucas said, still argumentative as they got back into the warm car.

"Look there," Jarrod said, ignoring the last comment. He turned the Pontiac until its headlights faced a row of sheds and fenced-in compounds that aligned the western riverbank near the point where its waters emptied into the immense lake. To their left, a derelict row of wooden piers jutted at right angles to the shoreline, the lake's frothy backwaters swirling around the rotted pilings that pointed skyward like a jagged line of black sentries. Whatever dock they once supported had either collapsed or been washed away by the fury of a nasty storm. The tall grass along the shoreline lay on its side, bent and matted from the weight of a recent blanket of damp snow.

"What's behind that fence?" Lucas asked, his interest piqued when he saw a series of shadows that resembled thc hulls of boats in dry-dock.

Wet flakes of melting snow sent water trickling along the crisscrossed wires of a chain-link fence that surrounded what appeared to be a storage yard for fishing boats. Even in the car's dim lights, Jarrod made out ten or twelve overturned watercrafts. Flipping on the car's high beams, the brighter light glinted off their shiny hulls. He assumed the boats were made of aluminum and hoped they didn't weigh much.

"Maybe you won't have to swim after all," Jarrod said, a cynical frown on his face. "But how do we get that gate open?" A heavy chain was wrapped around the thick metal post supporting the wide gate that provided the only entrance to the compound. The steel-forged lock and iron cross-beams that reinforced the gate made breaking in a formidable task.

Searching for a secondary entrance, or any possible access to the compound, Jarrod drove slowly along the fence line. Yet as usual, it was Lucas who was the first to spot the bulge in the chain-link fence. "Look, there's a split in the fence where that boat's pushed up against it," he remarked, pointing at the spot. Sure enough, a few of the bottom links had sprung open from the weight of the rotting hull of an old wooden scow that hadn't been afloat for many years. "

"Look in the trunk, Lucas. Maybe there's a chain or a rope, something we can use to pull that fence apart," Jarrod said.

Lucas quickly found what they wanted. A thick rope was coiled up in the wheel well, where a spare tire should have been. "How's this?" he yelled excitedly, holding up the coarse, prickly rope.

"That might do the trick. Stay back while I get closer to the fence," Jarrod said.

Maneuvering the old beater until the rear bumper was about five feet from the bulging fence, Jarrod noticed a warning light flicker on the instrument panel next to the speedometer. The engine was starting to overheat.

"Wind that rope through the wires next to where the fence is coming apart," he told Lucas. "Then crawl under the car and tie the ends to the frame, or the sturdiest place you can find. Can you tie a good knot?" As the car sank into the spongy, wet grass, Jarrod knew his own body wouldn't fit in the narrow gap between the car frame and the ground.

"I actually spent one summer in cub scouts," Lucas said, annoyed that his knot-tying skills were being questioned.

"Well make sure it won't slip. The way this engine's heating up, we may not get a second chance," Jarrod yelled over the rapping noise of the struggling motor.

His back soaked from the wet grass, Lucas slithered his slim body out from under the car and announced that the rope was secure. Steam was rising from under the Pontiac's hood when Jarrod slid the car into low gear and floored the gas. Like a spooked rabbit, the car lurched forward five or six feet until the rope tightened, bringing the car to an abrupt halt. Although stretched to its limits, the sturdy hemp rope held firm when, without warning, the left rear corner of the old car collapsed onto its wildly spinning tire. Fortunately, the agonizing screams of rusty chain links being torn apart meant a successful end to the mission. A gaping hole opened the compound to all intruders.

Sadly, the last few seconds produced a second casualty. Molly's car had reached the end of the line. Not only was steam gushing from its blown radiator, but the left rear spring had been torn from its mountings, leaving the shock absorber dangling like the broken branch of a dead willow. The old beater let out one last sigh before its engine stalled for the last time. With its final journey over, and its cargo of humans at their destination, the faithful old Pontiac spewed silent tears as steaming radiator fluid trickled over its lifeless headlights.

Lucas noticed the odd angle that the Pontiac had come to rest and hung his head sheepishly. "I guess that wasn't the best place to tie the rope." Evidently, he had secured the rope around the car's left rear leaf-spring and shock absorber, with devastating results.

"We'd better enroll you in an auto mechanics course," Jarrod said, feigning disappointment. "It doesn't matter much. I think the rad's toast as well. Hopefully Molly can grab some insurance money for her car being stolen."

"You're not mad?" Lucas asked.

"Only if we can't drag some boat through that hole and into the river. Come on. Let's get to work." Jarrod gave Lucas an encouraging pat on the back.

Without the car's headlights, searching the boatyard for a suitable craft became a difficult task. Despite intermittent clouds rolling across it, the moon provided a better source of light than the dismal rays cast by the town's few streetlights. Security lights in the compound were non-existent. Overcoming the poor lighting with eyes yet to be affected by deteriorating night vision, it didn't take Lucas long to spot a possible alternative to the heavier fishing boats. Overturned on wooden racks were several plastic, or fiberglass kayaks. They resembled low-slung, pointed canoes with seats sunken into oval cockpits. Due to their cocoon-like structure, only the upper body of the person, or persons, paddling them would be visible.

"Can we use those pointy canoes? I forget what they're called—" he asked Jarrod, expecting his suggestion to be quickly rejected.

Turning toward the rows of narrow, one- and two-seat kayaks, Jarrod nodded. "You might have a good idea. If we can find paddles. Those aluminum fishing boats don't even have motors. We'd have to break into another building—and then try to find gas. Have you ever used a paddle with two ends?"

"Don't you remember? I spent a summer in cub scouts. I even got a badge for paddling a canoe in a straight line. They taught us the J-stroke," Lucas responded proudly.

"I don't need to hear about your strokes. Just help me look for some paddles."

Not far to their left sat a lengthy storage shed with a corrugated metal roof that sagged in the middle like a sway-backed riding horse. The roof of the weather-beaten building extended over an additional storage area that was otherwise open to the elements. The add-on was enclosed by chicken-wire stapled to a rough frame constructed with assorted lengths of two-by-fours. It didn't take long for the fugitives to notice the rows of oars and paddles that hung on hooks along the wall inside the enclosure. Two large wooden crates most likely held lifejackets and floatation cushions.

"Look around for something to tear that wire apart," Jarrod said.

"What's this?" Lucas asked almost immediately, looking at the ground in front of him.

The five-foot length of metal conduit that lay on the wet grass next to his feet was exactly what Jarrod needed. Whatever wiring it would have previously housed had either been removed long ago or had simply disintegrated over time.

Pulling the pipe away from a tangle of dead weeds, Jarrod thrust the sturdy tube between several strands of thin chicken wire and made a circular twisting motion. The wire mesh tore apart like candy floss. One good kick with his boot heel opened a gap large enough to drive a motorcycle through. Moments later, two kayak paddles and two life-jackets were spirited away from their winter resting place.

After looking over the assortment of kayaks, Jarrod picked out a dark-blue two-seater. "In case someone starts looking around, this color will be harder to spot in the moonlight," he reasoned. Lucas already had hold of one of the craft's pointed ends.

It was easy to flip the lightweight kayak from its perch on the wooden rack and place it on the ground. The kayak's tough flat-bottomed hull made it not only sturdy as a rental unit, but also easy to carry and stable in all but the roughest of waters.

"Don't forget your bag," Lucas reminded Jarrod, who almost tripped over the frayed rope that still hung from the torn fence.

"You're right. I might need that. All my worldly possessions!" Jarrod couldn't help but laugh as he pulled his bag from the old beater. Rad fluid continued to trickle down the car's chrome grill. "But I guess it's a little more than what you've got . . . just the clothes on your back." He was almost apologetic.

"Well, I didn't have time to pack when we split from that friggin' farm. Miss Cass can keep those clothes I puked on. But without this ski jacket, I'd have frozen long ago." Lucas could not help thinking again of his brief encounter with Chris and his family. Their kindness and generosity were genuine yet already seemed so far in the past.

Thin wisps of vapor continued to rise from the stalled Pontiac's hood, and the smell of burning rubber hung in the moist, heavy air. Wet grass thrown up by the spinning tires clung to the shattered fence. Molly's car wouldn't be moving without the help of a tow truck.

Travel bag slung over his shoulder, Jarrod carried the front end of the kayak toward the nearby riverbank. The paddles and lifejackets were resting in the seating cockpits. Barely a minute later, he and Lucas reached the edge of the sloping bank, which dropped gradually toward the icy waters of the Rainy River. Just to their left, where the river emptied into the infinite blackness of Lake of the Woods, moonlight glinted on the peaceful waves that rolled in slowly, gently stroking the shoreline.

As they struggled to carry the kayak down a slippery embankment of mud and clay and then over wave-washed sand and rocks, Jarrod suggested they try to keep their feet as dry as possible. That proved to be a virtually hopeless task as they waded through a soggy mass of damp reeds and bulrushes near the water's edge.

"It won't take much to get your fever back," Jarrod warned.

Lucas merely grunted in reply, puffing from exertion.

The stark waters of the uninviting river lapped against the shoreline as the kayak's bow dipped into the frigid current. A late-autumn moonlit kayak ride was a rare occurrence, especially in that tiny hamlet. Jarrod was about to suggest that Lucas get into the front seat when a startling yet familiar sound broke the silence of the chilly evening: the shrill staccato barking of a large dog. The sound sent shivers up their spines. They weren't alone! The smell of the wood-burning fire must have come from somewhere close by.

"Let's get the hell out of here!" Jarrod yelled as he stuffed his travel bag into a waterproof storage compartment in the rear of the kayak. Neither of them took the time to fasten the straps on their lifejackets.

"I see a flashlight or something over there!" Lucas shouted, pointing his paddle along the moonlit shoreline as he slid into the front cockpit.

Straining his tired eyes, Jarrod could barely distinguish a beam of light that bobbed up and down far to his left, likely in the hands of someone hurrying toward them. The sharp sound of barking was amplified across the open surface of water.

In their frantic effort to get away from the shore, the amateur paddlers were unable to get any rhythm in their strokes. The curved ends of their long paddles kept banging together. With no time to practice, they had difficulty getting their arms and shoulders to move in unison. By quietly counting out, "One, two . . . three," Jarrod was eventually able to co-ordinate their strokes so the paddles dug into the water on the count of three before switching sides on the following stroke. Gaining momentum, the sleek kayak glided toward the Canadian shoreline on the opposite side of the river. Luck was on the paddlers' side when a dark storm cloud slid across the face of the November moon, blanketing the river with a protective cloak of darkness.

The yapping canine reached the riverbank well ahead of the person who was following it. Looking out over the water, the dog thrust its nose skyward as it searched for the scent of human intruders.

After making several stops to catch his breath, the animal's bearded and puffing master finally caught up. By that time, the dark-blue torpedo-shaped vessel was only a few yards away from being dragged through the reeds on the northeastern banks of the Rainy River. The man pointed his flashlight in the direction his dog was barking. However, the powerful halogen beam was merely reflected back into his eyes by shimmering fingers of mist that rose from the chilly water.

The bearded man was Kevin Monk, one of the coastal village's few permanent residents. Rumor had it that the tiny community was originally called Whalers Point, until someone pointed out that the nearest ocean was over a thousand miles away in the arctic. In addition to free accommodation during the long winter months, Kevin collected a small salary that had been previously split by the town's businesses and the government agency that patrolled the US/Canadian border. His duties were, more or less, those of an off-season custodian and unofficial security patrol. He never carried a gun.

What the heck is making that dog go crazy? Kevin had wondered earlier as he ran along the narrow beach near his home. Although he prided himself in watching over his town and the waters surrounding it, his dog, Charlie, was always first to notice any unusual activity.

In recent years, as surveillance of the border became more serious and more complicated, Kevin's menial observation efforts were replaced by sophisticated equipment that was often airborne. Although a powerful walkie-talkie and call number was all the American government would supply him as a gesture of his dedication, the local businesses still banded together to employ Kevin for security and seasonal clean-up duties. Yet as proven that night when one small kayak slid undetected across the international border, both the old and new systems were not exactly perfect.

"You sure there was someone there, Charlie?" Kevin asked, as if expecting a verbal reply from his faithful dog, who continued to pace anxiously along the river's edge.

At that moment, for a reason that could only have been instinctual, both man and dog turned toward the row of sheds and the fenced compound that was barely visible in the poor lighting several yards to their right. The outline of an old car that sat at a right angle to the fence caught Kevin's attention. Vapors of steam still rose from the vehicle's hood. As his dog bounded toward the car, Kevin reached for the two-way radio that should have been hanging from his belt. His hand came up empty! The radio must have fallen from its leather holster while he was trying to keep up with Charlie.

"Damn it. I'm getting too old for all this running around!" Kevin yelled skyward as he strolled over to check out the empty car. When he saw the rope and the torn fence, he was quick to figure out what had happened. Charlie's keen senses had shown their value again. His sharp ears had likely picked up either the sounds of the fence being ripped apart or the revving of the car's engine. Evidently, someone was either stupid or desperate enough to illegally cross the icy waters that separated the USA and Canada. Kevin was certain of one thing: Canada, with its small population and more trusting attitude, was not nearly as vigilant in patrolling its border as its southern neighbor. And with the long walk back to the landline phone in his home, he would be giving the fugitives a lengthy head start.

After taking a quick look around the steaming, dormant, pathetic old car, Kevin jotted down the plate number and removed the keys. Then he whistled to Charlie, who was sniffing around the rack of kayaks. "Let's get home, boy."

Retracing his route back to his warm home and crackling fire, Kevin hoped to find the radio along the way. If he had no luck that night, the custodian of Wheeler's Point would search for it again in the daylight.

Chapter 38

"Once we got our act together, we got this thing moving pretty fast," Jarrod huffed, winded as he pulled the kayak onto the Canadian shoreline of the Rainy River. Lucas, who had jumped out first onto the snowy riverbank, slipped on the wet reeds and dead grass, soaking his feet and legs up to his knees. Wet feet on a cold winter night did not augur well for someone who had recently recovered from a critical fever.

After letting out a curse, Lucas looked back to the opposite shore. "That dog scared the crap out of me. Do you think whoever had that flashlight saw us?"

"Let's hope not. Maybe the mist on the water gave us some cover," Jarrod replied, trying to be as positive as he could. "But it won't take long for whoever was there to find Molly's car. The border patrol in Canada will know soon enough about two American fugitives."

Jarrod wasn't aware that the village custodian had dropped his portable radio and could not make direct contact with the authorities. However, given the distance between the riverbank and the only highway that led north into Ontario, the extra time gained by the border jumpers might be of little value. Besides, traveling in the darkness of night with wet feet and clothing would be a serious detriment to their health. A sprawling, unfamiliar country now lay ahead of them.

"I can't believe I was so stupid, getting wet like that," Lucas lamented. "My toes are numb already. I can't even feel them." He was already beginning to wheeze.

"My feet are wet, too," Jarrod replied with concern in his voice. "Let's get away from the river and find a place to hide in the trees. You won't be getting very far unless we can get your feet dry. Remember what happened before."

"Don't remind me," Lucas replied, trying to hold back a sneeze.

After pulling his travel bag from the rear compartment, Jarrod dragged the kayak through the bent grass, doing his best to hide it under a mass of bulrushes and fallen trees that lined the lower riverbank. One good snowfall would conceal it from the view of any search plane or river patrol until spring.

While Jarrod was hiding the kayak, Lucas worked his way up the steeper section of the riverbank. By gripping the exposed roots of century-old trees, he dragged himself across an area that had been badly worn by years of erosion, the topsoil washed away to join the sediment at the bottom of the river. Although the exertion of the climb drained his strength, it also warmed his body. If he had remembered his old geography lessons, Lucas might have realized that the deep-red, three-pronged leaves that were strewn along the upper shoreline had fallen from a maple, Canada's official tree. One such leaf symbolically adorned the country's red-and-white flag. Unfortunately, lessons and schooling were all part of a fading past. At that moment, his only real concerns were warmth, survival, and the continual search for a place where freedom and happiness might be found.

Following his young companion's winding tracks through slippery wet patches of snow and clumps of colorful leaves, Jarrod worked his way up the embankment until he found Lucas. Kneeling on the ground, his head leaning against the trunk of a massive maple tree, the boy was throwing up the remains of his evening meal.

"Are you okay, pal?" Jarrod asked, trying to hide his concern. "Or is that what you think of your new country?"

"How old was that crap we just ate?" Lucas asked, his words coming out in a pitiful croak.

"Your guess is as good as mine. I'm more worried that your fever's coming back," Jarrod replied, still trying to catch his breath. "Let's get deeper into the trees and under some cover. I'll try to get a fire going—if I can find something dry to burn."

The upper corner of the wrinkled Minnesota map had extended into a small portion of southern Ontario. Jarrod assumed that the tiny red lines that wound across the grid were country roads or trails that led eventually to the only highway going north, which was a lower section of the Trans-Canada highway. Yet the distance, the wilderness, the severe temperatures, all those obstacles were more than one tired man could begin to imagine. Factor in one sick, exhausted boy, and the improbable task ahead was more likely an impossible dream. Shelter, the warmth of a fire, and a few hours of rest were the only details that held any relevance at that moment. It was hard enough to just convince Lucas to get to his feet and move as far inland and away from the chilling waters as they could get.

Keeping the late-autumn moon over their right shoulders, they pushed on through thickly wooded areas and craggy, uneven terrain. The trek would have been difficult in daytime, but it was almost impossible at night. Forced to practically drag Lucas along with him, Jarrod was on the edge of exhaustion when an opening thankfully appeared.

As if guarding a private estate, a tall stand of pine and spruce trees towered over the clearing. The immense evergreens acted like a fortress, blocking out not only any overhead view but also the bitter winter winds. Slabs of granite, lichen-covered rocks, and the rotting remains of trees that had toppled long ago lay strewn over the spongy, moss-covered opening. Under the circumstances, the place was ideal. It would certainly do as a hideout for the remainder of the chilly November night.

For two exhausted fugitives, it was time for rest.

Part 6
WHEN EARTH MEETS SKY

Chapter 39

Jamie Grogan was closing in on his fortieth birthday and hoping desperately that his latest girlfriend wasn't planning a surprise party. After graduating from police academy nearly twenty years earlier, his outstanding grades and exemplary character had made acceptance into the ranks of the Royal Canadian Mounted Police (RCMP) a mere formality. Being a city boy, Jamie was fortunate that riding a horse was not an actual requirement. Accelerating through the ranks by accepting a series of transfers and promotions, he never settled long in any one community. Although a nomadic lifestyle was necessary to advance his career, and normally his preference, it inevitably brought a rapid ending to a series of relationships with women he was just getting to know. So far, none were willing to follow him when a new assignment invariably led to a remote community in the widespread country of Canada.

As a result of his latest posting, one that had actually lasted for fourteen months, Jamie was settled comfortably in Rainy River, a scenic Ontario town situated on the border with Minnesota. An integral part of his duties was working as a liaison between the RCMP, the Ontario Provincial Police, and the federal customs and immigration department of the USA. Security and patrol of the land and waterways north of the international border were foremost in his job description. On call twenty-four hours a day, Jamie's sleep, not to mention his late-night encounters with the opposite sex, had been interrupted more than occasionally by the irritating beep of his pager. Yet on that blustery November night, the phone number that flashed on the nightstand next to his bed came as a complete surprise. It could mean only one thing. Sleep was over for Jamie Grogan.

"What is it, Marsha? You woke me out of the greatest dream—thanks!" Jamie mumbled into the receiver of his bedside phone. His normally fertile mind hovered in a state of semi-consciousness.

"Sorry to bother you so late, Mr. Grogan, but I just got a call from the American border patrol." Separated by several years of age and significant rank, Jamie couldn't convince the young woman to call him by his first name. "A guy named Jenkins wants you to call him right away. Apparently, there's been a breach of the border just west of here. He wouldn't give me any more information, but here's his number . . .."

Writing down the ten digits, Jamie's relative youth and experience quickly pulled him out of his sleep-deprived stupor. "Is it still snowing out there? I thought the snowbirds were supposed to be headed south, not trying to sneak across into Canada!"

"The snow's ended, but it's pretty cold out there," Marsha replied, ignoring his joke.

"Thanks. Tomorrow I might forgive you for waking me," Jamie said in his typical jovial manner before hanging up. He punched the Minnesota number into his landline. Although serious about his job, Jamie tried to keep life in perspective.

The conversation with Jenkins was curt, official, and contained little information. Apparently, a boat of some kind had been stolen from a summer camp on the American side of the Rainy River. Some fellow who patrolled the camp was certain the boat was headed to the Canadian side of the river, his dog barking madly at the misty waters. Any other information was purely conjecture, but Jenkins did mention a recent poster that Jamie's department was not aware of. The American official promised to fax the information on two wanted fugitives, a man and a boy. But a background of their records, descriptions, even the crimes they were accused of, was rather hazy. Although a deserted car had been discovered, no firm evidence linked the two fugitives with the border breach.

Before getting more concrete information, Jamie wasn't about to call out the cavalry. His only immediate call was to his partner, Henry Marais, with whom he had become close friends over the past year.

"Get your sorry ass out of bed!" Jamie bellowed when he heard the distant clunk of Henry's phone receiver hit the floor.

Groping in the dark for the fallen receiver, it took a moment for Henry to respond. "Do you know what time it is? Are you drunk? Do I have to bail you out?" Even half-asleep, it was apparent that Jamie's sense of humor had rubbed off on Henry.

"I got word that we may have a breach of the border, but not in a vehicle. From what I heard, there was a boat involved," Jamie began to explain.

"In this weather? Someone's got to be nuts—or madly in love." Henry tried to make sense of it all, but his mind was tired. "Do we have to go out tonight?" he pleaded.

"I've got the truck warming already," Jamie replied. "And you're right, I wish I was drunk and never heard the damn phone ring. Apparently, a boat was stolen from Wheeler's Point sometime tonight. Whoever he—or she—is, the person has a long walk ahead of them when they get to our side. I'm sure none of the camps near the border are open this time of year." His first instinct was to get on the road quickly in case a vehicle might be waiting to pick up the border jumper. Still tired, Jamie failed to mention that point to his partner.

"Sounds more like a rescue mission to me. Are we bothering to bring the artillery?" Henry asked in jest. As good a partner as he was, there were times when he didn't take his job as seriously as he should have.

Jamie played along. "No way. Just your bazooka will do."

Jamie and Henry had dealt with several illegal border crossings and had a good relationship with the American authorities. However, most of the unlawful entries took place on the vast expanse of Lake of the Woods, and most of them were unintentional. Tourists would rent boats, ignore warnings about wandering too far north in search of a trophy walleye or bass, and eventually be questioned and reprimanded by Canadian authorities, which occasionally included Jamie or Henry. Few charges were laid in those cases. The embarrassment of a temporary detention and a verbal lashing was enough of a deterrent to prevent repeat offences.

During his short tenure in the Rainy River area, Jamie was only aware of one other time when a person had attempted to sneak across the border in the dead of winter. The previous year, an agency promising true romance had found the perfect match for two prospective lovers, one American and the other Canadian. After months of correspondence, the American man was smitten. Since a criminal record made it impossible for him to enter Canada at a regular border crossing, the fool took it upon himself to trek across the border on foot in the dead of winter. A search team involving dogs and a helicopter located him just before he froze to death. His only reward was the loss of several frost-bitten toes and deportation back to the United States.

Jamie greeted his partner with a steaming cup of coffee as Henry slid into the passenger seat of the green, four-wheel-drive pickup idling in his driveway. Condensation from melting frost dripped down the rear window.

"Thanks, I could use that," Henry mumbled, buckling up his seatbelt. "Couldn't we have waited until morning? We'll never find anyone at night without aerial pursuit. Not a chance."

"I want to check the camp roads for any sign of vehicles. Someone could be picking up the border jumper, especially if drugs or other contraband is involved. Fresh tracks should be easy to spot in yesterday's snow." Jamie was firm in his decision.

"You never said drugs were involved," Henry said, a little perplexed.

"That's only one probable motive. Anything's possible until we get a better indication from the US border patrol. Maybe another lover? Who knows?"

"I'm betting against that one," Henry deadpanned, taking a sip of hot coffee.

With a detailed map of the area broken down into grids, Jamie drove carefully up and down a series of unpaved roads that, in general, led to seasonal fishing and hunting camps. Some of them were private residences, but many were commercial enterprises that were closed until spring. He asked Henry to mark off on the map all the roads they had checked. After almost two hours of driving, with only a few problem areas where snow had accumulated, they had covered all of the major arteries, avoiding the smaller roads that led into the camps. There was no sign of any vehicles or tracks in the snow other than those the green pickup left behind.

"That's about all we can do before sunrise," Jamie concluded, to his partner's relief. "Let's get an early breakfast. I'll call in a chopper and a couple of ground crews so we can organize a proper search. But if whoever crossed that border didn't have a plan for some transportation, they'd better be wearing the proper gear and be experienced in winter camping."

"Those whirlybird guys will sure be surprised," Henry added.

Despite their years of experience in law enforcement, both men failed to foresee two things. One was the dogged resolve of two desperate and determined escapees. The second was an unexpected circumstance that not even the fugitives could have anticipated.

Chapter 40

Lucas shivered uncontrollably as Jarrod worked on the fire. With fingers that were curled up and numb, the skin on them cracking and raw, Jarrod crumpled up the sports section of a Duluth newspaper that he had stuffed into his travel bag. By adding dry kindling and small twigs he found among the sheltered piles of fallen trees, Jarrod created a flammable base. Several towering fir trees had succumbed over the years to some form of blight and were eventually taken down by high winds that tore their roots from the ground. The toppled giants were rotting and supplied larger branches and drier logs that could be added once the fire had taken hold.

After several futile attempts to ignite the kindling, Jarrod's frustration was beginning to show. His hands felt like blocks of ice, and his cursing came in a steady monologue. With moisture hanging thick in the air, matches that quickly sparked to life fizzled out as soon as they ignited, barely blackening the edges of the crumpled papers. It wasn't until Jarrod struck his second-last match that his reward came. Long-awaited flames curled up the football results on page thirty-two, and the smallest and driest of the kindling burst into a tiny inferno.

Using a flat piece of bark, Jarrod gently fanned the struggling fire, adding sticks and small branches as the blaze intensified. Afraid he might accidentally snuff out the flames, it was several minutes before he dared to add thicker logs and deadwood. Eventually, the process of drying wet clothing and warming frigid bodies began in earnest. Because of the tall evergreens and thick growth of deciduous trees surrounding the campsite, the glow from the sizeable fire could only be seen from directly overhead. Hopefully, no commercial airplanes had flight paths anywhere nearby.

Fearing that Lucas was falling into a feverish state, regardless of the good blast of heat he was getting from the fire, Jarrod had a suggestion. "I've got some pills that might help you with your cold or fever or whatever you've got," he said, digging through his travel bag. "That fire should warm you up, but we've got to dry out our wet clothes. There's no point in trying to get anywhere tonight. What we need now is a few hours of rest. But I've got to keep this fire going."

"I think I've finally stopped shaking," Lucas said, his voice hoarse but steady. "Maybe getting rid of that crappy hot dog helped," he added, swallowing an Aspirin as well as a cold-remedy pill.

Steam rose from their jeans as the two fugitives sat next to the roaring fire on a mound of moss covered with flattened boughs and dry leaves. Jarrod had scavenged branches from the base of a lofty elm tree. Two pairs of bare feet rested close to a pile of glowing embers, and four wet socks made hissing sounds as they dangled above the flames from a makeshift hanger fashioned out of the green branch of a sapling. Their damp footwear leaned against a stump next to the crackling fire. With swirls of water vapor rising from them, even Jarrod's recently purchased winter boots were saturated.

Ten minutes later, he finally spoke. "My feet seem to have finally thawed out. Maybe I'll try to gather more of these softer branches to cover our moss beds. Should be almost as comfy as the Hilton." Jarrod's attempt to sound encouraging made no impression. Lucas's eyes were drooping shut, and his breathing became more labored.

"You stay put and try to get warm." His words were unnecessary, as the exhausted boy was not going anywhere. Jarrod felt the inside of his boots before slipping them on. Although warm, the lining remained damp.

While tramping through thick foliage on the way to the clearing, Jarrod had noticed clumps of low bush with dark berries hanging from the branches. The wet fruit glistened under the light of the full moon that peeked between the towering spruce trees. Feeling had returned to his feet as he set off to gather some of the berries, hoping they were safe to eat. He remembered gathering chokecherries and boysenberries as a child, but that night he wasn't sure what he was picking. Mixing fresh snow with a handful of the blackish-red berries and simmering the concoction over the red coals in his tin cup, Jarrod produced a hot tea that he offered to share with Lucas. The taste was sharp, both bitter and sweet, but at least it warmed the stomach.

Barely awake, Lucas was hesitant to taste the hot liquid but then sipped it slowly. A short time later, a surge of warmth filtered through his body. Perhaps the heat from the fire, the pills, or maybe the purplish tea had taken effect. Although his eyes continued to droop, Lucas's wheezing subsided.

"That tea, it tastes like something I had before," Lucas said softly, breaking a long period of silence. "That woman . . . Miss Cass, the one with the strange eyes, gave it to me. I feel so . . . so tired . . . do you think we'll ever see morning?"

The question was spoken with prolonged syllables like a melodic overture, as if Lucas was suspended in the middle of a dream. Or was it possible that every tea Lucas drank caused him to hallucinate? Following a few more incoherent words, Jarrod saw no reason to reply to his peculiar ramblings. Similar to the midnight ride along the railway, it was evident who would be stoking the fire throughout the night.

Green willow boughs crisscrossed over a bed of moss and lichens made a comfortable resting place. Jarrod laid Lucas on the makeshift bed as near to the fire as possible. He slipped dry socks from his travel bag onto the boy's bare feet and wrapped his legs with the last of his flannel shirts. Although warm from the fire, Lucas's forehead felt neither moist nor feverish. Hopefully the answer to his curious question, spoken either unconsciously or from a hazy dreamland, would turn out to be positive.

Jarrod stared up at the starlit sky as firelight flickered across his face. He wondered how a person so young could show such determination. Just when he thought the boy was about to give up, he would bounce back with renewed drive. Overcoming illness might be a factor of youth, but fighting though despair and hopelessness took a special brand of inner strength and fortitude. Perhaps his young friend was slowly teaching him to focus on the positives in life, showing him that a future did exist, and no past was so terrible that it could not be overcome. Had Jarrod discovered an inner spirit that allowed him to put others ahead of his own problems, his own needs? Could there ever be a light at the end of the long tunnel in which he and Lucas were trapped? One thing was certain: If he gave up, it could never be found.

Jarrod formed his own bed in a more upright position so he could keep watch over the fire as well as look out for any predators that might be lurking nearby. Unfortunately, in his tired state, he found that his eyes began to close far too often as the night wore on. Although his body ached for sleep, distant noises in the night air jolted him awake on several occasions. Those brief intervals of attentiveness allowed him to throw fresh wood onto the glowing embers of the fire, which threatened to die from neglect.

The ongoing transition from sleep to wakefulness resulted in the night dragging on forever for Jarrod, who kept sporadic vigilance as flames continually faded to glowing coals. But the still solitude only magnified the distant cracking of dry branches, the imminent warning sign of danger looming. Did wolves lurk nearby, pacing stealthily as they picked up the scent of easy prey? Was a cantankerous bear wandering the woods in search of accommodations for winter hibernation? Yet no eyes appeared that night, potential predators perhaps discouraged by the steady glow from the flaming logs. When dawn emerged, lighting up the highest tips of the tallest pines, Jarrod was relieved that the never-ending night had passed without incident. It was time to move on.

One look at Lucas reminded Jarrod of a Christmas pageant in which he had played a part as a child. Why was he suddenly reminiscing? Why did a boy sleeping soundly on a bed of moss and willows suddenly take on religious overtones? Jarrod shook his head. Was he searching for help from above, or was he simply overtired? He gave Lucas a gentle shake, trying to wake him. Forced to increase his efforts when the boy wouldn't budge, Jarrod was pleased when the initial groan he heard was not some delirious rambling but a complaint.

Lucas awoke slowly, beginning with a series of coughs. "Thanks, you just wrecked my first real kiss in a great dream." He mentioned a freckle-faced blond girl.

"Sorry. I didn't have much choice. We've got to hit the trail. The sun has been up for a while, and the weather looks better. How are you feeling?"

"Like crap since you woke me, but I don't think I've got a fever. Is there anything to eat?"

"I'm boiling water for some tea, and there's a package of powdered donuts that I got from that store last night—and a couple of chocolate bars. Sorry, no bacon and eggs." Jarrod dumped the remaining berries into the hot water.

"That tea reminded me of the poison that witch, Miss Cass, gave me to drink. I think I'll pass on it," Lucas replied. "But I'll try some of those donuts."

"I heard that the bark of certain trees can be used for tea. Want to try?" Jarrod suggested.

"No thanks. Sounds horrible. Maybe just some hot water and one of your pills. It seemed to help last night," Lucas sounded stronger, and his coughing had almost stopped.

"Good. There's no way I could have carried you today; my energy is just about gone," Jarrod said as he sipped his tea. "At least our shoes seem to be dry. Maybe you've started a new fashion trend. That shirt of mine hangs below your knees. How's your fancy new hat fit?" Jarrod had purchased the orange knit toque from the thrift shop for fifty cents. The word "armadillo" was woven into the material.

Lucas stuffed a second donut into his mouth, icing sugar getting all over his hands and face. "Maybe I should join a reggae band," he deadpanned. "Or do you think I'm ready to pull a bank robbery? What's your choice?" With a smug grin, he pulled the toque down so it covered his eyebrows.

"I saw your talent of robbing a drunk motel owner, but I'll go with the band. Of course, you'll have to braid your hair. And you'll look just great with that white powder all over your face," Jarrod said, feigning a smile.

As the reality of their situation sank in, his face became serious. He could only hope that the rest of the day might be as carefree as the start. The fact that Lucas was in good spirits, and relatively healthy, was encouraging.

What was this continuing concern about the wellbeing of another person, especially a boy he barely knew? Was his obstinate personality beginning to soften? Could it be his internal clock was telling Jarrod that time was running out to settle down and raise a family? The bizarre thought made him laugh out loud regardless of his present situation.

Without asking what his friend found so funny, Lucas was lost in his own thoughts, his mind confused as he sipped the hot water and polished off the last of the donuts. Had he finally found the person he could trust? One whose promises meant something? Doubts about ever finding his foster mother, the only person from his past who seemed to care, crept into his mind. What Lucas really wanted was a place to settle down, go to school, and live the life that most boys his age had the opportunity to live. He was tired of running. He saw Jarrod as the one person who could give him any chance of achieving his goal.

After smothering the remaining embers with several scoops of snow, Jarrod was confident that the fire was not going to spread. Only a few threads of smoke still rose from the coals. He and Lucas donned every piece of clothing from his travel bag, doubling up wherever possible. If only they had more insulated footwear. Without a compass, the sun was their only indicator of the direction they would be traveling. Only an hour past dawn, the yellow glow on the upper tips of the tallest trees gave a rough estimate of where east was located.

The top right corner of Molly's tattered map showed that northeast was the direction they had to travel to reach the main highway heading north into central Canada. Jarrod was aware that trekking the entire distance to the highway on foot was unrealistic and probably impossible in winter conditions without food or shelter, especially with no road or even a trail in sight. But at least walking toward the sun was a start and a way to keep warm. No opportunity would ever come from staying put.

Jarrod poured the remainder of the melted snow into a plastic juice container he found in his bag. At least they would have some liquid to quench their thirst. "Are you ready to go?" Jarrod asked. "We'll save the chocolate bars for later." He pointed. "See where the sun hits those trees? That yellow light should be opposite to the direction we're headed, so remember to keep checking the treetops so we don't screw up. I seem to have a knack for making wrong turns."

"How far to a road or a town?" Lucas asked, coughing briefly.

"I'm not sure, but probably a long way. We're in the middle of nowhere," Jarrod admitted. "I think those tiny red lines on the map are trails of some kind."

There was little conversation as the hikers trudged wearily over ground that was uneven and unforgiving. Many spots were soft and mushy, not yet frozen, as winter was only in its early stages. Other stretches were steep and rocky, the rising sun sending rivulets of water from higher, more exposed areas over the face of granite outcroppings, many coated with spongy moss. The footing was treacherous, involving frequent slips and slides and an abundance of cursing. In areas where snow had accumulated overnight, clumps of delicate flakes shrouded the outstretched branches of evergreens in a cloak of shimmering white. The dancing rays of sunlight gave the appearance of sequins on a royal wedding gown. Nature's picturesque beauty could not be avoided, even in the bleakest of circumstances.

"How are you doing?" Jarrod asked, his words coming out between puffs and grunts. "I'm actually sweating with all this hiking."

"I'm warm, too, but aren't we going off direction a little?" Lucas asked.

Looking around, Jarrod noticed the sun's position and then nodded. "You're right. We veered south toward the US again. Let's head more to the left. Do you need a break?" he asked, hoping for confirmation of his own wish.

"Yeah, I could use a drink of that water, please."

"Where did your manners suddenly come from?" Jarrod asked, as if surprised.

"I took a special course long ago, but around an old grump like you . . .." Lucas paused to take a swill from the water container. "Not afraid of getting my germs?" he said, handing the water back to Jarrod.

In an odd way, it appeared Lucas was relaxed talking to the "old grump" like he was someone nearer his own age. For a young person, it was more a sign of bonding, a feeling of comfort and wellbeing rather than a lack of respect.

"At this point, it won't make much difference if we can't find our way out of here," Jarrod replied, trying not to sound discouraged. Then, without warning, he pointed over Lucas's shoulder. "Turn slowly, and look what's behind you!"

His eyes widening with apprehension, Lucas turned his head slowly. A few feet away, a doe and her young offspring stared back nervously at the two intruders. The mother and her two fawns stood motionless, their oversized ears twitching. Their doleful eyes were swollen to the size of saucers. The encounter ended as suddenly as it began when the mother and her little ones turned in unison and bounded into the safety of the forest. Their white tails flicked back and forth like windshield wipers running at high speed.

"Wow, you had me scared," Lucas stuttered.

"I just wish I was a hunter; we could have eaten for days out here." Jarrod said apologetically, his words awakening distant memories of his one attempt to hunt as a youngster. Falling silent, his mind drifted back to his faraway childhood. His father, a sportsman and avid hunter, had spent weeks showing him the intricacies of loading, aiming, and squeezing the trigger of a rifle. Jarrod practiced for hours, shooting at rows of tin cans when, finally, the day came to show off his newly learned skills.

However, it wasn't until a young buck stood in the crosshairs of his scope that Jarrod realized his mistake. Tears welling in his eyes, he couldn't squeeze the trigger even though he wanted to please his dad. Without a word, he laid down the gun and walked away. Although disappointed, his dad restrained from criticism, instead choosing the power of silence as he picked up the rifle. He neither scolded his son later nor brought up the subject of hunting again. Ironically, Jarrod's respect for his father grew from that day forward.

"Is something wrong?" Lucas asked. "You got quiet suddenly."

"No, nothing. Just thinking," Jarrod replied, shaking his head slightly as his thoughts slid back to the present.

"It's time to get moving. We've got to find a road, or at least a trail that leads somewhere. Those chocolate bars we just ate were the last of our food," Jarrod explained. After walking for an hour and a half, his legs were starting to ache, and his feet were wet. The long night tending a fire had left him worn out.

"Maybe I can snare us a rabbit or fat squirrel. We'll eat like kings." Lucas spoke with more enthusiasm and displayed more stamina than his older friend. It was obvious he was feeling better, his brief coughs coming further and further apart.

It wasn't long before the soggy terrain began to show some change. Footing became firmer and more level, and the taller trees thinned out. Stands of birch, oak, and aspen spread out in the distance. The deciduous trees were stripped of most of their leaves by the early stages of winter. Scattered clumps of moist, colorful, composting leaves gave off a pungent odor.

Within the next half hour, the foot-weary travelers discovered the first sign of any human presence in the area. Although they had seen narrow, winding paths that deer, moose, or other animals had worn through the trees, likely leading to water or a food source, the opening just ahead of them was much wider. It was apparent that a plow or some other vehicle had forged a clearing through the brush, creating a pathway with a base of flattened grass, smooth granite rocks, and fledgling trees. Whether it was used in summer, winter, or in all seasons, Jarrod wasn't sure. However, he was certain that civilization must be lurking somewhere nearby.

"See that trail, Lucas? It must lead somewhere. We'd better keep our eyes open," Jarrod said, his voice tense.

"You think there's a herd of deer or buffalo roaming around here?" Lucas replied flippantly, indicating the trail's width. "But really, maybe there's a camp or cottages nearby."

Jarrod nodded. "You can bet on that."

Turning left and following the trail, which appeared to angle northeast, the worn-out hikers became more suspicious of every sound and movement along their new pathway. The silence was broken only by the twittering of tiny finches and wrens, the birds flitting through the brush in search of tasty berries. Although frequently covered with drifts of melting snow, the path was wide and reasonably flat. After less than twenty minutes, an opening in the brush revealed yet another surprise: a gravel roadway not much wider than the groomed path.

"A road, finally!" Jarrod almost shouted.

Lucas scanned left and right along the narrow, curving roadway. "Someone drove through here not long ago," he said with excitement. "See the tracks in the snow? They've gotta be fresh. You can still see the tread marks."

Jarrod knelt to examine them. In the last fifteen minutes, clouds had moved in and obscured the sun. The trail's meandering direction left him struggling to get his bearings. Looking up from his kneeling position, he noticed a startled look on Lucas's face. "What's wrong?" he asked.

"Don't you hear that?" Lucas queried, looking upward. It was apparent his ears had picked up a distant sound. "Listen . . . what's that whirring noise?"

Turning his head slightly, Jarrod made out the faint humming noise, which was getting louder as it closed in on the anxious fugitives. "Quick, get under that tree. It's coming from up in the sky. Someone must be looking for us!"

Backing away from the road, Lucas hurried after Jarrod. They ducked under the outstretched branches of a towering fir tree. Both man and boy remained motionless, their mouths suddenly dry as the spinning shadow of a large propeller slid across the needle-laden boughs of their lofty shelter.

Was nature's peace about to be shattered?

Chapter 41

The late-night drive along deserted country roads tired him out. Jamie had barely fallen into a deep sleep when his bedside phone rang its irritating, pre-dawn wakeup call. Although at the end of her ten-hour shift, Marsha still sounded sharp and alert. "Good morning, Mr. Grogan, I just received another call from Jenkins. Do you still have his number?"

"I do Marsha, thanks. Looks like I'll have to put my sleep time in the bank for a while," Jamie replied, trying to suppress a yawn.

Jenkins sounded anything but sharp and alert when Jamie was finally able to get through to him, after getting busy signals on his first two tries. The stolen car found near the docks at Wheeler's Point was traced to Duluth, the owner having reported it missing just yesterday. Apparently, the man described on the poster that Jenkins mentioned previously had been spotted that day at the downtown bus station, but the pursuing officer was unable to apprehend him. Only catching a quick glimpse of a young boy next to the man, the officer assumed him to be the twelve-year-old runaway also mentioned in the poster. Jamie jotted down a detailed description of both fugitives. He promised to keep Jenkins informed on how his search was progressing. He emphasized that, if the fugitives weren't dressed properly and lacked minimal survival skills, it was more likely to become a rescue mission.

Rainy River was a small town with an understaffed yet busy police presence, the duties of which were undervalued. As with most places in the lake area of western Ontario, it was primarily a summer tourist area. More recently, the town was becoming a retirement community for many people who craved to escape the larger cities, searching for a quieter, rural life closer to the lakes. Small bungalows and condos were springing up all over the place. Its location right on the American border brought many foreign tourists through town, more so during the summer months.

Jamie would be hard-pressed to gather an experienced search party together from Rainy River, especially on the weekend. The situation he faced would not be considered critical, requiring compulsory overtime for all local law enforcers. There had been no shootings, no abductions, no bank robberies, and no citizens appeared to be in danger. The nearest town of any size that could supply extra help was Kenora, well over one hour's drive to the north. He could request a search helicopter from Sioux Narrows, a picturesque tourist area located half the distance away in the middle of lake country. However, Jamie's first call was to his partner.

After several rings, Henry managed to answer the phone without dropping it. "What took you so long? I hardly slept just waiting for your call."

"You've got a few minutes to get ready. I've got to gather up a few warm bodies willing to trek through the brush on the weekend. I'll request an experienced search-and-rescue group from our Kenora detachment. It might take the guys a couple of hours to get here. Hopefully, the copter should be here in less than an hour. Coffee's on you this time. See you soon."

Straining to assimilate all possibilities, Jamie's organizational mind was being stressed to the limit. Yet keeping calm when unforeseen circumstances arose, as well as directing others to perform whatever tasks were necessary, were two of his strongest assets.

The early-morning call came as a complete surprise to both Travis and Brady, the only experienced search-and-rescue helicopter team in the area. Generally, at that time of year, the lakes were devoid of human intruders and lost canoers. Hikers and wilderness campers were almost non-existent. Snowmobiling season was at least a month away. Typically, in late fall and early winter, their services were only required for serious car accidents or other medical emergencies when a doctor or nurse accompanied them.

However, after listening to Jamie's request, Travis was quick to respond. "I'll get Brady up. We were out with the girls last night, but that's no excuse. It'll take a little while for us to get the copter airborne, but I'll call the emergency channel as soon as we're in your area. Shouldn't be long. Are you organizing a ground search?"

"I hope to have a crew out as soon as possible. I'll keep my handheld with me and that channel open in case you get delayed. Henry and I are driving out ASAP. We'll retrace our route from last night and check for fresh tracks. By the time the others get organized and their ATVs out here, I'll have a search grid mapped out. They can meet us in the southeast quadrant. It's too early in the season for the trackers to use snowmobiles. Not enough snow." At times like now, Jamie's history of promotions came as no surprise.

Steaming coffees in their travel mugs, Jamie and Henry retraced most of their route from last night. Hot air blasted through the truck vents, and swirls of powdery snow flew up behind them, eventually settling into the fresh tread marks of the pickup's winter tires. Satisfied he had rechecked all the major arteries, and in half the time it took last night, Jamie pulled over to the side of the road to await the helicopter's arrival. There was no sign of recent activity in the area.

Travis pampered his five-year-old Sikorsky search-and-rescue chopper like the owner of a classic car. Its twin-turbine Pratt and Whitney turbo-shaft engine shone like a vintage Harley Davidson. Both the interior and exterior sparkled. Even the instrument panel was polished to a mirror finish. The rigors of harsh Canadian winters had little effect on the well-equipped and well-maintained machine.

"Travis and Brady should have their rotors spinning by now. No point in us running all over the place before they arrive," Jamie rationalized, finishing the last of his thermos of coffee.

"Do they have heat sensors in that whirly-bird they're flying?" Henry asked.

"I'm sure they do. I know they have lots of experience and have turned down offers of better-paying jobs in bigger communities. They both told me they like the peace and quiet around here, away from the rat race, as they call life in the big city." Jamie agreed with their attitude, his outlook on life very similar.

As expected, moments later, Jamie's radio crackled to life. With the screaming sound of spinning propeller blades in the background, Brady yelled into his microphone. "We just spotted your truck, Jamie. The tracks were easy to follow."

Hearing the whirling noise of the blades above him, Jamie was quick to reply. "You guys don't waste any time. The others are at least an hour away."

"Where do you suggest we start our search? The heat sensor picked up a lot of wolves in this area last week. There's a pack of eight or ten not far north of here," Brady advised. It was a good thing Jarrod and Lucas didn't hear the conversation.

"Circle back to Wheeler's Point, and work your way back to this road. Try to cover an area at least a kilometer either side of the straight-line route. Whoever is down there may be disoriented trying to get through this wilderness area. They're not likely to have gotten far since last evening. There's no sign of vehicle tracks along these camp roads." Jamie knew the experienced flight crew needed few instructions. "By the way, the Americans are aware that you'll be in the area. I just have to keep them up to date with our search."

Jamie's mind had shifted into high-gear.

Chapter 42

Sharon Price could have been the perfect match for Jamie. Although five years younger, she was bright, adventurous, and dedicated to her job as a junior officer with the Kenora RCMP detachment. After four years of working as a phone dispatcher answering 911 calls, she felt smothered in the office. When an opportunity arose, Sharon enrolled in the police academy's intensive training program. Although few of the other recruits expected her to survive the course's physical demands, the petite blonde proved her doubters all to be wrong.

After graduating in the top third of her class, Sharon was prepared to hit the road in a cruiser. She longed to get into the action. Almost immediately, her smarts for coming up with unique solutions to awkward situations proved to be rather uncanny. She was especially good at calming domestic disputes that were getting out of hand. Although physically attractive and always wearing an infectious smile, her tailored uniform concealed a muscular build. Daily workouts in the gym sculpted a powerful physique. More than one belligerent drunk learned his lesson the hard way when he was tossed to the ground and handcuffed by the no-nonsense, yet down-to-earth female.

Although some women on the force were harassed and ostracized in their male-dominated jobs, the men in Sharon's department treated her with respect. Certainly, her positive attitude and willingness to lend a hand to her fellow officers, whether at work or giving advice on their personal problems, put her in good standing with almost everyone she encountered. Regardless of her physical skills and strict principles in upholding the law, Sharon was a softie when it came to consoling others. It was no wonder that she was well liked.

In her two and a half years of working for the Kenora RCMP, Sharon had problems getting along with only one male. Chris was one-year younger than her thirty-three years, yet he had two more years of experience and seniority. He was already in charge of one of the department's important assets, a Belgian Shepherd tracking dog named Abby. She was his pride and joy and obeyed all his commands. Perhaps that was one reason Chris was not enamored with Sharon. She was far too independent minded for him. On top of that, she was given assignments that Chris considered more high profile than those allotted to him. Among them was helping to quell some touchy domestic disputes as well as minor detective work. Her superiors often sought out her opinion as well as her innovative solutions. Chris was jealous, feeling his opinion was generally overlooked. Yet he always had his dog. No one could take her away from him.

When the unexpected call for help came in on that Saturday morning, Chris was one of the first to be contacted. With Abby by his side, his leadership abilities did not go unnoticed. He stood out as a take-charge kind of guy, yet he continued to be intimidated by his junior officer's charm and abilities. He was not impressed that Sharon was included in the search team that was headed to the American border. Certainly, she was not an experienced driver of the off-road vehicles required for the pursuit of two escaped felons, the imaginative category in which Chris boldly placed the illegal border jumpers. As well, what experience did she have in shooting a revolver should the situation get out of hand?

Keeping his opinions to himself, Chris quickly organized the search crew of six mostly younger officers. He had the authority to sign out the equipment necessary for the manhunt. His sergeant had explained that an officer named Jamie Grogan would direct the ground search in the Rainy River district next to the border. The sergeant agreed to let Chris take along an eager young recruit he was mentoring. Since the two suspected males who had breached the border crossing (one apparently only a child) had not committed any known assaults, and no weapons had been involved, they were not considered the most dangerous of fugitives. Hence, a senior officer would not be accompanying the crew to the border. Jamie's experience handling similar situations was well recognized and would keep him in charge of the search. Sensing her master's excitement, Abby was anxious to get going.

Rather than sit around waiting for the ground-search crew to arrive, Jamie and Henry began to check out the remote roads that led into summer camps and private residences. Traction wasn't good along the narrow driveways as the pickup plowed through frequent drifts of fresh snow that was turning to slush as the sun rose higher in the sky. Although their vehicle was four-wheel drive, the weight of several sandbags piled in the cargo box over the rear axle aided with winter traction.

Henry was just stepping out to check around the lodge of the first camp when the radio speaker resonated with Brady's voice. "Our sensors just picked up a hot spot not far from the water. It seems there was a fire here recently. We can still see a few puffs of smoke. Sorry, there's nowhere to touch down to investigate, but I can give your crew the coordinates."

Jotting down the longitude and latitude figures, Jamie marked an X on the location on his grid map. "Have you spotted any tracks or come across the groomed trail that the hikers and snowmobilers use?"

"Nothing yet. The pine and spruce are pretty thick around here," Brady replied. "No signs of any wolf pack either."

"I'm expecting the boys to arrive shortly. We'll focus our search between Camp Road Thirteen and the hot spot. There's no way someone could hide their tracks in these conditions. Even if the snow melts, the tracking dog will pick up the scent." Jamie suspected the intruder, or intruders, were cold, disoriented, and could be wandering in any direction.

"No sign of any human activity around this camp," Henry announced, breathing heavily as he returned from circling all the buildings visible on the property. "The only tracks I saw were made by deer, rabbits, squirrels, and small birds. No sign of wolves."

"Hop in the truck, pal. I want to check the spot where the snowmobile trail crosses the camp road. I have a hunch that whoever we're looking for may have accidently stumbled across the trail." Jamie's mind was sorting through all possibilities.

Tires spinning, the pickup fishtailed as it raced down the deserted driveway from the camp to the main road. Following the curves and landmarks on a detailed map of the region, Henry provided navigation as they searched for the footpath. Barely five minutes later, he shouted for Jamie to pull over.

"There's the trail next to that giant spruce tree."

As his mind continued to sort out various likelihoods, Jamie barked out orders like a seasoned veteran. "Are you up to another little job, Henry?"

Without giving his partner time to answer, Jamie continued. "Do a quick check of the trail before the others get here. Tracks made by humans should be easy to spot in the fresh snow, but the sun's starting to melt it. Head southeast first, since that would be the direction the illegals would have to come from."

"Hey partner, you're trying to wear me out. I was planning to laze around and watch hockey this weekend," Henry replied, hoping to get some sympathy.

"Just think, you can put your overtime money toward that fancy camper you've had your eyes on," Jamie countered. "Sorry, I'd go with you, but the boys from Kenora could show up at any time."

Sure enough, with his winter boots stomping through sticky clumps of melting snow, Henry had just disappeared around the corner of the trail when a garbled message crackled over the static of Jamie's two-way radio. The six enthusiastic young officers who made up the Kenora search party were approaching at the highest speed that road conditions would allow. The chase was about to begin.

Chapter 43

"That was close," Jarrod said from his kneeling position under the overhang of a sprawling spruce bough, its pristine needles fanning out in the form of a giant umbrella.

"I'll bet that copter was just our first warning. They'll track us down like we're a couple of murderers. What about our footprints along that trail?" Lucas spoke as though their fate was already determined. Was his mind envisioning high-powered rifles being aimed at their heads? His voice, just recently filled with enthusiasm, was flat and emotionless.

"Maybe those few steps we took on the trail will blend in with the deer and other animal tracks. We weren't on the trail for long, and we sure won't be walking on it now." Sensing that all energy and hope had been sucked from his despondent friend, Jarrod did his best to inject some optimism.

"They're sure to have dogs with them—and those machines with fat tires on them. We're worn out now, so what chance do we have?" Lucas asked, his mind rambling. All he could visualize was the inevitable return to his grim past. He couldn't imagine any possible escape route, and the thought of captivity in a strange country scared him so deeply that his knees began to shake.

Either unable or afraid to respond to his young friend's lapse into apathy and dejection, Jarrod continued to trek ahead, his eyes focused on the next ridge, the next mound of earth, the next toppled tree. He tried desperately to come up with any possible way out of their situation. Moments later, something in the distance caught his roving eye. "Look, what's that over those trees?"

Raising his head, Lucas stared in the direction Jarrod was pointing. His eyes were cloudy and unfocused. Sure enough, thin spirals of smoke floated above the outstretched tops of a cluster of white birch trees. He briefly recalled Julie's farmhouse and her warm hospitality.

"There must be a home or cabin up ahead. Whoever's chasing us wouldn't send up smoke signals," Jarrod said, a trace of hope in his voice.

"I guess we may as well check it out," Lucas said, his body aided by a much-needed boost of energy.

Trying to keep out of sight behind the cover of tree trunks and the little foliage that had survived the late-fall weather, the fugitives worked their way toward the dark-grey puffs. As they got closer, it was evident that the smoke was rising from a stovepipe that had turned black from the layers of soot that encased it. Jarrod was reminded of a gingerbread house when he caught his first glimpse of the tiny cottage. The time-worn walls were constructed with roughly hewn tree trunks sealed together unevenly with grey mortar. The cement sealant had dried and weathered over the years, creating a spider web of cracks. The logs were so discolored and covered in moss that it was almost impossible to tell they were wood.

Years of resting without a foundation had caused the structure to sink into the ground, giving it the appearance of a dwelling for dwarfs. The grey, asphalt shingles that protected the roof were cracked and badly curled. In all likelihood, it was only the spongy growth of colorful moss that prevented rain from leaking into the home like water through a spaghetti strainer. The only window visible was the color of a deep-purple haze. It was doubtful that anyone inside the archaic cabin could even make out the form of an adult bear, should one wander across the property.

"What next? Should we knock and say we're selling insurance?" Jarrod suggested.

"Look over there," Lucas whispered, ignoring the question. "What's that thing with the wide track on the bottom?"

Turning his head, Jarrod could hardly speak when he saw the machine sitting next to a pile of chopped wood. "That's a snowmobile. It's perfect for a winter climate, except there's not much of the white stuff yet." His heart beat rapidly as he sensed an opportunity.

Jarrod must have raised his voice just enough to disturb the sleep of an animal inside the cabin. Behind the moss-covered walls, a low, guttural growl was barely loud enough to be heard on the outside.

"Are you dreaming again, Wolfy?" The deep, gravelly voice was hardly audible, but it was enough to freeze Jarrod and Lucas in their tracks.

Seconds later, the shuffling sound of the footpads of a large dog moving slowly across a wooden floor made Lucas retreat toward the safety of a thicket of brush. Jarrod was slower to react and stumbled as Wolfy let out a series of warning barks, low in tone but serious in nature.

"What's there, boy? Another squirrel?" The dog owner's voice showed little concern.

However, as the man forced the poor-fitting cabin door open a moment later, the look of shock on the faces of the two grown men who faced each other was enough to spring Wolfy into action.

Fortunately, just as his dog, who was aptly named in terms of size and appearance, was about to pounce on the intruder, the owner yelled firmly, "Down boy, heel!"

The well-muscled dog obeyed immediately and returned to his master, who grabbed him by the scruff of the neck. His wet tongue drooping from the side of his mouth, Wolfy sat obediently.

"Sorry to startle you," Jarrod said. "I'm not here to rob you," he added, thinking quickly. "We're just lost and cold."

"Who's we?" the dog owner replied as he looked around.

"My nephew's over there." Jarrod pointed to the bush. "We got turned around and can't find the road." He turned to see Lucas emerge from his hiding spot.

"Bull crap! Nobody wonders around these parts this time of year. You'd have to be crazy." The bearded man, his full head of hair wild and unkempt, spoke with a powerful voice, then shook his head and waited for the real explanation for the strangers' sudden appearance.

Lucas moved next to Jarrod and put his left arm around Jarrod's waist, a gesture that seemed to relax the bearded stranger.

"Okay, so you're just wandering around looking at the wildlife. Well, you're sure not dressed for this weather. Look at your shoes, boy." The man's tone was softer, but he was still far from convinced.

"The truth is, we're both on the run." Jarrod admitted. He decided that further lies would get them nowhere. The man would see through any ridiculous story.

"You're on the run? From who? From what? I'm sure it's not the wolves around here." The bearded man seemed rather surprised that the truth came out so quickly. Yet fear of the strangers never entered his mind. Introductions were the only logical way to continue their conversation. "Whatever you're running from ain't a big concern of mine. My name's Matt. I'm supposed to be a licensed trapper, although the money's not too good these days. But it beats living in the city. My days around those crazy people are long gone. Local kids like to call me 'Matt the Hermit.' I'm sure they got the name from their parents. I couldn't give a shit what they call me. What are your names, and where are you from?" The bluntness of his questions demanded an honest answer.

As eccentric as he seemed, Jarrod was already beginning to like the man, but he would have preferred 'Matt the Trapper' as a nickname rather than 'Matt the Hermit.' "My name's Jarrod. This is Lucas." Using their real names, he managed a slight smile as he squeezed Lucas's shoulder. "We're from the United States and crossed the border last night by boat. You might call us illegal immigrants."

"None of that stuff means anything to me. I'm not much of one for rules and authority. Who gives a damn where you're from? We're all just humans. It's only what's in your heart that counts. Why'd you leave your country? Are you fugitives?"

It was evident that Matt hadn't talked to any humans for quite a while. He seemed anxious to let off steam. A first impression of the hulking man would make "opinionated" and "stubborn" his most striking characteristics. The real warmth of his heart would take longer to uncover. Ignoring the travel-weary adult, he stared at Lucas, a boy he sensed was mature for his age, which the trapper assumed to be pre-teen.

"Sonny, what are you running from?" Matt asked.

Lucas found that the few moments of listening to the burly, unshaven, old trapper with the wild greying hair had reinforced his doubt that all people were required to live within the narrow rules of society. He witnessed an adult living alone in the wild who looked him straight in the eye when he talked. Not only did the gruff, giant man seem to be just as stubborn as Lucas, but he shared a similar attitude about laws and authority.

"I'm running from a group home. It was filled with kids with no real homes. I hated it there. I have no family. Right now, Jarrod is the only friend I have. He's been good to me, but we keep getting into trouble. Does that make us bad? I don't know." Lucas's answer was not only candid but also summed up their situation.

Matt listened with interest and more than a hint of admiration. "And how about you, Jarrod? Did you do a bank heist?" he asked, expecting he wasn't far from the truth.

"Not quite, but I did leave my company on short notice. Something about some missing funds." Jarrod shrugged. "I'm sure I don't have to spell it out."

"I see . . . two hardened criminals. I'm sure the border patrol and half of our esteemed law enforcement agency is hot on your trail. You realize that if you're found here at my lovely estate, where I hide from humanity, I could be considered an accomplice." It was evident that Matt spoke tongue in cheek. His numerous encounters with the authorities over the years had left a bitter taste in his mouth.

"Don't worry, we can't stay long. There's a helicopter buzzing around, and a ground search can't be far behind." Jarrod said with a sense of urgency. "Do they—I mean the authorities—know about your cabin?"

"Sure they do. They've been trying for years to figure out how to evict me. They can't get any taxes off me out in the middle of nowhere. Did you follow that stupid trail they cleared so people can run around on their noisy machines?" Matt's voice rose, his frustration with the mindset of the human race becoming more evident.

"We tried to stay off it as much as possible, but I'm sure they'll bring out the dogs. We don't have a chance on foot," Jarrod said, unable to hide his desperation.

Matt paused a moment to collect his thoughts. "I'll show you something in a minute. But first off, come inside. I've got a pot of rabbit stew over the fire. You both must be starved. If you came on foot, you've had a long hike from the river." No doubt, Matt was pleased to have some company, regardless of the trouble they were in.

Over the years, with no foundation, the weight of the cabin had caused the log walls to slowly sink into the spongy ground. Matt had to pull up firmly on the sturdy iron handle before he could swing the heavy door fully open. Continuing to wear a deep grove in the hard-packed soil, the bottom edge of the door scraped a semi-circle design as Matt forced it open. The wood flooring inside was warped and uneven.

"We don't have long, Jarrod. They must be closing in," Lucas warned as he reluctantly entered the old cabin, feeling like a noose was tightening around his neck.

Much to their surprise, the two visitors discovered the inside of Matt's home was like stepping inside a previous century. How long ago did the fur trade exist? It was barely one-hundred-and-fifty years earlier that both the French and English were virgin settlers of the land. They exploited the untamed wilderness of the unpopulated and vastly unexplored country. The early settlers and fur traders showed considerable respect for its indigenous population, often depending on them to stay alive in a climate that could be very harsh. After sharing their survival and hunting skills, the indigenous people eventually became viewed as expendable, future settlers and the military treating them with less and less regard.

Was Matt a throwback to a previous generation? His tiny home was a virtual museum of artifacts, including snares and traps of every description. Jarrod held great distaste for the spring-loaded leg traps that hung like trophies on the cabin wall. Was any animal safe from Matt's arsenal?

Yet pelts were still being traded or sold to satisfy the fancies of the upper echelon on every continent. As opposed to the big-game hunter, who relied on taxidermy to display his trophies, the shelves and walls of Matt's home were littered with a multitude of skulls. The jawbones and teeth of beaver, muskrat, otter, lynx, skunk, and the skeletons of every small mammal that ever roamed the northern woods were on display. The place had the atmosphere of a prehistoric family's cave dwelling, where they proudly displayed their hunting trophies. The only thing missing was hieroglyphics.

The trapper's steel-grey eyes had a sparkle in them, perhaps brought on by his encounter with the two intriguing fugitives. Even more noticeable to Jarrod were the man's powerful hands. Their size, even their shape, resembled meat hooks wrapped with weathered skin that stretched like parchment over the skeletal bones beneath. The tips of two fingers were missing, the result of severe frostbite in a distant past. Yet as the conversation continued, it became apparent that Matt was not simply a rugged outdoorsman. Beneath his hardened surface dwelled an intelligent man, well-read and knowledgeable but not in tune with society, its attitude, and its multiple governments with their never-ending laws. A verse from an old renegade song ran briefly through Jarrod's mind—*Signs, signs, everywhere are signs.*

All conversation ceased as Matt's guests devoured their bowls of hot stew, quickly realizing how hungry they were.

"How's the stew, boy?" Matt asked, adding another scoop to Lucas's half-empty bowl. "You won't find any of my seasonings on a store shelf. I grow my own herbs, and the carrots came from my vegetable garden."

"It tastes great, thanks," Lucas replied, his words garbled by a mouth full of meat and potatoes. He was so famished he could have chewed on the innards of a dead skunk.

Wolfy lay in the corner on his tattered mat. He was quite relaxed around his master's new friends, enjoying the sounds of unfamiliar voices. Although company was rare around the cabin, the faithful dog never had a problem adapting to strangers.

During dinner, Matt carried most of the conversation, including questions about how his two guests had met each other. He tended to ramble a bit, talking about how he had been living out here for twenty-five years after tiring of society's rules. He also included his own poor decisions, including his few choices of relationships. Trapping was clearly a dying livelihood, but Matt managed to earn enough income for supplies and rations to get Wolfy and himself through the winter. Their meat supply was generally of the wild variety, and he grew his own vegetables. In most years, an abundant supply of berries kept his wine carboys topped up at the end of autumn. His biggest problem was keeping his glass away from the supply long enough to allow it to age properly. After Matt encouraged Jarrod to taste a sample of dry red from the home vineyard, both visitors were anxious to get on their way.

Jarrod and Lucas were finishing their stew as Matt continued his one-sided conversation. "Winter's just too damn long and dark around here. We go through lots of firewood, and there're a few noisy snowmobiles but nothing like the summer when all the tourists are out. ATVs, those four-wheeled buggies with balloon tires and loud mufflers, roar all over the place. They never stick to the trails and cause lots of damage. I'd like to shoot out all their damn tires."

"Thanks, Matt, the stew was fantastic," Jarrod said, "but I know you'll be getting some unwanted company soon. We have to leave. I don't want you getting into trouble because of us."

The words were barely out of Jarrod's mouth when everyone heard the whirling sound of propeller blades. Wolfy jumped to his feet, his ears stretched upward.

Sensing his guests' anxiousness, Matt started toward the door. Ever since he had brought the strangers into his home, he had been mulling over his next suggestion. "Come with me. I may have something you'll be interested in seeing."

Wolfy lumbered slowly after the others. It was clear that he enjoyed the new company and wanted to know what was happening outside. Yet when everyone scanned the sky over the treetops, there was no sign of a helicopter overhead.

"When winter comes, a few of those snowmobilers roar by here on their sleds and scare the hell out of my dog. One almost ran him over. But a few years back, I met a nice couple who stopped by on their machines asking for directions. We hit it off, and the fellow dropped by two or three times a winter. He would bring me supplies if I was running low, and he enjoyed a few glasses of my wine." Matt gave a little wink.

As Matt continued with his story, Jarrod noticed the sparkle leave his eyes. They took on a sad, vacant stare as he gazed off in the distance.

"About four years back," the trapper reminisced, "this fellow got cancer and died the next winter. He left me his snow machine in his will, the only thing I ever inherited in my life." Matt paused to collect his thoughts. "We used to sit here for hours and talk about life. Great guy. I really miss him. His widow drops by occasionally, but it's not the same. No woman I ever met could live this life. I don't get much romance anymore, that's for sure," he said, forcing a twisted grin, though his eyes remained sad.

A moment later, they all stood in front of two machines that neither Jarrod nor Lucas had ever seen up close. The one called a Skandic was obviously much older, its body square and its paint a faded orange. The second machine—or sled, as Matt called it—was much newer, black, and had a larger rounded frame. A decal on the engine hood displayed the name "Polaris" in bold letters. Lucas imagined the machine to be a combination of a toboggan, motorcycle, and dirt buggy. It had a windscreen and a comfortable seat that could fit two people, one sitting behind the other. The handlebars were not unlike those on a motorcycle and were attached to two short skis that steered the machine. The accelerator was a small trigger under the right handgrip that the driver squeezed with his thumb. The brakes were controlled by slim levers on the handlebars, much like bicycles and motorbikes.

"But how do those things run without wheels?" Lucas asked.

"There's a track underneath that spins like a treadmill that joggers use at home," Matt explained. "It's got metal runners across it that dig into the snow and ice when you gun the engine. But watch out for the power. That Polaris accelerates quickly."

Matt had already given some thought to his next offer. "Since I never really needed this machine, you two can use it. My old one still gets me around. And walking out of here won't get you very far. The gas tank is full and should get you to the road that runs north to the Trans-Canada Highway. That's the highway that will take you to civilization, if that's what you're looking for."

"We can't take your inheritance; that wouldn't be fair," Jarrod argued. "You might never see it again."

"You know, it would please me and Wolfy just to see you both get out of here. I'm just passing on what was never really mine. Trust me, my friend who left that sled to me will be looking down on you." Matt was not about to take no for an answer. If the RCMP found the snowmobile wrecked or abandoned, they would trace it back to the previous owner. Matt never had it registered in his name. Even the plates were three years old.

"One more warning," the trapper continued, "It's a bit too early in winter to use this machine. The sprockets that turn the tracks need to be cooled, so try to drive in the snow as much as possible, or you'll have problems with the bearings overheating."

Both Jarrod and Lucas were dumbfounded by the generous offer of the talkative recluse. Jarrod wished he could introduce Matt to Molly, the other person willing to give up her vehicle to help them.

Tugging on the Polaris's starter chord, the old trapper made a comment that Jarrod would always remember. "You guys remind me of a song by the only singer I ever liked, Harry Chapin. I think it was called 'A Better Place to Be,' and I hope you both find it. I'll think of you."

As Matt began a series of pulls on the starter chord, Jarrod shook his head. Was that not the same song he recalled when he walked out on Tammy and her orange cat flashed him the evil eye? Still, neither he nor Lucas could ever be confused with the love-struck midnight watchman portrayed in the song.

It was Wolfy who heard the sound first, a high-pitched whistle that only a dog's ears might pick up. He cocked his head and turned to look behind him, the fur on his back rising ever so slightly.

It didn't take long for the others to hear the distant hum of approaching engines. The starter chord slipped out of Matt's hand as he pulled it too quickly. A cold shiver went up Jarrod's spine. He looked over and saw Lucas's legs shaking as the ominous rumbling grew louder. Was this the beginning of the end?

Chapter 44

The speed at which the group of officers from the Kenora detachment approached caught Jamie off guard. They arrived over fifteen minutes early in a three-quarter-ton truck moving so quickly that it drifted sideways around the final corner, almost sideswiping Jamie's stopped vehicle. A spray of wet slush hit the side of the green pickup.

"Hey, you guys, take it easy!" Jamie shouted out his open window. "We're not chasing the Dalton Gang." His reference to the notorious Kansas bank robbers went over the young officers' heads.

"Sorry about that, but everyone is pretty excited to start tracking down some fugitives," the driver exclaimed as he stepped out of the truck, "except maybe for Jacob, who would rather still be sleeping."

It took Jamie a moment to assimilate the young search crew that poured out of the filthy turbo-powered vehicle that came to a stop only inches away from his truck. Kenora, the town the officers came from, was situated on the northern edge of Lake of the Woods. Larger than Rainy River, it was basically a tourist area that doubled its size in the summer months. Its major employer was a pulp-and-paper mill, an industry that was, unfortunately, dying slowly in the Kenora area. The search crew consisted of five enthusiastic young men. Jacob, by far the oldest, was only in his late thirties. The sixth member, a bright-eyed woman with a pleasant smile, appeared to be about the same age as the youthful officers.

It became evident quickly that whatever this bunch lacked in experience they made up for in exuberance. Anxious to make a good impression, the crew straightened their uniforms and adjusted their holsters as they approached Jamie. They were all eager to meet him and get on with the chase, which to most of them was a whole new adventure. The crew was not the experienced group Jamie had expected to meet.

Apologizing once again for driving so recklessly, Chris was the first to introduce himself. “Good morning, sir, the boys and I are ready to get to work—and Sharon, of course,” he added as an afterthought, nodding toward her.

Already aware of the man’s reputation, it was clear to Jamie who was in charge of the Kenora crew. As the senior male in his group, Chris showed a lot of confidence (Jacob showed little interest in advancing his own position). The others jumped to work when he instructed them to unload the two all-terrain vehicles from their truck. The ATVs—or quads, as they were called—were off-road machines with large, balloon tires, low gear ratios, and all-wheel drive. The tire treads were raised and angled for better traction. A plastic windscreen was the driver’s only protection from the elements. The vehicles were ideal for rough, steep terrain. Not only did they handle rocky, uneven ground with ease, but they dealt with soft, wet conditions as well and weren't slowed by a couple of inches of snow. However deeper, wind-drifted snow could cause some problems with steering and traction.

"It's good to meet you all. Welcome to our wilderness home," Jamie said before introducing himself to the group. Henry had not yet returned. "Thanks for getting here so quickly. We should be in for an exciting day." He emphasized that everyone call him Jamie. He was never one for formality.

While the others unloaded the ATVs, Chris went to get his dog from the cab. Speaking with obvious pride, he introduced her to Jamie. "This is Abby. She's the finest tracking dog in this area, maybe in all of Ontario. Not only can she track, she's faithful and a good attack dog as well."

Hearing her master speak, Abby relieved herself on the spot, almost peeing on Chris's boots. Undeterred, he continued. "She's already won a couple of awards. People say I know more about her than my girlfriend."

"What girlfriend?" Sharon couldn't resist the comment. She had no doubt that Chris would have preferred she stayed at home. The rest of the Kenora crew tried not to laugh.

Jamie seized the moment to address the group. "Don't get too excited about the border jumpers. They're not bank robbers or dangerous felons. It's very unlikely they're even armed, so don't be too hasty pulling out your weapons. In fact, this may turn out to be a rescue mission. I don't want any accidents with firearms. My information says that one of these so-called fugitives is only a child."

It was clear that Jamie was already acquiring a degree of empathy for those he was pursuing. It was not the first time it had happened and seemed to be the only real weakness he had in a career that embodied his heart and soul. His training had emphasized that emotional involvement with the public, particularly those who had broken the law, was to be avoided under all circumstances. Over the years, Canada had become a haven for many American fugitives and draft dodgers. Only recently had increased supervision and sophisticated patrolling methods, as well as enhanced documentation, made illegal entry into either country much more difficult. But once an intruder had breached an official border, it was the foreign country's responsibility to apprehend the culprit. Of course, help from the person's homeland could always be requested.

Just as Jamie unfolded a detailed chart of the area, Henry finally emerged from the cleared trail next to the roadway. His boots and pants were saturated from the soggy terrain. "Jamie, I found some footprints along the trail to the southeast that were fresh and definitely human," he explained, breathing heavily. "One set of prints was smaller than the other—fits in with your info about there being a child. The footprints lead to this road but don't seem to cross it. These people might have gotten spooked and tried to erase their tracks—the snow is pretty messed up in that area. It's likely they took to the bush and changed their direction."

"Good work, Henry." After complimenting his partner, Jamie introduced him to the others who had just finished unloading the ATVs.

"If Henry's right, we should be able to narrow our search and toss out a lot of possibilities," Jamie said. Then he made it clear who was in charge. "Before we tear around in those noisy machines and destroy any tracks or clues that those guys may have left, we'll do some footwork first. Let's see if Abby can pick up a scent. Chris tells me she's the best dog in these parts."

"Best in all of Ontario, I'll bet," Chris interjected.

Sharon rolled her eyes.

"We're about to find out," Jamie continued. "Here are two maps showing the network of roads leading to all the camps, cottages, and private homes in the area. Four of your men can take their machines and check out possible hiding spots. Those two must be cold and hungry, and breaking into one of the camps might be their only option. I would suggest leaving the ATVs at the head of the driveways leading into those places. Just hike in on foot. The transmitter base in my truck is charged up, so I hope radio contact won't be a problem. There are lots of trees and rocky outcroppings in the area."

"I'll get the boys right on it," Chris replied, taking the detailed maps from Jamie.

"After you get your fellows organized, why don't you bring Sharon along with Henry and me?" Jamie said. "The four of us and your dog will do a little footwork." Being a friend of a senior officer in Kenora, Jamie was aware of the innovative ideas the young woman could come up with. "Then we'll put Abby to her big test," he added. Jamie didn't mention that the only other time he had been involved with a tracking dog in a search, the canine had led its handler in the opposite direction of their target.

Chis had hoped to bring Alex, the youngest member of the team, along on the ground search. At twenty-one years of age, he was the newest recruit in the Kenora division. Impressed with his brash enthusiasm and willingness to learn, Chris had taken him under his wing and tried to get the young constable involved in many of his assignments. However, he went along with Jamie's suggestion. He nodded to Sharon before giving her a "Miss-know-it-all" look. It was evident that his actual concern was about being outperformed by a woman.

Chris briefed the four men on his team who would be taking the two quads to check out the small roadways that connected the camps and private cottages in the area. Repeating Jamie's instructions, he emphasized that imminent danger was not necessarily a factor. The "illegals" were more likely in trouble than a threat to anyone. He cautioned his men to walk slowly into the camps, be diligent and alert, but only consider force as a last resort. Henry was careful to circle the camp on the map that he had already visited. The searchers would find plenty of fresh tire tracks all over the area. Jamie assumed their field training would have clarified how to distinguish human footprints from the tracks made by wildlife foraging for food.

Although his first impression was that Chris was self-centered and a bit cocky, Jamie was beginning to like the confident officer who seemed to be comfortable directing others. His friend on the force had mentioned that Chris interacted well with the younger recruits. However, Jamie did notice some tension and abruptness in his attitude toward Sharon. Hopefully, the land search would not become a contest between her, Chris, and his loyal dog, Abby. The skills of all three were needed for a successful outcome.

Speaking up for the first time since she had given Chis a little jibe, Sharon put her hand out toward Jamie's. "It's nice to meet you, Officer Grogan. Just let me know whatever I can do to help out." She flashed a confident yet pleasant smile.

"Please, call me Jamie. We go by first names around here. Since you and Abby are the only females on this job, I'm sure you'll have the sharpest eyes and be spotting any clues or tracks before the rest of us do. Just keep alert; that's my only advice." Jamie gave her a reassuring grin as he gripped her sturdy hand.

Chris controlled Abby with a leash when the ground search began in earnest. Henry led the group toward the footprints he had located in his earlier walk up the path. The extended leash allowed Abby to pick up scents along the trail as she darted from side to side. Her time to run loose would come soon enough.

After remaining quiet while all the organizing was going on, Henry finally spoke up. "Not too far ahead, there's another opening to the roadway. You'll see what's left of some footprints that lead that way but appear to end at the road. I think our fugitives backtracked and tried to erase their tracks using a tree branch."

"Wait, Abby's got a scent; she's starting to tug," Chris said, excitement in his voice.

"Release her if you think it's time," Jamie suggested.

Snapping off the quick release, Chris watched expectantly as Abby bounded into the bush to the right of the trail. Moments later, everyone cringed when an overpowering odor stung their nostrils. Apparently, Abby had disturbed a sleeping skunk. Fortunately, the renowned tracking dog was able to retreat before the startled animal could unleash the full force of its potent defensive maneuver.

"I promise not to bring this up in my report," Jamie said, suppressing a much more caustic comment as he covered his mouth and nose with his jacket sleeve.

Abby tried to cuddle up next to her handler while Chris did his best to keep his distance from her, obviously embarrassed by the incident. "Now that's something that has never happened before. Training school never prepared us for this," he explained lamely.

"Just remember, everyone," Henry said, "whatever happens in the bush stays in the bush."

The spur-of-the-moment remark silenced Chris who was unable to come up with a good response. He only managed a sheepish grin while the others had a good chuckle. Sharon was careful not to make her own comment.

"How far away are those tracks you saw?" Chris asked, trying to forget what had just happened. "Let's give Abby a real chance to show her stuff." Vowing a better outcome, he was still perplexed by what his dog had done.

"I think we're here," Henry announced, spotting the orange mark he had sprayed earlier on the trunk of a gnarled oak tree. A broken branch from a spruce tree lay nearby, many of its needles missing. The fugitives had likely used it to wipe their tracks.

Only having been involved in one other search party, Sharon approached the scene cautiously but with the enthusiasm of a new recruit. Her eyes scanning the ground to the left of the trail, she was quick to point to the outline of two sets of footprints. The larger of the two appeared to be made by either hiking boots or winter boots with deep treads, but the smaller tracks could only have been made by sneakers or canvas running shoes, not recommended footwear for wintery conditions. The prints led away from the trail, where the terrain was rocky and hard-packed and would be impossible to follow with the naked eye.

"Okay, Abby, show them what you can do," Chris said, with less confidence than before.

Getting a pat on the head as she was released, Abby began to sniff enthusiastically, quickly picking up a scent from the footprints and brush along the edge of the trail. Calling her back, Chris pointed Abby toward the slope that headed up the rocky terrain to their left, following a northwesterly direction. Her nose working hard as she climbed the outcropping of rock, Abby stopped suddenly and looked back at the others as she waited for them to follow. It became apparent who was in charge at that point. Perhaps canines of the future might start their own union.

"I think Abby has picked up the scent. If I'm right, all we have to do is follow her," Chris announced, his voice showing renewed confidence.

"That's a girl who doesn't give up," Jamie said, gaining admiration for the tracking dog. Like most of the others, he was puffing as he attempted to keep up with Abby's rapid pace.

After almost thirty minutes of winding around and brushing against the spiny needles of an mixture of fir trees, not to mention climbing over thickets of thorny underbrush, the weary search group suffered numerous scratches across their hands, faces, and any unprotected areas of their bodies. But Abby was on a mission, darting back and forth, constantly sniffing the air and any foliage she encountered. Everyone but Sharon was gasping for breath. Daily workouts on the treadmill had kept her in superior shape. It was no surprise that she was the first to spot the wispy threads of smoke that rose above the trees.

"Look," Sharon said, her voice showing excitement, "Could that be a campfire?"

Looking over the treetops, Jamie thought for a moment, then slowly shook his head. "No, Sharon, but I'm quite sure I know where the smoke is coming from. It's a place I should have thought about much earlier."

Almost at the same instant he spoke, the whirling noise of the helicopter filled their ears. Jamie's radio crackled to life. Even Abby stopped her sniffing and looked up at the sky.

"Jamie, do you read me?" Brady yelled over the screaming propeller blades.

"I can see you. You're almost overhead!" Jamie shouted.

"So, you must see the smoke. We can see the outline of a small cabin."

"Our tracking dog is on a mission. She's headed right in that direction. How's your fuel supply?" Jamie asked. "We may need you in a short while."

"We're okay for fuel. We'll hang around the area until we hear from you," Brady replied.

Jamie and Henry looked at each another with similar looks of bewilderment. Each of them knew exactly what the other was thinking.

"Damn," Jamie mumbled, silently scolding himself. He should have thought of the possibility long before. It never occurred to him that Matt, the zany hermit who trapped for a living, would enter the picture. That had to be his cabin just over the next rise. If they had followed the trail, it would have led them right toward it in half the time. The overland route was simply a diversion. Could the American fugitives have known Matt all along? That probability seemed rather remote, as the isolated trapper had little contact with the outside world. Jamie had never actually met the man, but Henry knew more about Matt's past, his dislike of contact with society and its prejudices as well as any form of government and all its laws.

"Chris, I have new respect for Abby. She's a genius for leading us here. I knew this place existed, but the thought of it never occurred to me," Jamie confessed. Chris leashed his faithful dog, who was getting more anxious by the moment.

"Do we spread out and try to surround the place?" Sharon asked innocently. She was getting increasingly excited as well, her heart beating rapidly. Chris struggled to control Abby, who was refusing his commands to heel.

"No, not with just the four of us," Jamie replied.

"I think we should get at least one ATV to come as backup," Henry suggested. "I heard through a friend that the old trapper was given a fancy snowmobile a couple of years ago. If the fugitives get hold of it, we'll need a way to pursue them. Travis and Brady can follow them overhead and give us directions." Henry was earning his overtime bonus.

Jamie nodded. "Makes sense. Chris, get hold of your other men. We may need both machines, so get everyone to come here. Just tell them to follow the groomed trail as it angles to the northwest. Sharon, you can intercept them before they get too close. The less noise we make, the better. The rest of us will try to get as close as possible and see if Matt has any company."

Chris radioed the others with instructions while trying to calm Abby.

With Sharon making her way toward the trail, the others moved cautiously toward Matt's cabin. Abby continued to focus on her job, but the dog's progress was slowed as Chris held tightly to her leash. It wasn't long before she became overly anxious in her pursuit, and her master was forced to use a high-pitched whistle to control her. The sound it emitted could not be heard by the human ear, yet the training method got Abby to sit obediently. Her schooling well ingrained, she finally began to move forward at the same pace as the others. What Chris didn't realize was that the high-pitched whistle might be heard by an older yet still protective canine.

Not only was the entire group fatigued from trekking over the rough terrain, their progress slowed considerably as dry branches snapped across their arms, and bushes laden with overripe berries slapped against their tired bodies. Approaching the cabin quietly was a difficult task, but everyone was convinced that Abby had led them to their quarry, and the search was about to come to an end.

Chapter 45

Lucas had his head turned toward the rumbling noise of engines when he noticed some unusual movement in the tall saplings that grew not far from the cabin. The smoke from Matt's cook stove rose almost straight into the sky, so a breeze wasn't causing the trees to sway. Could it be a deer, wolf, or any wild animal coming their way? The boy quickly had his answer when Abby, who was more anxious than her training had taught her to behave, let out a low, harsh bark that was meant to be a warning to the group that followed her. Like cloaked figures in a three-dimensional movie, the forms of three uniformed men emerged from the trees. His eyes widening, Lucas didn't need binoculars to recognize the serious and determined looks on their faces.

Jamie and the others had increased their speed when they heard the approaching ATVs. Chris had not expected his men to react so fast, but their motivation and fervor was too high to allow them to hold back until they were, in fact, needed. The noise they made was enough to alert any living creature, human or otherwise, in the area.

"The boy saw us. He must have heard those damn machines!" Jamie said, annoyed that they had lost the advantage of a surprise approach.

"They're here!" was all that Lucas could say, his voice hushed, yet penetrating. Jarrod and Matt turned in time to take in the scene.

Just as Lucas spoke, the black Polaris roared to life on Matt's fourth pull on the starter chord. The snowmobile's two-stroke engine chugged roughly as it idled in anticipation of an impending adventure. The pistons were warming quickly.

"Frenzied," "impulsive," and "unrehearsed" could only begin to describe the following moments of frantic activity. Mere seconds of extreme stress could put more strain on the human body than running a marathon. Six humans and two animals reacted on instinct, all trying to move at the unmatched speed of a predator in pursuit of easy prey.

As might be expected, the canines displayed the fastest reaction. Abby was a tracking dog and was expected to obey commands. For the second time that day, she took charge, ignoring her master. Chris had unintentionally slackened his grip on her leash as the three officers made their final approach toward the cabin. With little formal training as an attack dog, Abby acted intuitively, pulling loose from her handler and then bolting toward the fugitives. When the dog whistle fell from his hand, shouted commands from Chris to "heel" were totally ignored. Then it was Wolfy's turn to react. Without doubt, a natural instinct took over when it came to protecting Matt and his friends. The two dogs collided like runaway locomotives.

Wolfy may have had a disadvantage in terms of age and speed, but he was a powerful and determined beast. The dogs stood on their haunches and clutched briefly, like two boxers in a sparring stance. That is when any comparison to humans ended. Sharp fangs were bared, and the growling and snapping began in earnest. Chis made the first move to put a quick end to any canine carnage by drawing his service revolver. Wolfy appeared to be overpowering his precious Abby. What the officer didn't foresee was the resolve, not to mention the unexpected speed, of a sixty-year-old trapper. With one short stroke, Matt's powerful left hand struck Chris across the wrist just as he was about to take aim. The revolver spun in circles as it skittered across the wet moss at the officer's feet.

"No need for that, son," Matt said sternly. "Control your dog, and I'll get mine off her." He turned to the struggling canines. His booming voice yelled, "Down, boy!"

Wolfy released his grip on the tenacious Abby, allowing Chris to grab his dog's leash and pull her back. Although young, fit, and willing, Abby would not have won the fight. Fortunately, it was stopped just in time, with the overmatched female only receiving a small puncture wound in the back of her neck, and no shots were fired.

Time seemed to stand still as the scene took on a tone of serenity. The entire group froze momentarily, likely to give their minds time to recover from the mayhem of the dog fight. Even the noise of the approaching machines seemed to diminish.

Jamie was the first to snap back to reality. He suspected that, in their rush to get to the scene of the action, the anxious ATV drivers had passed the cabin as they flew along the trail. It turned out his hunch was correct. The fire had burned down, and only a few strands of smoke came from the chimney, making it harder to locate, especially at the speed the machines were traveling. And where was Sharon? How had she missed the others?

As Chris scrambled to pick up his revolver, Matt ushered his dog into the cabin, holding Wolfy firmly by the scruff of his neck. With her tongue hanging from the side of her mouth, Abby panted nervously as she nudged her master. There was no fight left in Ontario's greatest tracking dog.

"Put your gun away, Chris. We're just going to talk to these guys," Jamie said firmly. "They don't look dangerous to me."

Henry and Chris rocked nervously as they stood less than thirty feet from the two people who were the objects of their strenuous search. The young boy glared back at them before his eyes began to dart in every direction. Was he searching for an escape route? Lucas was seated alone on the black machine that idled roughly beneath his tense body. The man who stood rigidly next to him looked just as uncomfortable. However, rather than threatening, both man and boy looked equally pathetic. They were dirty and disheveled with forlorn and resigned expressions on their faces. What in Jamie's training would help him diffuse this peculiar yet tense standoff? Before approaching the fugitives, he had to say something.

"I'm sure you both know why we're here. You've done well to get this far on foot," Jamie began calmly, even showing some admiration in his voice. "You must be tired of tramping through these woods. The terrain around here is awfully rough. I'm exhausted, and I haven't come nearly as far as you guys have."

When he got no response, Jamie continued. "The US border patrol alerted us to your illegal entry into Canada. I assume you are both Americans. Unless you have reason to fight it, the extradition procedure will be a formality."

Although he hardly felt like talking, Jarrod finally broke his silence. "You've got it right. We are Americans, but we don't want to return there. They think we're dangerous felons, but all we want is freedom. We can only find that up here in your country."

"I only wish it was that simple—just cross the border and start a new life. I'm afraid I don't have any choice but to take you both into custody and alert the American authorities," Jamie replied. Although he tried to sound authoritative, his tone showed a hint of remorse.

A tightness caused by fear of the inevitable gripped the chests of both fugitives. Lucas was so tense that the tendons were knotting up on both sides of his neck. His stomach cramped so badly that he came close to being sick.

Matt had calmed down Wolfy in the cabin, and was just emerging from his home when Henry and Chris moved forward, releasing the handcuffs that were clipped to their belts. What happened next came as a complete shock to everyone.

Somewhere in his youthful brain, a warning signal told Lucas that it was now or never. Fear and an overwhelming urge to escape gripped his mind, causing his body to react rashly and instinctively. A wolf caught in a leg trap does all it can do to free itself, even gnawing off its leg if necessary.

In its frenzied state, a caged animal will destroy his teeth trying to bite through the bars. All Lucas had to do was squeeze the plastic trigger beneath the right handlebar of the shiny snowmobile on which he was sitting, and that is exactly what he did.

Matt was certainly right—the machine had power. It lurched forward so quickly that Lucas almost tumbled off the back. Chris dove to try and grab hold of the boy or the grip bar at the rear of the double seat, but the exuberant officer wasn't nearly fast enough as the speeding Polaris catapulted over two small fir trees, careened off the edge of Matt's woodpile, and shot off the property as if flung from a slingshot. The plastic windscreen cracked as tree branches slashed against it, several dead ones snapping off, their shattered remains sent whirling into the surrounding brush.

After escaping the immediate danger, Lucas let up on the accelerator before causing more damage to the machine. A slash from an errant tree branch had opened a gash on his forehead, and blood trickled slowly over his cheek. His heart was pounding, but he wasn't about to look back. His eyes watered from the rush of air across his face, and adrenalin coursed through his knotted body.

After making a sharp turn to avoid a clump of poplars, the snowmobile slowed quickly when the boy's small thumb slipped off the throttle. At first, Lucas feared that the machine had stalled, but the sputtering sound coming from the two-stroke pistons confirmed the engine continued to rev. What next? How could he desert the only friend he had? Guilt, anxiety, the multitude of emotions that flooded his young brain only led to total confusion. As much as he cared for Jarrod, Lucas convinced himself that his friend would not want him to give up, but continue to fight for the only thing that mattered—freedom to do what he wanted with his life, to chase his dreams, and maybe, one day, find happiness.

As if directed by fate, the snowmobile had come to rest in a shallow gully, an open area where there was separation between fir trees, berry-covered bushes, and outcroppings of rock. The Polaris was sitting in an ancient streambed that had ceased flowing centuries ago. Water still cascaded through the area occasionally when an early spring of high temperatures followed a long winter of heavy snow.

With little time for thought, Lucas came to a quick decision. He would ignore the consequences and continue his journey. He figured the opening straight ahead, although winding, uphill, and strewn with rocks and tree limbs, was his best choice for an escape route. When his ears picked up the muffled sounds of an ATV somewhere in the distance, panic struck once again. As if hit by an electric shock, his right thumb jerked on the accelerator. The powerful machine responded immediately, lurching forward, its tracks spinning for traction in the matted grass and slippery moss that blanketed the age-old streambed.

While watching the novice driver zigzag randomly as he sped away from his pursuers, Jamie and Chris both grabbed their radios. Shouting almost simultaneously into their mikes, the two men had to separate from one another so they could be heard.

"Brady, do you read me?" Jamie roared.

"Go ahead. What have you found?" Brady asked.

"The boy took off on a snowmobile. I'm sure he's never driven one and could crash at any time. He was headed north from the trapper's cabin, but he's swerving all over the place. That machine is far too powerful for him. The kid's plowing over everything in his path, so he should be easy to follow. Let me know if you spot him."

"I expected we were after drug dealers or bank robbers, not kids," Brady answered, somewhat surprised. "We're not far away from the cabin. I'll get back to you shortly. How old is this kid, anyway?"

"About twelve, I think, but he sure freaked out. I'm concerned he's going to hurt himself."

Chris was equally loud as he tried to locate his men. "Where are you guys? You went flying right by us, and we need you right away. One of the fugitives escaped on a snowmobile."

"I realized we missed the trail to the cabin. We're on our way back," replied Jacob, the most senior of the other four men.

"I thought you would have seen Sharon. She was supposed to meet you. Make sure Alex slows down and doesn't miss the turnoff again," Chris said, a bit annoyed. "No one else can meet you. We have our hands full here."

"We'll be going slower. I don't want to screw up again," Jacob replied remorsefully. "We'll look out for Sharon and bring her with us."

With the others busy on their radios, Henry was responsible for handcuffing the older fugitive. Jarrod had little fight left in him. Physically, his energy was sapped, and mentally, he had just about given up hope. Without resistance, he merely put his shaking hands behind his back. Freedom meant little to him at that point. His only concern was that Lucas didn't hurt himself in his frantic attempt to escape. The kinship, the connection that had mysteriously developed over the last week with his young friend, was overpowering his own wellbeing. But why, and why at that point in his life, did he suddenly care? He had no more of an answer to that question than he had an explanation for why he had stood up in the dirty aisle of the Silverfox bus to begin with.

Chris was amazed at how quickly his men returned on their quads. Sharon had hitched a ride with them, her legs hanging off the back of one of the machines. She had missed intersecting the others by seconds as they flew up the trail past the narrow path leading to the cabin.

The four returning men turned up the plastic face screens on their protective helmets, exposing faces that showed varied shades of embarrassment. When everyone was together, Jamie spoke first, having already thought out his next action. "Chris, who are your most experienced drivers?"

Chris pointed to Jacob and another fellow named Chad, who was easy to spot with his thin mustache and goatee. "What do have in mind, Jamie?"

"With the help of the copter, Henry and I will go with your men and try to follow the path the snowmobile took. It shouldn't be too difficult, considering the way that kid was driving."

"His name is Lucas," Jarrod said. "Please don't hurt him. He came to Canada to look for a woman he considers to be his mom. He hasn't had many breaks in life." Jarrod shook as he spoke, having difficulty containing his emotions. The thought of returning to the United States, likely to prison, was furthest from his mind.

"I have no intension of hurting the boy," Jamie said. "I only hope he doesn't harm himself. He knows nothing about the machine he's driving or the area he's driving through." Jamie could not conceal the concern in his voice.

"I know this area better than any of you," Matt said, his voice powerful, yet gentle. He had returned from his cabin and overheard the end of the discussion. "I'm worried about the direction the boy is headed. The only real opening follows an old creek bed, but there's a cliff in that area, a place called Zeller's Summit. It drops off well over a hundred feet. At the speed he's going, the kid will never see it coming. It's not like there are signs up there."

"What do you suggest?" Jamie asked, sensing the trapper's apprehension.

"I should come with you," Matt said. "Remember, I've been roaming these woods for a long time, so finding a lost kid on a snow machine shouldn't be a problem."

"He's right," Henry agreed. "Take Matt with you, and the rest of us will keep an eye on this fellow." He glanced briefly at Jarrod, who was leaning silently against the cabin, staring at the ground.

Nodding in agreement, Jamie let Jacob and Matt take the lead while he sat behind the bearded driver on the second ATV. Matt's booming voice could be heard as he yelled instructions into Jacob's ear. The off-road machines crunched over broken branches and deadfall as they followed the twisting route that Lucas and his machine had forged through the woods. Both drivers' skills in handling their ATVs were put to the test.

Chapter 46

While the others were tracking the speeding snowmobile, Henry was left in charge of guarding Jarrod. Four officers from Kenora remained with him, including Chris and Sharon. The young rookie, Alex, showed signs of anxiety, likely wishing they had brought another off-road machine so he could have joined in the chase. Evidently, he got bored and agitated in situations where he was forced to sit around and observe. Activity kept him stimulated.

Wolfy remained in Matt's cabin, which was so small and cramped that everyone else remained outside, either standing about or sitting on one of the numerous stumps that dotted the yard next to Matt's vegetable garden. Sensing how worn out and dejected his prisoner was, Henry saw no need for the handcuffs and instructed Chris to remove them.

"Are you sure we should do this?" Chris asked. Abby lay on the ground next to him, her chest heaving, still shaken from her encounter with Wolfy.

"You think this guy is going anywhere?" Henry replied tersely.

"Do you know much about this area? That place the trapper was talking about, is it a high cliff or drop-off?" Sharon asked Henry, changing the subject.

"I've never been that way, but I hear Zeller's Summit is the highest point anywhere around here," Henry replied.

"The kid doesn't have a chance," Jarrod said, his voice barely above a whisper. "When he gets spooked, there's no stopping him."

"The way he was driving, he'll likely hit a tree or lose a ski long before he reaches the drop-off," Henry reasoned, hoping he was close to the truth.

Bored with the conversation, Alex started pacing. He even threw a few logs back onto the woodpile that the snowmobile had knocked loose. A conspicuous silence fell over the group.

Sharon, who had participated in calming numerous domestic disputes, was aware that casual chatter could break the tension of any situation. Recognizing the concern on Jarrod's face, she addressed him with an easygoing attitude. "So, how did you get involved with this boy? Are you related?"

Hesitant and unwilling to respond at first, Jarrod eventually decided to speak honestly. It was as if he had to get something off his chest. He also sensed compassion lurking within the officer. Sharon stood out from the others, especially Chris who seemed to relish being in charge and was very much by the book. Jarrod also sensed the competitiveness, approaching animosity, that lingered between the senior officer and his female associate. The two of them certainly had opposing personalities.

An unrestrained monologue rolled out of Jarrod as he described his last several days, including the onrush of events that never seemed to let up. Even Alex was mesmerized by the unbelievable tale. Each listener was affected in a different way. Like hearing folklore from a bygone era, the spellbound group found it difficult to believe the saga unfolding before them had actually taken place. Yet in one way or another, from that day onward, Jarrod's audience found his or her attitude toward life changed. Some were impressed by the fierce loyalty that bonded the two unlikely friends, while others reveled in the tenacity against all odds both desperate fugitives displayed. Either way, none of them would forget that prolonged moment.

Only seconds after his decision to continue up the old streambed, Lucas noticed a shadow hover over him briefly before moving off to the side. He was aware that danger loomed just overhead. It was apparent that the helicopter pilots had located his trail and were relaying the information to the men on the ground. The sight of the whirling blades only added to his panic.

The four-wheelers, weighted down with passengers, were difficult to maneuver over the rough terrain. As a result, they were unable to keep up with the torrid pace of the powerful snowmobile that careened off every obstacle in its path. Although Matt had no trouble following Lucas's route up the winding riverbed, his machine could not gain any ground on the fleeing Polaris.

His concern growing with every moment, Jamie had his driver slow down so he could give instructions to the helicopter search team. "I'm worried you guys may spook that kid even more than he already is. I suggest you pull away and return to your base. I think we have the situation under control. And thanks for all your help. I'll talk to you both later."

"I copy you, buddy. We'll head home. Travis asks that you keep us informed about how it turns out. I just hope we won't be involved later in a recovery mission."

Brady signed off, and Travis did a little loop with the Sikorsky to acknowledge the camaraderie of everyone involved in the day's events.

Still well ahead of his pursuers, and with his heart still pounding, Lucas refused to let up on the accelerator. He hardly noticed the blood that oozed from the wound on his face, trickling over his numb lips and into the corner of his mouth. A rush of air flowing through the gap in the shattered windscreen distorted the skin on his face. Yet his mind remained focused. Escape and freedom were his only thoughts. At that moment, neither past nor future existed. Lucas was fixated entirely on the chase, which was the only thing that mattered. Bouncing over rocks, smacking into tree branches, his wounded yet determined machine showed an equal resolve.

Still unable to gain any ground on the fleeing Polaris, the two quads took a pounding as they bounced along the dry creek bed. From his seat behind Jacob, Matt motioned to the ATV following them to slow down while also instructing Jacob to ease up on the accelerator. He wanted to chat.

After both machines came to a stop, Matt spoke to the group. "I don't know how that snowmobile keeps going. That kid has hit almost everything in his path. The skis should have been torn off by now. I'm sure your fancy quads are taking a beating as well."

"Is he still on target for that cliff you were talking about?" Jamie asked, ignoring the steam that rose from the overheated ATVs.

"I'm afraid so. This creek bed leads straight to Zeller's Summit. If we could only get him to slow down," Matt replied, unable to comprehend the fear and panic that held a firm grip on Lucas.

"How much farther?" Jamie inquired.

"I would guess it's less than half a mile away," Matt replied. "Maybe we should hold back for a few minutes. There's nowhere for him to go once he gets to the ridge. Hopefully he can stop in time. If he doesn't hear our machines, maybe he won't be in such a panic. Or else that drop-off might really spook him." The trapper showed a real concern for the boy who had dined on his rabbit stew barely an hour earlier. He now wished he had never suggested using his shiny snowmobile to get away.

Jamie agreed without hesitation. As the four men sat in silence, a poignant picture raced through each of their thoughts. The sight of a black airborne machine carrying a small, terrified passenger was inescapable. Without a doubt, uncertainty and anticipation were two sentiments that connected the divergent group of men who began pacing the ground next to their machines.

For his part, Lucas knew nothing about the danger he was approaching or the fact that his pursuers had slowed to a stop. Every muscle in his body was stretched to its limit and ached from the constant bouncing of his machine combined with the exertion and strength required to steer it. Only fear-induced energy kept his body functioning and alert. His head throbbed. It took all his concentration just to maneuver the machine up the winding creek bed. The tip of the right ski had broken off, making steering even more difficult. The bolts securing the other ski were about to fracture.

Although inevitable, the ensuing event was not only catastrophic but occurred at the speed of light. One last tree branch exploded as the left ski separated from the snowmobile. Without warning, only blue sky and cumulous clouds filled the panorama that emerged dramatically in front of the startled boy. What Lucas could not have foreseen appeared as quickly as a comet whizzing across a starlit firmament. In a fraction of a second, his path ended in the outstretched arms of oblivion. No longer did pine and fir trees line the sides of his route. The scene that burst into view was not only an intensely blue sky but also the pointed tops of towering evergreens that reached up from a valley far, far below. At the speed Lucas was travelling, putting the brakes to his determined sled was not an option. As if controlled by giant lungs, the cool, moist air from the yawning gorge seemed to inhale as it welcomed the wingless Polaris. The broken machine was airborne.

There are many theories of what goes through the minds of humans when they see that the end of their lives is inescapable. Survivors of serious car and airplane crashes have experienced a diorama of their life flashing across their minds, followed frequently by an intense white glow and then a feeling of peace and acceptance. When Lucas felt his hands slip from the snowmobile's handlebars, its tracks still spinning defiantly as it launched into the cool air that rose from the vast chasm below, his first thought was disbelief. Then, as his mind raced with an endless flood of emotions, reality came crashing down. Dreams of a future faded to nothingness. Behind eyes that were closed as he accepted his fate, the faces of many people flashed through the mind of the airborne boy. There were dozens of faces, but only two seemed to have bodies attached and arms that were reaching out to him. Visions of both Tracy and Jarrod stood apart from the others. Were those the two people who cared about him, or was some distant, magical force simply wanting to find peace for his bewildered, tortured mind?

A split second later, all mortal thoughts dissipated. With the devastation of an exploding bomb, a massive tree limb crashed against the airborne boy's head, knocking him unconscious. His helpless body tumbled down through the boughs of a towering evergreen. After rolling and bouncing from limb to limb like a rag doll, Lucas came to rest at the base of the colossal tree, his lifeless form collapsed on a bed of moss, cones, and pine needles. Disturbed from their job of collecting a supply of pinecones for the winter, two plump squirrels scurried to safety. What was once a bright and encouraging autumn day descended into darkness, complete and impenetrable darkness.

Following a respite that lasted several minutes, Jamie's search team resumed its pursuit of the young runaway. In varying degrees, each of them was fearful of what the search's outcome might be. Anxiety tugged especially on the minds of Jamie and Matt who were not only the most aware of the danger lurking ahead but also, for reasons personal to each of them, felt the most compassion in their hearts. Slowing their machines to a stop on more than one occasion to see if they could hear any sounds in the distance, the team was stunned by the vast and surreal silence that surrounded them. They did not hear a single dry leaf rustle on any tree, a bird chirp, or a squirrel chatter. The stillness, especially the deathly silence, was so eerie that it bordered on the supernatural.

Matt found the incredible serenity especially unusual as the group made one last stop before their final approach to the peak of the rise and Zeller's Summit. "This is strange. You could hear a pin drop out here. I've never felt it this still before," he said, his voice barely above a whisper. "What happened to the birds?" Matt was unsure if he was witnessing the calm before the storm or if they all were approaching the gates of heaven.

Both ATVs crept up the remaining few yards of the streambed, no one knowing what to expect at the summit. Filled with apprehension, nobody spoke when they braked their machines one last time. The trail had ended, and yet there was no snowmobile, no runaway boy, only silence. A broken limb dangled from a lonely tree that clung precariously to the edge of the precipice. A curious aura hung over Zeller's Summit that was neither scary nor serene. Jamie could never find the words to express what he felt. He could only describe a supernatural presence that appeared to envelope his body. The feeling could not be explained, yet the warmth that spread throughout every blood vessel in his body was indisputable. Had the boy finally found his "better place to be?"

Matt spoke first as he stared over the edge. "See the tops of those trees, the broken branches? I've never been to the bottom, but you can see the drop."

"Is there a chance of getting down there?" Jamie asked, feeling hopeless.

"Not without climbing gear and ropes," Matt said. "It's a sheer drop-off, like a bottomless pit." His voice trembled when he spoke again. "How long would it take to get a rescue team in here?"

"Far too long, I'm sure. We're not equipped for this type of rescue. The wolves will likely feast long before a team can get anywhere near the boy." Jamie said. The tone of his voice showed little hope of a happy ending. "But first, let's give Travis and Brady a chance to do an aerial search."

"Who gets to tell the boy's friend, the fellow he was travelling with?" Jacob asked, his question heartrending yet relevant.

"I don't know, Jacob, I simply don't know," Jamie answered hesitantly. Slowly shaking his head, he stared at the ground. "I'm not sure if I could find the right words."

Jamie's mind was still trying to comprehend what had happened in the last couple of days, especially what he had just witnessed. Would he grow from this experience, without doubt the most devastating of his career, or was his job having too much of an effect on his private life? Was his career becoming more than he could handle? Each lost in his own thoughts, four grown men stood in stunned silence at the edge of Zeller's Summit.

Jarrod and the others remained outside the moss-covered cabin. Storytime had ended, and conversation ceased. The despondent fugitive found himself staring into a sky that had taken on an intensely blue hue, so bold it was stunning. Tightness gripped the pit of his stomach. As a ghostly stillness enveloped the camp, a compelling suspicion told him something had happened. Wolfy let out a strange whimpering sound from inside the cabin. Was he dreaming, or did the dog sense tragedy had struck? Jarrod could not convince himself that Lucas, who had beaten so many odds, escaped so many threats, dodged so many obstacles, and had enjoyed his first love-struck experience could be gone forever. Yet deep down, he knew the truth. Feeling much older than his years, he squeezed his eyes shut.

From accountant to gambler to crook to itinerant to passionate lover to a person who cared, his life had run the gauntlet. Without doubt, Jarrod had just reached a major crossroad in his life. The next direction he took was up to him. Although jail time was inevitable, at least a future did exist. Still, he would never be able to erase an inescapable vision from his mind. The sly grin, the quirky remarks, the indomitable determination of a skinny boy was urging him ahead. As life continued, would Jarrod prevail? The answer was indisputable. How could he ever let his young friend down?

In the bowels of a deep ravine, a squirrel and a rabbit cavorted among scattered clumps of pine cones and fallen needles. Almost in unison, their ears perked up, and their furry heads turned toward the base of a lofty, snow-capped spruce tree.

The squirrel scurried up to safety on a nearby branch. The rabbit froze momentarily, unable to move. Then, suddenly and without warning, it sensed something move.

And yes, the rabbit did jump!

The end?

ACKNOWLEDGMENTS

"When the Rabbit Jumps" would never come about without my inherent love of travel. My parents, Margaret and Jock got me on the road at a very young age. My wanderlust has never ended.

My grade school teacher, Naomi Hersom, challenged me to broaden my horizon with a barrage of fancy, new words. She pointed out that writing with imagination seemed to come naturally. Unfortunately, school only became more and more boring as the years went by. As my interest waned, so did my marks. Education was of little interest to me.

My writing of this story has stalled on many occasions, at least until I met the Writer-in-Residence of the Winnipeg Millenium Library for 2015-16. Without the encouragement and persistence of Di Brandt, both during the Residency and afterward, I might never have completed the novel. Thank you, Di, the trips out to meet with you were well worth it.

Thanks to my bridge friends who took the time to read the manuscript and supply their helpful and knowledgeable advice. I appreciated all your input as I struggled through a series of rewrites.

I cannot forget my favorites, my many "Little Brothers," who, in their own ways, all became part of the fabric of Lucas. Each of them struggled to find his own identity, and, believe it or not, they all succeeded. All of us remain a part of our own extended family—and we don't drink special teas.

A few of the book's characters may have a slight resemblance to the zany cohorts I met during the working part of my life. Thanks "Toothy" and "Klem" for allowing me to use your nicknames. Many suggest that work never did fit into my life. I will argue that point.

Finally, perhaps my most important dedication is to the Allan Mowat KIN (kids-in-need) Fund, which, through the Winnipeg Foundation, was established to help youth in the community, either through education, health needs, job opportunities, or simply a fun summer at camp. A portion of every sale of the novel will be donated to the fund.

Thanks to all of you for taking the time to read "When the Rabbit Jumps." Perhaps, "The End?" does hold a message.

Allan

Allan and Marion

Printed in Canada